The

NOTHINGNESS

Addictions Of The Eternal: Book One

By
J.C. Stockli

First Edition: January 2015

BlueFae Publishing – Dartmouth, MA

Cover Design & Images by J. Coulombe

ISBN 978-0-9862688-0-9 (paperback)
ISBN 978-0-9862688-1-6 (e-book)

TABLE OF CONTENTS

DEDICATION

To Mishky—for taco parties in a box, toe nail clippings, and of course reading my first thriller in second grade.

PROLOGUE

June 22, 1872

"You look nervous, friend."

"I'm not nervous," I said. "And I have yet to decide whether or not you may consider me a *friend*."

"It doesn't even matter. What's done is done."

The man's grin made my skin crawl. There was menace hidden behind his gleaming white teeth and exotic accent, the kind held in high regard only by a madman, as though he held a secret no one else on God's precious Earth could comprehend. Though, he told me, God wanted nothing to do with me any longer.

I hated his grin. I didn't trust him, but he assured me a way to keep her forever. Therefore, I had no choice.

I'd sat back, forced to endure the insult as she married another man, shared his bed, and bore his child. I slaved over that man's traps and nets through treacherous squalls, securing his fortune, while he ascended to the captain's helm. This madman promised me that no one could ever take Evelyn away from me again. The need to possess her overwhelmed my love for her.

Yes, the heathen by my side was the key.

1

I glanced down at his hands, questioned where he came from. Despite all of our late night consultations held in the dim lit corners of the pub, he'd yet to add color to his background. I only knew he surfaced around the docks not so long ago. The man was a drifter, a nomad, no one of consequence, scarcely worthy of acknowledgment. I think he may have mentioned something about the new estate just outside of town. He said he was an associate of the lord of that manor, a man by the name of Carver. My new *friend* lacked the polish attached to the town's aristocratic pukes, though. His hands were coarse, but not weathered like mine. Rough. Seasoned. Capable of actions I found… intriguing.

My mind clouded, like a thick fog rolling across the harbor. My eyes burned, ready to weep blood. I became increasingly aware of my body's aches. Forget the man's hands—I needed to switch to tonic once my whiskey was gone.

"I would not drink much of that if I were you, friend," he said to me. I sipped my whiskey regardless. Its bite was strange, different from the countless times I'd let it carry me away. It burned a little more than usual. His eyes danced with excitement from my disregard.

"Would you care to explain to me what is about to happen?" I asked.

"Can't say I know, friend. It is different for everyone, I suppose. I remember little of what life was like before, and I love the pain. You may feel otherwise."

"Pain?" What I felt was not pain. Illness, perhaps the onset of a common cold, but not pain.

"You will be the man you were destined to become. More controlled. More self-aware. You will notice a change in your…" He snickered. "What a glorious awakening you are about to experience. But know that always, you will desire more.

"You harbor a vivid memory for someone who claims not to remember."

"Selective memory, friend."

I sneered at the heathen again and shot the whiskey back in my throat. As the spirit cascaded down my esophagus, I was washed over with a fiery current that seized my stomach in knots. I would've done anything to expel the toxic contents of my guts all over the bar, but my body betrayed me the release.

The son-of-a-bitch laughed at me.

I could have torn his fucking heart from his chest. In fact, the thought of it mildly amused me, distracted me from my discomfort. I pictured the look of utter shock that would cross his face, the hard crunch of his breastplate shattering as my fist cracked it open, the warm throbbing goo of his heart shuddering in my hand. And his blood—I salivated from the thought of my arm drenched in his blackened ichor. Its taste, warm, bitter, nauseating and thick. More than mild amusement, I felt myself outright aroused by the thought of tearing into him.

"Why me, again?" I asked.

My new and worldly friend with his wild accent, tanned skin, and oddly hardened hands shook his head and grinned as if I should have known his answer.

"Fate. Karma. Choose your faith, friend. Your lust has revealed her. It is more of her doing than yours, but you have provoked her essence."

"How is it that my condition enables me to take Evelyn away from her husband—and keep her?"

The sneer that creased the man's face was absolutely infuriating. I envisioned scratching that smug look right off his skull. Again, I found my blood rushing at the thought.

"She is meant for you. She cannot deny you. Wish it were I whom she prefers, but I know that is not the case."

Faster than I had ever remembered being able to, I lunged at the man with clawed hands. Grabbing him up into my hooks, the bastard snickered. His fear remained at bay.

"What do you know about what she prefers?" I growled.

He laughed heartily. "I know it is not me. I know it is not her husband. I have heard her whispers, her secret prayers for his ship to be lost at sea. But then she would lose you, and that is not what she desires. I do wish I could have her all to myself, but I will remain dutiful to you, as always."

"You won't be having anyone, *friend*." I spat in his face and thrust him back in his seat. When I looked around, several townsfolk were staring. I didn't give a shit for what they thought of me. I no longer needed this town. I needed only Evelyn. Replacing the nausea from the whiskey, the new gnawing in my gut urged me towards her more than ever. I jumped to my feet.

"Easy, friend," he said, and sat me back down. "You're not quite ready."

I growled back an inhuman sound. One of the greenhorns within earshot of us fidgeted in his seat. Out at sea, he was quick to follow at my heels. On land he distanced himself from me. He was as useless as this damn town.

"What else can you tell me?" I asked.

My friend shrugged the question off his shoulders.

"You should know there is another who will try to stop you. History has proven your dichotomy to be volatile. You must be better this time."

The bastard and his obscure comments infuriated me. I vowed to rip his heart out when all was said and done, when Evelyn was by my side.

The dark fog rolling into the harbor of my mind descended like a death shroud, and in no time, all went black.

***

I awoke from a red haze days later. My lips, dry and crusted over. My hands, stained burgundy. My friend had propped me up against a tree in the woods.

"What happened?" I asked with a broken voice.

"History has repeated itself, friend."

"Riddles, you heathenness bastard."

My body felt weak, though somewhat virile. My bones, old. Yet, the more I stretched in my skin, the better I felt. My body took time to adjust, but my mind sharpened quickly. She was gone. I knew it. I did it.

My friend stared into my eyes, seeking connection, which I reflexively obliged. I felt the muscles in my face pull my gore-caked mouth into a crooked grin. He smiled wide with recognition.

"The fog is lifting, is it not? Yet the eye of the storm has yet to roll in."

His enigmatic words amused me more than my last memories of his annoying drivel.

As I continued to acclimate, my wild friend inundated me with unbelievable truths—my memories, my past—*her*. It was absolutely wondrous. All the while, my body was like a barometer, adjusting to the decreased pressure of her distance.

"So now we wait for the eye of the storm to come upon us once more."

ONE

Present Day

The darkness was thick, heavy, rushing over Evie in waves. She lay back on her pillow and searched through the darkness for nothing. No purpose. No direction. Just searched. As her chest rose and fell, the sound of her own breath rasped in her ears—inhale—exhale. The impenetrable darkness slid in and out of her throat—inhale—exhale.

An undertow of black dragged her down, rippling between her toes, behind her knees, through the gap in her thighs to her navel. It swirled up past her breastbone and across to the back of her neck. Her hair lifted and swirled around her as the water rose. Earlobes, cheeks, temples awash in the nothingness.

Mind blank, eyes wide open, she searched as it pulled. She was wrapped in it, felt like a part of it. And, in the midst of her limbo, was soothed by it. Tides of black, rolling waves of emptiness, the ever-present echo of her breaths chased her through the dark.

A new rhythm, a hiss layered over the music of her breathing. Tiny pins pricked her body. She flinched, then calmed. The sensation, the flickers were pleasurable—inhale—exhale. And then she felt it.

A presence, company she'd not expected emerged, suspended in the black. A body, faceless and unfamiliar,

7

loomed overhead. Its breath met hers. Its weight laid heavy on her chest. And she wanted it.

Phantasmic fingers traced along her hips, up her taut core. They moved along her with intent and possession.

The breath of her faceless lover quickened to panting, as did her own in rhythm with the furious beat of her heart. Its body arched over her. She saw the mist of their breaths collide in the near-tangible darkness, deep in the nothingness. She reached out to touch it. Each time, her hands merely swatted through the dark, the figure fading to black with each pawing swipe.

A warm hunger gnawed at her belly. She wanted it. She needed it. She moaned and cried out with sound that echoed only in her mind. Every nerve ending in her body tingled and pulsed. She felt her skin aflame against the cool darkness, looming, suffocating and dense. She sank deeper into the nothingness.

Her lover drifted across her body again. The weight of his darkness excited her beyond belief, and the vibrations of her body rippled through the dark. Another swipe of her hand and he was gone. She yearned to writhe beneath him, envelop him in her limbs, her fleshy vise, to command him into her, but her synapses were overwhelmed by the dissonance of his formless gravity. She could only lay still, rasping breath pinging behind her eyes—inhale—exhale.

Eyes blazed within the darkness. Dazzling bright orbs, like wild starlight reflecting on a black pool in the dead of night. They hypnotized her with their growing intensity, tearing through her. Her head twisted in anguish from the glare of her lover's gaze.

The eyes vanished into the dark.

Her desire faded. Anxiety clutched at her heart and lungs. She was restrained, arrested by her own fright.

Breathing became a daunting effort. The blackness, which once slipped cool and viscous down into her lungs, now immolated her throat. Beams of red light singed her floating body. Her moans turned to howls. They split her head in two. Evie cried out, wild.

Fucking hangovers—never again.

***

Daylight screamed a violent prism through the window pane. Morning came. Always prematurely, but it came. Evie buried her head back under her pillow, wanting nothing more than to escape the cruel rays burning her into consciousness.

She peeked through a slit between her eyelids. The alarm clock chided her, a digital red admonishment that the day had begun without her. It was already eleven o'clock. Evie struggled herself awake. Her night had only ended sometime after six in the morning.

She took refuge in her sanctuary of down and cotton, safe from the offending light and cold air. Taking a deep breath, her lungs filled with scents of lavender fabric softener and fresh linen. A faint whiff of alcohol snuck in, an unwelcome interloper in her safe haven.

April showers lingered through the late spring season, as did the crisp early morning air, a stark contrast against the rays of light tearing through her corneas. As she stirred, a draft of cold air pinched the flesh of her leg, setting a wave of goose bumps coursing across her entire body. She withdrew further into the warmth of the white down comforter. It weighted on her like a clumsy lover, suffocating her. She relished the claustrophobic sensation that encased her naked body, the linen starchy and warming.

She lay safe in her cocoon taking in the pitter-patter of rain on the roof. The white noise soothed her tortured head. It helped to stave the pounding against the back of her eyeballs. Alcohol-tightened blood vessels drummed against her temples.

Fucking wine, she thought. *When will you learn? Never again.*

Of course, her very hollow promise was directed solely to the specific choice of drink. Then again, when that's all that's left at five a.m., that's what you drink. You drink the damn white zinfandel, because even though it goes down sweet and fragrant, it has a way of biting back the following morning, and accepting that consequence is always better than the sober alternative.

Her body twitched. She groaned. Evie felt the warmth of Nate's own nakedness against her rear end, a large and fuzzy mass by her side. A low growl erupted from underneath the covers. Nate planted his giant hand on her ass, patting it with affection.

Evie clung to the warmth of the comforter and the sound of rain. Even with her stronghold compromised, she could have slept long enough to escape the clutches of her nasty hangover. It was then that the time registered in her still slightly inebriated head.

"Shit," she said with a cry, propping herself up on her elbows, evaluating her surroundings. "Shit, shit shit shit shit. Shit!"

She sprang up off her belly and out of bed. Full exposure to the chilled morning air shocked her, like falling over a boat's starboard side. Evie hustled towards the bathroom. Shoes and empty bottles thumped and clinked as she kicked them out of her way. Loose articles of clothing wrapped around her ankles, and she stumbled, nearly dragged to the floor by the jetsam. As she clambered by, Evie caught Nate out of the corner of her eye. He jolted upright, rubbing away the grogginess from his face.

"What? What?"

"Blythe's going to be here any minute to go to the gym," Evie stuck her head out from inside the bathroom.

"What the fuck, Evie? Just text her and say you can't go."

Nate flung himself back onto his belly with a thud. He pulled the comforter over his massive shoulders. Both of his feet protruded from under the comforter off the foot of the bed.

"I can't. I've blown off her *and* the gym all week. She'll kill me."

Evie brushed her teeth and hopped into the shower, testing her recovering balance. Water sputtered, then spewed from the shower head. She scrubbed herself as the temperature rose to scalding, any burns sustained deemed worthwhile. The spray felt wonderfully antiseptic, like thousands of tiny razors scraping away layers of booze-soaked skin. She stuck her face under the water jet. It suffocated, and she loved it.

Properly sanitized, she wrapped herself in a soft white towel and approached the medicine cabinet. Wiping the steam-condensed mirror, a pale, sickly phantom revealed itself. Her heartbeat steadied as her reflection diluted the adrenaline that pulled her from bed minutes earlier. She paused to regard her image with its bruise-colored circles under bloodshot eyes. Her normally plump pink lips were a thin purple gash across her face. With her hair slicked back her feminine features hardened, aging her by a decade. At that moment, she looked just about as dead on the outside as she felt on the inside.

You look like shit.

"Why are you doing this?"

Pretty pathetic, Evie.

She hated her reflection, cursed it on a daily basis. No matter how many times she blinked, it glared steadily back in the mirror. Taunted her. Judged her. But that wasn't always the case. She was vibrant once, when she was younger, before Nate, before she was alone. Her reflection used to smile back. That was all before Evie discovered the sweet release of getting high, the blissful weightlessness of inebriation. Nowadays, absent the two experiences, she was miserable. And her inner voice knew it.

She stood there judged by her phantom self, desperate to be rid of its mocking smirk. She obscured it with the recollection of her dark, faceless lover. The image left her wanting, wondering. The memory of her building orgasm still throbbed down in the base of her freshly cleansed body. The image in the mirror glared back at her with an insidious smile she didn't recognize as her own. For a moment, she stared back at this stranger in the glass and reveled in the memory of her lover's breath.

Why did you wake up from that delicious dream?

Evie shuddered from her own perversions.

The honk of Blythe's SUV outside pulled her from her trance. With no time for her hair, Evie grabbed her bandana from the vanity drawer, wrapping it around her head. She slapped some deodorant on haphazardly.

"Shit. Shit. Shit."

She dug through drawers and laundry piles—dirty, but not *too* dirty, collecting her workout gear. After pulling on her tank top, she plopped down on the bed, minutes

12

earlier a holy refuge, now a mere prop for an ass she hoped to whip into shape.

"Why did you bother taking a shower when you're going to work up a sweat at the gym?" Nate mumbled with half-hearted interest from under the comforter.

"Because, jackass, I'm not going to work out with your stank between my legs."

Nate popped his head out from the comforter, wide-eyed and wearing an ear-to-ear grin.

"Yeah, Babe, that's so fucking nasty. I love it."

"You're gross," she said, teasing him back. "Don't forget to lock up when you leave."

Evie grabbed a sweatshirt from the rocker-recliner in the corner of the bedroom and ran for the stairs.

"Ay! Oh!" Nate summoned her back with his low bellow. She poked her head around the doorway. He'd flipped onto his back and lifted himself up on his elbows to reveal his fur-covered chest.

"What?"

"You're working tonight, right?" He grabbed a filthy ashtray and untouched joint from the nightstand. He had every intention of smoking it last night when he rolled it, but was derailed by a much more primal need to bend his girlfriend over the bed and violate her from behind. He rested the ashtray on his burly chest and inspected the joint, admiring his craftsmanship before lighting it. Evie surmised it looked like a toothpick between his massive digits.

"Yes," she snipped in frustration. Why would he make her even later with such an obvious question? He knew full well that she worked every Sunday night.

"We're shipping out early, so the guys and I figured we'd go to the club beforehand."

"Okay, whatever. I'll see you later." She rolled her eyes and ran down the stairs, out the door to Blythe.

Two

Evie collapsed in the passenger seat of Blythe's SUV with its fancy new car smell and sleek wood grain interior. The sudden flurry of action and overwhelming odor of leather and phthalates proved to be at immediate odds with her hangover.

"So sorry to disturb you before noon," Blythe teased. "I'm glad to see you could make it today."

"My pleasure," Evie grumbled, eyes pinched shut to block out the light. "Do me a favor and drive through North Star Café." She figured some caffeine and grease might help her shake her lingering buzz.

Blythe dug into her gym bag, and tossed Evie some aspirin and a bottle of water.

"Maybe we should go back to wake-up calls and text messages?" Blythe said shaking her head, playing up her disdain. "Here, you need these more than I do,"

Evie happily accepted the pills. The water would serve its intended purpose at the gym.

***

The SUV's floaty suspension over the soaked and bumpy roads lent a tinge of seasickness to Evie's nausea. She found it difficult to choke down her breakfast sandwich. Thankfully, the iced coffee went down without a fight. The slick weight of the meal helped her unsteady stomach—a little.

Wouldn't you like to top that off with a coffee stout?

Evie shook the thought from her head. Her stomach was treated, her pains managed. She turned to look at her best friend with appreciation in her eyes. Blythe huffed back at her. Evie worried maybe she read her mind.

She realized Blythe abhorred her extra-curricular activities, often using words like **alcoholism** and **detox** in conversation. Evie rarely paid much attention, because Blythe had a flair for the dramatic. True, she often carried a drink in her hand. And yes, she preferred to be drunk, discontent with the real world. Surely, no one would consider that *addict* behavior, would they? She knew her friend meant well. Then again, why should Blythe resist the urge to judge her? They were polar opposites.

Fucking Miss Prissy thinks she's too good.

Evie dropped her gaze to her lap. Much to her inner voice's express disapproval, she could never blame Blythe if she did pass judgment. Evie was alone, suffered from her own warped form of depression, and likely could be labeled an alcoholic. In fact, very little kept her from living like her mother had done. One of her saving graces was her best friend.

Evie looked over at her once more as Blythe focused on the wet roads. Their friendship was free of ridicule—most of the time. That was, when Evie could manage to shut up her inner voice. It never used to scoff at Blythe when they were younger, when she smiled more. Evie and Blythe spent their pre-pubescent nights gossiping over who kissed who; if a girl let a boy feel her up; who smoked cigarettes and drank from their parents' liquor cabinets. If—*if*—Blythe had an inner voice nattering at her like Evie did, Blythe had managed to find the MUTE button. Nate, on the other hand, was a 600-watt amplifier, who night after night poured Evie full of booze, smoked her up, and did much more than just cop a feel.

Blythe deserved better from a friend; someone who could reciprocate her thoughtfulness, not someone she felt compelled to care for day in and day out.

What makes Little Miss Prissy so much better than us?

"Would you just shut up?" Evie said in a soft whisper to her reflection in the passenger window.

"Did you say something, Evie?"

"Me? Nope. Not me."

Blythe nodded and pulled into the parking lot.

Ha! You're fucking crazy. She knows it.

***

Once in the gym, Blythe dragged Evie towards the treadmills. Several minutes of jogging forced beads of alcoholic sweat from her body. Her leaden bacon-and-egg-on-multigrain lurched its way up her throat, stopping just south of her uvula. She was on the verge of exhaustion and gooey muscular failure.

"I've met someone," Blythe said.

Evie huffed to keep up with Blythe's aggressive pace. Perspiration trickled into her eyes and mouth, dry and salty.

Of course she did. Only she could meet someone in this fucked-up town.

Blythe was upper-class, gregarious and wholesome. Men loved her big brown doe-eyes and perfect brown curls that cascaded down her back. Men *lusted* after Evie. There was a difference

"Who?" Evie managed to blurt the question out between burning gasps for air.

17

"Evan Carver."

Evie's face twisted beyond her exertion, puzzled. The only Carvers she knew of in town were long gone; a wealthy family who owned a large waterfront estate just on the outskirts of town. Secluded on its own private acreage off Black Cross Road, the property was abandoned decades ago. Its nineteenth century Stick-style homage to nature left to rot as the town spiraled into drug-induced decay. It was now a decrepit party den for teenagers, littered with broken glass and graffiti. Urban myths of eerie disappearances and devil worshippers had branded the property taboo.

Evie went out there once with Nate, during daylight hours, of course. She made him stop halfway down the driveway. The steep pitched rooftops pierced the tree line, masking the skeletal body of the mansion before they could get too close. He was more than willing to drive all the way in, but Evie made him turn around. She was still young and scared. Nowadays, she'd set up camp on the front lawn if it had enough booze to keep her numb for a day or two. But no, she had never heard of Evan Carver.

"Sorry, Blythe, I don't know him."

"Yes you do. You know the old Carver estate? That's his family's place. He moved in to renovate, '*reclaim its former glory*,' he says. That kind of thing. I met him down at the town hall when he stopped in to apply for some permits. And to think I almost called out sick that day."

"I didn't think the Carvers were still around here?"

"They're not, technically. He's just fixing the place up."

"So how long has this been going on that I'm just hearing about him now?" Evie asked.

"Not very long, actually. I met him a few weeks ago. We've had a couple of coffee dates here and there, getting

18

to know each other and whatnot. He just recently took me out to dinner. I think he's really interested, he was asking about my family—and you," Blythe answered, love-struck. Evie could hear it in her voice; revolting girlish swoon.

"Just be careful. Don't fall too fast, Blythe. He may be a devil worshipper."

As amusing as she found it, Evie's dark-humored joke went unacknowledged. They often did when discussing Blythe's love life. Poor Blythe, she was a hopeless romantic who fell hard and fast. She likely had their wedding invitations printed out already; classic cream heavyweight paper with black Engraver font—maybe their names in Edwardian Script for a little flourish.

Evie slapped her hand against her forehead to wipe away the sweat before it dripped past her brow and burned her eyes.

"No, he's the one who hasn't stopped calling me," Blythe said. "He always wants to be around me. He even wanted to come to the gym this morning to meet you. I told him this was our girl time. If he's going to see me sweat, I'd rather it not be at the gym, if you know what I mean." Blythe winked over at Evie, and she rolled her eyes back, huffing along. "Anyway, I think he's the one in love already," Blythe continued with a cocky grin.

Evie shrugged. If Blythe was happy then so was she. Though their conversation did little to ease her leg muscles, now searing with lactic acid. Each breath wasted on conversation denied oxygen to her body. She looked down at the treadmill. They still had another mile to go.

"So what does the sensational Evan Carver look like?" she asked with a heavy breath. Blythe wanted to continue gushing, that much was plain on her face, and Evie was a little intrigued. Tales of murdered teenagers and occult rituals at the Carver estate gave her a welcome cheap thrill.

What kind of guy would want to live there alone?

"He's adorable," Blythe answered. "He has the softest features, a real baby face. Pretty average height and build. Brown hair and the biggest brown eyes. He's just adorable."

"Sounds dreamy." Evie did her best to project a whimsical voice, but exhaustion getting the better of her, she wheezed instead.

"Well, we all can't expect to land a catch like Nate," Blythe said, teasing back. Both girls giggled at his expense. "Honestly Evie, why don't you break up with him?"

A simple question with a not so simple answer: why didn't she break up with him? Nate was a fisherman, a drug addict, a stereotypical man's man in a town full of them. Why did she stay with him? For years she'd tolerated his nonsense. His influence alone was to blame for her drinking binges. That's all they had in common. They got drunk, got high, and fucked. Day-in and day-out; that was the extent of their relationship as far as Evie was concerned. So why stay?

"I mean," Blythe said, huffing, finally relenting to her own over-exertion. The treadmill slowed. "He's cute, in a big lumberjack sort of way. And I'm guessing his big hands mean he's... umm, you know?" Blythe flashed a playful smile to which Evie shook her head.

"Yes, Blythe, he's got a big dick," she said. "Speaking of, how about Evan? Have you slept with him yet?"

"No. Thanks for reminding me. He's very reserved. Maybe there's something wrong with me?" Evie laughed the notion off as preposterous. Blythe was beautiful.

Who wouldn't want to fuck Miss Prissy?

"That's crazy talk, Blythe. Maybe he's a gentleman," she said.

"That would be a change from the guys around here." The girls laughed as their treadmills came to a stop. "Right, time for Nautilus."

Legs jellied, belly in upheaval, booze dripping from pores, Evie was ready to collapse.

THREE

The rain had let up, unlike Evie's hangover, and the not-doctor-recommended combination of exertion and alcohol-induced dehydration left her with a floating sensation.

Sweaty and famished, the girls crossed the street to the diner. Blythe devoured her garden salad, topped with cottage cheese and a side of watermelon. Evie fought hard not to gag on a Cobb salad topped with blue cheese dressing—hadn't she asked for the dressing on the side? *Fucking morons.* It smelled just as God-awful to her nose as it looked to her bloodshot eyes. With a queasy stomach, she pushed her plate to one side and sipped her coffee instead. If Blythe noticed Evie's green pallor, she was kind enough not to mention it.

"Have you ever thought about what you would do if Rob ever made a move on you?" Blythe asked out of the blue.

"Excuse me," Evie said, sputtering into her mug. "Where's this coming from?"

Of course she'd fantasized about him. What girl could resist? But what would she do if he ever made a move on her? Probably cream her pants in his more than capable arms.

Where is she going with this?

"I'm thinking about what you said at the gym. Nate may be hung, but Rob has a thing for you. It's so

22

obvious. Have you ever thought about what you would do if he ever made a pass at you?"

Blythe stared out the window with lustful eyes, and Evie followed her gaze across the street. Rob emerged from his beat-up old pickup truck, practically on cue, and strode across the parking lot as he chatted it up with his lifting partner. Both girls gawked with hungry and offensive expressions. He was more than twelve years older than them, but still had such sweet boyish charm. Evie damned her timing—thirty minutes later, and she would have been free to ogle him at the free weights during her cool down. He would have been a welcome distraction from Blythe's laments and her burning limbs. His large biceps and trim waist were a testament to his dedication to personal fitness. The dampness in the air encouraged his white undershirt to cling to his musculature.

Why don't we just fuck him and get it over with?

"No," she said to herself and turned back to Blythe. "He wouldn't ever make a pass at me. You're wrong. Him having '*a thing*' for me would be like incest. He's my best friend, for Christ's sake." Blythe shot her a curious look. "Best friend in guy terms. You're my best friend, of course."

"Well, I think you're wrong." Blythe sat up, regaining her prim-and-proper posture. Her fingers fiddled with her straw. Evie rolled her eyes with a huff and a smile.

"Look, it doesn't matter. I wouldn't do that to Nate anyway."

"But you want to. That's my point." Blythe bounced gleefully in her seat. Her constant cheerfulness had its moments with Evie. Currently, Evie wanted it to fuck off.

"Fine, yes, Rob's hot. Okay?" she said, her annoyance from Blythe's pestering bubbling over. "And he's sweet and he cares about me a lot. I know that, but I could say all the same things about Nate. It's not in the cards."

Blythe giggled. "That gives me an idea. We should go get our cards read."

"Oh please, you don't believe in that shit, do you? C'mon, I need to get home and get ready for work."

What she really wanted to say was that she wanted a drink, but home and work were good excuses. She stood up and pulled her sweatshirt around her waist and patted down her sides to make sure she had all her belongings. Blythe paid no attention and continued to leer at Rob from across the way.

"He does take care of himself, doesn't he?" she said, biting her lip. Rob had rolled up his shirt to compare lower back muscles, or whatever, with his friend. There was little regard for cause when the effect was so delectable. It was the perfect opportunity to admire his sculpted physique and an intricately executed tattoo. Evie chanced a peek back at him. A warm thrill washed over her.

She had been fortunate to accompany him to each session. Rob's tattoo covered most of his back, a monochromatic depiction of a beautiful geisha amidst cherry blossoms. She stood with her back to the viewer, head turned to stare her admirer down with a wanton glare. Dangling from her hand was the head of a samurai, a serpent twisting through his ocular cavity and out his mouth. The geisha held a dainty wagasa in her other hand to shade her porcelain complexion. She was breathtakingly malevolent. Evie often caught a glimpse of the geisha when the club was closed. She liked to stay behind while Rob cleaned up or conducted maintenance after hours. Sometimes, she could feel the geisha's eyes glowering at her, scolding her for coveting what was not hers to covet. More nights than not, her inner voice hated that tattoo.

Evie blinked and turned away. Staring was bad for both her and Nate.

She sighed.

Poor Nate, he was a good soul, unable to grow up, lost to the town's underbelly of drug abuse. But he did love her, she knew that with absolute certainty. He took care of her, for all intents and purposes. Still, her inner voice told her he wasn't enough. There was more out in the world, somewhere, something waiting for her. The gnawing in the pit of her stomach and the spectral glare in the mirror had convinced her of that many inebriated moons ago. Sometimes, most times, she fantasized Rob was that *more*. But both men had known each other for so long, had both become such integral parts of Evie's life. Guilt consumed her when she thought of leaving one for the other. It would be the ultimate betrayal. She couldn't.

Okay. So that's a no to Rob, but how about that drink?

"Evie?" Blythe called out. Her wallet and the food bill were in her hands. "How are you paying? I only have my debit card."

Without a word, Evie blinked and dug into the zippered pocket of her sweatshirt to produce the change left over from breakfast. She tossed a ten and five ones down and looked over to the gym again. Rob was gone, safe from her prying eyes for the time being. Blythe pocketed the ten, left the ones for the tip, and stood to pay the bill with plastic.

"Ready?" she asked. Evie followed her to the counter.

"By the way, why are you so hell-bent on Nate and me breaking up?" Evie asked.

"What do you mean?"

Evie paused in her step with one eyebrow cocked. "What's with the sudden urge to push Rob on me? What's wrong with Nate?"

"I think you need a better man in your life. Someone to help—"

"Clean me up?" Evie interjected.

Blythe smiled and batted her lashes. "Take better care of you. Rob does seem to do a pretty good job of that. And that body *is* amazing. You can't say Nate's big grizzly bear body is sexier than those muscles."

Evie whacked her best friend on the arm as they exited the diner.

"You just worry about Evan Carver's body, okay?"

Blythe sighed. "I will when I get to see it."

The two girls laughed.

***

During the drive home, Evie feigned interest in Blythe's repetitive ramblings about Evan Carver, his cute quietness, his chivalry. A small, compassionate part of Evie tried to break through. Normally, that part was drugged by her inner voice and induced to comply. As much as that part of her may have wanted to, she cared nothing for her friend's newfound happiness. She was just too selfish, or more so, apathetic.

The drizzle that served as the girls' accomplice earlier had picked back up into a steady rain. She watched the showers bounce off the passenger window as they drove across the bridge. They passed by Sirens and the fishing docks across the harbor. Evie recognized faces and recoiled in her seat as they recognized her. She wished she could sink into the concrete of the streets. She yearned to be invisible to the scrutiny of people who knew where she worked and who her mother was. She sat low in the passenger seat and tried not to make eye contact.

"Oh, I almost forgot," Blythe exclaimed. "My mom said the hospital's hiring for clerical help. You know, receptionists and stuff like that. You should fill out an application for the night shift. I know you don't sleep much. It's better than what you're doing now."

Evie's eyes went vacant. They focused on some distant vantage point beyond their scope. What *was* she doing now? She was up all night that was for sure. Solid sleep eluded her since her grandmother passed.

Working for Rob at Sirens kept her scattered mind occupied at night. He always kept a watchful eye on her, tending to her needs as only Rob knew how to. When forced to go home, she drank or smoked herself into a stupor to avoid her solitude. Still, the thought of her life changing made her cringe.

Not work for Rob?

Everyone deals with their issues in different ways. This is how I deal with mine.

She physically shook the thought from her head. Blythe pulled the SUV behind Evie's little white coupe in the driveway. "I have to get ready for work," Evie said quietly as she stepped out of the SUV.

"Say 'Hi' to Rob for me," Blythe smirked.

FOUR

An intangible weight crushed down on Evie's chest as she crossed the threshold. Nate had left, and she was alone, greeted by worn and dated floral wallpaper with equally worn and dated furniture. The décor was left untouched since her grandmother was her age. The fireplace sat dark and cold.

They were the last of their line, Evie and her grandmother. Her mother had fallen victim to the drug-dependent persuasions of the fishing docks when she was young. Her grandfather was a fisherman, his boat lost at sea during a hurricane. Such was the stereo-typical tale of the people of Fallhaven. The rest of her family was preserved via photographs atop the mantle, an unintentional shrine. Some pictures were stark black and white, others aged sepia, images of dead relatives who had lived—and perhaps died—in this very house. The more recent photos were color, including a Polaroid of Evie, her mother, and her beloved grandmother. Evie couldn't have been more than one year old in the picture, and her mom was barely sixteen. *What a fucked up family portrait*, she thought, choosing to focus on her grandmother. She frowned at the picture. Her grandmother was healthy then. That was before the cancer fed on her insides.

All the other faces meant nothing to her.

She paid little attention when her grandmother tried to introduce her to their photos. She only knew one: her namesake, Evelyn, the original owner of the house. She and her husband built their home to serve as a vantage point from which Evelyn and her son would have an unobstructed view of the harbor. They'd watch their family's fleet of fishing vessels come and go.

What Evie also knew of her namesake was that she'd died in the house, in the very bedroom where Evie slept. And she died young, taken from her family too soon under mysterious circumstances. Then again, maybe that was just Evie not paying attention to her grandmother's stories. Thinking back to the urban legends that haunted the Carver estate, Evie was intrigued by Evelyn's death. She held her photo in her hand.

What was your drink of choice back then? Evie shook her head with a chuckle. *Absinthe.*

She replaced the sepia photograph on the mantle and turned towards the kitchen. This place used to be a home, had once been warm and welcoming. Now it sat echoing and empty. It had been passed down from one generation to the next. And it all ended with Evie.

Once in the kitchen, she opened the refrigerator. She should have sought a healthy snack to nourish her body following her workout, but health food was the last thing on her mind. Utter joy spread across her face when she looked inside. A cold six-pack of cheap beer awaited her. Next to that beer sat a grapefruit. She should have gone for the fruit, told herself to go for the fruit, reached for it, but passed.

He bought beer.

Evie smiled at the brown glass bottles in their cardboard case, dizzy with excitement. Every now and then, Nate proved himself a doting boyfriend. Overwhelming love poured from her thirsty heart, for the beer of course. She popped the top off on the edge of the

Formica counter. The cold brew trickled down her throat. It left a sweet and satisfying trail from the inside out. On the table, a small singed roach sat on top of a note. She swigged down half the bottle of beer and lit the roach. While she puffed, she deciphered Nate's cryptic handwriting.

> Hey Babe, thought you could use a cold one after the gym. Stay sexy!
>
> -Nate

Evie shook her head with a crooked smile. The big oaf had used the half of a brain cell he had left to consider her. He probably used her money, found her stash of tips on her dresser. Usually, the thousands of dollars he made from each fishing trip were lost to the docks before he even got off the boat. But at least he left her a little something. He always left a little pot behind. A green bud here. A bag of shake there. He left her half-smoked joints all over the house. The fact that he went out to buy her some beer was a real treat. She finished the roach and grabbed the remaining beers. Precious cargo in hand, she made her way upstairs, avoiding the photographs.

Evie circled around the back of the house through the hallway to the stairs, thereby circumventing the living room and mantle altogether.

It had taken her over a year to find comfort in her own silence following her grandmother's death. Even then, she'd found self-medicating the only way to tolerate herself. With the rain beating a steady rhythm against the house and her mind buzzing, she preferred to be alone.

***

Evie's bedroom looked much like she had left it earlier in the day. The bed linen was strewn across the bed. Pillows lay like misshapen bodies on the floor among piles of laundry both clean and dirty, like an orgy of junkies leftover from the night before.

As with the rest of the house, her bedroom decor had not been touched in decades. Floral wallpaper peeled from the walls. A battered and threaded area rug belied years of pacing feet. The metal headboard and worn cherry wood dresser were original to the room, dating back to Evelyn's time. The mattress and nightstands were newer, but had still served several generations. The aroma of dust and lilacs permeated the senses upon entering the room. Just the way Evie liked it.

She navigated her way through the piles of laundry to the bathroom. If her down comforter was her sanctuary, this pristine white-tiled space was heaven itself. The antique claw-foot tub, the cloud in which she floated. While morning showers were hectic and unrewarding, her bath time was as close to a religious experience as she was willing to admit to.

Evie suckled at her beer bottle as she plugged the tub's drain and ran the faucet. The room quickly filled with hot steam. She emptied the remainder of the bottle and spun back into her room to turn on the stereo. Soon the house was filled with the wailing cries of a tortured musician and his guitar. He sang songs of love lost or never found in the first place, songs of love and death.

Eyes closed, she swayed her hips to the music. Her body contorted to peel away layers of sweat-soaked clothes. Free of their constraints, she paused to regard herself in the mirror. Though taut and trim, her naked body appeared

31

tired and worn. The curves of her body didn't please her. Her chest was too small. Her ass, too big. Her hips, larger than they should be. Releasing a self-loathing huff at her reflection, Evie refused to acknowledge the hip bones that protruded from the lower perimeter of her core, the collarbones that shone below her neckline, the obvious ridge of her spine.

Scrutinizing further, her skin was pale. The sun could diminish the purple mapping of veins which traced across her body, but only if she ever found the sun. She assumed she looked much like a corpse—a pity, but night owls had no time for the sun. The hollowness of her physique matched her worn face. At the very least, her workout had rushed some blood back in her cheeks. She wasn't totally dead.

Stay sexy, my ass, she thought as she popped open another beer, sucking hard at the glass tip.

Steam billowed from the bathroom, and the tub neared overflow. Evie placed her accoutrements on a tray before lowering herself into the antique bath's depths. The water burned. Her body flushed, and she sank deeper and deeper. Her stomach somersaulted as she initiated her baptismal ritual.

Evie inhaled deeply, willing her body to adjust to the water's temperature. She removed her bandana before submerging her body completely. The hot water stung her face, sucked the air from her lungs. Evie pushed her head back up above the water, gasping for air. Her hands remained on the rim of the tub at all times.

Content with her water torture, she recovered another roach from the bath tray and lit it up. Her dry fingers kept it intact. With a satisfying exhale, Evie grabbed her beer and took a large swig before lying back against the wall of the tub. The roach tasted sweet, sticky and piney, laced with a tinge of ash. The beer was a bit hoppy, but Nate enjoyed pale ales. Being that he bought the beer, pale ale would have to do.

Peace came with the security of the water and smoke intertwining with rising steam. Both intimately hugged her body, knew her contours like a lover. She closed her eyes and let her other senses take over.

Her body, though meant to be purified by the bath, sweat from the temperature. Her heart rate quickened from the haunting guitar licks blaring from the stereo. The music called to her and pinched at her skin. Her head swayed back and forth. Her mouth moved to lip-sync the lyrics. She relished these moments. This was her time. No one else penetrated the sanctity of her bathtub. Nate had tried to hop in the shower with her once or twice. He even tried invading her bath. Each time, she vehemently protested. This was her temple—her God. He'd been warned to leave her be during her time of prayer. Water, drugs, music; they were all she needed.

Her mind roamed this way and that. She thought about Nate and their exhausting relationship. She thought about her grandmother and her mother. She thought about work and her boss—about Rob. Evie paused there. She may have hated her job, but she loved him.

Waitressing at a strip club wasn't what Evie had envisioned for her life after high school, but she had little choice. Her grandmother's health diminished quickly. By the time she'd turned eighteen she had graduated high school and lived alone, and she needed a solid source of income. Fallhaven offered little opportunity. It wasn't equipped to support the photography-school and drama-class dreams of silly little girls. The town catered to the fishermen who fueled the town's meager economy. Men at sea for weeks on end with large paychecks to spend need entertainment, and the strip club near the docks was a great place to unburden their swollen wallets.

Rob inherited the bar—and its reputation—from his father. But unlike the original proprietor, Rob was a gentle soul. He wasn't meant to have been dealt the cards he got. When he first took ownership of Al's Gentlemen's Club, he changed the name. Erasing his father's name from the signage was the first step to improve the club's reputation, and by extension his own perception of his newfound profession. Rob felt responsible to protect his girls—his *Sirens*. And they were all his, but none more so than Evie. She knew that.

Rob hired her under strict conditions, more his than hers. He knew her mother and family well growing up. He said he hired her to keep an eye on her, to keep her from suffering the same drug-induced fate as her mother. She was allowed to wait tables, but that was all. Many a club patron would request a private dance or throw a pass at her. If they failed to catch the first emphatic hint, Rob would kick the jerk out into the cold. Evie always thought his knee-jerk reactions were a bit extreme given his job, but she liked to imagine his protectiveness was spurned from hidden jealousy or desire more so than anything else. Actually, the idea thrilled her. As her mind whirled in the tub, her body warmed from thoughts of Rob's potential hidden desires.

The waters wrapped around her body, holding her safe and secure. With the next inhalation of smoke, she left her lips parted. Smoke wafted from her mouth and up through her nostrils. She held in her breath and listened to the thrumming of her own heart.

Memories, images of dreams from earlier in the morning rushed to the back of her eyelids. She had dreamt of a faceless lover. A dark figure whose touch sent shivers throughout her body. She remembered the tingling sensation experienced during her dream, the lover's breath against her skin. His eyes were dark and deep like the ocean waters just past the harbor. His face was left forever shadowed and unknown.

There had been a shared excitement between them, a recognizable mystique. She was certain Nate was absent in her dream. She could recognize his rough hands and touch in any form. Could it have been Rob? No, the depthless orbs staring down at her had scorched with menace. They electrified her. Rob's eyes were gentle. She knew those eyes. In the end, Evie decided the nameless figure was just an ominous metaphor for her life, her mind playing off of her own desires and fears. The pulsing rush of blood to her labia, on the other hand, was very real.

Nothing like a good wet dream.

Evie lowered a hand down her body. Her fingertips retraced the path carved out by her faceless lover's. They ran across her breasts, down her torso. She dragged them back and forth against her hip bones, teased herself before caressing her delicate folds. With a small hesitation, she slipped two fingers inside. Bathwater crashing against the sides of the tub, she passed off her own hands as those of her dark lover. Evie pushed her mind back as far as she could to the nothingness that enveloped her body. Golden orbs flickered in her mind's eyes, bright flashes that did little justice to the figure from her dream.

Her breath quickened. The screams of the tortured singer intensified as her face contorted. Releasing a forced grunt, frustrated by the loneliness of her own inner silkiness and the inadequacies of her thin fingers, Evie whimpered and with much effort found her release. A hollow feeling was left in her chest. Her eyes searched the ceiling. She willed the water to wash her away. It left her wanting. Feeling less than whole, she once again sunk below the water's surface.

Evie lay in the tub long enough to guzzle the remaining beers. Her body stiffened as the water cooled around her. Church was over. She washed and shaved ahead of the night's work. When she emerged, her roach was gone, her beer bottles empty.

Five

Evie wrapped herself in a towel and gazed at the ghost in the mirror. She searched the crystal blue irises staring back at her.

What the fuck are you doing?

The question plagued her as one day bled into the next. Sleep, work, drink and fuck. Lather, rinse and repeat. What was the point of it all? When would it get any better? The ghost in the mirror stared. It offered no answers, save for filling her empty void with more poison—such an easy answer to fall upon in a small town full of sin. She hated that ghost. Anxiety churned in her stomach, tying her in sickening knots.

Nothing a drink can't fix.

Relenting to her cursed inner voice, she wished she had one more beer. Something to help numb the ache in the pit of her core, settle the tempest brewing inside.

Without any distraction to speak of, she opened the medicine cabinet in search of some mouthwash. Her eyes danced at the sight of the curvilinear bottle. She grabbed for it. Her lips were eager to press up to the sticky rim. But her pathetic attempt of masking her true feelings ended with the realization the bottle was empty. Her brow furrowed as she peered down into the hollow vessel. Discouraged, she tossed the bottle into the wastebasket. Evie closed the vanity and watched the ghost in the mirror mock her.

Stupid girl. Stupid, stupid girl.

She shuddered and turned into the bedroom, away from her reflection's judging eyes. A melancholy tune played from her stereo. A sad and lonely acoustic guitar drifted across the dull air in her room. She sang along under her breath to lyrics she knew by heart. In lieu of booze, the music pacified her, a playlist she'd compiled over the years: Evie's greatest hits of *the-best-ways-to-die-a-sensual-death-type* music.

She curved and twisted her body as she dug for her work clothes, choosing black vinyl and torn fishnet stockings. The shiny and cold outfit complimented the wet weather outside and hid little from the imagination, but just enough for modesty's sake. It would render decent tips for the night. Her outfit was finished off with a tall pair of patent leather Doc Martens, her favorite. Their thick and chunky soles offered plenty of comfort for a night on her feet. The tops of the boots came up under her knees where she fixed a tiny pocket on the inside of her right boot. That's where she'd stash tips, much more discreet than tucking dollar bills into her vinyl bra top.

Medicated by the music, Evie forgot about her thirst for a moment. Whirling her hips to and fro, she looked at herself in the mirror, signing along with an artist who died young, about her age, and allegedly from his own alcoholic tendencies—*allegedly*, or so she preferred to think. Evie knew the tune by heart. She turned, twirled, and paused at one point to regard the set of wings across her shoulder blades. Her one and only tattoo, she hoped they'd someday let her fly away. Away from Fallhaven. Away from her life. But she had yet to spread those wings. The ornately feathered pinions remained etched into her skin, immobile. Her thirst returned.

Wish we had just one more drink before work.

She turned back into the bathroom to style her hair and make-up. It was amazing how a little foundation and eyeliner could chase the ghost from the mirror. Soon, she had transformed the gaunt, grey specter into a more sprightly creature altogether. She outlined her gleaming blue eyes with smoky eye shadow and thick liquid liner. Some pink lip gloss returned life to her ashen lips. Applying a tiny bit of glitter along the rim of her eyelids and along her collarbones, and her reflection glowed. Life was restored.

Evie teased out the cropped mop in the back of her head into an auburn mess. Donning her trusty bandana once again by folding it into a long ribbon, she wrapped it around her head like a headband to keep her hair from her face. Such considerations would make her night more tolerable. She pulled through a few wisps of bright red-dyed tendrils to frame her face, hanging loosely across her shoulders.

Sickened by thirst—legitimate, *only-coffee-and-beer-after-a-workout-and-a-hot-bath-and-a-fingerfucking* thirst—Evie descended to the first floor. She passed through the living room to the kitchen. Her namesake's portrait made her pause. She glared at the stark contrast to her current visage. Innocent and beguiling eyes assessed her.

"Don't judge," she scoffed. "I bet you had a laudanum dependency." The comment was meant to instill confidence in herself, but did little to deter the photo's glare.

Who's judging whom?

In addition to her thirst, the effects from the pot lingered. Evie was famished. Inside the kitchen, she opened cabinet after cabinet. Little could be found beyond old bread and stale cereal. She grabbed the grapefruit from the fridge. A lonesome box of baking soda remained. She promised she'd find her way to the grocery store soon.

She didn't care much for the bitter taste of grapefruit. Evie winced and choked it down nonetheless. Like the beer, Nate had left it for her. He must have forgotten she hated grapefruit—it was just *half* of a brain cell he had, after all. Once finished, she ran a glass of water from the faucet and guzzled it down. The water successfully rid her mouth of the fruit's bitter taste. She checked her flat belly for signs of bloating. Pulling big tips when you felt like a heifer was difficult.

Once reassured her body would remain intact, Evie collected her tote—huge, but only containing her wallet, cell, and a few other random items. She grabbed her keys and a green plaid shirt Nate had left hanging on a kitchen chair.

Evie headed out the door.

***

The sun was just over the horizon when Evie made it to the club. The building didn't look like much on the outside. It had high solid brick walls, the faded outline of the club's original name, *Al's*, barely visible behind the neon glow of *Sirens*.

Back in the seventies, Rob's father found promising opportunity for financial gain wrapped around the club's brass poles. That's when the drugs and debauchery blossomed in Fallhaven. After he died, Rob wanted to close the place down. He wanted to save the town from its own depravity. But it was a source of revenue for Fallhaven, and the fishermen would have rioted if he tried to bar the doors shut. So it was that the sympathetic former high school all-star moonlighted as a strip club owner.

Actually, Evie credited Rob for changing the name of the club. She was always fond of the mythological reference to the femme fatales who would lure sailors into the jagged shores. His wit and charm, it's what made Rob who he was. And it's what made it all the more tolerable to enter the sinful building.

Those lured into the temptation of the strip club were greeted by a foreboding six-foot, three hundred-pound beast named Jerry, a personal friend of Rob's who served as the club's bouncer. He was a sweet teddy bear and put the girls' safety above all else. She passed by him with a small curtsy and a smile.

"Good evening Jerry."

He held the door open for her with a squinty-eyed grin. It was easy to pretend she was happy around Jerry, the big loveable guy that he was.

"Miss Westvale," he said. He mimicked the movements to tip an invisible hat.

A few customers sat in the club. Raunchy dance music thumped between the walls. Bathed in soft red light and adorned with metal poles, the stage jutted out from the left of the entrance. Several tables spread across the remainder of the floor. Beyond the stage, a row of curved booths lined the wall for most of the length of the building; they were a preferred locale for those seeking discretion. The bar was located across the club from the stage and overlooked the entire layout. A few private booths were concealed by curtains in the shadows. The dressing rooms and kitchen were behind the stage, as was Rob's office. The whole building reeked of musty old linoleum, vinyl and wood paneling. Not to mention alcohol and sweat. Like Evie and her house, Rob deemed renovation unnecessary.

Evie made her normal route past the stage. She wove between empty tables to the bar. There she found Rob, always found Rob, waiting for her with a smile.

"Hello there, Gorgeous," he said with his boyish grin.

She smiled in return. More so than even Jerry, Rob was easy to smile at. She shifted her eyes from him, remembering her conversation with Blythe, and blushed for fear he could read her mind. His eyes remained warm and inviting. How could she dream of working for anyone else? He was the only person in town who seemed to really care for her.

She made her way around the bar with a flirtatious swing of her hips, sashaying side to side with each step. Her bag and plaid shirt were tucked under a small cubby behind the bar's corner.

"My my, we seem to be in a good mood tonight," Rob said, chuckling.

"Only because of that cute little smile of yours, sir."

And thanks for the inspiration in the bath.

She bit her bottom lip to hide the devious smirk evoked from her inner voice's comment. He looked back at her while toweling off his hands. His smile vanished as she stood before him like the air had been sucked from his lungs.

"My God, Evie, you're going to get everything you want in life because of those eyes."

Her inner voice batted her lashes with a coy smile and a curtsy.

"Think they could get me a drink?"

Evie felt guilty for causing the frown that distorted Rob's face. He'd made it clear on more than one occasion that he opposed her excessive drinking habits. But she also knew he hated to see her want or suffer for anything, particularly something he could provide with ease. Her hands were shaking. He saw it. She watched him stare right at them. She let him witness the telltale signs; if that's what it took to get what she wanted, so be it.

"Okay, is that a double or single?" he asked with reluctance, knowing her shtick.

"A double, if you please," she replied.

He grabbed a double shot glass and proceeded to pour her favorite, Jim Beam.

"Your drink, Miss. That'll be one kiss."

Each time she grabbed for the shot, he pulled it away and smiled. The taunting game was a familiar one between the two. It always ended with a wet kiss on his right cheek, both blushing, and Evie tossing her head back as the golden liquid burned her throat. The drink swirled through her stomach. A horrid reaction ran across her face as her whole body shook. She jumped from side to side, pumping her fists with alcohol-induced excitement. As it settled into a burning node in the center of her belly, she felt the blood rush to her face.

Mmm... better.

"Okay, boss, let me at 'em."

Rob threw up his hands to shadow box, and then crept down into a grappling position and motioned towards her. She flinched before they made contact and both laughed.

"Easy there, champ. You're the only one on the tables tonight. I'm sorry, Carrie called out. I don't think it'll be that busy tonight anyway."

Evie looked around at the few customers they had, but it was still early. Nate had said he and his friends would be dropping by later. There was plenty of time for things to pick up and make some decent money.

"Aye, aye, captain." She saluted with a wink and grabbed an empty drink tray. Evie turned and walked out in front of the bar.

"And stop swinging your hips like that," he yelled out after her. Evie spun around to walk backwards, winking once more at him. Her inner voice smiled, and Rob smiled back with a shake of his head.

Six

The evening went on as any other. Evie waited tables as they filled up throughout the club. By eleven, they had a full house of drunken fishermen and local lowlifes. A few college kids with questionable identification showed up as well. Most of their customers were regulars and knew Evie, her family, and Nate very well. Those that didn't know her ogled her bare assets, but paid more attention and money to the dancers.

The music played on as people came and went, mostly men, but a few women came in as well. Some of the women came out of curiosity. Some were working in their own right. Escorts didn't usually get to pick out the night's entertainment; those women Evie easily identified. A small chamber inside her heart ached thinking about her mom.

Rob tended bar, which gave him the advantage of overseeing the entire layout of the club. It also meant Evie could chat with him whenever she came over with an order.

She approached the bar with a full tray of empty beer bottles and cocktail glasses. As she emptied the tray, her hips gyrated to the bassy hip-hop thumping all around. They moved like a separate entity from her body. Rob shot her a cautious glare to cease her suggestive movements. She puckered her lips, blowing mock kisses in the air, and kept dancing.

With a concerned brow, he nodded over to the corner booth farthest from the bar. It had been occupied by three shadows. Evie looked over her shoulder for a quick glance. Very little could be made out from their silhouettes.

"What's up?" she asked.

"New customers, they must have just sat down. Did you go over there yet?"

"No, I was cleaning up some tables. I'll head over right now." If she was going to do her job, she could at least do it right.

Rob huffed. "Yeah, okay. Be careful. There's something about them I don't like."

"You think there's something wrong? You can't even see them that well from here."

Evie re-evaluated her first sight through squinted eyes. The three bodies were still shadowed blobs hidden under the darkness of the booth's corner away from the stage lighting.

Rob shook his head.

"Yeah, I don't know. I'm just getting a bad vibe, I guess."

Finding little caution in his words, Evie grabbed her tray and headed to the booth. Here and there, a customer stopped her to order a drink. She wrote everything down on her little notepad.

Evie twisted and twirled through the tables and the shadows. She bobbed her head to the music and lip-synced along. Beyond taking orders, the music overwhelmed any attempt at conversation. Familiar patrons nodded or winked a greeting as she walked by. After a curvy course, she'd arrived at her destination.

When Evie reached the corner booth, she stopped dead in her tracks. Tray in hand, mouth gaped open, Evie stared down at whom she gathered to be the most beautiful man she had ever seen.

The stranger reciprocated her stare with a devious smirk and dark eyes. The sandy scruff of a five o'clock shadow framed his face. His dirty-blond locks hung down the side of his jaw line, ends resting just across his shoulders. His sharp, angular features guarded deep dark irises. They created a sharp line above his eye sockets, like they were meant to purposely shield those dark pools of mystery from the club's lighting. He held one eyebrow cocked indicating his amusement at her obvious fascination.

Look away, dammit. You're embarrassing yourself.

Evie forced herself to look away from his hypnotic features, but not too far. She dropped her gaze to his well-cut shoulders. His lean frame was shrouded under a soft grey sweater and worn leather jacket.

Dammit. Stop giving him the once over, she demanded of herself again.

Evie averted her eyes once more. This time she stared straight down to his lap. Weathered jeans concealed what Evie presumed was something much more offensive to stare at than his face. She lifted her surprised gaze back up to meet his. The sly side smirk across his face widened. Clearly, he delighted in her awkwardness. Exasperated, she broke the silence and forced herself out of her reverie.

"Hi," she said, yelling over the music. She had to lean closer towards him so that he might hear her. By doing so, she caught a faint but pleasant scent overpowering the rankness of the club. "What can I getcha?"

The stranger looked back up at her in pure delight. Eyebrows lifted, he propped himself up with his elbows, one against the table top and the other against the back of the booth's bench. They cradled his thin but muscular frame. He stretched himself up to her. She leaned in even closer. Her senses now identified his aroma of orange blossoms and mint.

Delicious.

"I was thinking I might like you," he replied and licked his lips.

Evie snapped upright. His dark gleaming eyes held her in place. His smile haunted. Evie's pulse quickened. Her heart threatened to burst from her chest. And she softened deep between her thighs at the thought of serving herself up to the devilishly tenebrous stranger.

She moved back a little, allowed herself a moment to register his order and shake off his scent. Fighting a quiver, she replied, "Sorry man. If you're looking for a girl, you'll have to request one of the dancers. I just bring the drinks."

She forced her composure and feigned cockiness with her hip shifted to the side, waiting for a new order. All the while her body trembled with anticipation.

"I can't say I'm interested in any of these girls," the stranger said. His dismissive hand waved through the air. "And I don't care for alcohol myself."

He reached into his pocket to reveal a large wad of cash and placed it down on the table. She looked at the generous fold of twenty-dollar bills. At least a few grands' worth. She gawked at him in amazement.

"I..." she stuttered. "I can't accept that. I'm just your waitress."

"Should that matter?" he asked. His constant smile made her shiver. "You asked for my order, and I'd like to order you."

I'll drink to that.

Night club clamor faded into the background. Laughter came from across the table. Evie turned and noticed the two other individuals in the booth. One was a male, shorter and stockier than the stranger in front of her, his features just as handsome. Disturbing though, concealed by a thick beard and a short, shaggy hair cut. Though the lighting in the club was poor at best, Evie could tell his skin was much darker than the handsome stranger's whose pale complexion shone through the lighting.

The dark man smiled wide, exposing gleaming white teeth. Like his smile, his laughter startled her. It was a haunting chortle, low and ominous. His belittling grin made Evie think he was also amused by her awkwardness.

Between the two darkly handsome men sat the long figure of a woman. She was tall, much taller than the men flanking her. Her features looked simple, with soft blond hair and a tired face. Her frame was emaciated like an addict's. Evie returned the animosity projected towards her by the woman. It was plain the woman was annoyed with the attention her companion gave her.

Don't worry, bitch. I'm sure you'll still get paid at the end of the night.

She broke free from the tall blonde's glare. The woman wrapped her long arm around the beautiful stranger's shoulders with obvious possession. Working hard at pushing that customer loyalty program of hers; buy five rides, get the sixth one free. Evie dared to look back at him. He gazed up with his persistent smirk. A million tiny pin pricks tickled her body. She was locked in his stare.

Chest heaving and cheeks flushed, Evie felt Rob's strong arm wrap around her waist. He pulled her away and positioned himself in front of her, using his own body to shield her from the booth. His chest puffed out, arms crossed over, muscles flexed.

"Hi, I'm Rob, the owner. Is something wrong here?"

The beautiful stranger's demeanor shifted from playful to indignant as he offered an open hand for Rob to shake.

"Rob, my name is Lucca. I don't think anything is wrong. I'm simply placing my order with your lovely waitress," he replied and motioned towards Evie.

Lucca, her inner voice echoed. The name lingered in her head. Her heart raced. Her entire body throbbed.

Rob looked down at the wad of cash, then up at Lucca. He took stock of the others around the table. The woman scowled at him. Her arm was still draped around Lucca's shoulders. The dark man sat back with his arms crossed, mirroring Rob. Chin lifted, the dark man stared down the length of his nose at him, sizing Rob up. He let the man stare and turned back to Lucca and pointed at the money.

"Unless you were planning to buy everyone's rounds tonight, I'd say that looks like you're ordering more than drinks. As long as you're keeping your requests to dancing, we can arrange that. We have very talented girls at your disposal."

Rob reached out and pulled aside a dancer who passed by. Natalia flinched with surprise, but calmed after acknowledging it was her boss who grabbed her, not a customer. She positioned herself by Rob's side and in front of Evie, and smiled.

Evie wasn't a big fan of Natalia, or Natalie as far as the Department of Motor Vehicles was concerned. She was tall, dark, and one of the club's favorites due to her Amazonian physique. She made Evie self-conscious most days. In front of Lucca, Evie felt particularly deflated by her presence.

"I'm sure you'll be more than happy with Natalia," Rob said.

She was offered up like a lamb to the slaughter. Lucca appraised her, considered her for a moment. With a shake of his head, he looked back up at Rob.

"Thank you very much, but my order is for your waitress. Though, I'm sure Natalia is very skilled at what she does."

Natalia's shoulders slouched with disappointment. Meanwhile, Evie's ears perked up. The thought of going behind the curtain with Lucca and grinding up against those dirty faded jeans resurrected the pulsing pain between her legs.

Do it, dammit. Dance for him.

She chimed in Rob's ear from behind, "That's a lot of money. What could it hurt?"

Rob's body stiffened, subtly jolted mere inches from her. Evie flinched and regretted the comment as soon as she made it.

He tilted his head back to her. "This guy's a creep. I don't care how much money he offers. You're not going anywhere near him."

Her inner voice scowled at the back of his head. *You're not my fucking father.* That was a lot of money. Stepping back, Evie peeked around Natalia's curves at the money and then over towards Lucca. She gnawed at her lower lip anticipating Rob's response. She knew what he was about to say and hated him for it.

"Sorry man, you got the wrong idea," he said with a laugh. "Evie's not for sale. Order your drink or get a private dance from Natalia, but that's all."

Lucca's eyes widened. Evie noticed how they gleamed in the dim lights.

"Evie?" he repeated with a piqued interest.

His tongue played inside his mouth, tracing the edges of his teeth.

"That's all." The dark man chimed in with a snort. He'd yet to release Rob from his glare. Evie noticed a strange twang in his accent, exotic and unfamiliar. Lucca's eyes flicked from her to his friend, then back to her. He beamed with pure excitement in the darkened hues of the club. With a contented huff, Lucca slipped the wad of cash back into his pocket. He licked his lips once more. Each time he did so, Evie was washed over in warm, wet waves of thrill.

"I'd say, based on the way she moved her hips over near the bar, that Evie is more than capable of fulfilling my requests," he said.

Rob's teeth could have turned to diamonds from the pressure of his clenched jaw. He glowered down at Lucca. Conversely, Lucca paid no attention to him, but continued to stare at Evie.

With a huff, Lucca relented. "I'll have a Bloody Mary."

The lithe blonde, still wrapped around him, rubbed Lucca's shoulders before chiming in with a low pleasing voice, "If you want a dance, baby, I'll dance for you."

Natalia stood by Rob's side, speechless over her rejection. Evie wondered if a man had ever rejected her before. *Probably not*, she thought and fought back a little chuckle from the notion.

The dark man stared at Rob, who met the man's glare with obvious disdain before turning to Evie.

"Just get this asshole his drink and get him out of here."

Evie nodded and looked back over to Lucca. He held his smile at her. She wanted to smile back, but something about him and the lingering tension unnerved her. She stumbled a moment, weak in the knees, and forced her composure as best she could.

"Bloody Mary, okay. Does anyone want anything else?" she asked.

The dark man shrugged his shoulders, apathetic. The lithe woman didn't acknowledge her, rather focusing all her attention on Lucca.

***

Still mystified, Evie walked back to the bar and stood at the end farthest from her new admirer. Even with the entirety of the club between them, she felt his eyes on her. His stare was ferocious and pierced through the poor lighting, smoke, and booze-soaked bodies.

The strange woman with Lucca stood to give him her own version of a private dance. She twisted her long, bony frame around in circles. Like a charmed snake, she swayed to the music. It was apparent he paid her no heed. His sights remained locked on Evie.

She tried to calm her nerves. Her stomach turned. Her legs numbed. The heat from the glowing node inside her intensified. Evie needed to slow her pulse. Never had she felt herself at a loss for words with anyone. Yet there she was, tongue-tied and goofy. No man had *ever* come into this club and made her feel so out of control.

Stupid girl. If you'd listen to me, I'd tell you what to do with that man.

Evie fell deeper into thought, into a dark desirable place. She heard her name being called out, but it was muffled by the buzzing of her thoughts.

"Evie," Rob yelled out from behind the bar.

She flinched, blinked, and looked to Rob who anxiously awaited her attention.

"Jesus, Evie. Are you okay there? Look, those college kids are back." He pointed over to a couple of well-dressed boys walking in. "I thought I told those fucking idiots to stay away from here. Can you look after the bar while I take care of them?" He huffed. His shoulder nicked her as he passed by.

"Quiet night, huh?" she said, but Rob was already gone.

She made her way behind the bar and looked back to watch the confrontation. He was already in front of the boys, whom she recognized. She'd had a run-in with them in the past.

They'd come up from the state college south of Fallhaven. A few hours' drive through winding forest highway, it wasn't a fun or easy ride. The boys, like so many of their collegiate brethren, came to town primarily for the drugs. The strip club was just a bonus. The dancers were lucky to get any kind of tips out of them after they'd scored. These particular boys were never spoiled with manners for all their wealthy upbringing. They came into Sirens high as kites, drank too much, and disrespected the girls, dancers and waitresses alike.

It all came to a boiling point a couple of weeks ago. The tall one with glasses took a shining to Evie, shamelessly hitting on her all night. Too much liquid courage led him to smack her ass as she leaned over the table to collect their empties. In doing so, the guy cupped his hand in between her legs. He attempted to slide his fingers up inside her, and would have had it not been for the thin layer of cheap vinyl from her booty shorts. Rob blew his top. It took Jerry and a couple of regulars to pry his hands off the kid. When Nate found out what had happened, it took both Evie and Blythe to stop him from driving down to the dorms to deliver a death warrant to the blond-haired, four-eyed pervert.

Evie watched as Rob argued with the two doped-up kids. Jerry stood close by, waiting to regulate if the need should arise. She was relieved Nate hadn't arrived yet.

SEVEN

In Rob's absence, Evie fumbled behind the bar. She popped bottle tops and poured draughts. Both were easy self-serving tasks. Though she had never taken formal bartending classes or possessed the requisite license to tend bar, she knew how to work the beer taps. She knew the liquor behind the bar at Sirens like the back of her hand.

Tension twisted along her shoulders. With no new orders but her own, Evie snatched up a pint glass and turned to the Guinness tap. Filling the pint halfway, she then grabbed up a shot glass to mix the perfect measure of Bailey's and Jameson. Evie ducked behind the bar and with a *plop*, dropped the shot into the pint glass. Wasting no time with the rapidly frothing concoction, Evie chugged. The Car Bomb was amazing—rich and creamy. It loosened her as it rushed down her throat. Safe behind the bar, she sighed. The thirst-quenching moment was divine, licking residual foam from across her lips. She resurfaced to find Lucca sitting across from her. The moment was gone. Her drink threatened its way back up her throat. His smile was wicked.

A crisp shattering sound crackled in her ears as she inadvertently whacked the glass underneath the countertop, shattering it in her hand. Her hand was cool, wet. She looked down to find her palm slashed open. Blood followed. The visual registered in her brain, and her hand began to throb.

"Motherfucker," she yelped, recoiling from the pain. She cradled her blood-soaked hand close to her chest.

Lucca's eyes widened. The golden rims lining his irises danced at the sight of the red stream. It flowed profusely. His smile disappeared. His body stiffened.

Evie was too busy to pay much attention to his reaction. She ran her palm under the faucet, searching wildly with her eyes for a towel while her left hand tended to its wounded friend. The hand towels were filthy; the mix of spilled alcohol, body fluids, crumbs, and whatever-the-fuck-else in their fibers not suitable to introduce to her bloodstream. Napkins were too thin and would be rendered useless in seconds. Evie pulled the bandana from her head and used it to fashion a makeshift bandage, wincing as individual nerves shouted their damage reports.

Her tattered hand was still a useful tool, though. It was effective in removing her awkwardness in his presence, the pain pulsing in her palm too great to care about being self-conscious.

"I'm so sorry, Bloody Mary, right?" she said as she scanned the back of the bar, formulating a plan to grab a glass and mixer from the cooler to pour the cocktail with her wounded paw. "Extra bloody okay?" she said, exasperated.

"Please don't." Lucca waved his hand to dismiss the drink. She looked back at him, annoyed, her endorphins pumping in rhythm with bass shaking the club. "I already told you, I don't drink alcohol. It was just an excuse to bring you back to the table without your boss on your ass."

"Oh," she said and turned her head down. The damned awkwardness returned.

He perched up on his barstool, leaned towards her, and took her injured hand in his. Evie marveled at how coarse and firm his grip felt. Yet, oddly enough, it felt warm and nurturing at the same time. She wondered what those hands might do for a living. They were chapped, like a fisherman's, hands that spent hours upon hours pulling salt-corroded lines and rusted traps from rough seas. But they moved like a surgeon's, expertly incising the body and adeptly fondling its insides only to stitch it back up with care. His rough appearance indicated to her that he was a fisherman come to town for quick and easy money. Not an inconceivable occurrence in Fallhaven. The reputation of its lobstering operation spanned across the country.

I'll tell you what those hands could do. Let's have another drink and find out.

Evie looked up at him as her stomach turned to butterflies.

"Pretty nasty cut you got there. Was it worth it?" asked Lucca.

"Everybody has their poison, I guess."

She blushed, mortified he caught her with a drink behind the bar. Lucca snickered and unwrapped the bandana. Evie refrained from pulling her hand away, lost in his crooked smile.

"Indeed, we all have our poison." His finger traced the wet wound. The pressure of its tip made her a little nauseous.

Evie stood silent a moment, watching his movements. There was purpose in his inspection. Perhaps he was a surgeon after all. He sat back straight on his barstool and released her palm. His red-stained fingertip lifted to his lips. They parted to allow it entry as his tongue stretched out to meet it. His gaze on her, unwavering. Evie found herself conflicted, unsure if she should be repulsed by his actions or turned on. Despite the protest taking place on her palm, the ache between her legs somehow became more urgent.

Lucca's brow lifted with thought. "Well Evie, the offer remains open. I would love to take you behind those curtains."

You can take us anywhere you want.

Flushed red, consumed by the building heat inside her vinyl shorts, Evie laughed with nervous embarrassment.

"I don't think Rob's going to go for it. He's a little protective of his girls," she said, hoping to deflect the conversation onto her boss. Her body remained gripped by Lucca's eyes.

"I've noticed that. Very protective... of you in particular, Evie."

His low, smooth voice poured over her like top-shelf bourbon poured over rocks, slick orange-zesty moisture forming as she warmed to his temperature. Her mind buzzed. She wanted to sink in deep, get drunk off of Lucca's company, but Evie glanced over to the doorway at Rob.

She sighed. "I guess he is a bit more protective of me than the others."

Lucca laughed under his breath, toying with the bloody bandana in his hand.

"A bit," he said. His eyes widened with sarcastic emphasis. Evie noticed how the small action brightened those dark pools. She caught the gleam of a gold rim around his irises.

Absolutely beautiful.

Before the conversation went any further, a throaty shout came roaring across the club.

"Evie!" Nate yelled with his fists raised in the air. Several clubgoers stopped to observe the spectacle. Those who knew him tipped their glasses as he walked by.

"What the fuck?"

Evie was shocked at her own voice, expecting that quick lash of disdain to be private. Lucca heard her, no doubt, as he raised a single eyebrow and turned. He glanced over his shoulder at Nate and his four equally inebriated crewmates. They stumbled through the crowd.

"Friend of yours?"

Evie found herself less than willing to admit the truth aloud.

"Yeah." she said. "Yeah, my boyfriend." She looked down in shame. Her palm was still bleeding. She wrapped a paper towel around it like a gauze dressing. She paused for a moment, and shook her head. "He's not going to like me dancing for you either."

A ruckus of laughter erupted from Lucca's core for just a brief moment before he regained his composure. A cocky grin remained, testament to his amusement.

"No, I'm quite sure he wouldn't," he said, wrestling his amusement back behind pursed lips and lifted himself from his barstool. "Right, well the offer stands, Evie. Boyfriend or not, it's your choice isn't it?"

His knuckles rapped the hardwood bar top with a *barrump bump*. When Lucca turned, he came face to face with Nate. The drunken sailor swayed back and forth in a stupor.

"Well, hey man, whatcha doin' there with my girl?" Nate slurred.

Evie rolled her eyes.

"Not as much as I'd like," Lucca said. His arrogant smirk, too sweet to hold in.

Nate froze for a sobering moment. The two men stood, staring each other down. Nate's broad, bear-like stature towered over Lucca's leaner build, but the audacity of Lucca's confidence was enough to choke the room.

"You better watch yourself, motherfucker. This is a small town, and everyone here's got my back."

"Not everyone," Lucca snorted as he turned back to his quarry. "It was a pleasure, Evie."

He dipped his head and walked back across the club to his booth. Bemused, Nate watched him navigate through the sea of tables and drunkards.

"What the fuck was that?" Nate asked. He turned to Evie for an answer. She stood bewildered behind the bar, watching the stranger glide through the crowd, carefree as a tern riding the breeze.

As Lucca settled back into his seat, he returned Evie's stare, spicing it with a most alluring and ominous smile. The alabaster blonde scowled at him as he lowered himself back into the booth. The dark man offered a frightening sneer in Evie's direction. He leaned over the table to say something to Lucca. It was likely not a compliment in Evie's favor.

***

Nate and his crew closed the place down. They left only after Evie's insistence that they take his drunken ass to the docks. They were well past curfew, and his boat was scheduled to shove off soon.

Some dancers had already gone home hours earlier. Those that remained became Jerry's responsibility to deliver safely home. Evie and Rob closed the register, cleaned the bar, tabletops and various nooks and crannies of the club.

"Some night, huh?" he said with broom in hand while Evie stood nearby, tidying up behind the bar. "How's your hand?"

"It hurts like a son-of-a-bitch, but nothing a stiff drink can't fix, right?" Evie chuckled under her breath, but Rob found no amusement with her comment. He approached her to rest a gentle hand against her arm along the crook of her elbow, a wave of wildly inappropriate thoughts washed over her with his touch.

"No drinking. Just go home and get some rest," he said. "Please, for me, Evie, at least try."

She answered with a long pause and hesitant smile. "Only for you—I'll *try*."

"We had some real creeps in here tonight. Do you want me to walk you out to your car?"

Bring him home. Bring him home.

Evie eyed Rob, her licentious fingertips tickling her vinyl lined hips. Her inner voice's suggestion didn't sound half bad, but no. She couldn't do that to Rob—or Nate.

"Creeps aren't anything new around here, Rob. I'll be fine," she said with a more reassuring smile than before. He released her arm.

She hoped he'd pretend not to notice when she grabbed a few beers from the cooler, stashing them in her bag. No one ever ordered the chocolate stouts but her; what would it matter if she took a few for the road? She knew he'd rather know he supplied her with what she needed rather than face the alternative. Dirty little secret in hand, Evie walked out to her car.

***

By the time Evie made it home from work, it was almost four in the morning. She plunked herself down at the kitchen table, tossed her leg up on the split and worn top and pulled a wad of cash from the lining of her boot, fanning the stack with one hand while the other maneuvered a bottle opener, the hiss of carbonation and the stack of bills in competition to satisfy their master most. Her tips consisted mostly of singles, yielding just over three hundred dollars. The release of pressure from the wad of cash jammed in her boot felt fantastic. Not bad for a slow Sunday.

She grabbed the remaining beers from her bag and made her way upstairs, aided only by the moonlight beaming through the windows. There were still a couple more hours before sunrise, and Evie rarely found sleep prior to that.

She turned on her stereo. Building percussions and echoing vocals filled the darkness as she changed out of her work clothes into a soft cotton tank top and undies, and made her way to the bathroom, the moonglow reflecting ethereally in the white tiles. After she washed the makeup off her face, the phantom Evie was revealed again. The ghostlike image in the mirror declined the opportunity to scold its twin.

She turned away from her shadowy reflection. A chill ran down her spine. She felt its haunting stare fixed on her back as she walked away. She made her way to the bedroom window and climbed through to perch on the front porch's roof. She watched the lights and movements of the fishing vessels across the way. She recognized Nate's boat. It pushed past the lighthouse into open waters, then it faded into blackness. Relief washed over her knowing he'd be gone for a while, followed by an immense amount of guilt for finding such solace in his absence.

"Good bye, Nate," she whispered.

Useless as he may be, he accepts your flaws.

She scowled at her inner voice. It was right. Nate was good to her, always had been. He didn't judge. But they were numb. Their relationship had fizzled from exciting to complacent. Or was their relationship just an unfortunate casualty of her general lack of feeling? Apathy won out in the end. She decided it didn't matter.

Down to the last of her ill-gotten beers, Evie knew she'd be off to bed soon. She sat in the cool early morning air as the dew dampened her skin. She sat with her legs tucked up in front of her, hugged them close to her chest, and nursed her final beer with her injured hand. The cold bottle soothed the ache from her cut palm. Her head leaned back against the house. Her chin tilted up in the air. Her eyes closed. The salt air was familiar and intoxicating. She breathed it in with a heavy sigh of contentment. Her tongue ran across her lips. She savored her salty taste, courtesy of the seaside mist seeping into her pores. The crooning of hoarse vocals wafted out from her bedroom window.

She re-ran the evening's episode in her head again and again. After Nate's drunken arrival to the bar and awkward run in with Lucca, Rob returned to her side. He tended to the gash in her palm and cleaned up the broken glass from behind the bar. Nate, conversely, laughed at the incident. He goofed around with his friends. They jabbed each other, high-fived, and recounted random fishing stories that made no sense through their slurring and scatter-brained broken statements.

Rob had kicked out the college kids as soon as they walked in. Insulted, they spat crude words and hollow threats while walking away.

Evie paid little attention to Rob or Nate, though. She remained ever-conscious of watchful eyes from across the room. Fearful she might lose it, she stayed locked on Lucca's gaze. The threat of losing their invisible connection proved too great a risk to her pounding heartbeat.

The blonde woman with him continued to fight for his attention. His dark friend entertained himself with multiple dancers throughout the duration of their stay.

At one point, Evie noticed Natalia approach the booth again and exchanged a few brief words with Lucca. He stood from his seat and followed her over to the private booth closest to the bar. As he followed Natalia, he kept an eye on Evie. His wicked, sly grin remained plastered on his face, taunting her. He settled in. Lucca left the curtain open, fully aware Evie was bound by his hypnosis. She watched him as Natalia performed her not-so-private dance. Her hips twisted and curved around Lucca. All the while, he smiled Evie's way. She glowered back at him. Even from across the room, she could feel his cold, deep, soulless orbs like—like—

Son of a bitch—those eyes.

EIGHT

The sun rose. Evie was unaware of how she made it inside. Her memory failed to save her path back to her bed. It lost her climb into the linen cocoon of her down comforter. It recalled only Lucca.

Not quite a blacked-out night like so many others, she mustered the scant memory of strong arms lifting her. She dreamt of floating to her bed, of being eased down reverently, like a coffin into a grave. There was the firm sensation of his body on top of hers, the earth piling on, pinning her down, sweet suffocation. She looked up into the deep darkness of his eyes, saw his beautiful facial structure made more angular by the early light of daybreak. He beamed down at her, true longing relayed in his expression. His touch eluded her, his voice was mute, but she knew it was Lucca.

The music was off, yet there was sound. Evie heard a predatory growl erupt from deep inside of him. His expression turned menacing and cold. Her breathing increased in intensity, but not from lust. Overwhelming dread flushed over her. She pushed up on him. Lucca held her down. She pushed again. He cackled. Panic set in.

***

Evie awoke sometime after noon. In a show of gratitude, the beers she liberated from Sirens left the mere hint of a hangover. She was grateful for that. She remained in bed in silent solitude for what felt like hours, her heart still racing from the glorious nightmare. Below her pounding chest, her belly was in knots. That physical pain was caused by something more tangible, more reliable than her emotions running rampant. She groaned and rolled over. Her period was due any day. She whimpered from the pain before a soothing thought occurred to her. At least Nate was gone; that would spare her the expectation of performing oral during her menstrual cycle.

"Thank God for little miracles," she grumbled into the knotted comforter in her arms.

It wasn't until mid-afternoon that she decided to rise out of bed. The temperature was still cool outside as showers continued to pass intermittently through the area. Monday and Tuesday were her days off. Evie decided to coronate her empty schedule with an extra-long shower. Pink from scrubbing and near-scalding temperatures, she emerged from behind the curtain, wrapped herself in a towel, and stood in front of the bathroom mirror. The image that was but was not her seemed less pale and worn than the day before. It stared back at her. A certain flicker danced in its eyes.

What a delicious little dream.

She turned from the curious comment, unsure whether or not she appreciated the image's opinion. She switched on the stereo, her iPod summoned to play her personal favorite *slit-your-wrists* melodramatic musings. Anguished moans of a singer echoed throughout the house, wrapping around her, soothing her as she made her way downstairs. A not-unwelcome tingle coursed through her. Disturbing. Rousing. She thought of him, the man who'd introduced himself—forced himself to be known—as Lucca. Who was he? Where could he have come from?

Throughout her young life, Evie thought she knew everyone in town. Not a fisherman passed through that she did not have the misfortune of meeting.

She recalled the blonde woman, perhaps becoming more statuesque in her memory than she was in reality. She *was* beautiful, though, tall and heroin-thin. She made no effort to conceal her desire for Lucca or her disdain for Evie. The compulsion to vomit seemed the appropriate response to the image of her twisting her body like a serpent around him.

And then there was the strange man sitting in the corner. There was nothing extraordinary about him, save for the spice in his accent and the dark glow of his complexion; she guessed he was from some place warm, a desert, a jungle, somewhere primitive and exotic. It was difficult to say. Regardless, his facial features were as attractive as Lucca's. Their sharp angular structures mimicked each other, but his malevolent, bizarre laughter made her cringe, nothing like recalling Lucca's countenance. Nothing at all.

The image of Lucca evoked a burning in her core. An undercurrent of thrill rode the impulses down her spine. It lingered warm and wet in the deepest and softest crevices of her body. Lucca, a complete stranger, made her come undone.

She remembered her last thought before dreaming about him last night. She felt in her subconscious as though she'd met him before somewhere, but that was ridiculous. Had they met before, there was no way she would have forgotten him.

But those eyes... those eyes are unmistakable.

She pictured his devilish smile, his cold stare that pinned her from across the room. His eyes were the same glowing orbs from her dream, the same golden rims dancing in dark pools. She knew it. Her inner voice told her so, the same voice that called out to her from the mirror. Now the voice didn't chastise her. It held back judgment of her reaction to him. It welcomed the dream she'd had last night. It welcomed the fear that gripped her.

Welcomed with open arms.

Evie held onto the intensity of fending off Lucca at the bar. She reveled in the wake of his attention. She would have loved to have danced for him, would have been glad to discard her monotonous existence for a chance to get closer. Her hips swayed like a metronome to the soft humming of music filling the house as she glided into the kitchen. A devious smirk lined her face. As she lifted one hand to the cupboard, the other slid underneath the waistband of her panties, toying with the lace trim against her skin. Her body halted as she opened the door.

Empty.

She'd forgotten; there was not one bit of food left in the house. Evie slouched her shoulders, the fog of her daydream burning off. The thought of going grocery shopping made her eyes roll. She hated leaving the house on her days off. To be out in public meant to subject herself to glares from nosy neighbors who knew enough not to approach her, but were too stupid to keep their prying eyes off of her. When necessary, she would ask Nate to conduct such plebian tasks for her. But he was gone, and there was not one crumb to eat in the house. The deed needed to be done. With severe hesitation, Evie collected her tip money in her wallet, and with iPod in hand she headed out the door.

***

Evie paused in the grocery store's automatic doorway. The doors flung open, closed, and then opened again. She didn't enter, not until she inserted her ear buds. Her iPod shuffled through the soundtrack of her life. The same somber music she blared through her house would serenade her as she shopped.

She tossed one bag of junk food after the other into her cart. Any food she bought had to be ready with a bare minimum of human involvement; idiotproofing was more important than flavor. Nate cooked. While he was gone she subsisted on cookies, chips, fruit, milk and cereals. She bought bread and eggs out of compulsion, because that's what you're supposed to buy at the store when you're an adult, not because she'd use them. They would have to wait for Nate to come home. She grabbed some bacon, and steaks were on sale. The meats would get tossed in the freezer. Nate often returned from his fishing trips with an extra lobster or two. There was nothing better than some surf and turf with a cold beer and a tightly rolled joint.

Evie paced through the aisles. She felt eyes on her. A woman whose daughter worked with her at the club snapped her gaze away when Evie looked at her. Another young woman with her daughter by her side scowled when Evie smiled at the little girl.

Her mother made her own reputation as a town tramp and notorious addict. Apparently, to be a waitress at a strip club was equally offensive. That's what they all thought. Or at least she felt that they did. That's what her inner voice told her.

The music hummed in her ears. A woman sang about the lingering touch of her lover, a song that Evie had always enjoyed—soft, sultry, and somehow tragic. In an effort to dismiss the negativity surrounding her, Evie let her mind drift to thoughts of Lucca. She smiled, conjuring the image of the way his body moved as he walked away from the bar, his confident gait. She thought of his wicked smile aimed directly at her—for her—while Natalia danced for him. She stifled a giggle, bit down on her lip, and fought not to make even more of a spectacle of herself in the middle of the grocery store than she already felt. She wondered if she'd ever see him again.

The only attraction that grocery shopping offered was the well-stocked liquor section inside the store, quite convenient for those like Evie. Her cart was already lined with a sufficient amount of things that would pass as food. She perused the bottles with thirsty eyes. A case of microbrew stout and a bottle of cheap whiskey topped her cart. The hard stuff was a no-name brand on sale. For the price and for the proof, she'd be crazy to pass it up. It was a good start to her week. If she bought more than that she'd just call for more glares from unwanted onlookers. As always, she expected to return in a day or two for more provisions as needed.

A vibration in her back pocket made her jump. Her reaction startled a nearby stock boy whom she recognized as a club regular. She shot him a toxic glare. She knew his look. She'd seen that expression time and time again and hated it. He stared at her ass like he recognized it, committed its curvature to memory, probably filthied a gym sock or two back home thinking about it.

Dismissing his stare, Evie pulled her phone from her jeans. She huffed at the phone's caller ID; Blythe was trying to get a hold of her. A row of tiny icons glowing at the top of her screen indicated a series of text messages and phone calls were missed. She'd been too wrapped up in the music to notice. That and daydreaming of Lucca.

What the fuck does she want?

Evie scowled, her inner voice doing the driving, waiting for the phone to cease vibrating as she let the call go to voicemail. She scanned through the text messages:

What are we doing today?
Are you awake yet?
Got an idea. Call me when you get this.

Seriously, this girl needs to get laid already, Evie thought. With much reluctance, she called Blythe back, scowling at the stock boy still staring at her ass. After just one ring Blythe answered the call.

"She lives," Blythe said, her voice screeching through the tiny phone speaker.

"Hey stalker, I'm at the grocery store. What's up?"

"I wanted to take a ride, but it's too late now."

"What do you mean it's too late? Where'd you want to go?" Evie snipped with playful exaggeration, or at least what she thought was playful.

"Really, Evie? Attitude? I've been trying to get a hold of you all day. I—Whatever, I wanted to head down to the city earlier today, but it's too late now. So I booked an appointment for us tomorrow to get a tarot card reading with this woman who one of my co-workers uses. She's supposedly wicked good."

Evie thought of a million others things she'd rather do than get a tarot card reading on her day off. She had thirteen bottles of those million things in her shopping cart. Without a doubt, she hated the idea of the city. The onset of an anxiety attack threatened her just thinking about it.

"You know I'm not into fortune tellers," Evie said.

"Scared of what you might hear?"

"Scared of who we might see in the city," she corrected, eyes fixed on her shopping cart.

"Well maybe you should've thought about that before you decided to prance around in rubber underwear for a living."

Hey, that's a low blow, fucking bitch.

"The appointments are booked for noon tomorrow. Make sure you're up in time," Blythe said before hanging up. Evie stared at her phone as the screen went to resting black. For once, she agreed with her inner voice.

Dammit.

NINE

"C'mon, Evie. This is going to be fun," Blythe said.

Her SUV roared through the winding roads out of town. Evie sat quiet in the passenger seat, flicking through static radio station after station. The white noise quieted her anxious brain, usually too nervous to stray too far out of town.

The city was at least a few hours' drive through winding forest highway. Just about anything outside of Fallhaven was. The ride was beautiful this time of year. The trees awoke, budding bright green vegetation creating a shadowy canopy over the twisted highway roads. The drive itself could be treacherous though. Several vehicles were swallowed by the roads' serpentine passageways each year, college kids for the most part, too drunk or high to make it back to campus.

The roads, however, were not what made Evie nervous. In truth, the city terrified her, swarms of strangers coming and going, a cacophony of beeping horns, sirens, and chatter. The metropolis to the south was home to many of her less savory clientele. Just like the stock boy, they recognized her. Too often, they felt no shame in asking her for a lap dance, commenting on her outfit, requesting their usual drink. The college kids were notorious for crude remarks. Being closer to such taunting filled her with dread.

Being of presumably more rational and sound mind, Blythe had chided Evie for her agoraphobia in the past, much like her predilection to drink. Evie couldn't believe it—wouldn't believe it. No, her inner voice told her otherwise. She was being judged. Such paranoia was warranted, so long as her inner voice confirmed it for her. And it did. **Repeatedly**.

"I'm telling you, a friend from work had a reading done with this woman and said she was dead on."

Evie took very little stock in tarot card readings or fortune tellers. She went to see one a few years ago, before her grandmother died. She was told of fantastic new beginnings and opportunities. Apparently, Madame Whatever had either misinterpreted the cards and neglected to foresee her grandmother's death, or was beyond enthusiastic about Evie's budding career at a strip club.

"I still think it's a rip-off." Evie pouted as she settled on the nearby college radio station. Heavy metal filled the SUV's interior, wicked guitar licks and the thundering of a double bass pedal. Evie's inner voice kicked back to the aggressive rhythm, but Blythe killed the music with an annoyed flick of her wrist.

"This is going to be fun, Evie. Try to keep an open mind."

"And what are you hoping to hear about yourself?" Evie wondered, was Blythe hoping to hear affirmation of her beauty? Her optimistic personality? Or that she would always succeed in life?

I know what Miss Vain is looking for.

Evie's eyes narrowed as the jigsaw pieces clicked together.

"You're looking to hear something about Evan, aren't you?" Of course she was. Blythe's coy smile validated her claim. "You know, I still have yet to meet this dream boy."

"I know. He keeps asking to meet you, but you're always sleeping or something. And then you go to work, and forgive me if I don't think taking my boyfriend to Sirens is my idea of a romantic evening."

Evie gasped and widened her eyes in mock offense. She knew Blythe understood why she worked where she did.

You know why she doesn't want to bring him by the club.

"Afraid Evan's eyes might wander?"

Evie regretted the joke as soon as it passed her lips and damned her inner voice for letting it slip out. It hung in the air like a rotten egg, and she watched it register on Blythe's fragile expression. "I'm sorry Blythe, really, I didn't mean anything by it."

"I know what you meant, Evie. But I like this guy, and well... I don't want him to meet you in your underwear."

"You're crazy. No guy in their right mind would choose a cheap trick over you," Evie said.

Who are you calling a cheap trick?

Blythe responded with a glower, one that warned Evie to tread lightly, that harkened back to the sins of her past. Two years ago Blythe was engaged. Foolish young love with a guy she met while away at college, never meant to last, but that was her style. Blythe brought her fiancé home from school after graduation, and being so excited to introduce the two most important people in her life to each other, Blythe brought him to visit Evie at Sirens as soon as they arrived in Fallhaven. The joyous visit turned into a frequent occurrence for her fiancé, and without much coercion had transformed into a full-fledged drunken affair which went on for some time before Blythe's naïveté wore off. Blythe discovered him one night tangled like a slippery seal in Evie's fishnets and vinyl, the two wasted beyond comprehension, courtesy of some Oxy that Nate had scored, which Evie stole. That short career of experimenting with opiates was the darkest time of Evie's life.

Those were the days, her inner voice swooned.

Rather than ratting her out to Nate, Blythe kept Evie's dirty little secret. They were like sisters, of course, and their history far predated her infidelitous fiancé. Nate would have been too doped up—Evie took *some* of the Oxy, not *all* of it—for the affair to register anyhow. Blythe scolded Evie, pressed her to get help, sober up. And as far as her opiate abuses were concerned, Evie did.

Blythe said she placed more blame on her fiancé, whom she shouldn't have fallen so hard for in the first place, but Evie knew better. She could never forgive Evie, not one hundred percent. Blythe also never forgave herself for being foolish enough to flaunt her half-naked best friend to any man she cared for. Blythe had yet to trust any man since, for that matter, and hadn't been able to carry on anything resembling a sustainable relationship, though Evie knew she wanted one more than anything.

Why do you keep apologizing for that? She should have known better.

Contrary to her inner voice, Evie hated herself for her misdeeds. And though she should have taken her mistakes as a learning experience, should have cleaned up her act completely, she found she drank more and smoked more because of it, fought fire with fire, inclined to let the motherfucker burn.

Now sitting in silence as her friend drove, Evie could feel the air between them getting heavy, carbon monoxide-poisonous. She needed to find humor. Fast.

"Okay," Evie said, placing a hand high on Blythe's right thigh, "I get it. You want to fuck me. I get it. I like you too, Blythe. But not in a lesbian kind of way. I mean, unless you're willing to wear the strap-on. *Then* we might be in business."

"Ha ha. Very funny," Blythe said, whisking her friend's paw off her leg as playful little fingertips spidered their way along her inner thigh. She grabbed the shift lever to initiate a parallel park, giving it a not-so-subtle jerking motion before engaging reverse. "You'll just have to wait and see what this fortune teller says."

Evie raised her brow and tented her fingers, a cartoonish lupine expression on her face. The toxic atmosphere in the SUV's cabin was replaced by nitrous, and the two girls burst into laughter as they exited the car and made their way on foot towards the seer.

***

The fortune teller was located in a dark, unlit alley. Only a crazy soul with no self-preservation instinct would venture down there after darkness fell. The lost. The confused. The damned. Evie felt at home.

The entrance to the shop was unmarked. The fact that Blythe managed to locate such a remote locale was bizarre. Sweet innocent Blythe, amongst the damned.

I'm working on that.

Once inside, the thick aroma of incense and waxy smoke assaulted the senses, a scent so strong it burned like a harsh bong rip. The shop was lit by candles of various shapes and sizes. The chipped concrete walls were draped with a rainbow of silken scarves. They hid the hideous desolation of the commercial space. Display cases held cards, crystals, incense, jewelry and other trinkets. The soft hum of new age chanting echoed through the space.

Blythe, what the hell have you gotten us into?

An elderly woman with long white hair pinned up with a seashell comb emerged from a batik curtain behind the counter. Her golden brocade tunic hung on her shoulders like it was still on a wire hanger, concealing a skeletal frame. She wore a peaceful look upon her face. Arms wide, she smiled unto the girls.

"Ladies," she said. "Welcome to my home."

Evie was taken aback. "Your home? You live here?"

"I do. My name is Hope," the woman said. "You must be Evelyn."

Evie would have snickered at the convenience of the woman's name if not for the sudden booming of her pulse between her ears. "I'm sorry, how do you know my name?"

"I think I already gave it to her, Evie, relax. I made our appointments ahead of time. Remember?" Blythe said. Evie tried to believe her friend's interjection.

This is bullshit.

"Shall we?" Hope gestured towards black shadows behind a purple curtain. She smiled at Evie, her serene facade unwavering. Merciful pleas shrieked inside Evie's head.

"Yeah, you go, Evie. I can wait to go second." Blythe pushed her forward, clearly enraptured by the metaphysical wares all around. Evie acquiesced with obvious hesitation. The woman paid her reluctance no mind. Evie followed her, buffeted by the chants piped in through overhead speakers, into a dimly lit room. It was much smaller than the reception area, adorned with a small round table and two plain wooden chairs.

"Please sit," Hope said as she motioned towards the chair with its back to the purple curtain. "You have a lot of weight on you now, Evie, don't you? There is a heavy air about you." Evie held her nerves at bay. She refrained to comment, denying the woman the satisfaction of any response.

Hope shuffled a deck of cards and fanned them out across the tabletop. "Please pick three cards," she said.

Evie scanned the curved row of ornately designed cards, all face down. She fingered two from the fan without much thought or effort. As she extended her index finger for a third card, one leapt across the table towards Hope like the alpha of the pack.

"This one feels compelled to join us," Hope said with a jovial, squinty-eyed smile. Evie refrained from rolling her eyes. "The card is choosing you, Evie. Let's listen to it. Go ahead and pick one more." Her voice was more urgent now. Evie obeyed.

Hope shuffled and fanned the cards out again. She requested Evie to pick three more, which she did. Hope then closed her eyes before continuing with the reading, taking in a deep, whistling breath through her nostrils. She cradled Evie's selected cards, paused and frowned.

"You carry a heavy load."

Yeah, tell me about it.

"Your destiny has been lain before you. I fear for you, child."

Yeah. I fear for myself too. Damned to life as a skanky strip club waitress.

"To resist him is to resist yourself."

Wait, resist who?

"Your past is heartbreaking."

80

Hope's voice trailed off, strangled into silence by the images projected through her mind's eye. Tears welled in her wizened eyes. Her sympathies relayed within the crevices of her crow's feet.

"My family is dead," Evie said. This, she presumed, would explain her sorrowful past. "But who are you talking about? Who is *he*?" The old woman seemed reluctant to answer.

"No, dear, not this life. Your *past* life. When *you* died." Her voice trailed off again. "I try very hard to block out past life tragedies, but yours is... unavoidable. Oh my dear, you poor thing."

Evie flushed. Goose bumps washed over her body. Hope was quite the actress, a real Stanislavski System success story. She had the hairs on the back of Evie's neck on end.

"What happened in my past life?"

"Evie, understand that what we've experienced in our past lives repeats in our current. We must understand our true nature to learn from our past and accept our future with an open heart."

What the fuck, lady?

Hope spread the cards out. The first was the Hermit placed upside down.

"Why do you keep away from others? This reclusive path of self-destruction is no good for you."

Evie marveled at Hope's theatrics.

"What do you mean self-destruction?"

"You, Evie; the Hermit is you. You close yourself out from others. Your habits are unhealthy for you, child. You must know this to be true?"

Of course Evie knew Hope was right. But for a complete stranger to quite literally lay it out on the table rattled her down to the bone. The old woman knew her name, knew her habits. Evie felt another stone laid upon her chest. Her lungs struggled to fill.

Hope continued. The next card was the Chariot.

"Face up, this is good for you. There are changes that need to be made, changes in you. This card here, the Chariot speaks to the situation at hand. There is no mistaking your current lifestyle choices must be addressed."

Evie leaned in closer. "How?"

"Let's see the next card. This was the card that jumped out at you, called for you. Let's see what will bring about change."

Hope placed the Devil card next to the first two; she gasped. Evie flinched. The Devil stared upside-down through slanted cat-like eyes. He had the head of a goat. His body was contorted. His characteristic spiked tail curled around him. Two naked figures, a man and woman, stood below the Devil. They wore horns atop their heads and thick iron collars around their necks, tethered by a chain to the Devil's grasp.

What? What? What the fuck do you see?

"He comes. To resist him is futile. He will bring the change you need."

"The Devil is coming for me?"

"Yes, dear. The Devil represents a new beginning, perhaps the change you've fought so hard against in your past lives? Don't try to resist. He is you and you are him. This will bring the change you need. Understand it is inevitable."

The woman placed the fourth card above the others. She worked in a clockwise motion around the center figure, the Hermit. The fourth card was revealed as the Lovers, face up.

"Ah, you see, there it is. Do not resist. Even if you do, your inner voice will draw you to him. To love the Devil is to love the good and the bad. Your connection to him is undeniable."

Hope's voice was soft, calm, like her grandmother's. Evie hated her for it. Moreover, she was undecided as to how she felt about the woman's performance. Some of her words were frighteningly accurate. Her intuition was eerie. She wondered why Hope was so disturbed by her *past life*. The gasping, the cryptic messages, the tears, if it was all an act, then contact the Academy Awards.

What if the crazy bitch isn't faking? What if she's a bona fide spiritual medium? Then what?

Another stone pressed Evie's chest down harder. The walls of the tomblike room closed in around her.

The next card revealed to Evie was the High Priestess. Then the Death card. All six cards had been laid out to create a cross-like shape. The woman placed a seventh card in to the top right corner of the formation. The Wheel of Fortune.

That one has to be good right?

"There you have it. Your inner voice, she is your High Priestess. Listen to yourself, Evie. You know the answers are in your heart. You can feel them all too well. When you can embrace yourself, can be true to yourself, you can embrace those changes. The Death card is indicating the change. Something new comes your way. I suggest you reconcile with yourself, because you do not control it. The Wheel of Fortune indicates all will be well, *if* you can manage the changes in store. All Major Arcana;

83

this is a very good spread, Evie, *if* you can embrace it. *If* you can embrace yourself."

Embrace my foot up your ass, lady.

Evie connected with Hope's gaze, searching her old eyes for further meaning. There had to be a better explanation. She sat at the edge of her seat, bemused by the peculiar woman's interpretations.

"Evie, you've been searching. You've been looking for meaning. My dear, the time has come for you to discover it."

Evie allowed her body a visible tremor and thought of her inner voice, the ghost in her bathroom mirror. Each night she was unable to sleep, every day afraid to be sober and alone with her thoughts. She had, in fact, searched for a purpose, a meaning to it all. Hope offered her one, but Evie was unsure what to do with it.

"He's already a part of you. You must search within yourself. Listen to your inner being. Take the reins over your emotions. You will find your purpose. Change is fast approaching. You need to be in control of yourself. You won't see the good in your sacrifice, but you must understand, it is all for you. For you to understand and for you to love. The Devil comes regardless."

Evie sat as though strapped to the chair, mouth agape. Hope could be throwing her best mumbo-jumbo in Evie's face, but act or not, it hit a nerve buried so deep within her body she was unable to deny it.

"So, things are going to change... I have to keep control over my emotions... the Devil will come for me... and I *love* him?"

Hope let out a sigh. "Evie, I don't normally feel so compelled to reveal a reading quite as I have with you. But, my dear, you must take heed. Your path was etched in stone before you ever came to be in this life. You cannot escape a destiny as strong as yours."

Hope's voice wavered. Evie's sights narrowed in on the faint quivering of her pursed lips. The more Hope spoke of her destiny, the more upset she became.

"I don't understand how you can talk about love and the Devil at the same time? What kind of change is that? What is my destiny?" Evie asked, perturbed the woman insisted on maintaining her act.

"No, no more." Hope threw her hands up in front of her face. "I won't have this in my house. No more."

Hope's raised, insistent voice startled Evie. She transformed from a calm and controlled sage to a crazed old coot.

What is wrong with this lady?

Hope rose from her chair, grabbed Evie's upper arm, and escorted her back into the reception area. Blythe was bent at the waist, her nose inches from a glass display case perusing an assortment of crystals, as she turned her head to greet her friend. The anticipatory spark in Blythe's eyes smothered at the sight of them.

"I'll be just a moment, and then I will take you, Blythe." Hope excused herself and vanished behind the shroud.

Blythe approached Evie with a scowl. "What was that all about, Evie? What did you do?"

Wide-eyed and baffled, Evie shrugged her shoulders. "I have no idea. She told me my life was about to change and some shit about me loving the Devil."

Blythe shot a foreboding glare at her.

A re-composed Hope emerged from the reading room, and Blythe bounded forward at the seer's beckoning.

Once alone in the waiting room, surrounded by crystals and prisms, sigils and incense, *a real one-stop shop for all your mystic needs*, it was somehow easier for Evie to remind herself she didn't believe in this hocus pocus crap anyhow. Such half-hearted reassurance aided to lift the rocks constricting her chest. She scanned the dusty showcases full of jewelry and pewter figurines, *cheap trinket shit, probably came in boxes of 500 stamped MADE IN CHINA*.

When she glanced over the front counter she saw a book left open to show the day's appointments. At noon, the old woman was expecting two readings for a Miss Blythe Delaney and guest. There was no mention of any Evie—and *certainly* not *Evelyn*—to note.

How did that crazy bitch know our name?

TEN

"This is fucked up," Evie mumbled to herself. Her eyes drifted about the room when the purple brocade curtain burst to life, billowing and swirling before being shoved aside by Blythe's frantic hands.

"Are you ready?" Blythe scowled.

"Yeah, what happened?"

"Nothing. Let's just pay and get out of here."

Blythe shuffled through her purse for a couple of twenty dollar bills. As Hope came out to join the girls, Blythe tossed the money on the front counter and without a word stormed out of the shop. Heart thumping, Evie remained cemented in place, gawking at Hope, who countered her gawkiness with a mere docile grin.

"What the hell did you say to her?" Evie asked.

"Take care, child. Remember, it is all for you."

Evie glared sharply. Her jaw glitched, and she spun on her heels to chase after Blythe.

***

The girls sat in static, rigid energy as Blythe pulled out onto the city's main streets.

The route back onto the highway differed from that which brought them into the city, and just as Evie had feared, they navigated by the college campus. She hadn't realized how close it was to Hope's shop. Gaggles of perky girls and droves of fraternity pledges stood at street corners, sat across bus-stop benches, and commingled along the sidewalks. Her stomach churned with anxiety. She wrapped her arms tight around her waist to hold in the angst. No good. Acid burned up her throat as beads of sweat formed across her forehead. The panic clamped its hands around her throat. Eyes pinched shut; Evie pushed herself into her seat, begging the attack to subside.

Red light after red light, Evie pushed herself further down into the passenger seat. Her eyes scanned the cityscape for signage directing them towards the highway, but their path was brought to one screeching halt after another as Blythe slammed on the brakes, consumed by her own inner turmoil.

Blythe's SUV was positioned in the front of the final red light before releasing them to the highway back to Fallhaven.

Almost there, Evie told herself and begged her anxious heart to cease its wild rhythm. *Almost there, stupid girl. Keep it together.*

A pack of frat boys passed through the crosswalk, and within that pack Evie saw a familiar face, one she knew all too well—one of the college boys Rob had kicked out of Sirens on Sunday night. Blond hair and glasses, the one so keen on fondling her. Her thighs clenched tight as she fidgeted in her seat. He walked, chatted, and laughed with his fellow brothers through the intersection as they exchanged a brightly colored paper in their hands.

The longer Evie's eyes froze on him, the more frantic her heart pounded in her chest. She fixated on him, begging the red light to turn green. Damn the light, it offered no relief. His eyes flickered towards the traffic as he passed by, and damn him for turning his sights through the SUV's windshield, directly towards Evie.

A second of questioning. A moment to make the connection. His perverse grin made her cringe as he recognized her; Evie was certain of that. The cursed light didn't turn green fast enough. A wave of terror washed over her and swept her feet out from under her. Despite the green light and despite the honks from other waiting cars, Four Eyes took his sweet-ass time stepping onto the sidewalk, honed in on her wide-eyed expression.

Fuck the one slab of glass not tinted on this goddamn heap of metal.

Evie hated Blythe in a way she never had before as the SUV's tires chirped through the intersection and onto the highway.

***

Few words were spoken between the girls for more than half of the drive back to Fallhaven. Finally, Evie's racing heart eased off its redline.

"So did you get the reading you were looking for?" Evie snipped.

Blythe pulled the SUV off of the main highway and onto the state road leading them far away from society, back towards home. Seeing as how Blythe did not fill the ride home with mindless chatter about herself, Evie guessed she would've been happier with a fortune cookie from the Shanghai Dynasty.

"Hope kept telling me something about helping him for you. What is that supposed to mean?" Blythe said, exasperated.

"Me? Why help me?"

"I don't know. I think it means I should've gone first, that's what. Whatever that old lady read about you scared the crap out of her and she couldn't focus on me."

"Blythe, you can't believe what that woman said, right? It's all smoke and mirrors."

Blythe harrumphed and wrapped her little fingers tighter around the steering wheel, distorting their delicate nature. "You think what you want, but I've gone to a few readings in my life and they've been dead on. This woman is supposed to be the real deal, very connected, and she was obviously upset by what she had to say to you."

Evie remained silent. She knew continuing such a ridiculous argument with her best friend was useless. What were they fighting about anyway, who got the better tarot card reading? *Really?* It was absurd. Still, the woman's genuine reaction to her reading made Evie uneasy. She sat in silence and pondered the woman's odd ranting, and then noticed Blythe's heavy foot on the gas pedal. It seemed Blythe, alone in her own thoughts, took her frustration out on the road.

Blythe's hand fumbled through her pocketbook, producing an orange piece of paper and tossed it on Evie's lap. "And get this, I grabbed this from the front counter at the old bat's shop. They must be advertising it across the city to attract college students. What kind of hippie students would go into that shop anyway?"

Evie took the paper into her hands and held it up. It was a party flyer, the same citrusy hue as the piece of paper Four Eyes had in his hand when he found Evie sitting amongst the traffic.

Perverted hippies, that's who.

"Evan's throwing a party at his house next week?" Evie asked, reading through the details of the advert.

"Yeah, and he hasn't mentioned a damn thing about it to me. Why would any adult throw a party for college kids?"

"That's weird. His house is in the middle of nowhere and under renovations right now, isn't it?"

"Exactly." Blythe's voice cracked, "Why wouldn't he say something to me about this? It's next week, for Christ's sake."

"I'm sure there's a reasonable explanation," Evie said before being cut off.

"Don't say it, Evie. There's no reasonable explanation—and we're going."

There was no arguing with Blythe, not on this one. But Evie worked every Saturday night, so something had to give. Now was not the time to discuss logistics, though. She allowed her friend to drive and sat in silence.

***

It was almost dinner time when they arrived back in Fallhaven. Evie insisted Blythe run by the package store before returning to her house. Even though she had made a run the day before, she could sense that Blythe's negativity would obliterate her stash. The night promised to be long and painful, but self-medication was Dr. Westvale's specialty. She tossed together a variety bag of nips and all the fixings for Blythe's favorite margaritas.

The two girls sat at Evie's kitchen table for some time. Blythe continued to fume over the day's events. Tearing through the pitcher of margaritas that Evie mixed for her, she texted back and forth with Evan, or so Evie presumed. She paid little attention to Blythe's infuriated state and sorted through her bag of nips, and then sat silent as one shot led to two, led to three, to four, to five, six and seven, and then she lost count.

Blythe left Evie in her drunken stupor at some point later that night. Angry, tequila-fueled lust sent her in pursuit of her boyfriend's affections.

Evie grabbed what nips she hadn't sucked dry and went upstairs. It was time for church. As she ascended the stairs, her ovaries twisted, a reminder of the fun-filled week to come.

Sinking slowly into the piping-hot tub, her body was encased in its warm compress. She was glad to be rid of Blythe, to be alone in prayer. The water did more than soothe her aching muscles. It melted her insides, calmed her, and allowed her to forget the day's stressors.

Wasted, floating in the steamy depths of her religion and her mind, Evie lost herself in her weightlessness. The physical medicinal qualities of the booze and the bath chased away her pre-menstrual cramps, but did very little to cast out the haunting echoes of Hope's voice. A few nips later, and she had managed to dull those to a low murmur in the back of her head. The crazed fortune teller's blasphemy was not welcome in her sanctuary.

Satisfied, Evie crawled naked into her bed. Under her white linen cocoon, she drifted off into a heavy drunken slumber.

***

The first thing she noticed was the slipperiness of her inner thighs. She presumed her eyes were open and cast them about her bedroom looking for an anchor point. The clouds were too thick to allow any moonlight through. The room spun. She could smell the booze wafting from her pores. Her head lolled back and forth. Her body tingled from the alcohol. The rolling waves of drunkenness flipped her belly upside down. She loved the ride. Then she felt a tongue.

Too drunk to be distressed, too aroused to stop it, Evie felt a tongue flicker against the sensitive pleasure-spots hidden in the tender folds between her legs. It lapped up the wetness and massaged the muscles therein. A set of hands clasped down on her hip bones. Their fingertips dug into her flesh. Undiscovered pressure-points sent shivers across her body. She reached down to find long strands of hair entwined between her fingers that grew from a head in rhythmic motion. Her breathing increased. Pure elation flooded her senses.

Goddamn, that feels amazing.

Evie weaved her thighs in and out like a butterfly flexing its wings. Her back arched. Her chest pushed up to the cool, dark air nipping at her. A chilling thought crept into her inebriated mind, sobered her for only a split second. Her body's euphoria arrested.

Nate is still on the boat. Who the fuck is this?

In shock and drunken confusion, Evie laid there and allowed the assault. A hand released her hip and crept its way up. It cupped her left breast and pulled playfully. The other hand followed suit. She brought her hands up to grasp the ones fondling her, those phantom hands that handled her body like none ever had before. Her breathing quickened as she came closer and closer to euphoria. A moan escaped past her lips. Muffled laughter emerged from between her legs.

Evie squinted through the darkness, fought to focus. She saw dark eyes gleaming through the black, eyes she recognized.

"Lucca," she said his name, panting heavily. Evie tried to push him away from the cradle of her thighs, but found no purchase, no success. She was too drunk, too numb to move. "How did you..." Her words trailed off. Her body trembled.

"Shh." His soft voice lifted out of the darkness.

As Evie came down from her high, she fixed on his gaze. Her eyes adjusted to the night. She could make out his defined bone structure, beautifully angled, lined in shadow. As she focused, she froze in horror. Depthless pools glared back, but his eyes did not evoke the horror. Below them, his face was coated in a dark and sticky crimson. It glistened in the night like the golden flecks that danced across his dark irises. Blood smeared all over his face, his smile widened, delighted by the spectacle.

Frothy 80-proof bile lurched up Evie's throat, searing as it reached up past her uvula.

Evie awoke and flung her body to the side of the bed in desperation, vomiting just as she cleared the edge of the comforter. The cheap liquor burned as it spewed through her nostrils. She struggled to catch her breath. Time stood still as her stomach voided its contents. Once empty, she lay hunched on all fours over the edge of the bed, defeated.

A dream. She huffed. *A fucking dream.*

Still drunk, Evie stumbled through the darkness to the bathroom. She grabbed a towel and messily cleaned up her vomit. The room spun, wracking with twisted seasickness. With a great degree of difficulty and too drunk to care about her half-assed attempt to clean her mess, she flopped sideways on the bed and passed out for the remainder of the night. She stayed that way until late into the next afternoon.

***

Throughout the following day, Evie nursed a nasty hangover. She struggled between the physical discomfort of her menstrual cramps and the shock of what grotesqueness lurked in her subconscious. She blamed Hope's card reading about loving the Devil, her period, and her own wild imagination.

Don't blame me. That was wonderful.

The reclusiveness she normally faked her way through at work was too over-powering. Unless forced to do her job and fill an order, she hid in the dark corners of Sirens, arms wrapped tight around her middle to quell the protest going on inside.

Rob was called out past the bar by angry customers and confused dancers approaching him for drinks while the pretty little red-headed waitress went missing. Searching empty booths and behind pub tables, he found Evie hiding in the shadows. His comforting arms offered little relief to her ailments. She refused to look him in the eyes, climbing out from behind a booth. Fear that he might read her mind and relive her dream terrified her as he came near, too embarrassed by the workings of her own fancies.

"Evie's what's wrong?" Rob asked.

"Nothing. I'm just not feeling well." She feigned illness with a hand set dramatically across her brow.

"Do you need to go home?"

Do you really want to be alone with me right now?

"No," Evie protested. She couldn't see or hear Rob, just flashes of gaudy stage lights and the echo of her own voice. No, she didn't want to be alone with her inner voice, her fucked-up psyche. "No, please Rob. I'll snap out of it."

And she did. Evie forced herself around the club for the remainder of the night. Rob kept a cautious eye on her, more so than usual.

After closing, she retreated to her house. What better way to beat a lingering hangover than more booze? Evie skipped church and went straight out onto the roof of the front porch. The salty air was surprisingly gentle to her wrecked stomach. She passed out half-naked, propped up against the shingled wall while paint chips took purchase in her hair. As the day's first rays of sun peaked over the horizon, she was coaxed back to her bed.

ELEVEN

Evie awoke early afternoon to her uterus trying to rip through her body, thankful to feel only a mild hangover. More importantly, she was spared any more disturbing dreams.

She moaned in bed, suffocated herself under her pillow and hugged her mid-section, hoping to quell the clenching deep inside. She staggered to the medicine cabinet, winced and then grimaced at an empty shelf. Doubled over in pain, Evie fought the urge to hurl. She needed to pop a few pills to minimize her suffering, but was reminded then of the joy of dating a drug addict.

Fuck you, Nate. I fucking need those pills.

For the second-best option, Evie turned back into the bedroom and fumbled through the grab bag of nips she'd bought with Blythe. To her pleasant surprise, two little bottles of clear liquid remained. She hoped the tiny servings of vodka would be enough to settle the bloody knots in her belly. They both warmed and relaxed her muscles, if only a tiny bit. Hunched over, she went down stairs for a cup of coffee.

Evie sat at her kitchen table with a warm mug. Her phone buzzed on the counter; it caught her off guard, and she jumped in her seat. Cramps stabbed her, and she flinched from the pain before glowering at her phone. It bore glad tidings, however. Blythe canceled their session at the gym to spend some time with Evan. That was good. She was in no mood or condition to exercise. Evie wondered when she'd have the great fortune of meeting Blythe's new beau, though the question was of little consequence. Between the cramping and the shots of vodka, her stomach was a wreck. She had no desire for their drama.

***

The day drifted on, and Evie lingered on the sofa. She curled up in the fetal position and snuggled her weed-packed glass bowl, welcoming the peace her solitude brought. Such rest proved the best medicine for dealing with her cramps, but the THC wasn't any slouch, either.

Evie divorced herself from the world throughout the remainder of the week and into the weekend. She only left her house to go to work or the liquor store. She even ignored Blythe's calls and texts. If she had any more wet dreams about Lucca, she was either too tired or too bombed to retain any memory of them. She felt grateful for such a reprieve, repulsed by her own imagination's conjuring. Rain showers continued outside, and Evie remained a hermit.

The next week rolled around. Evie made it to her favorite time, her days off. With plenty of food and a decent amount of booze, she could stay hidden away. She sighed, contented on her sofa with a beer in hand. Her cramps disappeared. Her period was gone. Her company was limited to the ongoing set of artists she'd booked to her one-woman festival. Raspy voices and haunting acoustic guitar licks echoed throughout the house. She reveled in her cloud of sweet marijuana smoke.

***

Evie stood in front of the mantle. She stared at the ghosts of her family, mesmerized by her doppelganger. The similarities between her and Evelyn were remarkable. The bone structure, the pale-eyed stare, the body's shape; Evelyn could be her trapped in time like one of those vintage photographs you'd take at a carnival. Evelyn was wrapped in a dark shawl with boat masts and fishing nets behind her. Her fishing crew stood awaiting her orders. She was plain, simple, and much more pure than the stoner holding the photo.

She's judging you too.

Evie's brow creased with conflict. Her inner voice, her High Priestess according to that old psychic—what bullshit—mocked her day in and day out, told her to drink, told her to overindulge; why should she listen to it? How was that healthy for her? She shook her head and placed the photo back on the mantle.

"Crazy old bat."

Sometimes crazy leads to the best kind of truth.

Evie's enchanted state was suddenly broken by the clattering of her phone against the countertop. She released a breathy "fuck" of relief. She'd avoided Blythe's calls for days, but this time she raced for the phone, happy to be interrupted before her High Priestess could continue.

"Hey, Blythe. What's up?"

"Where have you been? I've been trying to get a hold of you for days."

"I've been around. I just haven't been in the mood to chat," she said, settling back onto the sofa.

"I figured that. Listen, it's Tuesday night, Evan and I are going to the Dynasty for karaoke and drinks. I want you to come meet him."

The thought of going out made Evie's taste buds sour. She brought her beer to her lips and anxiously fiddled with a green bud at her fingertips. Evie held her response from Blythe until she chased her swig of beer with a generous toke off her glass piece. She let the poisoned smoke swirl in her mouth, allowing Blythe to think she was actually considering her proposal.

"I don't feel like going out tonight, Blythe," she answered with a wheezy exhale.

"Please, Evie. I really want you to meet Evan. He's been asking since forever to meet my best friend. Come out, please… for me?"

Just give Little Miss Prissy what she wants. Let's go have some fun.

"Fine." She whispered to herself.

"What was that, Evie?"

"Nothing, I was talking to myself. Fine, let's go out."

"Hooray!" Blythe exclaimed through the phone. Evie cringed and held it out at arm's length to protect her eardrum the outburst. "Okay, I'll be by in a couple of hours to pick you up. We can take my car."

Blythe ended the call abruptly. Evie sat in silence, letting the sorrowful music wafting through the house hug her shuddering body.

Let's go out.

"I really don't want to," she said to no one as she peeled the corner of her beer's label off of the bottle.

***

Hearing church bells in her mind, she took the remainder of the six-pack into her master bath and cranked the tub's water valve to its maximum. This time, though, her ritual felt forced, unenjoyable. The anxiety associated with public appearances consumed her. She smoked to medicate, to numb her senses enough to be amongst the living. She chugged each beer hard and fast, willing the effects to kick in, and quick. Her body was barely self-aware as she emerged from the now-tepid bath, dripping onto the floor. She drifted to the mirror. Her reflection smiled back, defiant.

"You can be such a bitch sometimes."

And you're a fucking prude. Get over it.

A bitter beer face turned her reflection's smile down. She wanted to stay home, but Blythe was coming for her. She'd find her. She always did. There was no use hiding. So Evie inhaled deep and exhaled through pursed lips, emptying her lungs, and she cautiously took her hands off the controls. That's what Hope said to do. The High Priestess was driving. She took her bowl to her lips one more time, blew the smoke out in the mirror and snickered.

Evie turned to the stereo. Melodramatic acoustics had no place in her house at the moment, not for the night's purposes. Distorted guitars, a heavy double bass pedal and guttural screams were called for.

Better.

Fueled by the onset of a good buzz, she felt her muscles loosen as her body responded to the guitar-led war chant, and instinct took over as she prepared herself for battle. When she was done, her inner voice had transformed her. Her eyes were caked in black. Glittering gloss iced her lips, a glistening cherry gumdrop as she puckered them in the mirror. She pulled a t-shirt from a drawer, Billy Idol's *Rebel Yell*; actual vintage, not an ironic reproduction. The cut-off hem in the front of the shirt exposed her taut core.

Her inner voice chuckled at the sight of the brooding blond boy stretched across her chest.

Who's the rebel?

She squeezed into a pair of painted-on jeans, stuffing the cuffs into loose-laced combat boots. She pulled her reddish tendrils forward in messy pig-tail braids. Upon completion, her inner voice applauded what she saw in the mirror. She usually wasn't one to get all dolled up to go out, but this time, having escaped her usual attire, her typical Evieness, gave her a bit of a kick in the ass. She didn't feel like the pathetic and stupid girl she dealt with day in and day out.

Let's do a shot.

She killed the math-metal blaring from the stereo and went down stairs. With a shot glass and bottle of Tennessee bourbon in hand, along with her trusty glass bowl, Evie waited on the sofa. When Blythe's horn honked outside, she downed the shot and took one last toke off the bowl.

Rising from the couch and making her way to her front door, she felt the High Priestess press the throttle down—hard.

"God help me."

Not tonight, stupid girl.

Twelve

The ride to the bar was a blur of street lamps and traffic signals as the periphery of Evie's vision dimmed. Streams of rain ran across the windows of the car, turning the passing lights into a Technicolor kaleidoscope. Evie's head bobbed back and forth to the Billy Idol title track looping in her mind.

"For Christ's sake, Evie. Are you already drunk?"

Evie smirked, but declined to answer. She still had a ways to go before she was good and wasted, but she had a solid head start.

Just the calm before the storm.

"What the—," Blythe said, annoyed. "Evie, I'm going to introduce you to Evan tonight. I don't need him thinking what I already do."

"And what's that? That I'm an alcoholic?"

"I don't want him turned off by the company I keep."

"I'll try not to embarrass you, then."

Evie's reply surprised herself; she meant it. The blink of sober sincerity was obscured, however, by the haze thickening between the two. Blythe's brow furrowed as they pulled into the parking lot. As she recognized a vehicle in the parking lot, Evie's heart skipped a beat.

"Rob's here."

"Good, maybe he can keep an eye on you," Blythe said.

"Would you stop? I'm not drunk. I'm trying to forget that you're dragging me out in the first place. I'll be fine."

Both girls glowered at each other before stepping out into the dampened air.

***

They entered the Shanghai Dynasty, turning right in the foyer past the golden lions to the swinging double doors of the lounge. The food was rank. There was a thin dusty film on every surface. The Mai Tais and Scorpion Bowls, though were out of this world. Evie salivated as she strategized her night's consumption.

While the bar would be able to slake her thirst, she wondered what would calm the hunger she felt as she spied Rob at the pool tables across the room. His sweet smile shined through the red lantern lighting and gold-trimmed decor. Since Nate was always with her, she rarely had the pleasure of his smile outside of work. There were benefits to the grizzly being out on the boats for weeks on end; she'd gladly endure Rob's company in his absence.

Gladly, but first let's get that drink.

Evie followed Blythe to the bar as her friend scanned the room. Blythe plopped down on a barstool, deflated.

"Not here yet?" Evie asked, shouting over a woman's shrill rendition of a song she didn't recognize.

Evie looked towards the bartender with an expectant look in her eye, and showed an exaggerated grin back at Blythe as the bartender recognized her and selected two, three, four glass bottles from the shelf. Of any location outside her usual house-club-grocery store rotation, the Dynasty knew her best. With a final flourish of liquor and a flick of a lighter to the little ceramic volcano in the middle, the barkeep slid a brimming Scorpion Bowl towards her.

"I hope we're sharing that," Blythe said.

"Sure, for now."

Each girl's lips wrapped around the tip of their respective straw. Blythe took a short, dainty sip, unable to contain a shudder as the high-proof concoction boiled its way to her stomach. Evie's eyes crossed as she followed the cocktail's trip up her straw and sucked down a greedy gulp. Bitter gin and vodka offset by rum and juices singed her insides.

Both girls lounged at the bar and exchanged pleasantries with familiar faces. All the regulars were out, both honoring and disgracing their favorites through their performances, broken up by the deejay's occasional interjection of pop and hip-hop. The absence of local fishermen was a blessing—the lounge could be wall-to-wall when the boats were in dock. Still, there were enough people to set Evie's phobic side on edge. She sucked on her straw, denying Blythe her fair share of their drink. The large bowl was soon a basin of ice cubes. As her buzz grew into a full-throated roar, Evie's hips swayed to a beat all her own. Her head nodded. All the while, Blythe's face was lined with worry. Evie ordered a Volcano next.

"I'm begging you, Evie. Please behave tonight. I really like this guy. There's just something about him. I can't quite place it."

So you don't want me to fuck this one too?

Evie imagined that comment, if vocalized, would earn her a slap. "I'll behave. What are you afraid I'm going to do, anyway?"

"I'm just glad Rob's around here somewhere. At least I know he can keep you under control."

"What's that supposed to mean?" Evie scoffed.

Blythe frowned, lowered her chin, and raised an eyebrow, as though posing for the encyclopedia entry for "*Really?*"

"Well, you're the one who invited me out in the first place."

"I know. I know. Just be good."

Evie looked around. Rob was nowhere to be found. It was impossible to think he may have left without noticing her. Her rational side began to worry Blythe would be right. Without the safety of Rob's or Nate's watchful eyes, she'd get too rowdy.

"He's here," Blythe said with glee. She jumped off her stool and wrapped her arms around Evan.

After a sip of liquid courage, Evie turned to finally meet him. Her heart stopped. He was *adorable*, just as Blythe put it, though the "baby-faced" adjective may not have been the most suitable. He had big brown eyes like she had said, soft features, but Blythe neglected to mention how painfully beautiful he was. Evie was uncomfortable just being looked at by him. As they made eye contact, she felt as though his reaction to her was equally disturbed. He appeared stiff, pained even.

Do you smell that? Sticky sweet.

"Evie, this is Evan," Blythe said. "Evan, this is my best friend, Evie."

Evie found the best reaction she could muster under his pensive glare was to down her drink. Evan extended his hand. She let it hang in the air. She was frozen with an awkward tension she couldn't quite come to grips with brewing inside her.

"Evie, I'm glad we finally have a chance to meet. Blythe's told me all about you."

"All about me?" she asked with a side smirk. "So my reputation precedes me, then."

Evan dropped his empty hand and smiled.

Do you recognize that smile?

Evie felt anxious. Her nervousness was recognizable. She'd experienced such anxiety, and recently. She shivered. A firm grip wrapped around her waist, a shepherd's crook pulling her to safety from the wolves. Rob's warm palm stretched across her exposed tummy.

"Hey there, Gorgeous, you look like you could use this," he said. His other arm swung around her to present her with a fresh drink. Evie leaned back into his half-embrace and gratefully accepted the drink.

"Hi Rob. This is my boyfriend, Evan," Blythe said. Both men extended a firm handshake. Evie felt Rob's arm tighten around her waist. She noticed Evan's brow furrow.

"You must be Evie's—"

"Boss," she said, quick to cut Evan off. "Rob is my boss." His arm loosened around her.

Why are you sweating so much?

"Right, well, what brings you out tonight?" Rob asked.

Evie scanned her company. Both men stood upright, chests puffed up like wild birds asserting their territory. Blythe made no indication she noticed—her ear-to-ear grin at Evan's side was telltale of her obliviousness. Evie sipped on the drink Rob handed her as the tension crackled in the atmosphere between the pairs.

"Evie? What's wrong?" Blythe asked. She looked around. Everyone stared at her.

"I'm fine."

"Are you sure? You look like you saw a ghost or something," Rob said.

Evie looked up at Evan. He reciprocated her stare.

"No, no ghost. I thought I..." She hesitated to finish her sentence. She wanted to say she recognized Evan, thought she had seen him at the club. That was the only logical explanation, but she knew if she said that Blythe would freak.

Why are you so awkward, stupid girl?

Rob's fingertips squeezed white dots onto her belly.

"Who wants a shot?" he asked, clearing his throat and spun around to the bartender to call out his order. Rob turned back to pass out a round of Kamikazes. Evie's shoulders loosened with relief at his attempt to redirect the conversation. Rob knew what she needed, even if he disapproved. She grabbed her shot. Blythe accepted hers as well with a smile.

"I don't drink," Evan said as Rob extended his peace offering. Rob's hand hovered in the air, shot still in hand. Evie lifted her eyes to Evan's again.

This silence is killing my buzz.

Evie tossed her shot back before the others could do the same. She grabbed Evan's shot and lifted it up.

"To awkward introductions," she said. Blythe and Rob lifted their shots and repeated her salute with a stilted round of laughter.

Evan's features softened, but he kept his gaze on her.

THIRTEEN

As the night progressed, the tension in the air loosened. Everyone took turns buying rounds of this drink and that, paying little heed to mixing hard liquor and beer. Evan bought a round of Suffering Bastards, though he never actually consumed anything. Drinking in public carried a different meaning, and Evie enjoyed herself, even as she watched Evan with a curious eye.

Blythe, ever the lightweight, was drunk within no time. She clung to Evan as they sat in the corner, watching Evie work Rob over at the billiards table. She feigned ignorance of the game, pretending not to know how to hold the cue or how to line up a shot. Each opportunity brought Rob closer to her, caused him to lean behind her. She stretched her body under his and pushed her rear into his core. She relished his closeness and was high off of the feeling of his own excitement pressing up against the small of her back. His playing along indicated he knew her game all too well.

In between flirtations, Evie would pause to enjoy the latest round. Each time, she'd peer towards Evan to catch his furrowed brow fixed on her. Even through her inebriated haze, Evie easily discerned his glares.

Karaoke came to a close, and the dance floor opened up, the deejay spinning the same catalogue that Sirens kept in heavy rotation. Both Evie and Blythe bopped to the music that overpowered the small space. Rob handed out another round of beers to the girls, then removed the pool cue from Evie's hand.

"C'mon, I'm sick of you kicking my ass. Let's dance."

Without objection, Evie shimmied her way after him. Blythe dragged Evan to an empty table by the dance floor. She tried to coax him onto the floor, but after adamant refusal, Blythe left Evan in his seat to join the others. Every now and then, Evie would glance over. She thought she caught a tiny smile on his face watching them dance. When their eyes connected, his smile vanished, replaced by a furrowed brow that troubled her.

Thankfully, she had Rob. He wrapped his hands around her hips. Choreographed to the music, they leaned into each other. It was rare for such an opportunity to dance with him, or with anyone for that matter. Nate would never let her dance with someone else, and he had no rhythm. Rob sure as hell did. He adeptly moved in sync with her body. Blythe wiggled up behind him. The two girls sandwiched him and pawed playfully at each other around him, despite him, through him, **part ménage, part** torture session.

The night evolved into an outburst of positive energy. In her stupor, Evie forgot about her loneliness. She forgot about her curious dreams and desires.

***

Songs transitioned, and Evie kept close watch of Evan sitting in the shadows. She mock-frowned at him and danced her way over to sit across from him at the table. Rob went up to the bar for yet another round, while Blythe excused herself to the ladies' room. Evie stared at Evan through foggy goggles, waving her emerald-colored beer bottle in between two fingers at him.

"You don't drink. You don't dance. You don't look like you're having much fun at all, Evan."

He smirked at her.

There's that smile, again.

"You're having fun. Blythe seems to be enjoying herself. That's all that matters, right?"

"Yes, it is." Evie took the final swig from her beer. "That's the right answer."

Rob sat back down with a fresh round of fruity cocktails. Evie salivated bringing the straw to her lips, sucking a generous portion of her Mai Tai down in one large gulp.

"Blythe speaks very highly of you, Evie," Evan said.

"No she doesn't," she said with a bitter face caused by a disproportionate amount of lime juice in her drink. "That's sweet of you to say though. I promise, I'm not a bad influence on her. She has a much better head on her shoulders than I do."

"You have a gorgeous head on your shoulders," Rob said, tugging on her bright red pig-tail braid. Evie watched Rob's remark crease Evan's brow.

"That's your opinion," she said.

"That's a fact. Am I right, Evan?" he said, enjoying his drink and his up-close-and-personal view of Evie's flushed cheeks.

Evan paused to answer, eyeing her up and down. Evie felt her pulse quicken as he did so.

"That's a fact," he repeated quietly, gaze fixed with Evie's matching intensity.

There were far too many temptations left to linger in their conversation, and she'd flirted far too much with Rob for one night. Her interest in Evan's peculiar fascination with her increased with each disturbing exchange of eye contact. She was surprised to want to miss Nate at that moment.

Fuck Nate. He's not here, and we're getting Rob good and drunk.

Evie dismissed her inner voice, lost in Evan's big brown eyes. She wrapped her tongue around her straw, muscles working to coax the rum and juices back into her throat.

***

With her Mai Tai gone, she excused herself to the ladies' room, while Rob returned to the bar to make a pre-emptive sobering effort by picking up a round of bottled waters for the group. Evie meandered her way to the lavatories, where she found Blythe.

"Isn't he the cutest freaking thing you've ever seen?" Blyth said, slurring her words.

"He's fucking hot is what he is."

Both girls exploded into laughter.

"I'm gonna try to sleep with him tonight." Blythe adjusted her shirt, perking up her already perky little breasts in her pink top.

"You should. I would," Evie blurted.

"You won't," Blythe said, waving a firm finger in Evie's face. She batted it away.

"Of course I won't. Thanks for giving me some credit."

We've got our sights on someone else tonight.

Blythe cackled and walked back to the table. On her way out of the ladies' room, Evie paused in front of the mirror.

"Are you having fun?"

Aren't you?

Evie smiled. "I am."

You should listen to me more often.

"So what do you think of Evan?"

There's something about him. He looks like—

Her inner dialogue ended in an instant as a woman with an inebriated smile walked into the ladies' room. Evie excused herself and pushed through the door. She nearly vomited when she rammed right into him.

Lucca's wicked grin shone down on her like an interrogation lamp. Her blood raged through the veins in her temples.

"Evie," Lucca said, amused and looking her body over like a sailor returned from months at sea—famished. "And how *does* the rebel yell, exactly?"

Swaying back and forth, puzzled, she followed his eyes down to her chest and huffed, then mirrored the crooked smile on her t-shirt. "According to Billy Idol, she cries more, more, more."

"Does she, indeed?"

Evie stood drawn to his rosy lips and pearly whites hidden behind them. Her mind's eye blinked, and as it reopened, there was the image of those same lips, that same beguiling mouth, rising from between her thighs smeared with her menses. She saw the Devil card dancing in his dark irises. Transfixed by the image, she remained frozen.

"Is everything okay, Evie?"

She blinked. That wasn't Lucca's voice. It broke her trance, but it wasn't him. She looked over. Evan glared at the two. Evie heard a rumbling, the kind you'd hear from the depths of a cave in winter. It sent a shockwave of sensations through her body.

"Not here alone, I see," Lucca said. She watched his ever-present, defiant smile stir a raw nerve in Evan. It was etched across his face, jaw flexed. He stepped closer to Evie, protective, much like Rob.

"No, she's not alone," Evan said.

"And neither am I."

Evie looked behind Lucca. The tall blonde from the club stood next to the dark stranger. The room spun. Evie was drunk, scared and unnerved as yet another safe haven of hers was invaded.

Evan wrapped his firm grip around her arm. For the first time Evie felt the warm thrill of his touch. His hands were agile and firm, very much like hands she felt the night she met Lucca.

"C'mon, Evie," he said and pulled her away.

"Some of us will never learn our place," Lucca said, trailing off behind them as Evan pulled her along.

***

Evie thought to protest, but allowed Evan to guide her away. She presumed he would drag her back to their table, back to the others. He didn't. Evan led her outside to the parking lot. The cold misty air sent a wave of goose bumps across her skin. The fresh air sobered her spinning head, a little

"Where are we going?" she asked.

"To my car."

"Wait a minute," Evie said, yanking her arm away. "I think you've got the wrong idea. I don't know what Blythe told you about me, but she's my best friend. I—"

"Smoke pot," he said, cutting her off.

Her jaw snapped shut, containing a different answer entirely. "What are you talking about?"

"I don't drink, but I do smoke pot. It's my understanding you do too," he said.

Seriously?

"Does Blythe know?"

"She does."

"And she doesn't have a problem with it? Shit, I guess she really does like you," Evie said.

More willing than before, Evie followed as Evan led her to a shiny black sedan. She looked it over, marveling at its design. It was arguably the most expensive thing she'd ever seen in Fallhaven. She hadn't thought much of the Carver estate or its owners, but judging by what Evan drove, it appeared money still ran in the family. They stood by it, concealed in part by its shadowy structure. Leaning towards Evie, Evan opened the passenger door and bent down into the car to produce a bag from the center console. She staggered back from his approach. When he opened the small plastic bag, Evie was overwhelmed by the scent of sticky hydroponic weed.

"Wow, that smells amazing."

"Thanks. You'll never catch me smoking mid-grades." He chuckled, a sweet and spicy laughter that tickled her auditory senses just as the weed did to her olfactories.

"Well, that's all we have around here. Where'd you get this?"

"I have a guy."

Evan quickly rolled a thin joint, lit it, inhaled, and passed it to her. She lifted the end to her lips. It was slightly damp from Evan's first toke. His taste was fresh and tangy. She licked her lips, savoring the flavor.

"That tastes really good." Her lashes batted.

"You like it?"

Evie shut her eyes again and wrapped herself in the essence of the piney scent. A wide grin lined her face. Engrossed in the moment and his lingering taste on the tip of the joint, she allowed her silence to hang for his own interpretation. When she opened them, Evan's pensive gaze pierced through the parking lot's lighting. His soft features were masked by swirls of smoke wafting up to the sky. She melted under the shadowy smirk lining his face. Her body swayed back and forth, woozy. Whoever Evan was, he evoked a very similar reaction from her as Lucca.

He's in there, you know. He's thinking about us.

Evie's inner voice ordered her to leave Evan's side, to go back in the bar, to look for Lucca. But Evan's gaze was too inviting to break away.

Let Blythe have him. You have Lucca in there. And you have Rob.

"Rob," she said with a sudden jolt. Evan flinched. "I'm sorry. I shouldn't leave Rob in there wondering where I am."

"Your boss?" He paused. "Are you sure he's just your boss?" There was an element of hurt underlying the shock from her outburst.

"Well, I guess it's obvious he's a little more than that to me."

Evan nodded as he took the last toke off the remnants of the joint. "I think Blythe mentioned that."

He licked his fingertips and pinched the ashy end of the roach, extinguishing the burning tip. Evie watched his disappointment rise with the waft of fragrant smoke he exhaled up into the night air.

"We shouldn't leave them waiting," she said.

Evie pushed a foot forward and stared up at Evan for a moment. A lead weight in the pit of her core held her in place.

"Let's go," he said and turned away.

***

Deflated and a bit relieved, Evie was able to move again. She followed him inside.

They returned to their table. Rob sat, tipping a beer to his lips, not quite as happy to see her as he had been before. With a dopey grin, Blythe grabbed Evie by the hand and dragged her around the dance floor.

Evie's head whirled from the mixture of intoxicants flowing through her veins. The world slowed down around her. She could feel each inhale and exhale of breath as she slithered against Blythe. With her rear pushed up against her friend, she searched for Lucca's glowing eyes. She found him tucked in a dark corner, felt the familiar haunt of his stare from across the room. Her smile widened with excitement.

Through spiraling colored lights from the deejay stand, Evie continued to scan the room. She felt Lucca's cold glare. She could see him licking his bottom lip. Blythe's hands wrapped around her waist, twirling her around. Evie envisioned the tip of Lucca's tongue in place of Blythe's fingertips, flitting and flicking along the sensitive skin over her hip bones. Enthralled by the notion,

Evie's hands roamed across Blythe's skin while her eyes moved around the room.

She caught sight of Evan's creased brow. Her pulse boomed between her ears, synced up with the bass of the old-school hip hop bumping from the subwoofers. Blythe continued grinding against her. Evie was deafened by her drunken laughter screeching in her ear. Evan stared.

More pulses of light, strobes this time to accentuate the pounding bass of the bridge of the song reverberating between Evie's ears. Her eyes were a roulette ball bouncing and careening around the room, seeking a point on which to settle. She landed at Rob's face. He scowled. Finishing his drink, Rob stood and grabbed one of the bottled waters no one seemed to pay attention to amongst the empty glasses and beer bottles littering their table. He marched out to the dance floor.

"C'mon, Evie. It's time I take you home."

FOURTEEN

"What happened back there?" Rob asked.

"I'm sorry. Evan took me outside to smoke. I didn't mean to—I know Blythe said she wants to—"

"No, not that. I don't give a shit what Blythe is trying to do with her boyfriend," he said. "He's a creep, by the way. He couldn't keep his eyes off you all night. And then you went outside with him. What the fuck were you thinking?"

She remained silent, too ashamed to admit he was right, too drunk to formulate her defense testimony in a cohesive manner. She let him drive her home.

Through potholes and puddles, Rob's impaired driving nearly made Evie spew the contents of the water bottle he handed her on their way out of the Dynasty. The engine of his truck clanked and clacked along as he beat on the transmission. His angst only served to thicken the air between them and roil her stomach further. Rob hydroplaned around the corner of her street. Evie held her breath in, hands latched to the passenger door handle.

"Rob, watch out. What the fuck? Nothing happened between me and Evan. You can drop the protective big brother shit. You're drunk."

His truck came to a screeching halt in her driveway. It stalled, and he threw up the emergency brake.

"It's not '*big brother*' shit,'" he said with obvious frustration. "Look, the other reason I dragged you out was because that other asshole from Sirens showed up. I saw

119

him watching you. Don't think for one second I didn't see you staring back. God, where are these guys coming from all of a sudden, eye-fucking you like that?"

"What, should that be your exclusive pleasure?"

Rob's eyes widened. "Excuse me?"

She sat in his truck drunk, woozy, and conflicted. She blurted out words and instantly wished to take them back. But they were said, no going back on them. Her inner voice had the reins by the fistful and seemed perfectly content to drive off a cliff.

"I'm sorry, I didn't mean that. Will you walk me inside?" she asked, tail tucked between her legs.

His nostrils flared from his own ungoverned anger. Rob huffed and rubbed his hand across his face. "Of course. Anything you need, you know that."

Anything?

"Would you please stop?" Evie mumbled to herself as she flopped out of the truck onto the rain-slicked cement driveway. Rob was quick to her side.

"What'd you say?"

"Nothing. I was asking the ground to stop spinning out from under me. It didn't listen too well."

He laughed off her little joke, thankfully. She was afraid of what Rob might say if he knew she talked to herself. The two stumbled their way to and through the front door, letting momentum fill in the blanks in their balance.

***

Rob turned lights on as they moved through the first floor. Evie extinguished them behind him while they made their way into the kitchen.

"Are you going to be okay driving home?" she asked.

"Yeah, I'm going to grab a glass of water before I head out. I'll be fine."

She observed his body language. His words were clear. His eyes were alert. Yet, in his pursuit of water, he carved a crooked path to the kitchen. Her inner voice, a panther awoken in her cave, emitting her sweet scent, contemplated her approach. She watched his Adam's apple bob as he downed his drink, her tongue rolling along to the roof of her mouth.

"Would you mind tucking me in?" she asked.

Rob placed the empty glass down, wiping his mouth with the back of his hand and meeting her gaze in the shadows of the house. "Will I what?"

"You know, will you... *tuck*... me in?" she repeated and grabbed his hand.

She led him back through the living room, quick to evade the photos of generations past. Those eyes, judging. She led Rob towards the second floor. Evie, who could find the way faultlessly if she were struck blind, was led by the moonlight pushing through the scattered clouds outside as the rain subsided once more. Rob fumbled up the stairs behind her, but kept his hand locked with hers.

"Evie, what are you doing?"

I'm not done with you just yet.

She held in her inner voice's answer, ashamed of what she was about to attempt. The sober Evie would never dream of seducing her boss, her friend. She stopped at the foot of her bed and turned to face him. Before the blunt needle of doubt could penetrate the moment, Evie closed her mouth over Rob's.

He hesitated for a moment, but then fell on top of her across the downy comforter. Her drunken mind flashed images of his sweet smile, Nate's stoner grin, Evan's pensive glare. It settled on Lucca's wicked smirk. The image of the Devil tarot card danced across her mind. His cat eyes gleaming as he yanked the chains around the man and woman's necks. Her tongue lashed out at that image as she clawed the back of Rob's neck, pulled his shirt, and ripped it at the seams to gain better access to his broad shoulders. She dug her nails into his soft flesh. He groaned with arousal, only pushing back when she bit his lip.

"Ouch! Evie, what's gotten into you?"

"You don't want this?"

"That's beside the point," he said, rubbing the bright scratches on the nape of his neck. "But this is wrong."

"Why is it wrong?"

"Why? What's with the clawing? Evie, what about Nate? No, we're both drunk. This is bad. I need to go."

"Rob, wait," she said, calling out with pathetic desperation as he turned away from her room, towards the stairs.

Evie sat up, chased after him, stumbled down stairs she knew so well, and bounced off his back when he stopped at the front door. Rob turned to her, and she hated the hurt expression she saw, the expression she caused out of her own reckless selfishness, from her inner voice's brazen control.

"Evie, stop. We're drunk. This would be a huge mistake."

"I'm so sorry. Please don't hate me for this."

Rob tried to smile his usual sweet smile, but couldn't quite muster it. It stung her heart while he held her hand.

"I could never hate you, Evie. But I don't want you doing anything you'll regret. You're a good girl."

Not good enough for you.

Muted by shame, she dropped her gaze and let Rob leave, the throaty bellow of his truck dissipating into the night. She paused before closing the door. Evie saw eyes in the shadows across the street. Her own eyes drying out, she forced herself to blink. The glints across the street were gone.

Stupid girl, I'm so disgusted with you. Just go inside, get a drink and go to bed.

She pushed her hallucinations aside and did just that. Evie locked the door behind her, moped through the dark to the whiskey and shot glass left behind earlier in the evening, cursed her hormones, and then went up to bed.

***

Just before daybreak, Evie tossed and turned in her bed. Her head ached, but not as badly as the night's activities may have predicated.

She peered through a cracked lid and recoiled violently in her bed, certain she'd seen a figure in the corner of her room. The lithe figure was draped across the upholstered rocker-recliner near the front window. Evie propped up in her bed. Her eyes strained to focus. She was still woozy from all her drinking.

"Hello?" She called out into the purplish dark.

"What would you have me do with him?" the figure asked. It was a man's voice. A soft and melodic hum that made the most intimate parts of her body vibrate like a tuning fork.

"Lucca?" She struggled to find his eyes. If she could match the dark figure's eyes to his golden orbs she'd feel better. She'd know it was a dream. But there were no eyes,

123

just a figure. She could feel sweat beading above her lip, her heart pounding.

"Will you resist me when the time comes?"

"Evan?"

"You know you can't resist me." The figure voice's dropped to a low growl. Still, his eyes remained elusive. Her body throbbed. Her inner voice pushed against the confines of her chest. It begged to be set free. It wanted the figure. Evie gripped against her comforter, too afraid to emerge.

"Who are you?"

Her question was left hanging. Whatever effects remained from her night of overindulgence vanished. She was far too aware of all her faculties as she anticipated the shadowy figure's response.

"Evie... I am you."

FIFTEEN

As the next day rolled around, Evie hated to leave her bed. Her dream haunted her. She was so aware of her surroundings. Drunk or not, it was difficult to believe she'd experienced anything short of a ghostly encounter. Not just any ghost, the Devil himself visited her last night. She was sure of it.

Evie paced around her house, but found she'd finished off the last of her alcohol before heading to bed. Certain she had an extra bottle of whiskey around somewhere, she couldn't find it and grew frustrated. How could she have lost something so precious? She cursed herself again; her weed was gone, too. Her final toke before Blythe picked her up was just that, her final toke. Evie took a scalding hot shower, seeking equal parts distraction and restoration. She emerged detoxified and antiseptic, but still a tight ball of anxiety with trembling hands.

She stared at the ghost in the mirror. It offered an insidious smirk she'd seen too often as of late. She balled her fists, intending to threaten the grinning specter. It beamed wider.

Do not try to resist. He is you and you are him. Isn't that what the old lady said?

"Fuck off," she said in a hushed voice. She needed a drink, a smoke, anything. She needed out of her house. Shaky fingers laced her sneakers as she grabbed her iPod and headed for the door.

***

She set a slow pace, queasy from nerves and alcohol withdrawal. She jogged through her neighborhood isolated by the music pumping into her ears, vision tunneled to avoid any possibility of meeting a neighbor's watchful eye. The air outside was crisp and cool. Grey clouds overhead indicated a storm was rolling in. Within no time, Evie passed Sirens and reached the waterfront.

Once over the causeway, the town's appearance improved. Downtown commerce created the illusion of normal life. Brick buildings with lively decorated store-fronts were too busy earning their dollars to worry about who Evie was, or her lineage.

On the opposite side of the harbor, she came to a sweaty stop at the old fort. If she had bothered to count the miles she jogged, Evie would have been impressed, but her mind was plagued. For that reason alone, she hadn't realized how bad her thighs burned from the exercise. Now, standing still, her face grimaced from the sudden realization of physical pain. Her lungs burned.

How do you plan to run back now?

She turned off the music and pulled the earbuds from her ears. Heart rate slowing, breath normalizing, Evie stood a moment and stared out into the harbor. She found her house across the water with little effort. She was grateful her mind was finally empty of images and thoughts. She'd run from her problems—this time. The tranquility of the moment tingled across her skin like the impending rain showers. She took in a deep breath and was calmed.

"Hey there, good lookin', need a ride?"

Evie whipped herself around ready to release a torrent of anger at whatever idiot was crude enough to address her with such disrespect. It was common for a greasy drunkard or coked-up fisherman to make catcalls along the streets. Because of where she worked and her mother's reputation, some felt they could treat Evie like their own sweet little plaything. She never hesitated to lift a middle finger to those men, or even Nate if he deserved it. The only man who could get away with such bullshit would be Rob.

Speak of the Devil.

Her scowl softened into a smile when she recognized the familiar features of her provocateur. Rob hung his head out the driver's side window of his truck, arm rested across the sill. He wore his usual truthful and trusting smile.

"C'mon, hop in, or do you want to stand in the rain?"

Evie looked up. A soft mist tickled her eyelids. She was so wrapped up in hollow thought she hadn't noticed the cold droplets against her skin. Her exhausted legs thanked him even as they struggled to hoist the rest of Evie into the passenger seat. Her body eased, any trace of her anxiety vanished. Rob had that effect on her, just like he did the night before. Evie dropped her head down, averting her eyes in shame.

The engine of Rob's rusty pick-up bellowed, scaring a flock of gulls into flight. The jerkiness from the old transmission made for a bumpy ride. Evie felt her chest bobbing with the truck's suspension and wondered if Rob had noticed her **décolletage** bouncing softly above the neckline of her shirt. Every now and then, Evie thought she caught a glimpse of him noticing just that out of the corner of his eye. She flushed at the thought.

"I'm sorry about last night, Rob," she said.

His warm smile answered her in return. "What about last night?" She glared back. He chuckled. "It's okay, Evie.

We both had more than our share of drinks last night. I should apologize to you too."

"I shouldn't have taken advantage of you like that. I'm really sorry."

Rob reached out to take her hand in his. She grinned with appreciation, another line item on the laundry list of transgressions Rob was willing to forgive.

"I told you it's okay. It did make for an interesting story at the gym, though."

Her eyes widened. "You told your friends at the gym about it?"

"Not all of it, but it was a little difficult to think of a decent lie for the claw marks on my back."

A red tide of embarrassment washed across her face. She stretched her neck out to peer at the red marks poking out from above the back of his tank top, along the back of his neck where her nails left their mark.

"I didn't realize I was so rough."

"Very rough." He laughed. "But it's okay. I didn't give any names. Your secret's safe with me. Now let's just forget it happened. Like I said, we were both drunk."

It's not like this whole town doesn't know about you and Rob.

Evie's lips curved down to a frown, but she was glad he accepted her apology. The idea of more strangers judging her, equipped with such incendiary ammunition, made her nauseous.

"I hate going to the gym. I only go because it makes Blythe happy. I feel like people stare at me too much."

"Well, a beautiful girl in skin-tight clothing walks into a gym, what would you expect? I know that's why I go," he said, his eyes flickering downward for another glimpse at Evie's bouncing chest before turning his attention back to the road.

She hung her head and was silent a moment. She felt eyes on her, like those that followed her around town. The daughter of a whore, a drunk, a slut working at a strip club, that's what people thought of her. That's what her inner voice told her anyway.

"That's not what I mean," she said, her voice choked. Rob squeezed her hand. She covered his with her free hand. It trembled. She felt him squeeze tighter. He smiled again, soothed her as only Rob could. She smiled back and fought the urge to tear up.

"Whatever it is you're thinking, stop. Nobody is comparing you to your mom."

"But they are judging me because of her. Don't tell me they're not, Rob. I see the way people look at me. Men rape me with their eyes. Women shoot daggers at me in disgust." Evie's voice cracked. Regardless of her efforts, tears welled up in her eyes as testament to the conviction in her words.

"And what if some of them do?" Rob said. "What do you care anyway? Most of this town is made up of addicts and assholes. Don't you think I feel judged for taking over the club after my dad died? Don't you think I feel hatred from fathers all over this town, men who want to kick the shit out of me for putting their daughters up on the pole? Fuck them. They don't realize what I do for those girls. I watch after them better than they do. So they don't end up like—" Evie watched anger seize his usual calm demeanor. She knew what he was about to say. And she knew why he stopped short of completing his statement.

"Like my mom."

"Yeah." His voice softened. "Yeah, like her. I'm real sorry, Evie. I didn't mean to—"

"It's okay. You weren't my mom's keeper. And you're not the keeper of those girls either. You're not my—"

"I know," he answered before Evie could finish. But it was true; Rob wasn't her keeper. They both knew it. Maybe they both wished for it, but they knew it nonetheless. Last night proved it.

The two sat in silence, stuck in limbo at a red light. The rain came down harder, the pattering against the roof of the cab rising to a deafening roar. Silence was unnatural between them. Evie wanted to find the words to convince Rob he did more than most for her and the other girls, that each and every girl there loved him for it. That she loved him for it. But she held her tongue. If she continued the conversation it was sure to fuel the fire she could see building within him.

When the light turned green, he released her hands, left them to tremble in her lap and growled. "Fuck this."

Rob cranked the wheel one, two, three full rotations. Gears clanking, tires chirping, he whipped the truck around in a U-turn.

Within minutes they pulled into the club's parking lot. Evie turned to Rob, apprehensive, frightened even. She'd never seen Rob like this. His frustration dominated his appearance. Usually when Evie saw it, it was channeled towards a disrespectful customer, some idiot who overstepped his boundaries with one of the girls. Outside of such a scenario, his anger made Evie uneasy. His facial expression remained cold and foreign. With a fair amount of caution, Evie followed him inside.

***

The club was different during closed hours. The overhead lights that lit the space exposed the room's ugliness in its totality. The vinyl coating the booths was cracked and ripped. Scratches spread across the old and worn flooring. Dust collected in hidden corners.

Rob marched backstage to his office. Evie was just a few steps behind.

She wondered why he steered away from the bar. That's where she assumed they were headed. At that moment, she craved a drink more than anything. Anything to curb the edgy nervousness she felt from Rob's unrest. She clenched her own hands together to stave off the shaking. Her discomfort was building. Her stomach was in knots.

Rob flipped on the lights to the office and made his way over to a small coffee station. Without asking, he fixed two cups, one for him and one for Evie. Though not what she preferred, she accepted the hot mug of caffeine. She settled into a chair at the front of his desk. Rob sat in his chair, both hands clasped his mug. Not a word had been spoken since he lashed out in his truck and adjusted his course towards Sirens instead of Evie's place. She watched him, wondered if she should break the silence. He gazed into a swirl of wood grain buried deep within the top of his desk. His lost facial expression worried her even more than before. She had never seen Rob so... disturbed.

"Rob, if this is about last night. Again, I said I'm—"

"No one's heard from Natalie since last week," he said with his eyes squeezed shut.

Jaw snapped shut, Evie took in a deep breath. Of all the words to break their uncomfortable silence, those were not the ones she expected.

Natalie, or Natalia to the patrons; Evie didn't care much for her, probably because they were complete opposites. Natalie stood tall, confident, didn't seem to mind the men of Fallhaven ogling her. Hell, Natalie said she enjoyed it, even. "More money in the G-string," she'd say.

Conversely, Evie was pale and self-conscious. She steered clear from anything that drew anyone's attention. Natalie had gone missing. What of it? There could be any number of reasons someone kept to themselves.

"So?" she asked. Rob shot a look up at her in amazement. She sipped her coffee, carefree. Did he not realize even his precious little Evie with her big blue eyes could be so callous?

"*So*, I ran into Carrie at the gym. She said she's been calling Natalie for days and hasn't been able to get in touch with her. That's not like her."

Evie paused a moment, tempering her derisive response. The last thought she had of Natalie was pure jealousy. She wanted to be the dancer in the booth with Lucca. She wanted the opportunity to corner him a dark space to stare into those cool, gleaming eyes. So why should she care now that Natalie hadn't answered anyone's calls? Why was Rob overreacting?

"So nobody's talked to her. Has she blown off a bunch of her shifts or something?"

"No," he said. "She said she wanted a few days off because of her cramps or something."

Evie nodded her head. Natalie had uterine fibroids that made her menstrual cycle particularly painful, or so she claimed, anyway. She often requested time off to stay home

132

and milk it for all it was worth. Evie chuckled under her breath; the two polar opposite girls at least had the same cycle in common. She looked back up at Rob. He seemed not to notice her digressive thoughts.

"You're upset because Natalie's blowing people off while she nurses her period? C'mon, Rob. I'm sure she's fine. Where's her car?" she asked, betting Natalie was just being a baby with a heating pad across her belly.

"It's parked outside her apartment. Carrie said she even tried knocking on the door, but no one answered. Her boyfriend's out on the boats. It doesn't make any sense."

Despair increased in his voice. Knowing how much he cared for each of his girls, Evie could see how difficult this was for him. He was like a shepherd who'd lost a lamb of his flock.

She put her coffee down and walked over behind the desk, removing Rob's hot mug from his hands. He didn't even blink as Evie perched herself on the edge of the desk in front of him. His stare remained blank. She grabbed Rob's hands and pulled him towards her. He rested his head down on her lap. The heat from his erratic breathing sent warm shivers down her spine. She placed his hands at her side, running her fingers through his hair.

"Do you know if Natalie had a drug problem?"

His stubbled cheek rubbed against her thigh as he spoke. His voice was faint, frail, and very unRob-like. She knew he hoped maybe drugs could offer some reasonable solution to this particular mystery. It was so common in town that even the thought of drug abuse would be some kind of relief. But Evie had no answer to give.

"No, I have no idea, but I'm sure she's fine," she said with a soft whisper. Her body flushed, heated, and tingled with him so close. What would it take to bring back the strong and dependable Rob she knew? He pinched his eyes shut and pursed his lips. His breathing regulated. His short brown hair felt coarse in between her trembling fingers.

Gazing down at him, Evie couldn't help but marvel at how different Rob was from Nate. Aside from the obvious that Nate was a physical giant and Rob was short, stocky, pure muscle, their personalities were drastically different. Evie knew Nate would've had the same reaction as she did, thinking Natalie would show up to work tonight, and he wouldn't let the issue plague him a moment longer.

An employee, that's all she is.

Their coffees turned cold waiting for attention. Evie's neck strained from looking down at him. Her ass was numb from sitting on the edge of the hard wooden desk. For all she knew Rob could have fallen asleep in her lap. He never moved. He never said anything, just sat there with his head atop her lap. Evie checked the clock. It was getting late. She had to go home and get ready for work in a few hours. There would be no bath in her near future. She'd have to take a quick hot shower to peel away the layers of sweaty skin still clinging to her from her jog.

A twinge of guilt prevented her from lifting his head off of her, but she had needs. Plus, there was a stocked bar in the other room calling her name.

Evie edged her rear off the desk. Rob flinched as she did so, but remained silent. He shot straight up in his chair and grabbed her by the wrists, pulling her down on top of him in his seat. She fell clumsily. He hugged her tight, as she settled on his lap. Evie drew him in close to her chest, cradling his boyish features with more concern than she realized she had.

Her tone softened, doing her best to reciprocate the care he always bestowed upon her. "Rob, it's getting late.

The club is going to open soon. I still have to go home and get ready."

Her comment lingered between them. After a few minutes, Rob mumbled into her soft chest. It tickled. "I don't care. Don't go yet."

He clung to her tighter. Evie sighed at the desperation in his voice. It pained her to do it, but she pushed against him and pried him away. She lifted his face to meet hers and did her best to relay confidence in her smile.

"Everything is going to be fine. I promise." It took him a second, but his expression softened. Rob smiled back.

"Thanks, Evie. I needed that."

Did he need to hear her say everything would be okay? Did he need to hold her close? Or did he just need company for a little while? Whatever it was she had done for him, she was glad for it. Her own quickening pulse slowed, and she dismounted from his lap.

He was smiling. The strong, dependable Rob peeked through the gloom.

"I'm going to grab a drink on my way out, okay? I'll see you in a few hours," she said.

Evie stood and their hands released. She left him to his own quietude.

Evie stopped by the bar to pour herself a shot of Jim Beam, maybe two. Through the clinking and clanking of the glasses behind the bar, she hoped her statement rang true. She hoped she didn't just lie to Rob, and everything would be okay. Taking the whiskey down and finding peace in its comforting burn, she sighed before casting one more cautious glare towards Rob's office, and then left.

SIXTEEN

The club was halfway in between the old fort and her house. The bourbon whiskey did little to ease her mind, but they did curb her withdrawal symptoms. Her hands no longer shook. Those double shots would have to hold her until she returned to the club for a very long and awkward night at work.

Evie jogged down the street, across the causeway back into her neighborhood. The rain had stopped. She dodged puddles on her way around the harbor. Between the gaps in the rhythmic padding of her cross-trainers against the pavement and the echoing of her breath between her ears, somber tunes shuffled through her earbuds, complementing the dreary weather. The music set an ominous soundtrack for her jog back home. She turned away from the streets to cut through the marina.

As she ran through the boatyard, Evie weaved around vessels in dry-dock awaiting the warmer weather of boating season. Having navigated the nautical labyrinth, she set a slow pace through the open parking lot. The few boats that remained in the water year-round floated on their slips. She looked out into the harbor and was drawn to the calm, dark waters. Stealing what few minutes she had and compelled to get closer, Evie made a quick right turn to the water's edge at the end of the dock.

The air was cool from the passing rain shower. The pungent smell of seaweed hung in the air. She turned off the music and removed her ear buds to take in the tranquility of the harbor. It was still midweek. Barring a miraculous catch, the fishing boats wouldn't return for another day or two, at least. Without their penetrating hulls tearing through, the water was like glass, smooth and shiny across the great expanse of the harbor. She peered down into the murk below the wharf.

The crispness of the air tightened her skin around her frame. She remembered the dewy warmth of Rob's breath where goose bumps now ran rampant down her legs. What she saw from him today bothered her; she didn't know how to react. Should she have said something, done something other than to pass off his worries so easily? Her physical attraction to him dispelled, Evie's more protective instincts ignited. The fortune teller was right about one thing; her emotions were all over the place, and like her emotions, her thoughts were scattershot. They took her to dark places. And she was still haunted by those dreams, unlike any others she'd had in the past. The visions in those dreams had names to their faces.

Evie wondered what clairvoyance she possessed to connect her horrible dreams with a stranger she just met. Where did that damn card reading fall into place? The twisting ache in her chest fixated on Rob and her compulsive responsibility to take care of him, the same way he felt the need to take care of all the girls at the club.

And Natalie was *missing*. Then again, Evie was still uncertain about that. There had to be a logical explanation for why no one had heard from her. Being that Evie preferred to be alone, why would she judge Natalie for suddenly adopting the way of the hermit?

A week ago her problems were simple. Get drunk, get high, fuck Nate, and go to work. She stared into the water, searching for an answer.

You could just jump in. Let the water wrap around us. Sink into the darkness. Swim away. How cold do you think it would be?

Evie looked out past the lighthouse at the tip of the harbor into the blank horizon, its beam diffusing into a bank of fog rolling in towards the shore. How far could she go into that grey void? When would exhaustion take hold, or worse? Evie wondered what creatures lurked below the water's shadowy surface. Perhaps something would be kind enough to emerge from the water to drag her down and make the decision for her?

"It's a little cold for a swim. Wouldn't you say?"

For the second time in the day, a man's voice called out from behind her. A black figure sitting in her rocker-recliner flashed before her mind's eye. It wasn't the cold air giving her goose bumps anymore. Despite a lifetime full of them, the dread of facing this particular demon arrested her breathing. She stared at the water, unable to move. She missed the sound of footsteps coming down the dock. Released from the water's provocation, she turned to identify her new caller in wide-eyed wonder.

"Lucca," Evie said with disbelief.

Out in natural light and somewhat sober, she evaluated him up and down for the first time without distraction. In the misty daylight, he was a sight to behold. Sandy stubble lined his jaw line. His deep intense eyes gouged through her. And he wore his ever-present smirk. The sudden pounding of her inner voice's attempts to break through the prison wall of her chest cavity frightened her. And as it pounded, her chest heaved up and down.

"Did you have fun last night?" he asked.

"I—I'm sorry. I was a little drunk when I saw you."

"You keep interesting company. Dare I ask, was that Evan Carver you left with? Not another one of your boyfriends, I presume," he snickered. "And then did I see you with your boss?"

"How do you know Evan? I—he's dating my best friend. And yes, I left with my boss."

So many men. So little time. And yet you keep us away from this one. Stupid, stupid girl.

"Is he, now? Interesting."

Lucca made a wide stride forward to her side. He looked out over the harbor. "I was passing by when I noticed you standing here by yourself. You looked lonely, Evie."

His casualness disarmed her anxiety. She considered arguing about who or what Evan was to her, which was nothing. She thought to ask how Lucca knew him, but that wouldn't quite support her argument. Plus, she was far too confused about Rob to talk it out with Lucca. Evie turned back around so they could scan the waterfront together.

His nearness was thrilling. She wondered if he could sense her inner voice screaming out to him, begging him to reach through her ribcage and give her release. Did he know he'd been haunting her dreams? Even worse, was it possible he knew in what manner he haunted her? Did he know what he did to her in those dreams? A sudden rush of blood flushed Evie's face at the embarrassing thought. She noticed him smile down at her through a cryptic sideways glance.

Lucca took in a deep breathe of salty air and sighed. "I haven't been down here in what feels like a lifetime," he said. A soft chuckle escaped him.

Evie looked up, puzzled. "What, you mean here? The docks?"

"Yes. It's developed over the years."

"Developed?" she repeated, incredulous, quite certain she'd misheard him.

She stood with her arms crossed to stave off the chill from the encroaching fog and turned to stare up at his scruffy face. His eyes were fixed on the disappearing horizon, his hands in his pockets, a contemplative look across his face. Heavy in thought, Lucca's jaw flexed in the most delectable manner. In his cold and calculated stare, she thought perhaps she saw the silhouette of the figure from last night, but the angle was wrong, and he was not shrouded in darkness. She couldn't be sure it was him and waited for him to speak again. Her ears strained to analyze his sound waves for a comparison to her dream.

"Of course. The harbor looked much different the last time I visited it," he said.

No good; her memory failed to form a reasonable assessment.

Lucca dropped his gaze to the ground. He kicked at the wooden dock below his worn black boot and turned with a swift spin on his heels. With his hands nestled in his jacket pockets, he cocked his head to the side. Without a word, Evie obeyed and followed him away from the water as they made their way down the street.

***

He navigated through side streets with the secondhand nature of a local, at ease finding his way through the neighborhood. But, this was Evie's neighborhood—her *home*, dammit—not his to be familiar with. He acknowledged landmarks which Evie had never even noticed before.

Too fixed on matching his gait, she stubbed her toe against a raised piece of the cement sidewalk. Lucca laughed under his breath.

"My family lived in the area for a short time," he said.

"I'm sorry... your family?"

It was a simple enough question in her mind; in a small section of a small town, she felt like she knew everyone and their parents that hailed from these streets.

Her comment, though serious in nature, evoked a roll of laughter from him. Lucca tossed his head up to the sky and grabbed his belly in amusement. He wiped a small fleck of liquid from the corner of his eye.

"Yes, Evie, my family. Did you think I spawned from some primordial ooze? Or perhaps the depths of Hell?"

His mischievous crooked brow made her feel foolish for the impulsive comment. The dark shadow filled her mind's eye, dizzying her as it morphed into the Devil on the tarot card, yanking the chains of his captors. Evie took in a deep breath, forcing the anxiety in her throat past its choking point, and somehow summoned the energy to glower back at him. Her reaction widened his smile all the more.

"I don't recognize you from around town. It baffles me there are faces in this town I don't know," she said.

Lucca peered down the tip of his nose at her. His gaze burned through to her core, kindling something deep inside. His familiarity once more crept in through her senses.

"Yes, well, I suppose you wouldn't. They've long since passed," he said.

Perplexed once more, Evie was left tongue-tied. And with that, she decided to segue off the difficult subject of his origin.

"Do you mind if I ask how old you are?"

"How old am I?" He raised an eyebrow at her. "How old are you?"

"Old enough, but I asked you first."

Lucca stopped and turned to her. "How old do I look?"

Evie gazed up at his face. His body moved closer so that he stood just inches away. She felt the warmth of his body wrap around her, shielding her from the wind's cold torments. If she were unable to calm her breathing, her chest would collide with his.

The wind picked up. Bright red tendrils whipped her cheeks. They stung her with every tiny strike. Through the lashings, she found herself caught in the deep pools of his eyes just as she found herself dazed by the water's murky depths. Her heart pounded. Her knees wobbled. A rush of intense heat and wetness formed between her legs. She wanted to dive into the depths of his eyes, to plunge into their dark nothingness.

"Well, what'll it be then, Evie?" Lucca asked in a soft rasp.

"Y—yes,"

"Interesting. Is that saying yes I *am* old? Or are you reading my mind and answering a question I have?"

His response caught her off-guard. Willing herself to blink, Evie stepped back. She looked away in a poor attempt to regain what little composure she had in the first place and cleared her throat.

"What?"

Lucca shook his head and laughed. He led her up a small set of stairs, through a doorway.

"My age, Evie, or do you want to know the questions that I'm pondering?"

Before Evie had the time to think of an answer, she looked around and was shocked to recognize her surroundings.

"How did you know where I lived?"

Lucca perused the living room, grabbing a glass pipe out of the ashtray on the coffee table. He walked around the sofa and paused in front of the mantle, squinting hard to inspect the photographs on display.

"What are you talking about?" he said.

"My house, how did you know how to walk me back to my house?"

"I don't know what you're talking about. You led me," he said with a wily grin.

Evie opened her mouth to speak, but found no words, her tongue tied in a Gordian knot. She closed her mouth, held in her breath, bemused. Lucca continued to appraise her ancestry's portraits. From right to left, he passed by each face, pausing at the end of the line with a stern glower.

"This one looks like you," he said, observing her namesake. "Although, I think I prefer your wild red hair."

Lucca twisted his neck to wink at her. The glance sent her hormones into frenzy.

"But you led me through the door..."

Lucca stood tall and turned from the mantle, walking up close to her. He toyed with the glass pipe in his hand.

"Evie, have you been smoking more than weed out of this?" He waved the piece in her face.

"But—"

"Your keys are still in your hand," he said. Lucca placed the pipe on the coffee table. In turn, he took Evie's hands in his. They both watched as he released her key ring from her hand to join the glass piece on the table. Evie fought to recall having her keys in the first place. "How could I lead you in, if you're the one holding the key?"

Lucca held her hand, palm up in his. With the index finger of his free hand, he traced swirls along the scabbed gash that lingered from their first encounter.

Evie's mind raced to reconstruct the walk home. Did she lead him here? Did she lure him back to her house and invite him inside? Aside from fixating on the darkness of his eyes, Evie fought to even remember her own name, much less how they ended up in her living room or what they were talking about. Lucca continued to play with her palm. He traced an invisible rune that he saw somewhere within its creases.

"Where's your boyfriend now, Evie?" Every time he whispered her name her insides effervesced. Her palm was lifted to his lips. Her eyes met his.

"He's gone."

"Good. So we can pretend a bit?" Lucca licked his lower lip before running the tip of his tongue down the healing wound in her hand. He rocked side to side on his heels, subtle, playful.

Evie was lost again. A wave of heat washed over her as she watched his tongue, wide-eyed, wanting to synchronize her hips with his. He stopped smiling, dropped her hand down, and moved in closer.

"I don't want to hurt him," she said.

"Of course you don't. You're a good girl, aren't you?"

Lucca wrapped a hand behind her head and pulled her to him. He traced his tongue against hers as he had done with her palm. Evie closed her eyes and felt liberation in his grasp. He tasted cool and refreshing. It took every ounce of strength in her body to hold back. Her tongue, now loose and untied, strained to remain at bay, teased by his. Even as Lucca pulled away to gaze down on her, Evie's eyes remained closed. She savored his flavor.

"You're salty," he said in a low and melodic whisper.

"Fuck." Evie barely vocalized the stream of conscious thought. The word rolled off her tongue like a rogue wave across the sea. Lucca smiled in response. He glided his finger down the tip of her nose, across her lips.

"Perhaps," he said and stifled a laugh.

As he leaned in again, Evie prepared herself for his touch, anticipated it. Before their tongues could touch once more, Lucca straightened his posture. He glanced over his shoulder. His smile had vanished, replaced by a troubled scowl. He stepped back towards the door. Her inner voice wept as he moved away from her.

"Twenty-nine," Lucca said firmly.

"What?" Evie ached with inner chaos from the interplay between fantasy and reality, sensuality and stoicism.

"My age. You asked my age. Twenty-nine."

"I did?"

"You did." He chuckled.

"When?"

"On our walk."

"No, I didn't"

"Yes, you did."

"I don't remember that," she said.

"But you did, and now you know," he said.

He nodded at her before he opened the front door. Blythe and Evan stood on her stoop, a look of shock on Blythe's face as her hand hung in the air, knuckles-first in mid-knock.

"Evie, I didn't realize you had company," Blythe said and smiled at Lucca.

Lucca regarded her, then Evan, and then turned back to Evie. "Something about the red," he said flashing that wicked grin and a wink. Lucca bowed slightly to his hostess, "I'll show myself out."

He stopped in front of Evan. The two glowered at each other, teeth clenched. A guttural growl emerged from one of the pair, possibly both. It was difficult to tell. Without any further acknowledgement, Lucca slipped past the couple.

Evie watched through the window, numb, as he walked away back down streets he shouldn't have known.

***

"Who was that?" Blythe asked.

Evie, now free of Lucca's gaze, blinked and regained her awareness. "Just a guy I met at work last week."

She saw a frown line Evan's face as he and Blythe passed over the threshold. Evie considered asking him about Lucca, but thought better of it. Based upon their reaction to each other just now, she suspected bad blood between the two—something that was none of her business to begin with. Instead, Evie turned towards Blythe with a roll of her eyes.

Blythe giggled. "You met a guy at Sirens? Classy. Does Rob know?" she teased.

Evan looked Evie up and down. His once-over made her uneasy. She thought of what Rob had said about him, how he stared at her. How it pissed Rob off.

"No, and neither does Nate. There's nothing to know. What are you guys doing here?"

Under Evan's eyes, her spiteful tongue lined the inside of her mouth recalling Lucca's taste. Her inner voice delighted in his discomfort. Still, with her hormones on edge thanks to her previous visitor, Evie found it difficult to deny Evan was a pleasure to lock hateful glares with. His build was much like Lucca's, exquisitely trimmed. A freezing wave of guilt seized her spine; she shook it off with a subtle shudder.

What's the matter, Miss Prissy isn't enough to satisfy you?

Evan stepped out from around Blythe. "We wanted to make sure you made it home alright," he said.

"Rob took care of me, as he always does," Evie said.

"You two were both pretty wasted, I was worried," Blythe said. "You didn't do anything stupid, did you?"

"Define stupid. Aren't you the one trying to push Rob on me?"

Blythe gasped. "Oh my God, did you finally do it? Did you sleep with Rob?"

Evie scowled; this wasn't a conversation she cared to hold in front of Evan. She saw his furrowed brow deepen with concern, confirming his discomfort with the conversation as well.

Worry about your own sex life. What do you care who we fuck?

"No, I didn't. I don't want to talk about it," Evie answered Blythe while keeping her suspicious gaze fixed on Evan.

"Well, maybe next time. You two make a great couple. Don't you think so, Evan?" Blythe said, wrapping her hand around his and leading him further into the living room. Evie followed them over to the sofa. Her stomach

147

roiled under the shadow that descended upon his already dark brown eyes while he held back his opinion.

"Sure," he answered, quiet and dismissive.

"Well, I'm embarrassed to say I barely remember last night," Blythe continued with her usual gaiety. "I told Evan next time to stop me after just two volcanos. I never remember how strong they mix the drinks at the Dynasty. Man, my head is killing me today. Evan took me out for breakfast..."

The white noise of Blythe's voice faded into the background, overpowered by the static distorting the receptors in Evie's mind. She sat silent, allowing Blythe the opportunity to do what she did best: talk about herself. Evan appeared to do the same. The two flanked Blythe's one-way conversation. Evie struggled to decode his stare.

Determined to divert those big brown eyes, and with no weed left in the house, Evie pushed her empty bowl towards Evan. If he was going to ogle her, the least he could was make it worth her while. And remembering the tasty joint he'd rolled the night before, Evie hoped he had some of that weed on him now.

A little something to curb this edge.

He cracked a tiny smile. His shoulders softened as he revealed a small plastic bag of bright green hydroponic from his pocket. She salivated at the sight of the sticky sweet pot. His fingers packed the tiny glass bowl with care, then he offered her the first hit. With a deep inhale, she passed it back to him. In an instant, Evan reached out and took a hit. She exchanged a hesitant but appreciative smile with him.

Blythe sat between the two waving the smoke away as she was lost in her own self-centered recount of what she didn't remember about the night before, how hung-over she was today, and how she couldn't fathom how Evie functioned like this on a regular basis.

As Blythe rattled on and on about nonsense and herself, Evan rarely took his eyes off Evie. And much for her efforts, Evie likewise kept her eyes on him. His stare was cold and cautious. It lacked the thrilling menace in Lucca's eyes. Evan's were dark, matte, had no glimmering golden orbs flickering across their surface. It was like they were shrouded by a widow's veil. His stare unnerved her throughout their entire visit. A fleeting thought crossed her mind, a shadow sitting across her room, watching her. Evie wanted more than anything for Evan to pay more attention to his girlfriend than to her.

Judging, just like the rest of them.

Although his stare was unlike the others she suffered around town, there was a genuine look of animal interest in the lines around his eyes. She glanced over to Blythe, who remained oblivious, chattering on. She glared at Evan once more.

You don't get to fuck us. You have no right to judge us. Go fuck Miss Prissy instead.

Continuing her solitary conversation, Blythe drilled Evie for details of her night, of Rob, and of the man at the door when they arrived. With sparse one-word answers, Evie withstood her inquisition. As soon as Blythe took a second to breathe, Evie jumped up from her seat.

"Right, okay, everyone had fun last night, and Evie hasn't done anything regrettably stupid. Perfect," she said, directing the others to the door.

Evan's gaze had killed whatever buzz lingered inside her from Lucca's kiss. That damn curbed edge was too persistent for the pot to do much more than leave her with cotton mouth. She just wanted a hot bath before work. She could hear the church bells chiming in the back of her mind. If she could get Blythe to leave now, she'd still have some time for a quick ritual.

Blythe stood, mouth agape. "Why so pushy?"

"I'm not being pushy. I need to get ready for work."

"Well, I'm glad everyone made it home safe," Evan interjected. His voice was soft and melodic, a perfect harmony in tune with Lucca's. The church bells chimed louder. "Let's go Blythe, your car is still at the Chinese restaurant. We should pick it up and leave Evie to get ready for work."

"Fine. Call me later, Evie," Blythe said. Evie nodded, but knew she wouldn't call her later. She wasn't one to chat on the phone. Blythe knew that; her comment was rhetorical of course.

This time it was Evan who led Blythe by the hand to the door. His eyes roamed Evie's body one last time, just one more for the road before nodding to her and escorting Blythe to his car parked in the driveway.

Evie released a massive sigh of relief, collapsing her body up against the door. One, two, three deep breaths and Evie locked the dead bolt and headed upstairs to the bathroom.

Her baptismal ritual did little to settle her nerves or the tempest of emotions threatening to obliterate her from the inside out.

SEVENTEEN

When she arrived at Sirens, Jerry didn't greet her at the door with his usual jovial smile. The girls inside were huddled around each other. A cloud hung over the interior of the building. Evie looked around, had an inkling of what could be wrong, but was too scared to ask anyone.

Halfway to the bar, she was approached by Rob. He swooped forward and picked her up like a rag doll in his arms. His panicked appearance from the afternoon had returned. He held her close, closer than before.

"Thank God, Evie. It's awful," he said, digging his nose into her hair and taking in a deep breath. Evie accepted his embrace. Mystified, she scanned the room.

How bad can it be?

"What happened?"

"They found Natalie's body," Rob said into the nape of her neck, squeezing her tight.

"What? Where?" Shock constricted her lungs.

"They found her tucked away in the back of her bedroom closet. Crumpled up in a duffel bag. She'd been dead for days," He said. His quivering jaw belying his somehow steady voice.

"She's dead?" Evie asked, incredulous. Out on a bender, she thought of. Bruised up from a bad night with her addict boyfriend or some other asshole, maybe a customer who didn't want to pay to get her attention anymore. That tended to be a common occurrence around

Fallhaven. Christ, maybe appendicitis or something. But dead?

"The police think it was her boyfriend. They're working with the Coast Guard to find his boat," Rob said. Evie knew Natalie's boyfriend, Scotty, a friend of Nate's, who worked on one of the fishing boats. He was a coke-head and had been known to use steroids in the past. He had his anger issues, sure, but Evie had a difficult time picturing him as a murderer.

"Fucking asshole must've been all jacked up and wigged out on her," Rob continued. "I hope they catch him and fry the bastard."

Evie pried herself away, but Rob continued to hold her in his arms. She pushed against his muscular biceps and searched his eyes. She looked for an understanding, an ounce of the calm and soothing demeanor she had come to depend on from Rob. Only worry looked back at her.

"Wait, Rob, Scotty went out on the boats. He was here the Sunday before last. I know I saw Scotty leave with Nate. They were all here, drunk off their asses. Jimmy's entire fleet went out early that morning. How could he have murdered her?"

"Maybe he met back up with Natalie before he shipped out. Are you sure his boat left the same time as Nate's?" Rob paused. Evie thought about it. No, she actually didn't know the entire fleet's schedule, just Nate's. Scotty may not have left for another day or two. Her eyes went wide with disbelief as she held Rob's trembling body. "I'd close the place down for the night, if it wasn't for the fact that I want to keep all you girls safe tonight," he continued.

The desperation in his voice was heartbreaking.

"Rob, if it was her boyfriend, then we're all safe."

"I know that, but I can't help it. What if it were you and Nate? He's just as bad as Natalie's boyfriend. Just as capable of..." Rob quieted as his voice drifted off. Unwilling to continue his statement, he pulled her in close again. "God, Evie, it could just as easily have been you. Your face bashed in. Your body torn to shreds. I couldn't—" Rob dry-heaved in her chest. Evie reciprocated his intense hold. She rubbed his back, pulling the back of his head closer into the crook of her neck.

She knew what Rob said was true. All of the fishermen used. They were all coked up. There was no other way to work eighteen hours, sleep for five, and maintain such a pace for days at sea, for a week, two, three or more in a row. It was all part and parcel to the life of a modern-day fisherman. Evie also knew Nate was just as capable. She knew his jealous nature. She could share Natalie's fate. Her mind went back to the lap dance Natalie had given Lucca last week. Since Scotty was part of Nate's pack of boozehounds that night, he could watch his girlfriend work. Was Natalie as captivated by Lucca's gaze as she was? Could that professional courtesy have been enough to spark a drug-induced rage of jealousy in Scotty? If Evie were to be honest with herself, she was jealous of Natalie for engaging in something so intimate with him. If a twinge of jealousy gripped Evie, than what would Natalie's boyfriend have felt?

Evie thought back to her kiss with Lucca. If Nate knew, he'd kill both Evie and her mysterious stranger, with or without chemical assistance. A shudder of fear crept down her spine, and she pulled away from Rob.

"C'mon, we need a drink," she said. The two passed the bottle of Beam back and forth. The bourbon could only mask the horror and shock muffling the thumping bass and shifting lights of the stage.

***

A heavy pallor joined the mix of perfume and spilled alcohol in the club's atmosphere, the deejay's choices hopelessly outmuscled in the fight to turn the mood around. Regulars offered condolences at the news of what happened to poor Natalia. Some of the girls found themselves unable to perform. Rob made no objections to allowing them to leave. Those that remained attempted to maintain the charade and collect the extra tips.

Evie kept a watchful eye on Rob as she made her rounds. She could tell he was searching for a way to blame himself for Natalie's death. If he was this upset about Natalie, what would he do if anything ever happened to her? She wanted to hold him again, console him.

As the night wound down, one by one, patrons and employees trickled out of the building. Evie thought to linger after the club closed to spend time with Rob. Thinking better of herself, her emotions, his emotions, and Nate's jealous nature, she felt it better to go home alone. With much reluctance, she left Rob to himself.

***

Just past three in the morning, Evie was grateful to be home and alone with her thoughts. She resolved not to allow her mind to fester over what happened to Natalie, which was not a simple task given the morbid atmosphere at Sirens throughout the night. She chanted over and over in her mind: if this was something between her and her boyfriend, then it was an isolated incident, everyone else was safe. Evie locked the door behind her.

She didn't bother to turn any lights on in the house. Instead, she moved through shadows and moonlight through the living room, past the mantle and the jury of generations passed. She grabbed the bottle of Beam that she swiped from the club on her way out. Taking a swig from the bottle, Evie winced from the burning sensation of the fluid rushing down her throat. A pain shot through her gut. A gurgle bubbled up her empty belly. She missed more than one meal during the day. Fueled only by booze and caffeine, Evie grabbed a package of cookies from the kitchen and went upstairs.

The darkness and quiet of the house comforted her. She was used to its creaks, cracks, and musty odor. The darkness shielded her from the bathroom mirror and the ghostly image she feared would judge her. Evie lit a solitary candle on her nightstand, allowing her enough light to fumble her way to the bathroom and run a hot bath. She turned on her stereo to the same longing music as always and stripped down to her panties. She paused for a moment and stared at her rocker-recliner.

For the first time since she could remember, she was a little scared of the dark, too afraid of what she might find standing in the shadows. Lucca? Evan? Someone or something else entirely? Perhaps even a serial killer set to take out each and every one of the girls from the club. Her body trembled fervently trying to evict paranoia from her mind. She relied on the bourbon whiskey to work its magic on her nerves.

Evie climbed out onto the roof with her bottle. The coarseness of the shingling abraded her near bare bottom. The air was cool on her skin. She let her senses take in her cool surroundings, the one way she could in fact feel her body.

She looked out onto the harbor, a giant pristine black expanse unperturbed by any vessels at the moment, but the boys would be home soon, whether escorted by the Coast Guard or of their own accord. No doubt, Natalie's boyfriend would be in custody. For now, the harbor would remain still. The beacon at the tip of its mouth rotated reliably. The all-seeing eye of the lighthouse winked at her again and again.

Evie suckled at her bottle until her body warmed from the inside out and her lips were singed from the whiskey's fire. Again, she was grateful for the solitude. She scanned the shadows across the street and was relieved no glowing eyes stared back at her.

With a healthy buzz on the rise, Evie crawled back through the window. Pleased the booze had numbed her for the time being, carefree and alone, her head swirled as she found the bottom of the bottle. She discarded it, kicking it under the foot of her bed. Evie giggled a little at the sound the empty glass container made as it clanged off the bed's metal frame, spun on its side, and skittered over to her dresser.

By the time she made it back to the bathroom, the water had risen to the rim of the tub. She carried the candle in with her, a drip of molten wax trickling down her arm as she stumbled her way through the minefield of her bedroom floor, and settled it on the silver tray. The hot water against her malt-soaked skin tingled through her entire body like a tiny orgasm. She shuddered a little and moaned her way into the steamy depths.

Evie lay her head back against the cool porcelain rim, the water feeling like gelatin hugging her naked body. She remained ever watchful of the cushy recliner across her bedroom. It remained vacant.

Evie listened to the soft plucking of a guitar and the crooning of a lover lost at sea. Evie wanted to find the singer and hold him, keep him safe like Rob. The next song, a sultrier strum of the guitar pitted the same singer against a forbidden love. He tried to convince his lover to lie to everyone about them, to keep their love a secret.

Evie thought about Lucca, of the hypnotic eyes from her dreams. She knew those eyes that ravaged her in her slumber were the same eyes that beamed from his beautiful face. She thought of the dream she'd had of him prior to their first meeting. She felt his body over hers, but couldn't seem to reach it.

More satisfying than her dreams, she remembered how sweet his lips tasted earlier in the day. She thought back on how her mouth parted to receive his tongue, and she remembered the soft purr that emerged from deep within him. What she would give to make him purr like that again.

"God, that fucking tongue," she said in a soft whisper out loud to herself. Her clammy hand caressed her forehead and trailed down her cheek. It traveled past her chin and rested across her chest. Evie's mind drifted to the cryptic card reading she'd received with Blythe, ramblings about a past life, love, the Devil, and having already been confronted with her fate. She peeked back over at the rocker-recliner.

Black shadows blurred in the darkness. She squinted, forced her eyes to focus. If the Devil awaited her in the bedroom, then he'd delight in her drunken state.

Eighteen

Evie dreaded the return of Nate's boat. Word had it the Coast Guard would bring the entire fleet back at some point during the day. The tempest of events over the past couple of weeks dizzied her. Lucca Natalie; her tarot card reading with Hope; Blythe and Evan. And, of course, Rob. One good thing about Nate being home would be the normality he could bring back to her recently abnormal life. Though, considering what everyday life with Nate was like, Hope's reading and references to her habits hung over her head, threatened to guillotine her.

It was that angst, that raging storm inside her, which prevented Evie from finding any sleep. Following her ritualistic bath, she met the sun rising up over the horizon with bloodshot eyes. She tossed and turned until her buzz waned and her mind ached.

Staring up at the prism of light cast over the ceiling as daylight broke, she continued to obsess over Lucca, the Lucca from her dreams, the one who hovered above her in bed. What it would be like if he actually was on top of her? She squeezed her eyes shut, focused on recalling those tantalizing, shimmering orbs that fixated her so, but she found nothing, no images. Why was it so easy to see him in her mind at night, but during the day he vanished? Depression and digressive thoughts left her irritable, restless, but still unwilling to rise out of bed.

A soft buzz to the left of her head forced Evie to focus her fragmented senses. She leaned over to retrieve her cell phone from the nightstand. It was her 45-minute warning from Blythe that she was coming to pick her up for the gym. With a reluctant groan, she rolled off the side of her bed and dragged her feet to the bathroom. Following a scalding hot shower, scrubbing away the layers of dead and flaky epidermis, Evie felt no more awake than when she dragged herself to the bathroom in the first place.

She faced the mirror. Her colorless reflection gazed back. Life was as it always had been. Nothing had changed for her, nothing noticeable. Yet, she felt something was different. Something from the old woman's card reading made her somewhat optimistic. Change was coming, and neither her inner voice nor the image in the mirror had control over it. She let a half-hearted smirk cross her lips at the thought.

"You can't touch me much longer," she said to her reflection. A smug grin beamed back, mocked her like it knew a secret. Her smile faded. Her hand dropped down to the vanity and groped the cool white ceramic for something not there.

"Where the fuck is my bandana?" Evie bent under the sink, dug through the vanity's drawers for her favorite accessory. It was nowhere to be found. Propping her head back up, she looked at herself in the mirror again. "Did you take it?" She snorted in response. Shook her head back and forth at the absurdity that the bitch in the mirror was to blame. It could chide her, mock her, but move objects? Ridiculous.

She heard her cell phone vibrate again. That had to be Blythe's five-minute warning to get her butt downstairs. Unable to locate the bandana, Evie grabbed two hair elastics and fashioned pig tails out of the long strands of hair that framed her face. Punctual as always, Blythe's horn called for her outside just as Evie scooted down to the first floor.

***

"You look awful," Blythe said while Evie settled into the SUV's plush leather interior.

"I didn't sleep at all last night." Evie tilted her head back into the passenger seat and closed her eyes, hoping for just a few winks before Blythe murdered her on the treadmill.

"Thinking about what happened to Natalie?"

"Yeah... something like that."

Lights flittered over Evie's closed eyelids like warm rolling waves. She could have fallen asleep to the soft murmur of the engine were it not for—

Chatty Miss Prissy.

"It's just gruesome, what happened to Natalie," Blythe said. "See, this is why Nate is bad for you. Those drugged-up fishermen, God only knows what would happen if—"

"That's enough, Blythe," Evie ordered with a stern voice, but otherwise placid demeanor, keeping her eyes closed. Blythe's teeth clacked when her mouth snapped shut tight. The girls did not speak the rest of the way to the gym.

***

Fighting insomnia-induced fatigue, Evie barely made it through her first mile on the treadmill. Blythe began lamenting over Evan.

160

"You know he still hasn't invited me to that stupid party he's advertising all over the place," Blythe said in a snippy tone that made Evie's lip curl.

"Maybe it's not his party," Evie said, her tone coated in a thick layer of apathy and the hopes of ending the conversation.

"Oh come on, Evie, at his house? Why wouldn't it be for him? No, he just wants a bunch of college girls to head up from the city. That's why he doesn't want me there."

Evie huffed heavily, perturbed she hadn't circumvented the conversation after all. "Well, have you fucked him yet or not?" Evie slowed the treadmill to a fast-paced walk. Maybe Evan wasn't interested in Blythe at all. Maybe he saw through her superficial prissy exterior already and she just wasn't picking up on the clues.

Blythe scoffed and scanned their surroundings to be sure no one nearby heard Evie's remark. "No," Blythe answered, pained.

"What happened the other night at the Dynasty? You said you were going to try and fuck him," Evie noted, squeezing the burning stitch in her side.

Blythe sighed, regretful. "I tried, but he was all weird about it. He made sure I got home safe and all, but then he just left my apartment. I couldn't even get him through my front door."

"Have you even kissed this guy?"

Evie was beginning to think Blythe was just fantasizing about her relationship, falling too quick as always. Did Evan even know they were *dating*?

"Here and there, no real tongue action though," Blythe answered. "Do you think he's gay?"

Evie shook her head. The all-too-vivid image of Evan's russet stare quickened her pulse. Burning ache subsided, replaced by a new sensation, her pace increased to a jog as she futilely ran from the memory of his gaze.

"I don't think Evan's gay," Evie affirmed.

Blythe whacked Evie across the chest with a back-handed swing, nearly knocking Evie straight off the side of the treadmill's safety guard. Evie clung to the railing for dear life. "You don't suppose he's asexual, do you, like he doesn't even enjoy having sex?"

"What? No, Blythe. You're being ridiculous."

She saw the sadness lining her best friend's face. Blythe never handled rejection well, and Evan's rebuke was not only insulting, it was baffling to think he wouldn't find Blythe attractive.

"How long have you been seeing him, again?" asked Evie, a valid point just a few paces ahead of her, and she was closing the gap.

"It's been almost a month."

And there it was.

"Don't worry about it, Blythe. Give it time. If it's meant to be, it'll happen."

Traces of disbelief and sarcasm skimmed along the corner creases of Blythe's smile, slowing her pace to cool down. "Listen to who's preaching about fate now."

The remainder of the workout focused on low weights, multiple repetitions, and controlled breathing. They made no room for their usual chatter. Evie could see Blythe's self-esteem deflating with each squat and leg-lift. She knew that look well, the self-doubt, the despair. She'd seen it for years staring back at her in the mirror.

Evie almost felt bad for leaving Blythe alone for the evening, left to her own self-wallowing. Blythe was too light and carefree for her lifestyle.

That's what you look like, you know. Day in and day out. That's why she judges us.

***

Evie walked through the front door to find Nate sprawled out along the length of the couch, his gigantic feet hanging off the side, a fool's grin across his face.

"Babe, come here. You gotta see what this idiot's trying to do."

Evie approached. His laughter was directed towards the television at some ridiculous reality show. They were all the same, really. Evie rarely bothered to watch TV, but the show was amusing enough for a stoner, she supposed. Nate laughed in hysterics. She remained ambivalent, preferring her entertainment to generate from her stereo at one hundred decibels, along with a glass full of amber liquid and green bud on the side.

She sat down on the sliver of space on the sofa not engulfed by Nate's body. She gagged at the pungent funk of fish guts emanating off of his body. The coffee table was littered with half-eaten bags of chips and candy wrappers. Among the debris lay a couple of empty beer bottles and a Zip-loc containing a massive bud of marijuana. Next to the pot was a stretched-out, filthy paper clip that Nate used to unclog the glass bowl nestled on the adjacent ashtray. Evie had only been gone an hour or so, and already Nate had returned and made himself at home. By the looks of it, Nate had found the stocked cupboards and fridge she'd braved society to provide. At least he came with his own beer and bud.

He neglected to acknowledge her as she sat next to him. She grabbed a half-emptied bottle to relieve Nate the burden of having to consume any more of it.

"When did you get in?"

"Not too long ago. You should've seen the fucking greenhorns we had on deck. One of them was actually green, like I mean he literally puked everywhere."

Evie frowned. She felt bad for the fisherman who, by the sound of it, lived up to his newbie status. Greenhorns were called just that because they got green in the face with seasickness. Many of the town's young men had suffered such a label at one point or another in their life. Nate, on the other hand, proved a natural talent for the fishing boats and the fisherman's lifestyle. He never suffered the teasing that came along with the slang, but he loved to dish it out.

"Sucks to be him," she said quietly.

"It was wicked fucking funny. Where've you been?"

"At the gym with Blythe."

"You're working tonight, right?" he asked.

"Yes."

"Okay. I'm beat, and I don't have anything to eat at my place. I'm going to drop you off, pick up some food, and come back here to take a shower and unwind, if that's cool with you? I'll pick you up later," he said with a sniffle.

"You know you're going to have to get your car fixed at some point. It's been months," she reminded him.

"I know. I don't have the money for it right now."

Evie looked down at the bud and beers; it looked like a replacement alternator's worth, by her measure. One more deep breath, and she continued, "Did you hear about Natalie?"

"Yeah, pretty fucked up. I guess Scott doesn't even remember doing it. He's baffled by the situation."

"Do you think he did it?"

"He must have. The Coast Guard escorted us all back in. I heard they questioned a few guys, too. It's messed up. Now Jimmy's fleet is coming in short-handed."

Yeah, that mutilated dead girl's being a real pain in the ass.

The conversation ended. Nate stretched out to grab the pot, paper clip, and bowl. Without words, they passed the bowl back and forth a bit. Each took a generous toke off the small glass piece, content, innocuous, and lackluster.

Soon, the sun set and Nate drove Evie to the club. While she was at work, he would make himself at home eating her food, drinking, smoking, and using her shower.

NINETEEN

Evie stood in the entryway at Sirens. Jerry held the door open, quiet, sullen. There was no miming tip of his hat, not tonight. Instead he held his hand across his chest, pressed to his heart as he bowed his head down. Tension slithered its way down her back like a snake upon entry. The place looked different from a couple of days ago, before word of Natalie's murder. *How long can the mourning last*, Evie wondered.

The pall cast over the club slowly lifted—for strippers as for Shakespeare, the show must go on, Evie supposed—but like a child with a scabbed knee, the regulars couldn't stop themselves from picking away at the murder. Who was the last person Natalie was seen with? Where did she go after her last night of work? Had anyone spoken with her since she left the club that night? No one accepted the easy answer, that Scotty had killed her in a drug-induced fit of rage.

Evie struggled to push the controversy from her mind, but the lasting image of Lucca during Natalie's lap dance arrested her thoughts. Last she remembered, Natalie was bent over backwards and naked save for a G-string, mere inches from Lucca's face, and yet the newcomer seemed only interested in teasing Evie.

She cringed. She did poor Natalie no justice obsessing over those dark pools glistening with golden flecks of light from within the contours of Lucca's face.

She tried to force the memory out, but Evie's imagination took the opportunity to picture Natalie's body crumpled up in a bag in a closet, like a pile of dirty laundry, bruised and bloodied from the fatal beating Scotty gave her. It probably would have happened at some point anyhow. Natalie was always an exhibitionist, one of the few girls at the club who seemed to enjoy her job. Scotty's distrust could only lay dormant for so long before it became too much.

Evie told herself she saw Natalie leave with Scotty that night, him goading her to spend the night together rather than being stuck carting Nate's drunken ass to the docks. That explained it, and that was that.

Lucca's glimmering eyes gripped her mind again.

Keep convincing yourself that you care.

***

Finally, at the end of a barely profitable night, three a.m. approached. Evie stood out in the parking lot under the neon lighting of the *Sirens* sign. Nate had yet to show up with her car.

She stood with his green plaid shirt like a blanket of moss wrapped around her shoulders to stave off the cool air. Her eyes searched through the darkened streets hoping for a pair of headlights. She checked the call history on her cell. Nothing except for the five outgoing calls to Nate in the last fifteen minutes, all unanswered. A wave of sadness crashed into her back, stirred the ground under her feet, beckoned to drag her away in its undertow. Another girl's headlights flashed bright in her eyes, causing her to shrink back and shield her face from the painful glare.

"Evie, why are you still here?" Rob came out from the club, turning the locks to close up for the night.

"Nate isn't here yet."

Rob scanned the parking lot. Evie was afraid of this, afraid of what Rob might think if he suspected that Nate had abandoned her.

"Is he supposed to be picking you up?"

"Yeah, he'll be here soon, I'm sure."

She knew her statement was half-hearted. She presumed Nate was passed out in the living room, comatose from a mountain of booze and bud consumed over the last eight hours. Rob's shoulders dropped a bit. She cursed herself for allowing her distress to make itself so evident in front of him.

"Do you want a ride home?"

"I'm sure he's on his way," Evie said. She peered down the street, hoping to see a car she knew wasn't coming.

"Evie, it's the middle of the night. You know I'm not going to leave you here alone. C'mon, let's go."

Reluctantly, Evie followed Rob to his truck. As she settled into the passenger seat, she scanned the dark corners of the parking lot one last time. She only closed the car door after being certain no one was there. Buckling herself in, she noticed Rob. He watched her, worried, from the driver's seat.

"Why do you date that idiot?"

"What do you mean?"

"I mean the guy's a burnout. Evie, he left you stranded in the middle of the night at a strip club. What kind of boyfriend does that?"

"He's tired when he comes back from the boat," she said.

"Evie, the guy's a drug addict. He's no better than Scotty. When I think of Natalie..." He trailed off, choking on his words.

"He is not going to kill me," she argued, insulted by the comparison.

Rob's jaw flexed, but he remained silent. Evie took in a deep breath knowing the conversation teetered on the precipice of a nasty argument. "Evie," he said in a firm voice. "You *know* you deserve better."

Like who? Him? We tried that. He said it was "wrong."

His words cut to her heart. Did she deserve better? This town was nothing but deadbeats and drug addicts. If not Nate, then who? She bit her tongue. Her inner voice forced a smug grin, and she accepted his under-handed compliment before continuing.

"Thanks, but Nate's not that bad. He's not. He's just Nate."

Rob forced a smile back at her. It wasn't his usual warm smile. It was the kind of smile Blythe gave her when she was holding back the truth, a smile that conceded a point just to avoid a much more devastating argument.

When they pulled up to her house, the lights were on and the car was still parked in the driveway. She fumbled through her bag and realized her house keys were still inside with Nate. She saw Rob scrutinizing her behavior from across the old truck's bench seat. Her inner voice cackled wildly from within.

***

It took her a minute or two, but she convinced Rob to take off. She was grateful for the privacy. It prevented

Rob's witnessing her pummel the front door not once, not twice, but three times before it opened.

Nate fumbled to the front door to let her in. He rubbed his eyes, dazed and unaware of the time that had elapsed during his nap. Evie shook her head with disappointment as she passed by him into the living room.

"Babe, I'm so sorry. I had no idea what time it was," Nate muttered. Evie noticed the house looked the same as before she left for work: half eaten packages of chips and cookies, empty beer bottles, though the quantity had increased considerably. A dirty ashtray cradled a host of cigarette butts next to a near-empty bag of pot. In the midst of the mess, she saw a tiny orange prescription bottle, no doubt ill-gotten and of unknown origin. Judging by its lack of contents and his groggy state, it appeared Nate had already had his share of narcotic candy for the evening.

"Looks like you had a productive night," she said. A slight inflection in her tone revealed her animosity. Nate scratched his head and stepped closer to offer his giant open hand.

"I took a shower," Nate said, raising a packed bowl and yellow lighter as a peace offering in his massive paw. She frowned but accepted it. Flicking it multiple times with no success, Evie shook the lighter and finally took a flame to the bowl. She inhaled the smoke into her lungs, letting it spin circles through her mind.

Just breathe, Evie. Just breathe.

Exhaling a great puff of smoke in his face, Evie cast a disapproving glare up at Nate. The different attire and diminished stench of fish entrails verified his statement. So he showered. *Big fucking deal.* Her inner voice didn't need to convince her to glower at him. She dropped her bag on the floor in disgust, shook her head and walked around him to head up to her room, but not before taking the half-empty beer bottle from Nate's other hand. She chugged it down on her way up the stairs.

Nate followed and extinguished lights behind her.

Once upstairs, he watched her rip off her boots and chuck them towards the closet. She tossed her tip money on the nightstand, stripped down to her undies and changed into a tank top. She paced the bedroom back and forth, mumbling something to herself, not meant for Nate's ears.

"I'm sorry, Babe. I didn't mean it. I swear."

Evie stopped and stared up at him. The genuine guilt on his face both insulted and softened her. His scruffy, hang-dog look confirmed his lack of malice. She knew he didn't mean to abandon her tonight. His worn eyes and pouty lips lined by a ginger beard pinched at a tiny remorseful nerve. Evie sighed.

"I know," she said, reaching up and running her fingernails from his temple to behind his ear. "But just imagine how I felt when Rob had to drive me home."

The mention of her boss's name made his eyes sharpen and his back stiffen. He knew what Rob thought of him, that he wasn't good enough for her. Nate always said their relationship wasn't open to Rob's scrutiny as far as he was concerned. His scruffy and jolly features shifted to a hardened scowl. He wrapped his giant arms around her, pulling her close.

"I suppose Rob can thank me later for letting him save the day," he said with false bravado and bent down over her, closing his mouth over hers.

He pulled Evie onto the bed, and she instantly forgave Nate his faults. She had spent the last couple of weeks emotionally and sexually frustrated, left to her own devices and her fucked-up psyche. The need to feel something real inside of her was much more urgent than playing any guilt trip on him at the moment. His desires echoed hers. An empty beer bottle clanged to the floor before it rolled out of sight.

The two rolled over each other back and forth as they pawed layers of clothing off. Their mouths attacked each other's. In a moment's time, Evie had pinned the massive giant down to the bed and slid down onto him. She moved her hips up and down. They found their routine rhythm, and she was grateful for the familiarity of him inside her, something she knew and could trust. As a heavy breath of relief escaped her, she pushed her hands down on his chest, curling her fingers through his thick chest hair. She closed her eyes and tossed her head back in delight.

Under normal circumstances, she knew Nate had a tendency to rest his arms behind his head and enjoy the ride. But unlike normal circumstances, Evie felt hands clasp down on her hips, an unfamiliar and firm hold as fingertips dug into her rear, spreading her open, inflicting a thrilling pain. When she looked down alarm seized her. Nate's face was gone, replaced by a Cheshire grin as Lucca gazed up at her before easing his head back into the pillow in satisfaction.

What the fuck?

Evie slowed her hips. She felt his hands loosen their grip on her.

"Babe, is everything okay?" Nate's voice called out through the shadows.

Evie blinked twice to be sure she saw him correctly. She felt his chest again, thick curly hair still caught between her fingers. Satisfied she was seeing straight, she worked her hips again, increasing her rhythm. Her breathing quickened. She heard Nate's pants and moans building.

Again, she dared to peer down on him to find Lucca's perfect smile beaming through the darkness. Rather than slow her pace, Evie embraced her hallucination. She rode harder, grinding her hips harder into his, forcing him deeper inside. His moans were musical. Evie arched her back in pure elation.

"You fuck so good," he said, groaning and biting down at his bottom lip.

He pulled down on her, yanked her hips wildly on top of him. She throbbed. Her voice cracked as she peaked, fighting every urge in her body not to shout out his name.

Oh—my—God—Lucca.

She collapsed onto his chest, breathing in his musky sweat. It was then that Evie became aware of the chest hair tickling her nose. She looked up and her mouth met Nate's.

"That was intense, Babe," he said, kissing her forehead. Evie dismounted and made her way through the darkness to the bathroom. Her mind flooded with images. Her heart, still racing, was burdened by a barrage of emotions.

"Hey, Nate?"

"Yeah, Babe?"

"Where did you get that pot?" she asked, hoping it had been laced with something to cause her vivid hallucinations.

"From Jimmy. Why?"

With trouble lining her face, Evie made her way back into the bedroom. Nate had the covers lifted up to receive her. She crawled back into the bed and was enveloped into a bear hug.

"No reason, I guess."

The two lay in their familiar content.

"Babe?"

173

"Yeah, Nate?"

"I'm shipping out again in a few hours to help Jimmy recoup some of the losses from Scotty's situation. I should only be gone for about another week or so."

Evie thought for a moment and decided this affected her very little. "Okay," she whispered, and pulled his arm to rest around her waist.

She didn't drink. She didn't dream. She just slept, blissfully numb in Nate's arms.

TWENTY

Evie tossed and turned herself awake in what was now an otherwise empty bed. She managed to lift herself up, propel herself towards her white-tiled cathedral, and turn the holy water on full-blast. She languished in the bath while the droning of a love-sick singer serenaded her. Nate was gone. The sanctity of her ritual remained intact.

As she soaked in the tub, her mind drifted back to her hallucinations. She was left awed by the experience. She could feel Lucca, see his eyes beaming up at her, and she could smell his sweat. What triggered such vivid imagery? After all, his body was so different from Nate's. She recalled their stark contrast the night they'd run into each other at the club. Nate towered over Lucca. His shoulders were much wider. Nate was a built like a Kodiak and was just about as hirsute. She was certain what she felt last night was smooth, silky skin.

Gorgeous skin.

The more sharply she recalled his touch and the sound of his whisperings, the lower Evie's hands traced down her body, over her hip bones, moving further down to her center, teasing, parting her folds and curling inward, but her fingers proved a poor substitute for the girth at the center of her imagination's craving. She emerged dripping from the porcelain pool still frustrated.

Evie pieced together an outfit from the piles on her bedroom floor, clomped her way downstairs, and lounged catlike on the sofa, angling her frustration towards what little pot she could pinch together and the few beers Nate had left behind. All the while, the melodic cries from her stereo permeated the house. She was content to be alone for as long as possible.

When the time came, Evie made her way upstairs and finished a beer on her perch above the front porch, drinking in the view of the harbor. The briny seaweed scent from the low tide tickled her nostrils, not unpleasant, somehow familiar and comforting like the musty wallpaper on her bedroom walls. Steeling herself for yet another night in the club's ruined atmosphere, she downed the last of her beer and crept back through her window.

She strapped herself into a mini-dress, circled her eyes in smoky shadow, and braided her hair in pig tails, flows of lava cascading down over her shoulders to match the traces of red around her irises. She left Nate's green plaid shirt hanging on the kitchen chair.

***

As she had feared and expected, the night dragged on much slower than a strip club on Saturday night should ever be. New faces were scared away by what happened to Natalie, and the regulars were more interested in playing detective than playing doctor. The fishing boats had returned, but few of the crew came for a visit. Some of them would be out on the boat with Nate, making up for time lost to the Coast Guard and the murder investigation, but not this many.

Evie watched as Rob forced himself through his normal routine. The blame he carried on his shoulders pushed him down. His head hung low when he thought no one was watching. At one point in the evening she saw him stare into nothingness behind the bar. The bass of the music blared, the lights flashed, but Rob was deaf and blind to it all. Since there were hardly any customers to tend to, she walked behind the bar and stood by his side. On a normal night, Rob would have acknowledged her. The two may have shared some playful banter before she pilfered the bar. But tonight, such behavior would be thievery.

Evie stood beside him and held his hand, resting her head on his shoulder. The tension circling in the air around him like a shark dispelled the longer she remained connected to him.

A figure in her periphery appeared from the shadows. He sat alone at a pub table far off to the left of the stage. To Evie's best memory, she didn't recall waiting on that table yet. She squinted through the flashing lights to make out the details of the shadowy figure. Her breathing abated as recognition clicked into place, seized her. He looked just a hint less comfortable now than when he was draped across her cushy recliner.

Go. Go to him. He is you and you are him.

Her pulse boomed between her ears. The Devil danced with excitement in front of her mind's eye, his wicked, crooked grin gleaming, and leathery tail flailing. His arms swung through the air, yanking the chains that held his captives. The thought of finally revealing her devil's identity filled her with both thrill and dread. The anticipation sent a shiver down to her core. Her mouth dried. Her chest heaved. She lifted her head off Rob's shoulder and released his hand.

He looked down at her retracted hand with a frown. "Is everything okay, Evie?"

She jumped at the sound of Rob's voice, bewildered as she looked back to him.

"I'm fine. I'm going to see if that guy needs a drink," she said as casually as she could. She tempered her stride as she walked out from behind the bar. Rob nodded his head and grabbed a cloth to wipe down the bar top in his zombie-like state, going through the motions.

Trying to mask her anxiety, Evie stopped at a few tables along the way to check in on what customers there were, hoping to create the illusion of composure. Inside, her heart felt as though it would fail her at any moment. Each step forward brought her closer and closer to a destiny she felt helpless to comprehend. Her parched throat demanded a drink. Her mind begged for a light-headed high. As she closed the gap between their bodies, she saw his familiar devious smirk spread across his face. His gleaming smile reflected the flashing strobes as he licked his lower lip in anticipation of her approach. And the golden orbs of his eyes gleamed like an animal's in the Amsterdam-red lighting.

"Hi," Evie said in shock. "I didn't expect to see you." Her heart pounded.

"Really?" Lucca raised an eyebrow and smiled. "Are you surprised?"

Though the volume of their voices increased to yell over the pounding music, they didn't have to strain too much to hear one another.

"I meant... well, I don't know what I meant, what can I get you?"

Stupid girl. Pull yourself together.

Lucca chuckled. "It's dead in here tonight. What happened?"

She paused and looked around, Lucca's choice of phrase lingering in the air like cheap perfume. As Evie contemplated her response, the contempt she held for Natalie burned in the back of her head like a stray ember.

"One of our girls was found murdered this week. Everyone's pretty shook up by it," she said, straight to the point. "Actually, you met her. Natalie—err, Natalia. She gave you a lap dance the last time you were here."

Lucca's eyes scanned Evie up and down, a pensive stare. "Nope, don't remember her. All that I remember about the last time I was here was your tiny vinyl outfit."

She shuddered. A warm burn tickled between her legs. The memory, the sensation of his fingers tips digging into her as he pulled her over his hips in ecstasy threatened the structural soundness of her legs. Evie stifled the tiny moan aching to break past her lips.

Delicious.

And it wasn't just last night; her mind cycled through all the dreams she'd had of him. Blood rushed to her cheeks. She watched as he stared back, dragging his tongue across his lips, as if he could read her thoughts, his smile, slightly crooked, slightly evil. A knot formed in her throat as she lined up his silhouette with the shadowy figure in her room. It was impossible to believe Lucca was in her room that night, or last night for that matter.

His satisfied grin suggested otherwise.

How the fuck is this possible?

"You do have..." Like a snake, he consumed her from head to toe once more, "... *quite* the interesting wardrobe. Does your boss ask you to wear things like that?" The fact that Evie remained standing under his gaze was a miracle. Her breaths, erratic. Recomposing herself, Sisyphean. A verbal response to his inquiry was unthinkable. "But that's not what I came here for," he said. "I know a secret. I know why no one is here tonight."

She looked at him, curious and relieved to not be the topic of conversation for the moment.

"Because they're all here." He pushed a flyer across the table towards her. She picked it up. It was the same flyer Blythe had taken from the psychic's shop, the one promoting the party at Evan's.

"Everyone's at the Carver Estate?" she asked, bemused.

Lucca nodded. "I would guess so, at least most of the younger crowd you'd expect to see here tonight, I would assume. I'm shocked anyone can move around that place right now."

Evie presumed his two constant accessories, the blonde and the exotic brute, were there as well if he was here alone.

"Aren't you a little old to be partying with college kids?"

He snickered. "Perhaps," he said through his smile. "But there are plenty of others there who aren't in college."

"Then why are you here?"

Lucca puckered his lips through his unrelenting smile. "Maybe I wanted to see you. Maybe I was hoping you'd come to the party with me."

Evie's jaw dropped. Why did this man have the ability to make her come undone with so few words? Her dress made her breasts look spectacular, but did little to hide her labored breathing. She noticed a gleam in his eyes at the sight of her lilting chest.

Evie slipped the flyer into the tip pocket sewn into her boot, quite aware of the display she presented him by leaning down. She kept her eyes on him the whole time. His, in turn, followed her every movement. She was a rabbit scouted by a hawk.

"I have to work tonight." The invisible chain wrapped around her neck in his presence pulled her closer and closer. She pleaded with her inner voice to push back.

Lucca stood and walked over to her. Coming within inches of her, he looked down into her eyes, down to her cleavage, then back to her eyes. He cocked his head to a side, his eyebrows arched, a slight pout on his lips. "Evie, are you resisting?

Are we what?

"No," she said with a heavy breath in response.

"Find a way to get out of work, Evie."

Lucca turned and walked away. She watched his tall, confident stride as he exited the club. Jerry glared down at him. Lucca just smiled and patted him on the shoulder.

***

She took a deep breath, calming her pulse before walking back to the bar. She looked over at Rob; he was fixed on her body as she walked back towards the bar. She was hesitant to approach him. More than anything she wanted to race to the Carver Estate to see Lucca, to dispel the mystery behind her visions. She knew Blythe was more than likely sitting at home, stewing over the fact that Evan never invited her to the party. She could easily call her and be on the road in no time. But how was she going to get out of work? She hated to lie to Rob. The mere tremor of thought of deceiving him touched off a tsunami of guilt. Splotches of red tinted her flesh with each step.

"Evie, what's wrong? You don't look so good." Rob said and raised a concerned hand to her forehead.

"It's just—" She paused. *He's going to hate you for this.* "It's just, that was the creep Natalie gave a private

181

dance to last week, the last night we saw—" Evie dropped her gaze to the ground. Rob grabbed her hand and squeezed it tight. "I guess it's bringing up some heavy emotions."

"You haven't reacted to Natalie's death yet. It's okay to grieve," he said and ran his hands along the outer length of her arms. She closed her eyes. Tears welled up, not out of mourning for Natalie, but out of the guilt she felt for the deception at play.

"Go home, Evie. It's so slow tonight. I can take care of these guys. Carrie's here to help me." Evie looked up at him, incredulous.

You didn't even have to ask.

"Rob, I—"

"Go home, Evie. Get some rest."

It was a quarter past eleven by the time she got into her car. She pulled her cell phone from her bag and began texting Blythe.

Get ready and pick me up in 30 minutes. We're going to Evan's party.

TWENTY-ONE

"You can slow down, Blythe. We'll be there soon enough," Evie said as she gripped the door handle. Blythe's heavy foot pushed the vehicle through the curves of Black Cross Road at a frightening speed. The SUV's pitching and yawing, combined with the anxiety brought on by her charade, coaxed bile to the back of Evie's tongue. "Please, Blythe, slow down."

Blythe's urgency would not be denied. "I still don't understand why he didn't tell me about this party in the first place."

"Blythe, what did I say at the gym? What if this isn't meant to be?" Evie asked.

"No," Blythe said. "No, I don't believe that. There's something about him, Evie. I know you can see it. And I confronted him about the party over the phone earlier. He said the party wasn't for him. That it was for his uncle's house guests or some nonsense. I didn't even know he had guests."

"I thought the house was under construction?"

"Well, I guess part of the house is complete enough to have guests *and* a party in their honor." Blythe huffed as the car hurtled down the road.

***

By the time the girls arrived at the estate's front gate, the long gravel driveway was a sea of cars. Floodlights lit up the front of the house. People were everywhere. They poured through the front door, sat on cars, stood under the spotlights on the front porch, crept through the shadows out towards the bushes. Evie's earrings vibrated from the loud bass of the music coming from inside the mansion. Seeing the estate up close, making it all the way down the driveway this time, was intimidating. The house, itself, was enormous. Its decrepit skeletal frame capped off with pitched roofs, buttresses, and wrought iron embellishments that reached up to the sky like spears ready to impale falling angels. It was huge and portentous. Much more foreboding than any local ghost story she'd ever heard.

Inside, the grand foyer was ornately decorated in mid-nineteenth century décor. When she heard that Evan was renovating the house, she presumed he was updating it; she saw now that he was restoring it to its original beauty, and beautiful it was. Even through the swarms of people, loud music and ruckus, she was compelled to gape at the oil paintings hanging on the walls and intricate woodwork. Delicate Victorian furniture lined the rooms. Rich colors and textures warmed the otherwise austere space.

Guests who occupied the delicate furniture looked up at her, some in disgust as they recognized the town pariah, others with curious longing expressions that made her uneasy. She looked up to her right to see several people lining the grand stairway that led up to a darkened second floor. The swarms of guests laughed and drank, danced and flirted, and enjoyed each other's company. She looked left and she looked right, but Evie found no sign of Lucca. She grabbed a hold of Blythe's hand as her friend made a determined line to the back of the house. It took her breath away to think a place like this existed on the outskirts of

Fallhaven. They ended in a large marble space Evie guessed was a dining area, a kitchen maybe, or possibly a waiting room somewhere in between.

"I don't see him. Where is he?" Blythe said, yelling out over the crowd as she scanned each face for Evan.

"Maybe he was telling you the truth and the party isn't for him. Maybe he's not even here,"

"No, he's here. And when I find him..." Blythe pursed her lips and shook her head at the thought of her next move. Evie scanned the crowd herself and, not having found Lucca, found the next best thing—a beer keg.

"Okay, you stay here, I'm going to grab a drink," Evie said.

"There he is. Evie, stay here. I'll be right back," Blythe replied.

Both girls walked away from each other.

***

As Evie stood in line for the keg, she continued to monitor the crowd. None of the faces were so familiar that she worried about word getting back to Rob. She still felt a shackle of guilt around her neck, knew the weight would only increase if she didn't see Lucca. There were so many people. He could be anywhere. She noticed a veranda off to the right of the dining area. Maybe he was outside. If her bearings served her correctly, that was the back of the mansion and faced the ocean cliff beyond the property. She thought maybe after she filled her cup, she'd head in that direction.

Evie turned her head the other way and saw Blythe in a heated conversation with Evan. Blythe's hands flailed in the air as her mouth moved at him. Her expression appeared a mix of pain and anger.

What is that guy's problem? God, I need a drink.

Right before reaching the keg she heard a familiar set of voices behind her. She froze in fear.

"You could bounce a dime off that ass," the first voice said.

"Touch it, man. Go ahead," Evie heard the second voice say. A sudden bump against her rear made her turn on her heels wide-eyed. She stood in front of the two college boys whom Rob kept away from her at the club, Four Eyes himself and his steady sidekick.

"It *is* her," Four Eyes confirmed, whacking the back of his hand across his friend's chest, an equally well-dressed boy with a slicked faux-hawk. His upper lip curled in a manner that made Evie's stomach roil. But Rob wasn't here, and neither was Nate, so who was going to protect her now? She felt her anxiety building, a drastic crescendo of heat rushing to her cheeks, threatening.

"Are you handing out free lap dances tonight?" The implication in his voice made Evie want to retch.

"Excuse me?" she snipped.

The two boys laughed. "I see how it is. Never off the clock, huh?" He paused to wipe the saliva-soaked edges of his mouth with two outstretched and wiry fingers. "Okay, so what'll it cost to get you off the clock and on my cock?" Four Eyes pulled a roll of cash from his pocket.

Anxiety morphed into rage, pulling a clenched fist back, ready to plow forward.

"You motherfu—" Evie's words cut off as the boy's body jerked backward, as though possessed. His pinstriped collar was drawn taut as a harp wire around his larynx.

"You wouldn't know what to do with her, *boy*," Lucca hissed in the kid's face, frothy spittle dotting his lenses.

Four Eyes' feet dangled off the floor. The boy motioned his friend to defend him. Fauxhawk froze in fear, sizing his competitor up and deciding it wasn't worth his friend—or the prize. Whatever was contained in the glare Lucca shot his direction was enough to keep him at bay. Lucca considered both boys, saw surrender in their eyes. He shook Four Eyes once, Alpha status asserted, and rag-dolled him to the ground. The boy asphyxiated on his own stupidity and abashment.

Lucca's cautious glare shifted to a humored grin. "Go get a drink, boys. Have fun, won't you?"

Dubious, both boys accepted his lenient judgment and departed with only the tiniest flicker of their eyes over Evie's body. Fear, rage, astonishment mixed in her bloodstream, pumping furiously through her veins.

As they were swallowed up into the sea of people around them, Lucca turned his attention over to Evie. Her jaw was agape, unsure of how to respond. He stepped closer and extended a hand.

"Not friends of yours, I take it?" he asked. Her lips moved, but no sound came forth. She shook her head back and forth. "Drink?" he asked, his brow lifted, entertained. He walked her still dumbfounded body towards the keg.

Heart racing, Evie watched him pour a beer into a red plastic cup. His mundane movements seemed too simple, too common. "Evie? Are you okay?"

She blinked for a moment and realized she had a beer in her hand. Finally, an action she knew well and that didn't require thought or speech, Evie slugged it down in a few short gulps. As long as the cup was up to her mouth she didn't have to talk to him.

That's better.

"Thank you," she said over the music.

He leaned down towards her ear. "For what?"

"For helping me with those assholes. They're kind of a recurring problem for me."

Lucca looked over his shoulder and back to Evie. He shrugged. "You're welcome. But I didn't catch what they said to you. Were they bothering you?"

"You didn't hear them?"

"No, I'm just a very jealous person. I saw two guys talking to you and I got jealous. Simple as that. Why? What did they say?" he asked, intrigue and indecency skittering along the tip of his tongue.

Evie looked up at him, confused. He was *jealous* of them? She felt her heart pounding again, testing the integrity of her breastbone. The thought of him being jealous of any guy talking to her lit a fuse leading from her head to her core.

"One of them recognized me from the club and was looking for a lap dance. Something about getting off the clock and on his cock," she said.

Lucca scowled for a moment before breaking into hysterics. He held a hand against a stitch in his side and used the other to hold in his laughter behind pursed lips. How easily she evoked such an uproarious reaction from him. His guffaw was like a madman's. Evie gazed down into her empty cup, hating the sight of its white bottom rimmed with a tiny ring of amber ale.

"I wish I had known that," he laughed. "I would have ripped the fucker's throat out." His grim smile made her shiver. His malevolence took her by surprise. He didn't notice she was put off, or seemed not to care. Lucca wrapped his arms around her waist and pulled her close into him. Her empty cup fell, left to be trampled by dancing feet all around. Closing the distance decreased their need to shout at each other, ostensibly.

"Doesn't he know, if anyone gets a private dance from you it will be me?"

He spoke with a wanting gleam in his eyes. She felt the same telltale wet and warm sensation between her legs that always accompanied his closeness. Words were so difficult to find when he was around. He looked down at her cleavage. That mad smile glittered across his face, an expression Evie had committed to blissful memory.

"You changed. I rather liked the tiny dress."

She felt her skin radiate red in response. "I just dress like that for work."

"You wouldn't dress like that if I asked you?" He raised both of her hands to his lips. She shuddered in response. Through the swarms of people around them, Evie felt as though they were alone, able to delight in their little tryst.

"You forget, I still have a boyfriend." She said with a coy smile. A sudden blast, right behind her eyes.

Still?

"That's right. The tall, staggering brute, yes? Looks like a real catch, Evie. You must be a lucky girl."

His teasing offended. For all Nate's faults, he was still a good person. He took good care of her—when he was around. The amount of shame and guilt that overwhelmed her in that moment was suffocating. She needed to level the playing field.

"Yup. That's him. The tall, *well-endowed* guy."

189

Lucca laughed. "Ouch, Evie. Are you challenging me?" He pulled her closer into him, rocked her back and forth against his hip bones. "Shall I take you upstairs and show you how well-endowed I am?"

Yes!

Evie's legs proved a shaky foundation to her throbbing core. She fought the High Priestess' compulsions, tried to distract herself from the thought of accepting his challenge. Lost herself in the memory of her hallucinations the night prior. Evie's eyes roamed the room looking for any excuse not to gawk at his groin. Off to her right, she caught the warm glow of light pouring through a multi-colored array of liquors Evie would've had to work the dance poles through the holiday season to afford. Lucca jostled her body to redirect her attention back to him.

"Would you like a drink, Evie?" His smile was unwavering.

"Good God, yes," she said without hesitation.

He squinted his eyes and peered down at her. "I'm not quite sure what a '*good God*' may have to do with this, but what would you like?"

"I don't care, as long as it's strong," she answered. She'd settle for anything.

Lucca stared into her eyes.

"Alright, Evie, I'll make you a deal. I'll get you '*something strong*' to drink, but I'd like my dance." The lights flickered across the dark pools in his eyes, glistening. She could see the tip of his tongue line the inside of his exposed teeth. He smiled, awaiting her response.

"Your dance?"

"My dance, Evie. I haven't been able to purge it from my mind since I met you. Something I've wanted for these last two weeks. I've even dreamt about it," he admitted.

He's dreamt about us?

Evie blushed from embarrassment. What was she to him that he dreamt about her? *Nate be damned*, her inner voice told her. She wanted that drink. And she wanted that dance. She wanted *Lucca*. After all, why else did she risk death by Blythe's crazy driving on the way up here?

"You've dreamt about me?"

"I have. What do you dream about?" The sly smirk across his face alluded to the notion that he already knew the answer.

That's absurd. There's no way he knows what we've dreamt about.

"By the look on your face, I'd say you already know what I've dreamt about."

Lucca snickered. "Well, one can only hope to know. Tell me, Evie, what have we done in your dreams?" Lucca continued to rock her side to side, enough so that their bodies rubbed together in the most delicately painful places. There was no stifling the moan that slipped past her lips this time, no matter how hard she bit down on her lip. And Lucca reciprocated with his own soft murmur.

"First my drink, then maybe I'll tell you."

The menace that hid behind the smirk pulling at the corner of his mouth should have registered, but her inner voice swooned nonetheless.

TWENTY-TWO

"What a luscious little treat. Who's your friend, Lucca?" A man's voice could be heard from behind Lucca's back. A twinge in his accent gave away his foreignness. Lucca released one arm from Evie's waist as the other steered her to face the man. He was no taller than Evie, but dark and handsome with olive skin, thick short black hair chopped across the top of his head, a thick beard growing along his jaw line. He had a stocky build not unlike Rob's, with large muscular shoulders almost disproportionate from his trim waist. And his eyes, his eyes were deep pools of heat, similar to Lucca's but deeper, darker like cooling lava. She recognized him as the same man she'd seen before with Lucca. He was gorgeous, in a frightening sort of way. Evie's pulse quickened at the sight of him.

"Khan," Lucca said. "This is Evie, my guest for the evening." His possessiveness made her feel small and bright, a diamond in the setting of his grip. But there was something about it that didn't sit well in her core.

"Really?" Khan acknowledged her with a grin that made her cringe. "Well, we always say what is mine is yo—"

"Not this time." Lucca said, cutting him off. "Evie's *mine*."

The way the two god-like men jockeyed for her attention unnerved her. She attempted a small step away from him, but Lucca wrapped his arm tighter around her waist, pulled her to him and locked her in place.

Khan smiled. "Is that so, friend? That won't go well with Mae, I think." When Lucca's smile appeared on Khan's face, it made Evie's stomach knot.

"What won't go over well with Mae?" The tall blonde, the *a trois* in their *menage*, looked down at Lucca's arm wrapped around Evie's waist. She stood there, an alabaster tower next to the stout immigrant, in a pair of white lace bell-bottoms low-slung around her waist, a gold chain encircling her around the stomach, clinging to her protruding hip bones, with a tight worn jersey knit that accentuated her unremarkable chest. "Well, well, Lucca. Found yourself the little skank from the club I see. I hadn't realized the bar was serving up Red-headed Sluts tonight."

Evie's eyes widened as though she'd been shot right between them. She saw the hate ripping through the woman's facial features, blaring from her hazel eyes.

A newfound uneasiness gripped her as the woman appraised her. Evie's desire to pull away from Lucca and his possessiveness was replaced by the urge to crawl behind him and shield her eyes from the beautiful blond Medusa standing before her. Evie looked up at Lucca for reaction. He laughed.

"I don't see how this concerns you, Mae," he said shaking his head.

"Not my concern?" Mae gasped, holding her porcelain marionette's hand to her thin frame. "Lucca, that hurts. You are always my first concern."

Evie was being fought over. She searched the room for an escape route, scoured faces in the crowd, there was no one she knew to run to.

Where the fuck is Blythe, she wondered.

193

"And who gave you permission to make me your first concern—or your last for that matter?"

Khan laughed, fueling Mae's anger. Evie watched as she closed her eyes, breathed in, calmed herself, and proceeded.

"Why, whatever do you mean, my love? We've never kept things from each other. Don't you love me anymore?" She batted thin lashes at him.

"Kept things from you? Who are you exactly?" Lucca said, oozing disdain in his forceful tone. "Love you? You stupid bitch. Who would ever love a whore like you?"

Evie glared back at him, dubiously. The razor-edged words sliced through the air towards Mae and shredded her to ribbons. All of Lucca's charm and allure was shorn away to reveal something much more primal, much more monstrous. His silhouette darkened, and Evie remembered the ending to all of her dreams. Each time his menace revealed itself and she woke in terror. He *was* terror. Hope's comments about loving the devil, or at least lusting after the devil, crystallized. The drumming of her pulse against the walls of her cranium blocked out all other sound. She wanted to be released from the hold he had on her. A mad current of shame and heartbreak sucked her down.

"Lucca, how can you say that?" Mae asked with a pout.

"What have I ever done that would make you think I have ever *loved* you? Why would I? I am not your lover."

The rising intensity of his chastising offended even Evie. She looked around. Their argument went unnoticed by any partygoers surrounding them. She was held captive, an unwilling audience to their sparring match.

"You were a distraction, something to pass the time, nothing more. You are not *her*."

Lucca spewed forth words which held no meaning to Evie. She tried to block out the argument, listening instead to the beating drum of her pulse in her head. She closed her eyes, focused on the din of partygoers. She needed a drink. When she opened her eyes, Evie saw Khan's hungry eyes upon her.

"How can you say that?" Mae said. "What I've done for—you fucking coward. You bastard. You call me the whore, when all you want is this fucking girl, this—this— she's the whore here, not me."

Evie stared incredulous at her assailant.

"Excuse me? Who the fuck are you calling a whore?"

"You watch your fucking mouth, bitch. I haven't even started with you," Mae said, pointing a needlelike finger in her face. Evie straightened her stance in defiance.

"Ladies, ladies," Khan interjected. "Let us not fight. This is a party. Does not everyone love a good party?"

He reached up to place one arm around Mae's shoulder, the other around Lucca's. His eyes coiled around Evie's entire body. She watched Mae as Khan pulled her close to him. The two girls bared their disdain through bitten tongues and squinted glares.

His touch seemed to dispel Mae's aggressions, though Evie still burned from the insult that had been thrown at her. She would *not* be labeled a whore. She refused to be placed in the same category as her mother. Khan's eyes widened, danced in her anger like pagans around a maypole. She felt Lucca's hand squeeze her hip bone. When she looked back to him, he shared an equally wild and aroused expression.

"Let us talk." Khan gestured for his cohorts to step aside for a private consultation. Lucca sneered down at him, shaking his head in the subtlest form of defiance. "Come, Lucca," he said and released his arm from around his shoulder.

Khan patted Mae's flat belly, used his muscular arms to pull her tall figure to his will. Evie felt his cold stare release her as he turned away.

"We're not done, bitch," Mae spat at her. "You're dead. Just you wait and see." She pointed at Evie again then looked up at Lucca. "Both of you—dead."

Lucca snickered.

What just happened?

Evie's guard faded as Khan and Mae disappeared into the crowd. Her frenzied breathing normalized. She looked further into the crowd for escape. Lucca looked down at her. A hateful scowl lined his jaw.

"Don't move," he said with a growl and stormed off.

The physical relief of his arm from around her waist was immediate; the emotional grip he held on her lingered. Evie hunched forward with a sigh. Whatever had just transpired should've been taken as a clear warning to Evie's inner being that she should stay away from him. But, as she watched him leave, she couldn't help but wonder where he was going. What was being said between the three? When would she be close to him again?

*****

Following Lucca's orders, Evie stood in place for a minute, then two, wondering what the hell she was doing. She searched the crowd of faces again, looked over towards the bar. Somewhere off to the entrance of the room she saw

Blythe and Evan still engaged in a heated discussion. Not caring for whether she was or was not interrupting their discourse, Evie sliced through the crowd like a scalpel, bisecting the two.

"I think we should go," she said. Blythe looked back at her in disbelief. Turning to acknowledge her, Evan stiffened to stone. His deep, warm eyes seemed to bulge out of his head like he was being squeezed.

"Evie's here too?"

"What? You think I just came up here in the middle of the night by myself? Of course Evie came with me," Blythe said, snapping back. "She's looking for that guy, Lucca. *He* invited us since you wouldn't.".

Evan's eyes flinted back and forth between the two girls. Muscular tension challenged his jaw's integrity.

She felt nervous in his presence, the same as she had with Lucca.

"Fuck this. You guys work your shit out," Evie said and turned back into the crowd, determined to make her way to the bar. If she was trapped in this hellhole of animosity, she was at least going be good and drunk.

"Evie, don't—" a voice said from behind her as she stomped away.

The crowd around the bar was thick. She looked up at the shiny bottles glistening in the lights from overhead. She couldn't reach them, though, at least not in time to find the relief she craved.

Evie looked back and saw Blythe and Evan pushing through the crowd, chasing after her. Rather, she noticed Evan chasing with Blythe lagging behind. She had no intentions of engaging in their argument after what had happened between Lucca and Mae. She had her own lovers' quarrel brewing within her between her natural instinct for self-preservation and her High Priestess calling out to find Lucca again.

As she pushed through the crowd to get to the beer keg, she thought about Nate. Poor innocent Nate, what was she doing to him by coming here tonight? And what about Rob? What about how easily she deceived him to make the trek out to the Carver Estate? To see who? To do what? And what of the shadowy figure stalking her, was it Lucca? Could that be possible? She was certain the figure was a figment of her overactive imagination, delusions, a parlor trick. But Lucca used that word, *resist*. That had to be more than coincidence.

He is you and you are him.

Evie shook her head fervently. Now was not the time to engage in debate with her inner voice. She pushed people aside, partiers who cussed at her as she caused them to spill their drinks. The loud music quickened her pulse with its wild cadence. She felt an anxiety attack clawing at her chest. The beer keg was close by. She just needed to reach it. As she closed in on it, she looked around once more. There was no sign of Lucca. Blythe and Evan had been swallowed up by the waves of partygoers in the room. And at the moment she was alone to indulge in the sweet sensation of cheap, fermented barley.

"Drink?"

Exasperated, Evie turned. She saw a hand gripping the top of a red cup full of beer. Without hesitation, she grabbed the cup and chugged its contents. When Evie removed the empty cup from her mouth she stared straight up at Four Eyes licking his chops at her.

"If you ask me for a lap dance again, so help me God, I'll punch those glasses off your fucking face," she said with warning. He threw up his hands in defense.

"Fine," he conceded. "We can take it slow."

"We won't be taking anything anywhere," she said and nudged past him towards the keg for her own turn at the tap.

"That's fine, kitten. I'll keep an eye on you though, you poor little thing, while your boyfriend walks off with that tall blonde pussy," he said, and his words made Evie freeze. The insolence he exuded in the way he addressed her, the inflection in the word *pussy*, infuriated her.

Evie whipped herself around to knock his wiry frames straight off his box-shaped nose. Her fist missed and nearly caught Blythe by mistake. Evie looked around, but Four Eyes had vanished. Instead, she found her best friend standing in front of her with a startled expression.

"Evie, I need to leave," she said and grasped Evie's hands in hers, knocking the empty cup to the ground. Evie watched it roll away, looked up to their hands pulled close to Blythe's chest, and then up to her friend's fragile features.

"Fine. Let's go."

"No, not with you," Blythe said over the music. Evie looked back, puzzled. "I need to leave and work things out with Evan. I can't let it end like this. Are you going to be alright? If I leave will you be able to get a ride back into town?"

Evie's jaw dropped. Never in all their years of friendship had Blythe ever left her out in the cold for anyone. What made Blythe think abandoning her in a crowd full of strangers and sociopaths would be a good idea?

Evie gaped at her friend. "What? No," she said, exasperated. "No, Blythe. How the hell am I going to get home?"

What the fuck is she thinking?

Blythe sighed. The feeble expression across her face made Evie nauseous.

"Evie, please? Listen, I'll just leave for a little bit and come back. I promise. Please do me this favor, Evie. I need this. I need him."

Evie found the distress in her voice pathetic; Blythe hadn't been so hung up on her ex-fiancé even, yet here she was, second fiddle to this rich boy. "Fine, Just please don't be gone too long. This party blows."

Blythe's face beamed. She clapped her hands and hugged her friend. "I love you, Evie. I'll be right back."

Evie was alone again in a sea of strangers. A heavy fog descended upon her vision. The room began to spin. As she noticed black splotches dart across her line of sight, she felt her chest tightening and her breath quicken. Evie knew the signs. She was going to have a panic attack. Her internal temperature rose and sweat beaded up on her forehead. She needed fresh air. She pushed her body in the direction of the veranda as the mass of bodies blurred.

TWENTY-THREE

The veranda was a welcome oasis. The salty air wafting up the cliffs from the sea tickled her taste buds. She ran her tongue across her lips to savor it. There were fewer people outside, but she still felt the need to escape their company.

Each movement felt forced. Breathing became a chore. Her rasps echoed in her head—inhale—exhale. Her body was shutting down.

Evie leaned herself against the cold stone wall of the veranda, pushing forward into the darkness. The overwhelming weight of exhaustion took hold. Evie's body grew heavy. Her arms hung limp at her sides, her legs like bags of sand as she forced each step forward. Her head lulled from side to side with fatigue as her eyes rolled to the back of her head. The light was extinguished.

***

She managed to pull herself around to a quiet corner away from the noise of the revelry. She collapsed up against the wall. Images flashed in front of her, of which she could no longer discern between dream and reality. A fog loomed in, dark and ominous.

Through the cloudy film blurring her vision, Evie managed to make out a group of dark figures approaching. She thought it was maybe four or five separate entities, merging into one then diffusing back out.

They moved around, wove between each other, made it difficult to focus. The black splotches in front of her twisted and whirled around like some demonic dance.

She tilted her head back and closed her eyes, the grip on her faculties loosening. She felt drunk. Beyond drunk. How much had she drank? She arrived not all that long ago. What little she had to drink was not enough to leave her as incapacitated as she was. The sensation of drowsiness seemed to come on quick.

No, this wasn't an anxiety attack like she had feared. She wasn't drunk. This weariness came on fast and heavy, like a freight train. Panic kicked in with the fear someone had slipped her something.

As her body fought what she was sure would be a chemically-induced slumber, she noticed the dark blob of forms closing in. She was able to make out but a few detailed observations. One, definitely a woman, moved like a waft of smoke from a snuffed-out candle. Two other figures made slow and controlled movements. There was maybe one or two more, staggering, lurching. They pawed at the lithe creature. She made out the faint sound of laughter as they approached, though her hearing had been muffled by the dark cloud around her.

Through her dimming vision, Evie fought to focus on the moving figures. All five figures were now right in front of her. Everything was black, but somehow she could still see their fuzzy profiles.

Their voices became louder but no more audible. She heard cackling, loud ominous laughter that made her want to jump, but her body was unable to respond. Evie was disconnected from herself. Panic continued to suffocate her like a heavy pillow. The cackling continued. Some other sound—screaming? She was sure she heard screaming, pleading, babbling. The figures darted about like striders on a still pond.

Evie fought to make out the voices, to assign ownership, but all that emerged from the black haze was a dissonance unrecognizable and most unsettling. She tried to cry out, but found her mouth wouldn't move. She was imprisoned inside her limp body. Then, as if emerging from the depths of the harbor, clarity.

Her heart thumped, terrified by what she hoped was nothing more than a lucid nightmare. A familiar voice drifted through the dark. It was soft, melodic and controlled. Her eyes burned, unable to focus through the murk. The voice moved in, dragging with it another figure. As the images grew closer, Evie made out more detail. Her heart pounded as she was able to recognize Lucca along with Four Eyes in front of her. He dragged the boy up to her face. Lucca's features contorted with anger. Four Eyes whimpered and twitched in fear.

"This," Lucca said, spitting in Four Eyes' face, demanding attention to Evie's disoriented state. "What the fuck is this?" He snarled and tightened his grip around the boy's neck, evoking a terrible choked wheezing from him. "Is this the only way you can get a girl to fuck you?"

She heard a loud bellow of laughter, feminine. Mae.

"No," the boy said crying.

"What was that, motherfucker?" Lucca said, releasing his grip on the boy's trachea just enough to allow his vocal cords to vibrate.

"No," Four-Eyes sniveled.

"You don't deserve sex. You sure as hell don't deserve *her*."

"No," Four Eyes continued to cry.

Evie heard a coarse growl rip through the dark. She heard muffled screams of excruciating pain. She saw flashes of movement in front of her. A rip. A crunch. The splash of warm liquid and film across her face and chest. The cries quickly cut off to gurgles. More cackling. More splashes of liquid against her skin. More gurgling and then silence. A faint metallic odor and taste danced across her lips.

Evie's mind continued to struggle against its restraints, fought to regain control of her limbs and emerge from the fog. Adrenalized fear flooded her. Her head continued to loll back and forth. Her mouth loosened, and her ability strove to match her will to produce sound.

"N—nuh—n—nuh—no—no—No!"

Finally able to create sound, Evie was able to object to whatever it was, or whoever it was, around her.

"Shit," she heard, Lucca's voice.

Evie felt her consciousness slip again. All the strength she'd used to speak out was exhausted. Her body was falling back into a shutdown state.

"Take—" said the woman.

"Let's all—"

"Fuck—" Lucca said.

Evie felt her body jostled around. Unable to fight any longer, she succumbed and coasted off into blackness. She didn't dream. She wasn't awake. She was numb.

This is what the water would feel like.

TWENTY-FOUR

Evie awoke sprawled atop a cloud of white, surrounded by woods. Her vision and her mind were sleepy—hazy, cool air nipping at her exposed flesh. A musty odor laced with a spicy tinge of incense tickled her nose. Not unpleasant, but unfamiliar. After a moment, her senses sharpened into focus. Her soft cloud was not a cloud at all, but rather a king-sized feather bed adorned in soft white Egyptian cotton sheets. The woods surrounding her were an ornately carved mahogany canopy with heavy brown and green brocade drapery. Evie focused in on the carvings. At first glance she guessed them to be cherubs, but at closer examination found the gleeful mouths of the infants contained fangs. Their eyes were manic, shaped like a cat's. Demons. A new odor, the smell of leather, drew her attention to the massive headboard and footboard.

Where the fuck are we?

Body still, one part strategy, two parts fear, her eyes roamed the room. The walls were covered in the same warm, dark mahogany wood and blended fabric. Antique tapestries hung along the wall to her far left, next to a door. To the far right were two huge windows. Outside, a low grey sky seemed to rap against the panes of glass, demanding entry. The drapery which framed the windows matched those adorning the bed's canopy. A blazing fireplace centered the wall across from the bed. Atop it displayed what looked like classic Renaissance oil paintings. In the middle was a large portrait of a man, centuries dead. On each side hung country landscapes. Between the fireplace wall and the bed were a large divan, accent tables and two high-backed chaises. It was the bedroom of an autocrat. The room was unlike any other place she had ever seen before. And it was so very quiet.

What the fuck happened?

Evie propped herself upright on her elbows, relieved to find the interference between her brain and her extremities had cleared. She was cold. She looked down and was surprised to find her navel looking back at her. Her clothes were gone. She was atop the feather bed's linens in just her bra and panties.

What happened to our clothes?

Too confused or alarmed to move, her eyes shifted. The sound of rushing water to her left called her attention, a running shower. Slow to move, she tilted her head to peer into a luxurious black marble-tiled bathroom trimmed with gold fixtures. Steam billowed out of it into the upper atmosphere of the bedchamber.

Her chest heaved with anxiety. Her eyes widened. Evie didn't feel any trace of toxins or hangover lingering. Her sight was crisp. Her movements were controlled. She dared not speak, but she knew somehow that she could scream. And she knew there was a huge gap in her memory, like a movie with a missing film reel, that would explain how she came to be sprawled across this bed in her underwear with God only knows who in that shower. Her pulse was a war drum between her ears, inciting the fight-or-flee inside her. As she searched through her memories of last night, the one possible answer as to who was in there suggested itself. The shower nozzle turned off. Panic increased. The mist that floated out of the bathroom abated, melted away, and then she saw him.

Lucca stepped out, dripping wet, from the stone-and-glass shower stall. His flawless, pale skin glistened fresh and new in the bathroom light. Unable to blink, her eyes fixed on his exquisite frame. He was not sickly thin, nor was he very muscular. His skin was stretched to perfection across the muscle. His body was built for efficiency, impeccably toned for optimum performance, applicable towards any worthwhile purpose—any. The sweetest sight was his beautiful midsection trailing down his hip bones to create the most perfect V-shape. Every inch of him was perfect. She gazed at his delicious nakedness, too afraid to move so as not to alert him to her prying eyes. She stared with her jaw agape in awe at his beauty. Her tongue traced the back of her teeth.

Lucca toweled himself off and brought his hands up, rubbing them over his eyes and face, down the back of his head, taming the wet locks that fell below his shoulders. He let out a loud exhale, followed up with a sniffle.

She watched him stare into what she presumed was the bathroom mirror. His profile was a thing to behold. His strong angular features were enhanced by the fresh shower sheen and hair wetted back against his head. Though his stance was tall and secure, there was a look on his face, a familiar look. He was still. She wondered if he was as mesmerized by his appearance as she was. When Evie searched her mirror, she searched for the girl inside the hollowed-out alcoholic shell that was her body. Her brow furrowed. What was it he searched for?

After a few minutes of silent regard, Lucca turned. He grabbed a pair of dark, worn jeans out from behind the bathroom door and slipped himself inside one leg at a time. As he moved to zip up his pants, he lifted his head in her direction and found Evie staring at him, exactly where he had left her. His mouth formed a smirk of filthy satisfaction as he stalked to the side of the bed. Having given away her position, and embarrassed for having been caught ogling him, Evie sprang up on her knees in the middle of the bed. Her heart pounded, unaware how to respond to his approach.

"Good morning Evie."

"Good morning. Where am I?"

"You're in my room."

"Yeah, I guessed that. Where is your room?"

"My room is right here, of course."

He gestured grandly across the room, taking every childish delight in toying with her open-ended questioning. Evie shot him a contemptuous glare which only stoked his glee.

"That's not what I meant," she said, volume rising with annoyance.

He continued to smile as he walked around to the foot of the bed. Evie twisted her body around on her knees to face him at all times.

"Did you enjoy yourself last night? I know I did."

Lucca looked at her through sultry eyes. She gawked back at him, unaware how to respond. If anything had happened between them last night, which it appeared it had, she harbored no memory of it. Part of her was ashamed and terrified by the thought of sharing something as intimate as a sexual experience unknowingly. Another part of her, her inner voice, cursed her for not remembering.

How could you let us block that out? Stupid, stupid girl.

Evie frowned, and a wave of revulsion made her body quake.

"What happened?" she asked in a whisper. Tears of fear and shame welled in the corners of her eyes.

"Well now, that hurts my feelings. You really don't remember?" She shook her head, embarrassed. Lucca grimaced back at her. "Well, doesn't that make me feel awful? I quite enjoyed myself. I'm sorry you carry no recollection of what we shared. You truly are amazing."

Evie blushed and her heart raced at the unknown. His cryptic responses had not outlined what happened, but the grin on his face indicated it was not at all anything she should have been doing.

"Where are my clothes?"

Lucca raised a hand and directed her over to a pile of clothes on a chair beside the windows. She stood. Her eyes locked with his as she edged sideways towards the pile.

"I wouldn't put them back on if I were you," he cautioned.

Evie paused, confused. "Why is that?"

"They're a bit... dirty. From last night," he answered. "Sorry about that, by the way."

Unnerved by his caution, but too curious not to see for herself, Evie turned from him. She bent down to grab her black tank from the pile. She heard him stifle a self-satisfied snicker as she bent over in front of him. Her clothes felt damp and gritty. They smelled awful, like sweet metal. Startled by the odor, she gagged and threw the shirt back down. Evie fought the urge to vomit when she looked down to find her hand covered in crimson.

Staring at the red stain on her skin, her hand trembled not from alcohol withdrawal, but from the surge of adrenaline coursing through her body.

"Oh my God, what is this?"

Lucca laughed. Threw his head back, thrilled by her reaction.

"I assure you, *your* god has nothing to do with this," he quipped with satisfaction. "You look frightened, Evie. Are you frightened?"

Evie had to stop and think. Was she frightened? Was that the best word? Should it have been mortified? Violated? Sickened? Ill with the thought of what she may have done with him last night? The rapid pounding of her heartbeat and the knot in the pit of her stomach indicated a meld of all of the above. But what of it? Even if she was frightened, she had yet to run screaming out the door. Not yet. She stood across from him, no longer hyper-aware of her near-nakedness, poised to flee if need be. Her inner voice urged her to stay. She had to stay, at least until she could come to grips with the situation at hand.

His body language paired with hers. Calmly, he moved forward to her like a wolf stalking its prey in the wild. She was reminded of the dark figure. Anticipating his movements, Evie sidestepped around him, weaved into the sitting area in front of the fireplace, and made her way to the door.

Doing her very best to keep her eyes locked with his, Evie allowed a fleeting moment to search the room. Lucca stood between her and her blood-stained clothes. What use would those clothes be now? Heat from the fireplace blazed behind, flushing her body in a heat which would have scorched her clothes off, anyway. She would take her chances in her underwear. But what chances were those? Through the nervous beating in her chest, her mind pleaded to find some reason.

What happened last night? Let's start there.

Lucca stalked forward as he closed in on her. Evie continued her backwards path across the room. She stopped with her back pinned up against the locked chamber door

"Evie, you're very quiet. Always so quiet. Are you frightened?" His voice was velvety soft and soothing as he extended his palms to lean against the door behind her.

Caged by his body, her chest puffed out, buffing against his as a result of her erratic breathing. The soft touch of his bare skin against the tender flesh of her cleavage was exhilarating. His breath was warm and syrupy. It coated the skin along her cheek and down her neck. He smelled like orange blossoms and mint. She tilted her head to the side, closed her eyes, and strained to control her breathing and her impulses. Under his suffocating proximity, the memory of his impossible form emerging from the shower moments ago and her body's desire to scream aloud in fear divided her like a war-torn nation. Her face contorted, hoping to reconcile the schism by force. She bit down on her lip before answering him.

"What did you do?"

Her words fell feebly from her mouth, but their freedom allowed her the courage to turn her head and face him straight on. The tips of their noses touched. His eyes blazed like the fire, and she was a moth, drawn by instinct to her own blissful demise.

Lucca smiled back at her in response, equally dazed by the crystal blue abyss of her stare.

"What would you like me to say, Evie?" he asked. The melody of his voice pulled at her body's senses.

He leaned his body against her, barring her in place. The closeness of his lips to hers melted the knot in her stomach. It trickled down in a warm wave between her legs. She gulped down a chunk of air and nerve before whispering her demands.

"Is that blood on my clothes?"

"Yes," he said, hissing.

"Why?" Her voice wavered as she fought the tremors running through her body. Evie clung to her conviction for dear life. If she was to understand him and her desires for him, she needed to understand why she was so afraid. "Is it mine?"

Lucca licked his lips. His features softened.

"No. You truly don't remember anything that happened?"

He was toying with her; she knew that, and in the moment hated him for it. She scowled. He let a little frown of amusement dance across his face before flashing a beautiful, gleaming smile.

"You were drugged, Evie, plain and simple. Those spineless bastards slipped you something in your beer." Lucca's demeanor never faltered. On the contrary, his voice was calm and soothing. Almost loving—almost.

"I suppose it's lucky for you that I find myself so fascinated by you that I happened to witness the dirty deed. Otherwise, who knows what they may have done?"

Lucca pressed his forehead to hers and closed his eyes. Evie savored the almost familial moment, a moment in which she may have fallen head-first with keen abandonment if the circumstances leading up to it didn't weigh so heavily on her. Closing her eyes, a single and solitary tear streaked down her cheek as images from the night before flashed through her memory. The boys from the club, they recognized her. Blythe ran off after Evan. For whatever reason he appeared furious the two girls had crashed his party. Evie almost bothered to wonder what

Evan's deal was, but let his insignificance fade. The college boys swarmed in like vultures. That did little to help answer how she woke up in Lucca's bed wearing nothing more than her underwear because her clothes were soaked in blood—blood not her own. Lucca said she was lucky. She remembered his reaction to one of the boy's crude comments, *I would have ripped the fucker's throat out.*

"What did you do?" she asked. Lucca's eyes danced as she connected the pieces.

"What would you have had me do, Evie?" he whispered, almost purring in her ear. "Would you have wanted me to let them defile your exquisite—" He placed a light kiss on her neck. "—little—" He kissed her collarbone "—body?" He placed a final peck on the opposite side of her neck an allowed his tongue to poke at the carotid artery pulsating under her skin. Evie shivered and let out a soft moan. Her legs wobbled.

What is this delicious sensation?

How had she managed to find herself lost in the arms of such an obscure individual? And how was she supposed to stop her body from feeling this way about a man who had yet to explain why her clothes were covered in blood?

The blood.

In an instant and before Evie could recover control of her body, Lucca scooped her up by the waist. He flung her onto her back along the length of the musty old divan by the fire. His body landed atop hers. A cloud of dust burst from the upholstery as they landed. In their rush to replace the air that was expelled by her rough landing, her lungs sucked in the miasma, the particulates coating her windpipe.

Lucca's body, much larger than hers, engulfed Evie, though she felt no weight on her, as though he were suspended above her, much like in her dreams. As if a natural inclination, she wrapped her arms around his neck to brace herself for the impact of falling down on the chaise. His skin was soft and warm from the steaming hot shower. His still-wet hair dangled over her face and tickled her. A playful smile parted Lucca's lips while Evie gawked up at him, wide-eyed. How was she supposed to make sense of her emotions when her dreams became reality through such a nightmarish lens?

"I've answered your questions, Evie. You should be polite enough to answer mine. Are you frightened?"

He bowed his head to hers, nudging his nose along hers and down the side of her neck. He took in deep breaths, inhaling her essence. The air rushing into and out of his mouth stroked her, sent her body tingling and her mind buzzing.

Evie fought tears, fought desire, fought panic at the unknown. Was she frightened? Yes. That would be the simplest answer to give. All other notions were moot. His intentions were so unashamed. His movements so exact. His touch so corporeal. She was lost in herself, unaware of how to respond to him, unaware of whether or not she deserved such treatment.

Yes, she was frightened—frightened that she may wake up at any moment, losing his warm breath to the cool, crisp morning air of reality, alone under her downy white cocoon. Yes, she was frightened, but there was more to it. As she felt his hand grip her side and rub against her rib cage, Evie sensed there was more to him that should frighten her. His darkened silhouette engulfed him like a dark halo. The stalking shadow, her devil, terrified her.

The blood.

She pushed him up away from her, pressed up at his shoulders to look into his face. Hoping for an earnest answer, she asked, "What happened to those boys? Why is their blood on my clothes? And what happened to me?"

Lucca gazed down on her with a content grin. He shook his head back and forth in amusement.

"Search your memory. You know what happened to them." He smiled down on her. "And there you were, passed out in their blood. Trust me when I tell you, Evie, this is not the place you want to find yourself in such a state," he said. She tried her best to calm her breathing, to listen to his words. *Search your memory. Search your memory.* Somewhere deep in her subconscious she had a vague remembrance of last night's events.

She thought of Lucca and the fear she felt during his argument with Mae. She thought of the uneasiness she felt meeting Khan. Evan was pissed when he saw her. The college boys came over, handed her a drink. *Yes.* They handed her a drink, a beer. She thought back to Blythe, who ran off on her. The house was packed with bodies. She remembered faces, ogling, hating, and calling at her. There must have been music, but Evie couldn't remember noise. Everything in her foggy memory was muffled and cold. *The cold.* She went outside. She remembered the sea salt air. Cold brick against her skin. It was so dark and—*Lucca.* His voice, it was angry. There was crying and then wet. *Wet.* Like sea spray against her face. But it wasn't salty. It was—coppery. *The blood.* What had Lucca done to those boys? What did he do to her? *I would have ripped the fucker's throat out.*

At that moment, Evie knew what happened to those boys. And at the same time, all that mattered was Lucca. The issue at hand appeared to be how far he took his abhorrent fascination with her body. Feeling ashamed of herself for indulging in his sick foreplay, she closed her eyes to tame her thoughts. Unconsciously, Evie licked her lips, a small gesture not unnoticed by Lucca. He dipped down to meet her skin again. Though refraining from kissing her, he dragged his parted lips across hers, over her face as he recounted the night's events.

"You looked so fragile lying with your back up against that stone wall," he said, whispering in a low and melodic rasp. "Not content, not sleeping. Frail. Victimized. And beautiful. I picked you up. You molded to my arms, and whimpered as I lifted you up. It was arousing. You were like a child in my arms. I won't say I didn't enjoy it. I brought you back to my room for protection from…" Lucca paused. "…the others."

Once again, panic faded and Evie rode along another wave of conflicting emotions. She focused on the soothing purr of his voice seducing her senses. Her breathing calmed as she imagined a very different side of Lucca, the thought of him whisking her away to safety, her savior. And yet she had no memory of this.

"You were breathtaking, covered in their blood," he said, continuing as a prominent bulge pressed up against her panties, the inner lining darkened now by her own moisture. Evie lifted her hips forward, beckoning him to her. Lucca once again placed soft, delicate kisses on the tender flesh along her collarbone and shoulders.

"I removed your clothes," he continued. "You have beautiful skin, Evie, so soft, so warm. And such a beautiful body. I'll admit, I enjoyed undressing you. I'd be lying if I said I wasn't tempted to do more. You were incoherent, mumbling and moaning. It was very… thought-provoking. But very clearly, you repeated my name several times. The sound of your voice whispering my name is distinctly… satisfying."

If she were to give in to him now, what would be the outcome? What more would she know of him? What more could she learn *from* him? Her blood pumped. Her breathing increased. Not out of fear now. Out of what? Lust? Wonder? Awe? The mental image of the tarot Devil spun into focus on the reel of images spinning through her mind. The horned tyrant stood hunched over, his sneer menacing as he gripped the chains restraining the man and woman beneath him.

He is coming for us, whether you're ready or not.

Evie shook her head in disbelief. Was it Lucca? Could he be her devil, and if so, what would be the use in resisting him, if he was just... so... inevitable? The low hum of his voice against her skin rushed a thrilling sensation through her body and the Devil card spun off the reel.

"I shouldn't tell you this, but I held you in my arms. I held you longer than I should have. I traced my fingers along your body using their blood to paint nonsensical designs all over you. A very sensual experience for me, Evie. I don't recall the last time I enjoyed myself so much. Then I lapped you clean," he said. A soft moan escaped on his breath. She lay pinned under a complete stranger who confessed to murder, admitted to fondling her unconscious body, and yet she still wanted him.

To resist him is futile.

"Is that it?" she asked. She held back tears and a deep pulsing between her legs.

"That's it."

"And what do you want to do with me now?"

A faint tone of longing from her High Priestess oozed out, and she hated herself for allowing such want to make itself evident. Lucca lifted his head from her chest to gaze into her face, deep into her pale blue eyes.

"I want to taste you," he answered, steel-eyed and menacing.

A new shiver shot down Evie's spine, quelled the desires that had emerged. Through all their teasing, all the purring and soft kisses, Evie saw in those wild eyes the Devil himself. The dark pools of his eyes, gleaming dancing golden orbs within.

Lucca, a furnace stoked, laughed out loud in excitement. His laughter echoed throughout the chamber, suddenly more resonant, pounding. His ears perked and annoyance swept over his face as he fell quiet, yet the pounding continued. The door, the echoing boom petrified her.

Who the fuck could that be?

Echoing her inner voice's dismay, Lucca turned his head to look over his shoulder at the doorway, perturbed.

"Patience has never been one of my virtues, Evie. You'd do well to remember that."

He stood up. He left her lying on the divan.

TWENTY-FIVE

In no position physically or emotionally to question him, Evie sprung from her perch. Without a word, she ran barefoot towards the door. Before opening it, she turned, checking to see if he would follow. Lucca stood still and refrained from making any move to track her. He stood in front of the fire with calm lining his face. Evie took one last look at his bare-skinned chest and ratty jeans hanging off the perfect sculpt of his abdomen before turning the lock, throwing the door open, and hurtling herself straight into Evan's arms.

He stood expressionless at the sight of Evie wide-eyed and breathless in his arms. She remembered she still had no idea *where* Lucca's room was, but the sight of Evan and the surrounding ornate décor indicated she was still at the Carver Estate.

What the hell is going on here?

She looked to her left down a long, dark hallway. Her gaze was met by glowing eyes a fair distance off in the shadows. Goose bumps ran rampant across her body wondering who or what glowered through the darkness. The haunting image of the shadowy figure, her familiar, made her freeze. She was compelled to pull Evan closer for protection, but hesitated. She looked back up at his poor delicate face. He released a heavy sigh before looking up to scowl towards Lucca, who reciprocated with disdain. A guttural growl erupted through Evan's throat before he latched on to her elbow and dragged Evie downstairs.

***

The musty air of the house parted around her as she stumbled down the winding staircase. Aside from the glowing orbs at the end of the hallway, the house appeared empty and, to her surprise, intact, as though the party never happened.

Though Evan didn't keep too tight a hold on her, Evie was cautious to follow in his footsteps. She had no idea what Lucca was doing in his house. Based on the manner in which they carried themselves around each other, they clearly harbored some sort of animosity. Never in a million years would she have guessed they lived together. He set a determined line down the stairs Evie's eyes traced the walls. Out of the warm glow of nightlife banter from the party, the house was dark, ominous, not at all welcoming. Evie felt her inner voice crawling in her skin. She could hear the High Priestess screaming for freedom. Urban legends of teen murders and devil-worshipping cultists flitted through her mind to stifle the voice's protest.

Go back to him! Stupid girl, go back to him!

She was relieved when they burst out the front door, escaping the morbidity of the place. Outside, the air was flat and reeked of low tide. A cool mist trespassed through the grounds.

Evan released her elbow and walked over to a black sedan. She recognized it as his car from the Dynasty, the one car left from the entourage parked outside the night prior. His silence furthering the nauseous feeling in her gut, she followed him onto the gravel driveway. The jagged edges stabbed at the balls of her bare feet. She hobbled to the side of the car.

Before getting in the driver's seat, Evan stopped. Their eyes connected over the ebony roof of the sedan. His shadowed eyes glared through her. He reached for his collar and pulled his sweater over his head, smoothing down his undershirt as he tossed it over the roof to Evie. She was, after all, still in her underwear. Perhaps that was what caused his look of consternation? Perhaps it was guilt for seeing his girlfriend's best friend exposed as she was?

That's not why he's staring, stupid girl.

A bit surprised but grateful, Evie dismissed her inner voice, accepted the sweater, and threw it on. The soft brown knit cashmere tickled her skin. She pulled it down across her chest. It draped over her round rear end, allowed her a mote of decency. It smelled of the piney scent of good weed, like Evan. She took in a full breath.

Before getting into the car, like a sixth sense pulling her, Evie looked up at the windows to the second story of the Carver Estate. She saw Lucca standing in his bedroom window. He stared down with his telltale grin. An explosion of wonder and dread burst from inside her chest and spread throughout her bones. Even through the distortion of the antique window pane, she could make out the details of his bare chest and torso. Her tongue played along the corner of her slightly parted lips.

His arm searched behind his body to retrieve an item from his back pocket. She watched his eyes close as he lifted it up to his face and breathed in deeply. She squinted, focusing hard on the object and paused, shocked. Wrapped around his fist was her blood-stained grey bandana.

***

"What the hell is going on here?" Evie demanded as the car coursed down Black Cross Road. Evan had yet to say a word to her. She did her best to ride in silence with him, which proved an impossible task. His face was contorted in pain, at least she assumed it to be pain. Tears welled in his big brown eyes. His mouth parted as if to speak. No words came. He looked at his white-knuckled grip on the steering wheel, back through the rearview mirror, but let Evie's demands hang.

"You shouldn't have been there," he answered. "I told Blythe I didn't want you two there."

Evie pulled her knees up towards her chest and hugged them tight, allowing only her eyes to look over at him. "Who are you people?"

"*You people?*"

"What just happened there?"

"You spent the night with Lucca," he said. "Did you drink so much that you don't remember?"

"He said some college kids slipped me something in my drink." She paused. "And then he said he killed them."

Evan stared forward, pensive and mute. In his quiet manner, he scowled and looked down towards the steering wheel as if it held the answer, hidden somewhere deep inside.

"He told you he *killed* those guys," he said, repeating and emphasizing the word. She took a moment to recall her conversation with Lucca.

Are you sure that's what he said? Or what you heard?

"Well, no, he didn't say *killed*."

"Well, that's good, because no, he didn't kill anybody."

"So what the hell happened?" Evie asked, exasperated.

Evan looked over at her. His eyes brimmed with tears that wouldn't fall. His lips parted as though he wanted to say something, but couldn't find his voice.

What was it that she felt under his examination? She searched his face for an answer, a clue even, but found nothing.

"Those guys—the college kids—they did slip you something," he said. "Lucca roughed them up—a lot—and he took you upstairs. You know better than I do what happened after that." Evan looked down at his lap before refocusing on the road. They were driving through town. Evie did her best to hide her face from passersby. Being carted around town by her best friend's boyfriend—in his sweater—in just her underwear—the morning after a party—after skipping out on work—would not exactly hold wagging tongues at bay.

Stupid, stupid girl.

"But he didn't say we had sex," she said. "He said he played with their blood all over my body…" Evie trailed off in her sentence remembering the way Lucca described what he had done to her. The sinfulness of his story warmed her from the inside out. The details felt far too intimate for her to divulge to Evan. She blushed and dropped her eyes to her lap.

"I honestly don't want to know. But you're still in your underwear so I assumed…" His sentence faded into the tension-filled air. Rapt with guilt, Evie squeezed her eyes shut and focused on the inhale and exhale of her breath. She opened her eyes again; Evan's worried expression had yet to diminish. She wanted more than anything to remember anything that may prove her innocence. Did she need to prove her innocence? Did it matter? Somehow, she found it did. Evan's opinion mattered. She forced her mind to focus once more, dug deep within the dark corners of her foggy memory for more details from last night.

"He also threatened to hurt me," she said, breaking the silence. "Or, he said he wanted to taste me."

Evan flinched and took a deep breath, registering what Evie said. His tears beaded up, ready to fall over the edge of his lids at any second. But still his face remained dry.

"Taste you? Is that the same as hurting you? Evie, I'm not judging. Lucca has his own... penchants, we'll call them. I don't—I can't—I don't like the guy." His statement made things all too obvious. Evie's guilt waned, replaced by anger. Her inner voice fumed.

This motherfucker is jealous. What's wrong, Miss Prissy isn't good enough?

"What do you mean you don't like the guy? He's staying at your house. Isn't he a friend? What are you, fucking jealous? You're dating my best friend, Evan."

"Wait, what?"

"Not going to happen, guy. Maybe in another lifetime, but not this one. I can promise you that."

"Evie, stop," Evan demanded.

Her head began to throb.

"I don't know what she told you about Adam, but that was a long time ago. I've apologized profusely. I've practically lived and died for Blythe since then. You can forget it, Evan. I'm not going to fuck you and that is final."

"I heard you, Evie. You can stop. Who's Adam?"

She paused her rant to evaluate his exasperated expression.

"She didn't tell you about Adam? Her ex-fiancé?"

"What? No, but I get it. You're not going to fuck me. You don't have to keep saying it, please."

She registered both insult and disappointment in his face. Evie presumed it was disappointment, anyway. The etchings in his brow grew deeper as they argued.

"Well, as long as you understand."

"I get it—not in this life. You said that. Listen, Evie, I... I'm not jealous... I worry about you and your safety around Lucca," he said as he looked her bare-skinned legs up and down.

"Well, it sure as hell sounds like you're jealous. And stop looking at me like that. It's not helping your side of the argument."

Evie threw her legs back down in front of her, crossing her left over the right. It only exposed more bare flesh up the side of her thigh. The two turned to face the street in front of them. Neither spoke for some time. It wasn't until Evan had pulled in front of Evie's house and killed the car's engine that he turned to face her.

"I don't know how to explain this without sounding like a lunatic, but I don't like him or his friends. They're staying with me at the request of my uncle. They are not my friends, and I wish I could ask that you didn't see him anymore."

Evie's jaw went slack.

You wish you could ask? Who the fuck are you?

"Why do you care?"

Evan pursed his lips in contemplation, shook his head fervently back and forth, like he was trying to shake the thoughts loose from whatever sticky substance was holding them back. There was more to his conflict than he let on; Evie saw it and was angered further by his discretion.

225

"I'm not judging you, Evie." She huffed loudly. Evan looked for understanding on her face. "I'm not. I swear it."

He cleared a knot in his throat and brushed little red wisps of hair away from her face. His words and soft touch set her skin aglow. When Evie looked back at him, she knew there was more behind his concern than he would let on. Out of love and respect for her best friend, she told herself, she would never pursue the truth any further.

Evan shifted his body around in the driver seat and reached out towards her again. Her eyes widened, and she found her oath challenged. Her pulse quickened. Her mind raced for an exit strategy. How was she going to break away from him before they both did something regretful?

Evan took in a long, meditative breath. After fixing the stray wisps of red around her ear, his fingers drifted down to the collar of his cashmere sweater.

"Thanks for the ride... and the sweater. You can have it back now." She motioned to pull it up over her head, but Evan quickly stopped her.

"Do you really think it's a good idea to get out of the car in your underwear?"

Dammit, he's right.

She conceded with a bashful smirk, gripping the collar close around her neck.

They sat in the car, the awkwardness morphing into something other. Once Evie felt she'd be leaving him on good terms, she pulled the door latch and swung her legs out of the car. Evan declined to stop her, but neither did he let her go. Rather, he followed her to the safety of her doorstep. There were no neighbors in sight, yet still Evie felt eyes on her. It was an unsettling sensation. It made her want to slink away and hide.

She produced a tiny silver key stashed under a dirty old plant pot inside the screened porch. She had keys stashed all over the place following Nate's little stunt the other night.

"Umm..." Evie started, unsure as to what she should be saying. "Do you want to come in? I still don't know what to make of everything that happened."

She wanted so much to prolong their silence. She looked deep into his curious gaze. A hopeful light flickered somewhere in the depths of his irises. Evan pursed his lips and his brow furrowed before he responded.

"I probably should go."

"Please, Evan?" she begged, inwardly shocked by the desperation in her voice. "I don't want to be alone right now. I'm so confused. And I don't have any—I thought maybe you could smoke me up." No truer statement had ever passed her lips. She was confused about what had happened last night, what happened with Lucca this morning. Most of all she was confused by a barrage of emotions and desires flooding her body for Nate, Rob, Lucca, him, and even Blythe. Some of Evan's sweet hydroponic weed was just what her body craved.

Evan lifted her hand and played with her fingertips before taking hold of her palm in a firm grasp.

"Okay," he answered. "But just for a little bit."

***

Evie went upstairs for a quick, dissatisfying shower. Evan sat in the living room, hunched over the coffee table. He played with a small plastic bag of pot and some rolling papers. By the time Evie had descended from her room, leggings underneath his cashmere sweater, Evan had lit up a joint. He took the first hit and passed it her way.

"So you want to know what happened?" he asked. The thought brought an alarming sense of fear back to the forefront of Evie's mind. She didn't answer, but accepted the joint.

"Lucca's friend, Khan—the foreign guy—he's a friend of my uncle's, so to speak. My uncle asked me to let them stay in the house while they passed through town." His tone was placid as he inhaled each toke deeply. He had yet to feed into Evie's nervousness while he spoke.

"How long are they staying?"

She may as well have asked, *"How much time do I have left to see Lucca?"* More confusion rushed over her. Through all the fear and obscurity of his role in her amnesiac night, her want to see his perfect flesh again was too controlling. She choked on her obsession.

Need—I need to see him again.

"Too long, as far as I'm concerned," Evan said under his breath.

Evie took a hit and passed the diminishing joint back to him. She held her breath and raised a speculative eyebrow at him, puckered her lips to hold back a smile. Evie then exhaled with exaggeration and a stifled laugh. A small amount of smoke escaped her lungs. Evan flashed a close cousin of Lucca's trademark grin before accepting the joint and inhaling. It made Evie remember what Blythe said about him.

He's just adorable.

"I don't know," he said. "They were supposed to leave a couple of weeks ago. Then I was asked to host that ridiculous party and invite some friends up for them."

Evan coughed as he exhaled the fragrant smoke. Evie focused on the smoldering cigarette back in her hand. Its embers burned the tip with a tiny stream of smoke twirling upward and dissipating into the air. She remembered meeting Lucca a couple of weeks ago. Had he not gone into the strip club, she may not have ever had the chance of discovering his beautiful face. She may not have had the opportunity to spy his perfect naked body. She would never have known her dark stranger.

"So why are they still here?"

She inhaled and passed the joint. Its effects taking hold, Evie's mind spun. Her pulse slowed down as she sank back into the sofa cushions.

Smoke wafted from his parted lips up through his nostrils as Evan scrutinized the tiny joint burning down to his fingertips. "I think Lucca wants to stick around." He looked at Evie with silent intent.

"You think he's sticking around for me?" She jerked her body forward.

"I don't see any other reason keeping them here." He wheezed and passed the joint back, exhaling a thick cloud of sticky smoke.

"Why?"

"Why not? He's obviously charmed by your beauty."

"Interesting," she said, amused, giggled a little. *"Charmed by my beauty*, huh? That's a first." The two exchanged a coy glance.

They settled back into their comfortable silence together. She watched him suck at the joint, now not more than a tiny spark of ash in between his fingers. She knew how the hot embers would be as they singed his rose-colored lips and wondered how soft those lips were. Remorse grabbed at her heart, repulsed by the warmth she felt building inside her. Images of Blythe's delicate face crept to the foreground from the guilty crevices of her mind. She thought of the heartbreak she caused with Adam a few years ago, a look she'd suffered and vowed never to cause again. She pulled her eyes away from Evan.

"I'm surprised Blythe hasn't tracked me down yet," Evie said.

"She knows you're okay."

"She does? How?"

"I told her I was going to drive you home when I spoke to her this morning," he said.

"She knows I stayed at your house?"

Evie sat up. Blythe knew about everything that went on? Did she know Evie was drugged? Was she cool with knowing a complete stranger brought Evie's incapacitated body up to his room?

Yup, fucking Miss Prissy abandoned you for Adorable Brown Eyes over here. Ain't that some shit? Stupid girl.

"I convinced her you would be okay. But Blythe thinks I'm jealous, too. Every time I tried to intervene last night she accused me of being envious or too protective," he said.

"So just like that, she let me stay? Didn't she think I was in danger?"

Evie's tone was accusatory. Evan looked back at her with a raised eyebrow and hesitant smile. His grin was so similar to Lucca's it made her insides squishy. Unlike Lucca's constant smirk, though, Evan's was quick to depart.

"Didn't we already discuss the fact that you really weren't in any danger?" he said. "I didn't want to worry her, so she doesn't know about what Lucca did to those kids. She just knew he took you upstairs. I'm guessing she thinks you're a big enough girl to handle what goes on behind closed doors." His regretful tone did nothing to hide the innuendo in his statement. Evie was not amused by his insinuation.

"And you didn't tell her that you don't trust him?"

"Evie, if I mentioned something to Blythe she'd accuse me of being jealous." He paused and dropped his head down. "Arguing with her is exhausting."

That's true, Evie thought and nodded.

He stuffed the bag of pot back in his pocket. She turned away from him and the conversation, but there was something else that had been eating away at her since last night. Something she'd not thought of to ask until now.

"Evan, who's Mae?"

He laughed out loud. "Mae?" Evie stared, intent and anticipating his answer. Evan appraised her reaction then sighed before continuing, "I think that she likes to refer to herself as his girlfriend, but I don't know how much he likes it."

"She threatened me last night at the party," Evie noted with sincerity in her voice. "And I think she meant it. She used a couple of other choice words that I'd rather not repeat." The force of her jaw nearly diminished her molars to dust.

"Just the ramblings of a jealous bitch, if you ask me."

She looked back at him and smiled a fleeting smile.

"Tell me the truth, Evan. Do you think Lucca will hurt me?"

She summoned all the gravity she could muster. It tore through Evan's softened expression. He paused, pursed his lips. He shook his head back forth before lifting his gaze to meet hers.

"No."

The pain behind his eyes resurfaced, but she felt his answer was truthful.

Satisfied, Evie stood up; Evan followed suit.

"Thanks Evan… for everything."

She walked him to the door. They stood in silence, an invisible force fixing them in place. Evie's mind ached to search through the fog of the evening.

Was it possible that she was overreacting to mixed signals? Could it be that Lucca's heretical tendencies were just that? Unorthodox and strange to her, without question, but not as menacing as she presumed? Chalking her morning up to misinterpretations and the lingering effects of unintended drug use, Evie dismissed her fears. One more night of work, then she'd have a few days off to mull it all over. She wondered if Lucca would still be around.

"Nice outfit, by the way," he said in the doorway and tugged at the cashmere sweater's hem.

"I'll go upstairs and change real quick if you want it back."

Evan smirked. "It's comfy, isn't it?"

"Very." She smiled.

"Keep it. It's yours."

TWENTY-SIX

Following Evan's departure, Evie locked the door and looked down in her hand. He left her with a tiny nugget of some of the tastiest weed she'd ever sampled. Nate never brought home anything this sweet. She studied its crystallized surface, a bright green bud with tiny purple veins weaving through it. Delicious, she'd ration it for sure.

Evie took stock of her liquor supply in the kitchen. Empty. She'd forgotten to make a package store run after drinking the rest of Nate's beers. To her relief, the clock indicated it was later in the day than she'd expected. She'd have to get ready for work soon enough. She'd sneak a drink there. Walking past the mantle, she flipped off the ghostly images perched there and marched up stairs to her room. She was in no mood to face their inquisition.

Blaring her stereo, she danced across her floor. Her body became serpentine in response to the sensual music. Her blood boiled with passion recalling the image of Lucca's dripping wet skin. Her body quivered at the thought of him wrapped around her, drawing sigils on her skin, atop his bed.

God, I wish I could remember that part.

Other curiosities pertaining to what happened the night before crept to the front of her mind. Her hips slowed while the building percussions of the music increased. She stalked over to the bathroom, but stopped in the doorway. A golden flicker caught her attention out of the corner of her eye.

Hello there, what are you?

Evie bent down to pull a tall bottle of golden whiskey from a pile of laundry. How long had the bottle been there, she wondered. She could have dropped it there months ago and forgotten about it. Regardless, Evie removed the cap and took a satisfying swig.

Better.

"You, my little friend, can go right here." She placed the bottle near the tub's claw foot, rose, and scampered over to the vanity.

She stopped and stared at the mirror. The image was pale, as always, the dark circles under her blue eyes prominent. Evie pulled and stretched at the skin across her face.

"Dear God, is this what I looked like at Evan's place?" Embarrassed, Evie watched the image in the mirror snicker at her. "Charmed by my beauty, my ass."

She dipped a hand into the vanity drawer, searched for her bandana and stopped. She popped her head up again, this time smiling at the mirror.

"He's got my bandana." She swooned and spilled back into her bedroom.

Evie twirled round her room again, using the music to help block away the bad images in her mind. She didn't want to think about what happened to those college boys. She didn't want to think about Evan and his obvious and unspoken fascination with her. She didn't want to think about what Nate would do if he found out she'd gotten herself into trouble last night and did God only knows what with Lucca.

God only knows.

Gnawing her lip, she skipped downstairs and sang along with a woman's voice. Together, they sang about a lover and the haunt of his touch. She circled around the house for her bag and cell phone. Where were her things? Where were her keys? She paced, flipping up seat cushions.

"What the fuck?"

Her belongings were gone. She paused in the middle of her living room, running her fingernails along her scalp. Where did she have her bag last? She brought it home from work, because she remembered pulling her cell phone out to text Blythe. She laughed out loud at herself. She'd run so frantically from Lucca that she left not only her clothes but also her cell phone, wallet, and all her belongings at the Carver Estate.

The thought of going back there to retrieve them from him sent a current of electricity through her insides. What would he want in exchange, she wondered. *I want to taste you.* She remembered his words and the soft moan with which they rolled off his tongue.

"God, I want to taste you too," she said aloud to herself, disturbed by her own conviction. Her own damn inner voice grew more and more prominent with each day, emboldened her. Images of her recent dreams played in her mind. Her knees wobbled at the remembrance of Lucca's face between her legs and the wet sensation she felt. Something savage gripped her throat at the mental image of his blood-smeared face howling above her.

To love the Devil is to love the good and the bad, but your connection to him is undeniable.

Hope, the old psychic; her words rang in Evie's ears. The shadowy figure in her room sat mute in the back of her mind. Evie flushed and made her way back upstairs to dress for work. She'd deal with her cell phone and all her belongings later. She'd deal with the dark shadow later.

Evie dressed for work. She pulled on a barely-there black tube top just covering her breasts. The word **TASTY** was scrawled across the front in bold, bright green lettering. She layered that with a black fishnet tank top and pulled up black vinyl booty shorts paired with her Doc Martens. She applied smoky eyes and a speck of shiny lip gloss and glitter. Feeling less than the hollow shell that had peered back at her earlier, she puckered her lips in the mirror.

Damn, I need a drink.

***

Evie pulled into the parking lot of the club. She was well over an hour early for her shift, and she certainly had no intention of starting early. She needed to blunt the tips of the emotions that needled her from all over. She needed to numb those sensations. She passed by Jerry. He tipped his invisible hat and smiled.

"Good evening, Miss Westvale."

"Good evening, sir." She feigned a curtsy and smiled, then marched to the bar.

Evie sucked in a heaping gulp of air when she saw Rob. He stood shirtless behind the bar. His back faced her as he swept. His expansive shoulders flexed as his arms worked the broom back and forth. She perched herself atop one the barstools and rested her chin on her hand, marveling at the fine artwork on display. The black-inked geisha stretched across the canvas of his back slithered on the muscular tissue of Rob's body. She thought of how many times she'd seen that grim courtesan mock her from across the club after hours. She hated her. She scowled back at the tattoo.

Without forethought, she licked her lips and compared Rob's thick muscular figure to Lucca's long, lean body. The thought of being sandwiched between the two of them, penetrated by the two of them, streaked through her mind like a comet. She whistled a loud, demeaning catcall at him. He turned and a mixed expression of surprise and excitement etched his face.

"Hey, Gorgeous. How long have you been there?" he asked, dropping the broom and fumbling across the bar for his t-shirt. Evie feasted on her view of his well-toned torso before he could hide it.

"Long enough to wonder what it would cost to get you in one of those private booths," she said with a wink. Flirting with Rob was fun, and she loved to make him blush, but it was all just more conflicting emotions.

He laughed, embarrassed. "Easy now, we decided that would be a bad idea, didn't we?"

"*You* decided."

Rob paused and snickered. "I don't think you can afford me. Settle for a drink?"

He grabbed a shot glass. Evie perked up in her stool. In the absence of human flesh, other earthly delights would have to do.

"Yes, please." She smiled.

"The usual?"

"No, something different. Surprise me."

Rob turned, produced two glasses, one for each of them, and filled them with a cool, dark syrupy liquid.

"I think I'll join you. This has been a fucked-up couple of weeks."

Together they lifted their shot glasses.

"To a fucked-up couple weeks," she said and let the Jägermeister burn its way down her throat.

"Are you feeling better tonight?"

Rob placed an open beer bottle in front of her.

He always knows what we need.

"Yeah."

"Sometimes it's good for us to be alone with our thoughts."

He wiped off a series of glasses before setting them up for the evening behind the bar. Feeling too guilty to answer him, she brought the glass bottle to her lips and sucked down the dark stout.

***

The night went on like most others. The regulars were friendly enough. The obnoxious college students that made the trek through the woods found what they needed. All whispers of Natalie had faded. The case against her boyfriend was said to be air-tight, though no one knew exactly what happened. Evie looked around and was grateful that no one looked familiar from the party, or what she could remember of it. If anyone did recognize her, they made no mention of it.

Halfway through the night, a few drunken fishermen got a bit too rowdy. Evie didn't know what it was over. She could hardly care, but Rob and Jerry jumped in to break up their fight and dragged each man outside. Without Rob having to ask, Evie jumped behind the bar for him and transitioned into a relief bartender until he returned sweaty and winded from the skirmish.

Draughts were poured. Customers were getting their monies' worth, and Evie continued to help clean behind the bar. Flickering her sights up towards the entrance, a familiar shadow emerged. It was petite, feminine, and filled

Evie with guilted heat. The hateful glower meeting her gaze did little to settle her trepidation as Blythe stormed forward, a second familiar figure in tow.

"Blythe, what the hell are you doing here?"

"Hey, pretty girl. What brings you in tonight?" Rob offered a warm welcome and tapped Evie on the shoulder to take over duties as bartender.

Blythe's scornful expression indicated to Evie that her cameo at the club was not her idea. Blythe rolled her eyes and folded her arms like a pouting child. Her disgusted stare prompted Evie to shift her attention to Evan who stood tall, an apologetic smile pulling at the corner of his lips. He pushed a bundle across the bar top.

"We were driving by and figured you'd want your stuff back," he said, as Evie sifted through the bundle locating her cell phone, wallet, shoes and pants. She looked up at him. Clearing his throat in his fist, he continued, "The shirt wouldn't come clean. I had to toss it."

She looked down at the pile again, then up at Blythe. She hadn't forgotten Rob had no idea she'd lied to him.

"What's that, Evie?" Rob asked.

"Evie spent the night at Evan's," Blythe said, spewing obvious hate.

"Blythe," Evie exasperated.

"What? Are you saying you didn't?"

Her snide retort made Evie shut her mouth. Evan looked over at Evie, guilt-ridden.

Rob scanned the faces of all three. "What is she talking about, Evie?"

She took in a deep breath. Her pulse quickened with anxiety. How was she going to get out of this mess?

"I'm sorry, Rob. I just couldn't sit alone last night—" she said.

"Yeah, so she had me drive her to see *him*," Blythe interjected. The hurt in her voice and the hate in her eyes was enough for everyone to think she was referring to Evan.

Why is she letting Rob think something happened between us and Evan?

Evie thought about it, and although she knew she'd burn for her lie, she allowed the masquerade to play out. Rob's jaw dropped. He eyed both Evie and Evan, who hung their heads low in shame. Evie knew what Rob was thinking; this guy Evan got dragged in by the balls by his girlfriend to hand over the evidence of his cheating.

"Blythe, I'm not sure what happened, but I think maybe it's better if you and your... uh... boyfriend leave for now," Rob said, lifting a hand out towards her. He glowered at Evan, who obeyed and put an arm around Blythe to coax her away. Rob did the same with Evie.

"Blythe, wait." Evie threw his arm back and ran out from behind the bar. She ran and pulled Blythe around with a jolt.

"Blythe, what's wrong? Why do you look so angry?"

"Are you kidding me?" Blythe snapped back. "Evie, *you* spent the night at *my* boyfriend's house. The two of you spoon-feed me some bullshit about that guy, Lucca. But who drove you home this morning, huh? All Evan and I did was argue last night, and then he drove you home this morning? How convenient. And if that isn't insult enough, I brought my *ex*-boyfriend to a strip club to return clothes you left at his house. Do you remember the last time I came in here? What happened? Tell me, why shouldn't I be angry?"

Blythe's lips began to quiver in anger. Evie felt her hatred scourge her face. Rob tried his best not to listen and turned away.

"Blythe, nothing happened with me and Evan. You know that. You were there."

Evie looked over to Evan to jump in and reaffirm her statement. He was silent, head down in penance, but Evie caught his eyes scanning her up and down.

What the fuck are you looking at, you asshole? Tell her.

"Yeah, I was there long enough for Evan to convince me to go home," Blythe said, sneering.

"Wait, he said he told you about..." Evie looked again at Evan. He remained lasciviously fixated on her outfit. Saliva wetted his lips.

"I never saw you with Lucca," Blythe yelled.

"Tell me, Evie, what happened to your shirt? What was Evan trying to clean off it?"

Rob's eyes widened, jaw dropped, and ears perked up. He gawked at Evie. She noticed his disappointment out of the corner of her eye and wanted to die in the moment.

"I left everything with Lucca. Evan, tell her."

"Yeah, that's what he said too—Lucca." Blythe's volume lowered, but her venomous tone increased. "Tell me why, oh why, Evie, did I see you wearing nothing but Evan's sweater when he drove you home?"

Evie, frozen in shock, had no idea how to respond.

"How do you know that? Did you follow me?"

"I followed *him*," she said and thumbed over her shoulder to Evan.

You fucking stalking crazy psycho-bitch. Here we've been making amends for years. I told you. I told you Miss Prissy wasn't worth it.

"Okay," Rob said and stepped out from behind the bar and wrapped his protective hand around Evie's core. "Blythe, I can see you have some things you need to work out with Evan, and I need a word with Evie. So if you don't mind, why don't you put your little tirade on hold until Evie's day off tomorrow? You girls can have it out, off the clock."

Though his words carried a light tone, Blythe scoffed at him and turned away. Evan moved to follow as Rob tried to pull Evie aside, but she pushed his arm away again and ran after them.

"Evan." She pulled his elbow to spin him around. He looked down at her, saddened. "Evan, what the fuck? Why didn't you tell her what happened?" She searched his eyes for an answer, but they were too shrouded in pain and guilt.

"I've never seen you like this. You look so… different."

"What are you talking about? This is how I dress for work. Who gives a shit? What the fuck happened, Evan?"

He paused, stared. It made her uneasy. He released a heavy breath.

"I tried, Evie. I swear I did, but she wouldn't listen."

As Evan spoke, his eyes drifted down to Evie's outfit, his lips parted as he stared through the fishnet to the cleft between her breasts. Evie snapped her fingers to bring his eyes back to hers.

"Well, you better find a way to convince her that nothing happened, because nothing *did* happen, Evan. And nothing's going to happen—not in this lifetime, right?" she said. Her eyes bulged out of her head to emphasize her point.

Evan looked as though he were about to say something. Blythe stormed over and hooked an arm around

Evan's. "Can't get enough, can you?" she said and dragged him away.

"A word, Evie," Rob said with a stern voice in Evie's ear.

She walked behind him towards his office. She tried to hide between her shrugged shoulders and looked around the club. Some of the girls were watching them, and only a few customers seemed to notice Blythe's little outburst. Judging by the way Rob stormed off to his office, she knew she was in big trouble.

Stupid, stupid girl.

Evie sat in the worn leather chair in front of Rob's desk. He leaned up against the side, keeping his back to her, staring up at the ceiling. Evie was left to fester in silence for what felt like hours.

"Evie, is what Blythe said true? Did you leave work early to spend the night with her boyfriend?"

"No."

"Did you leave work early to go see him? Blythe said that she brought you to his house last night."

Evie sighed. There was no avoiding it. She had to tell Rob as much of the truth as was necessary. Trying to skirt around the details, she explained that yes, she did have Blythe drive her up to Evan's house, but it wasn't to see him, it was to see Lucca. She neglected to fill in the details as to why. She felt it was better to let him believe she attempted to stay at home, but couldn't stand to be alone. She told him she'd spent the night at the house, but with Lucca, not Evan. She didn't divulge the circumstances that lead to her abrupt exit, but said she'd left the house in a hurry and forgot all her belongings there. Evan ran into her, offered her a sweater to keep her covered and warm, and gave her a ride home. What Blythe saw when Evan dropped her off was a misconstrued form of the truth, and she knew Blythe was acting out of an unjustified jealousy.

"Rob, you know I'd never do anything to hurt her."

Evie looked up to him with anxious eyes. She needed him to believe her. She told the truth, just not all of it. Her words were desperate, but they would suit her purpose. Rob remained still during her entire recount. His head rolled back so he faced up towards the ceiling, his eyes closed in deep contemplation. She could see he was trying to sort out what she'd just divulged to him.

"I believe you, Evie. I do. But why did you have to go see this guy, Lucca?"

The question made her panic. How was she supposed to explain something she found difficult to understand herself?

"I don't know. I felt like I had to see him."

"Has he done anything to you?" Rob shifted his gaze to the floor below his feet. Evie watched as his biceps muscles twitched and his jaw flexed.

"No."

"But you ran out of the house leaving everything, including your clothes, in his room?"

"I know that sounds bad, but I promise, I'm fine. Nothing's happened to me."

"And this guy is living with Evan?"

"He's a house guest of his uncle's. Evan says he doesn't like the guy."

Rob chuckled. "Well, I guess Evan and I have two things in common."

Evie looked up at him puzzled. "What's that?"

He turned to her, his arms still folded against his chest. She watched individual shocks of muscle twitch across his body from the tension he held in.

"Well, we both can't help staring at you when we shouldn't. And we both can't stand Lucca."

TWENTY-SEVEN

When Rob told Evie to go home early, she obeyed with reluctance and shame. The disappointment she'd stirred in him broke her heart to witness. He was unable to look at her. As she drove home she remembered the pained expression on his face when he told her to leave.

Go home, Evie. Grab your shit and go home. The sting of his words, callousness infused with betrayal, were hydrogen peroxide to the fresh wound in her heart. *Grab your shit and go home.* He'd never spoken to her like that before in her life. In one night, Evie watched two out of the three most important people in her life push her away, and for what? For a carcinogenic attraction to a man she barely knew.

You're a fucking mess.

"Please stop," she said, begging through a whisper to her inner voice.

It was midnight when she walked through her front door. She flicked the light switch on to illuminate the front hallway and living room, then switched the light back off. She dropped her bag on the coffee table and fumbled through it to produce two beers she'd managed to swipe on her way out of work. She moved over to the fireplace wall to flip a switch, illuminating the room with a soft glow from two old and tarnished brass wall sconces flanking the mantle. And in that soft light she sat, catatonic in the middle of the couch, two cold and capped beers in her hands.

No thoughts plagued her, just emptiness. Hurtful emptiness seized her mind and cracked her chest in two. Evie blinked. Moving just her eyes, her sights shifted to the tiny green nugget wrapped in a cellophane ball on the table. Her mouth parched at the thought of taking in the tangy taste of the weed Evan left behind for her. And so, trusting her natural inclination to numb the pain, she twisted the cap off of one of the beers and began breaking the little nugget apart to pack her glass bowl.

The cheap beer made her wince while the fine weed filled her brain with wonderful, poisoned smoke. She let it dance along her lips, swirl around her tongue, and envelop her taste buds. She French-inhaled the smoke through her nostrils, crossed her eyes to look down her nose to watch as smoke wafted up from within her.

She killed the two beers, but savored each hit from the pipe, taking her body down to a drug-induced stasis. She thumbed through her bag, checked her cell phone, and scrolled through a series of missed calls and texts from Blythe. Even in her texts, Evie could sense her hate. She placed the phone down on the table, unable to look at it. She closed her eyes, listened to the cacophony of ramblings in her mind. A titillating voice emerged from the chaos.

I want to taste you. Lucca's words sent a warm wave across her body, and it lingered in the pit of her belly, churning with the beer. Lucca's words echoed in her mind. She played off each silky length of smoke for Lucca's soft smooth skin as it passed through her.

Feeling warm and claustrophobic, Evie peeled the layers of fishnet, vinyl and cotton from her weak and defeated body. Leaving the living room aglow, she walked naked upstairs through the light of the moon. She made her way upstairs into her bedroom, riddled with piles of laundry, clean and dirty alike. Empty glass bottles poked out from under the masses, but Evie paid no attention. She dropped her exhausted body on top of her downy soft comforter. With her face buried deep in a feathery pillow, she groped along the edge of her bed to her nightstand to flick on her stereo. A coarse voice and acoustic guitar sang of the wondrous ability to love an enemy. The crying melody of his voice made Evie swoon. She curled her naked body into a tight ball atop her bed, pulling the comforter to wrap around her like the familiar clumsy lover she frequently shared it with. She breathed in a deep, suffocating breath, taking in the linens' faint lavender scent.

As she lay in bed, Evie cracked open an eyelid. She searched through the darkness and moonlight for the shadow, the Devil, herself, anything, anyone to keep her from her own solitude. Tonight her hermitage was a curse, not a blessing.

Close your eyes and dream of him. Fuck this night and dream of fucking him.

***

Despite Evie's desperate efforts to summon him, Lucca declined to haunt her dreams that night, nor did the shadowy figure appear in the corner of her room. She awoke feeling rejected, cold, and with an unaddressed ache between her legs.

For once, the morning air was warm. A sign of spring. Her bedroom was filled with unfiltered sunshine. Her body was sore, and she was grateful for that pain. It brought her senses to something obvious, immediate, something she could address with some aspirin, booze, or pot. Her body's maladies were a minimal nuisance in comparison to what her mind was about to endure.

She hopped in the shower, praying the drain would pull her down. Through the past couple of weeks she had allowed herself to lapse into a momentary bout of psychosis. She needed to make things right, to get her head out of her ass and repair the rift she'd caused between herself and the two people she loved most.

Her inner voice took more convincing. After her shower, Evie stared at its mocking glare in the mirror. Hateful blue eyes burned, glowering back at her.

They won't forgive you. They'll never fully trust you.

Tears welled up in her eyes.

"I have to try. I didn't mean to hurt them," she said to the mirror.

All you did was follow your heart and go to him. It is all for you.

"I followed my hormones. I followed my lust. My heart had nothing to do with it," she said, arguing with herself and losing.

He is you and you are him. Do not try to resist.

"Why are you saying that? What do you know that I don't?"

Evie heard her own voice cackle, reverberating off the bathrooms ceramic tiled walls. She rushed her head over to the toilet, ready to spew the contents of her stomach into the bowl. Nothing came up. She dry heaved once, twice, her cramping abdominal muscles folding her in two. Salty tears stung her eyes and the taste of bile coated the back of her tongue. Her naked body convulsed. She hunched over the bathroom vanity as she stared down the image in the mirror with reddened and puffy eyes.

"What the fuck am I going to do?" she asked of the image. It didn't respond. A moment later, she heard the doorbell ring. She flinched and stood rigidly. Her eyes squeezed shut. Her face contorted with effort as she shook her head from side to side. She threw on some clothes and ran downstairs to open the door.

A sense of relief overcame her when she saw her best friend's soft brown hair radiating in the sunlight like a halo on her front step, coffees from the North Star piping away in each hand.

"Let's talk," Blythe said as she walked past Evie to the kitchen table. Evie followed, head low, as they sat facing each other.

"Blythe, I'm sorry. I don't know what happened or where things got so mixed up, but I—"

"Save it, Evie," Blythe said, throwing a palm in her face. "Evan and I did a lot of talking last night. I came here to say something to you. Not the other way around."

Evie sunk down in her seat. "Okay," she said and accepted the hot Styrofoam cup Blythe handed her.

"Look Evie, I don't even want to know if you slept with Evan or not. I don't really care what your version of the truth may be. I think you've given me good reason to mistrust you with someone I care about. The fact is, I've been seeing Evan for a while now and you're the one who spent the night at his place. It's all bullshit." Blythe paused for a sip of her coffee. Evie stared into the table top.

"Even though I knew Evan said Lucca had taken you up to his room, I—I still—I didn't trust him. I had no idea Evan had people staying at his house, so I thought that was a cover-up. I took my dad's car and parked outside across the street from your house waiting for him to bring you home, like he told me he would. When I saw you get out of his car wearing nothing but his sweater—" Blythe paused. "Well, what would you think?"

"I'd think I slept with him too," she admitted. The truth did look that bad on the surface.

"Exactly, and besides that, it's just not going to work. There's something Evan's not telling me."

Evie knew where this was going. She just didn't want to admit it. The two girls sat at the table in silence for a bit longer before Blythe spoke again. Evie hated herself and her inner voice for the images of Evan flittering across her mind's eyes, hated herself for the comfort she felt around him. Even though she never intended to, sex or no, Evie had betrayed Blythe's trust yet again.

"Just do me a favor, Evie, stay away from Evan. I saw the way he looked at you at the club. I can't compete with that. I don't think it's your fault. I think it's him. Hell, I think it's any guy. Please, just don't."

Evie felt the urge to argue Blythe's comment. She wanted to remind Blythe that she was still with Nate. Even if she wasn't, she was already fucked up in the head over Lucca, and Rob for that matter. Evan never crossed her mind, not in *that* way. She remembered Rob saying something similar to her last night about how Evan looked at her when he shouldn't, how he shouldn't. She held her tongue, though. She was on the verge of losing her best friend; there was no need to antagonize her further.

"Deal," she said.

"This doesn't make things better between us. Not yet anyway. You have a problem, Evie. You really need to think about sobering up. You keep finding yourself in these situations."

Fuck you too, bitch.

"Blythe, I'm sorry. It wasn't my fault."

"I know. But you're going to allow me some anger here. I'm hurt... and confused." Blythe took another sip of coffee. "So did you sleep with Lucca?" Blythe asked with a hint of genuine interest in her inquiry. Evie slumped over her coffee.

"No, at least I don't think I did. I don't remember anything. He said he took me upstairs because the boys from the club slipped me a rufie or something."

"Jesus Christ, Evie, that sounds scary. Why didn't Evan tell me that?"

Evie smiled at the glimmer of sympathy in her voice.

"That's okay. He said he didn't want you to worry. I guess Lucca took me to his room to look after me. Nothing happened."

"But you left all your clothes there, so they had to come off at some point. You must have done something."

Blythe sipped from her cup. Evie thought of how to respond. Something had happened, but she couldn't repeat to Blythe what Lucca had told her. She couldn't tell her about the blood or about the way Lucca described fondling her unconscious body. It was far too intimate, entirely too grotesque, and might've been a lie just to fuck with her head.

"Yeah, I guess my clothes got dirty or something. He stripped me down to my underwear." Blythe's jaw dropped. "He said he didn't do anything bad. But I saw him get out of the shower the next morning when I woke up. He's..." she rolled her eyes to the back of her head and inhaled, "...*perfect*." She blushed while she drank her coffee, using the Styrofoam cup to mask her embarrassment. Blythe looked at her with amused surprise.

"Perfect, eh? In *all* the right places?"

"In *all* the right places."

The girls laughed out loud together.

"So Lucca, huh?" Blythe's open-ended question left Evie to fill in the blanks.

"Yeah, Lucca. But what am I supposed to do? He's only here for a short time, and Nate's going to be home any day."

"Well," Blythe said as she finished her coffee and rose from the table. "I guess you'll have to go back to said perfect man and find out more."

The thought of going to see him again thrilled and terrified Evie.

TWENTY-EIGHT

Evie hopped in her car with no idea what she was doing or where she was going. She knew that Blythe was right to a certain extent. Not that she needed to sober up; her habits were just fine as far as she was concerned. But she did need to know more. She would never be set free from the net she found herself tangled in if she didn't pursue Lucca to the bitter end. To do that, to find her release, she needed to call out to her inner voice to guide her, not chastise her for her actions. She needed to find her change. Like the psychic said, change was coming. She needed to look into herself and embrace it.

Her hair flailed through the breeze streaming through the open car window. The warm spring air and bright sun was invigorating. She pressed on aimlessly through town with a wary sense of determination. Dammit all, her inner voice was silent for once.

As she drove over the causeway, she saw Rob's truck sitting outside the club.

"Rob," Evie said in a whisper to herself as she pulled into the parking lot.

***

Forcing one foot in front of the other, Evie made a timid path towards the solid metal doors of Sirens, peering up at the muted signage hanging overhead. Inside, she found Rob cleaning up around the bar. He was alone and

254

shirtless with his back to her. The girl etched into his body watched Evie through malicious eyes and beautiful fury, forever carrying her trophy, shaded by her parasol in a blizzard of sakura petals. Of course, the geisha was fortunate to remain fixed in her youthful beauty to forever follow Rob. *There are worse fates*, Evie thought. Still the geisha's eyes glared at her.

I'd like to claw that tattoo's face off.

The sound of the door drew Rob's attention. He was surprised to see her walking towards him. His usual boyish charm and warm smile were nowhere to be found in the scowl lining his face. Evie froze in her steps for a second, but pushed forward. He leaned the broom against the bar in exchange for a hand towel, brushing off the dirt and sweat from his hands, face, and chest. He walked to meet her at the edge of the dancers' stage.

"Evie, what are you doing here?" he asked, head down to his hands, jaw clenched, nothing like the dependable Rob she loved more than she was willing to admit. His distressed tone thickened the air of the club. It set Evie back with a repentant frown, but the more he held back from her, the more her inner voice pressed her forward.

"I was passing by and saw your truck. I thought we could talk."

He shook his head at the idea, still filled with resentful disappointment.

"I'm glad you came, Evie. I am, but..." His sentenced trailed off into silence.

Evie huffed. She needed this.

"Rob, please. I can't have you mad at me or disappointed in me, not you, not even for a second. Please, can we talk?" The nervousness in her trembling voice made itself evident. Rob watched her for a minute, head tilted. Her hands quivered with her voice. His body lifted with an exaggerated and heavy sigh, forcing the air to pass through him.

"Wait here," he groaned before turning his back to her and headed towards the bar. The geisha followed.

He grabbed a bottle of Jameson and two glasses, then made his way back to Evie. Rob always knew what she wanted. He always took such good care of her. With the hint of hope pulling at the corner of her lips, the tension in her shoulders loosened.

She propped herself up on the side of the stage. The silence and dim stage lighting created an oddly serene atmosphere for their chat.

He handed Evie an empty glass and filled it halfway. Doing the same in the second glass for himself, Rob took a seat next to her. The outer edge of their thighs rubbed against each other. She watched his movements, anticipating something, but what, she couldn't quite say. So she did what felt natural in her limbo. Evie downed her drink in a single gulp.

Rob proceeded. "Feeling better?"

She smirked, suffocated by her own nervousness in his normally calming presence. Confusion clouded her already divergent emotions. "A little."

"You put me in an awkward position, Evie. You always come to me for comfort. The idiot that I am, I always give in to you. For what? I can't even trust you to be honest with me."

Anxiety pushed tiny beads of sweat from her pores, moistening her brow and under her arms. An internal heat scorched her pounding chest. She couldn't afford to lose him.

"I'll tell you anything you want to know and be completely honest, I promise. Where do you want me to begin?" She was afraid to look him in the eyes for fear he may see right through her thin façade of nerve, straight to her inner shame.

"How about with Blythe. What happened?" Rob's voice was cold, authoritative, and nothing like what she expected from him. She wanted to lash out at him, burst out with emotions in the hopes of eliciting a similar response from him to crack this unnatural hardened shell of his.

Instead, Evie sighed and responded by bringing him up to speed with their coffee talk from earlier in the day. She winced as he scowled knowing that she and Blythe would forever have a yet another barrier between them.

"So you expect me to believe that nothing happened between you and Evan. Really?"

Evie's eyes widened, desperate. "No. Why is that so hard to believe? Am I that untrustworthy?"

Rob shook his head and snickered, refilling his glass and shooting the whiskey back. He forced an apologetic smile towards her.

"So, then what about this other asshole, Lucca?"

Lucca. She let the sound of his voice on her mind's breath linger. *Where to begin with someone like Lucca?*

Evie's mind drifted along with her gaze. Rob huffed with a shake of his head and refilled both of their glasses.

"That bad, huh?"

Snapped back to reality by the sound of Rob's voice and the faint scent of Jameson tickling her olfactories, she flinched and looked over at him. Evie eyeballed Rob sitting by her side, shirtless and sweaty, thinking about Lucca, stirring a burning sensation in the pit of her core and the aching between her thighs to replace the one in her chest. It took her a second to break her stare away from his physique, but she managed to peel her eyes away to the golden liquid in her glass and brought it to her mouth, let the whiskey roll over her tongue. The sting of it numbed her impure intentions.

"I don't even know where to begin with Lucca," she said. "I feel different around him. I come undone, and I'm afraid of what I might do around him."

"Afraid?" Rob's face distorted with a disgust that pained her to witness. "What are you afraid you might do?"

She stared into his eyes, cautious, confused, and took in a deep breath. Verbalizing her thoughts, those of her inner voice, was a difficult task. "I'm afraid of what I want to do to him, or let him do to me. Just thinking about him makes me shiver."

Evie closed her eyes tight, allowed her body to tremble. She peeked through one eye, gauging Rob's reaction. He'd dropped his gaze to his hands clawing at the glass atop his lap.

"I haven't done anything with him though," she insisted. "I promise. I haven't done anything against Nate." Her pleading fell on deaf ears and Rob swigged his drink before filling their glasses again. That wasn't what he cared to hear, she could see that much smeared plainly against his face. She'd come by to erase that tortured look, not intensify it. Endorphins boosted, anxiety on the rise, Evie's pulse quickened. "It's an infatuation. That's all. I'm infatuated with him. As soon as he leaves town I'll stop thinking about him. I'm sure of it. I hope so at least. I hate being so drawn to someone and yet so afraid of them at the same time."

"Again that word—*Afraid*," he snipped. "Are you afraid of him or yourself?"

"Well... both, I guess."

"Why would you be afraid of him? You said nothing's happened between the two of you, right? Are you being honest, Evie, or has he tried something? Has he threatened you?"

I want to taste you. He comes. And to resist him is futile. Words swirled through her mind, pushing the blood rushing through her veins to pulse in a dark and warm place deep inside of her. Her honesty needed to maintain its limits if she were to salvage whatever it was she had with Rob.

"No," she answered. "No, he hasn't. It's just... it's a feeling so strong it scares me, because I don't understand it."

In Evie's vague response, she'd found the truth. There was a magnetism between the two of them, her and Lucca. She didn't understand it, therefore she feared it. And so logically, she feared him. Overwhelming relief washed over her like a wave. As her body relaxed, she heard a rumbling come from Rob's direction. She peeked over to find his eyes scanning her body.

"Why do you keep falling for these losers, Evie? When will you learn you're worth more?"

Evie held Rob's gaze, tearing up from the internal torture of holding herself back.

Worth more? But not worth you.

"Maybe Lucca is exactly what I deserve."

"That's bullshit, and you know it. I didn't like him for one second the night he came into the club. The way he looked at you. The way he tried to *buy* you—Disgusting. You just keep replacing one bad habit with another."

The building tears found their way over the crest of her eyelids, trickling down her cheek. *One bad habit with another,* Evie realized the truth in his statement. Regardless of her pull to him, she knew full well that Lucca was unsettling. She may not have known why, but he seemed capable of terrible things and presented a very real threat to her well-being. She knew she was better off without him, but still didn't want to let go. She couldn't let go. Not yet. Not without a taste, a hit, not without feeling that sweet release her bad habits always promised and delivered on.

Pushing away the tempest brewing inside, she shook her head back and forth. The High Priestess was roused. A million flippant remarks flitted through her mind, something, anything to break their tense silence, but Evie couldn't find the words, her emotions left to pour out through her tears.

All too aware of the empty glass in her hand, she lowered her eyes down to it. The glass was left wanting. With another heavy sigh, Rob removed it from her hands and rested it beside its twin next to the thin green bottle. He slid from the stage and stood in front of her. Evie's cheeks burned as he gazed down at her.

"I'm sorry, Rob," she whispered, hopeless.

In his firm and dependable grip, he pulled her legs around his waist. Trepidation present, lust overpowering, Evie's heart pounded under her black tunic. She'd never questioned Rob's motives in all of their years together, and suddenly, as he loomed over her, she did not recognize him at all.

"I know you are," he said in a tone one octave lower than his usual. He cupped her face in his hands.

"How do you stand me after all the shit I put you through?" she asked, searching his eyes, wondering where his fraternal familiarity had vanished to, replaced by a something that had her inner voice throbbing with anticipation.

He snickered under his breath. "Nobody's perfect, Evie."

"You are. You're too good for me."

"No, I'm not," he insisted. "Why do you think I have you working for me? It's not to let every other guy around here drool over you. It's because *I* want you near me. It's so *I* can see you. You're my siren, Evie, calling me— pulling me into your jagged shores," he said, leaning in and licking her whiskey-soaked lips with the outstretched tip of his tongue. "*My* siren," he repeated, grazing his lips across hers.

She released the subtlest of moans. Having recently been though such torturous waves of lust, a set of glowing golden orbs flickered in her mind's eye. She thought to push Rob away, stop him before the fissure between her mind and her body cracked beyond repair. "Rob, I—"

Eyes closed, head listing side to side, he hushed her and licked his lips. "I don't want to be just another one of your bad habits, Evie."

Like the tide, Rob rolled in over her, kissing her with a possession that rushed a current of electricity down through her bones, releasing years of tension in the one act. His lips were firm, but softened as their embrace lasted. His flavor, intoxicating; Evie lapped it up as water in a desert. Having gained temporary satisfaction from her mouth, Rob pulled away. Her inner voice celebrated, whirling through the dark of her mind, pirouetting through the light from the golden orbs floating therein. Those orbs vanished as Evie opened her eyes to find Rob's warm smile inches away.

"Please don't tell me this is wrong again," she said.

He let out a soft chortle. "No."

Rob leaned in again, this time pressing down harder, pulling her up to him with his hand cradling her rear. Evie wrapped her legs tight around his waist and reclined onto the stage. She clawed her fingers into the geisha, thrilled. The feeling it gave her was exhilarating. After navigating the troubled waters of confusing emotions and lustful compulsions, Evie was high off of Rob. As always, Rob knew what she needed. He felt soft, strong and warm as he enveloped her body.

This is what love should feel like, she told her inner voice. This was passion, the excitement she had been missing through her time with Nate. This is what the fear blocked from all her moments with Lucca. This was the change she hoped for.

Rob's hand ran in and out from under her shirt. He rubbed the soft skin around Evie's mid-section. She laid back and allowed him to tower over her. He stopped, lifted his head and paused.

"No, Evie, wait. This *is* wrong," he said.

Evie's eyes grew wide with shock. "What? No. Rob don't do this again, please."

"No, we can't do this here. I won't. You deserve better."

He stood up, releasing her from his arms. Evie's body deflated with disappointment as she sat up. Rob held up her face to his. Both hands held her jaw with a softness that drew tears from her eyes.

"I have wanted this for too long to allow it to happen here on this stage," he said with a reassuring smile. She beamed back at him. "Why don't you head home? I'll be by after I've finished cleaning up."

"Really?"

"Really," he said.

Rob lifted her up. The floor was like rolling waves beneath her feet, but she managed to stand straight. One last kiss pressed to her lips, one last flash of his familiar smile, and Rob leaned down to pick up the glasses and bottle.

"I'll see you soon," he said and turned away. Evie beamed back as the geisha followed him towards the bar.

Evie bit her lip to hold in her excitement, chancing a quick glance here and there as she made for the door. Rob grinned back from across the club, waving her on.

***

Evie walked out of the club towards her car with a hopeful smile lingering on her lips, laced with Rob's delectable zest. Unlike what she'd told Blythe in the past, she would have no second thoughts at pushing Nate away for him.

As she settled herself behind the steering wheel, a needle of anxiety pierced her heart, pinned her to the seat like a butterfly being mounted for display. Her eyes flicked to her rearview mirror, but showed her only the empty lot. Evie dismissed the sudden apprehension, chalked it all up to guilt for what she was about to do to Nate. It didn't matter anymore. For the first time since she could remember, she felt right about what she was doing with her life.

***

As clouds rolled in overhead, snuffing the sunlight that fueled her ambitions, Evie drove home elated.

She ran through the house with cleaning materials in tow; if a strip club stage wasn't good enough, a filthy house wouldn't do either. Giggles and light-headedness followed her as she transformed her space from bedroom to boudoir. She'd fantasized about this moment with him for years, and here it was, coming to fruition. She looked over on her dresser and saw a picture of her and Nate looking back at her.

Ugh, Nate. What are we going to do with you?

Evie decided that the feeling of Rob against her was too good. She'd find a way to break it off with Nate when he came back from his fishing trip. It had to be done. Nate and Rob hated each other already, but she couldn't fight the excitement she felt at the thought of getting her chance to be with Rob. Nothing was going to stop her now.

She was stopped by the scowling image in the bathroom mirror as she passed by. The image of the Devil card flashed in her mind.

He comes. And to resist him is futile.

"What do you want?" she said to herself in the mirror. "You've wanted this with Rob for years. Isn't this the change you want? Isn't this what you need?" The anger she projected at herself made the image smirk back.

He comes. And to resist him is futile.

"You mean Rob?"

Do I?

"Why don't you just tell me to grab a drink or something like you always do?"

I'll tell you what I'd like to drink. I want to taste it.

"Fuck you." Evie pegged her middle finger to the mirror, inflamed at her inner being for not allowing her this moment to rejoice.

Evie stormed away from the mirror and paced through her bedroom, mumbling nonsense to herself as her temperature rose. She glanced over to the clock on her nightstand. Her jaw ached from clenching it so tight. Bile lurched up her throat.

"Fuck!" she exclaimed and turned back to the mirror in the bathroom. "Rob will be here soon. What the fuck do you want?"

You cannot resist.

"Resist what? Resist who?"

Lucca, stupid girl.

"Lucca? You want me to confront Lucca now? Are you fucking crazy? What if Rob comes here and we're gone?" Her pulse boomed against the walls of her temples. The image in the mirror sneered back, mute.

"Answer me! You crazy bitch, answer me!"

You cannot resist.

"You want me to risk everything with Rob right now for someone who is obviously bad for me?"

You cannot resist.

Evie growled, primal. Without any idea of what she was about to do or say, she turned away. Afternoon faded into evening as Evie ran downstairs, hopped in her car, and headed to Black Cross Road.

TWENTY-NINE

Even as Evie skittered her car to a stop in the gravel driveway of the Carver Estate, her conviction wavered. Her head leaned into the steering wheel as she argued with herself. "Should've just gotten drunk. None of this would be a problem if I kept to myself. I need to go home and get numb. It would be so much easier that way. Just go get fucking drunk."

It's futile to resist. I want to taste him.

Evie knew the likelihood of leaving the mansion without falling into his pull was minimal. Whatever Lucca was, whatever she thought he may be to her, the fact remained she felt something for him. It was an unquenchable thirst, greater than any withdrawal she'd known. She was sick for him. She was sick with him. Every minute near him tempted fate, and every minute away, sanity. She looked for answers hidden in the faded grey plastic of her dashboard but found none.

The words of Hope and those of Lucca played like a broken record in her head. The Devil printed on the tarot card laughed at her. Her heart raced. The wind threatened to topple her little car over on its side; the gusts were treacherous this close to the cliffs. The car lilted and Evie's reflexes jolted her up straight as she gripped the steering wheel. She looked up to the mansion to find Lucca sprawled across a bench by the front door.

He sat with both arms resting along the length of the back of the bench. His legs were stretched open wide. She couldn't help observing the way his dirty worn jeans hugged him in all the right places, and a faded black t-shirt covered the softest, warmest flesh she'd ever felt up against her. The pull, the magnetism hit her.

She looked at his gleaming eyes, the dark pools that haunted her dreams. They called out to her with a hunger she'd never before experienced. His lips were parted in soundless satisfaction. The faint shadow of his tongue traced the edges of his teeth from behind.

Evie's breathing deepened, and her body shivered as a warm wet sensation built between her legs. She was pulled. His face was so familiar, so menacing. She knew that look. That devilish—

Putting the pieces together there, stupid girl.

The contorted figure on the card morphed into the sculpted body sprawled along the bench. She could make out the dark shadow's sneer in the back of her memory. He smiled down on her the way the grotesque figure on the card smiled down on his chained prisoners. And Evie was his prisoner. She was leashed to him by unseen shackles whenever he was near.

The Devil represents a new beginning. Do not try to resist. He is you and you are him.

"A new beginning," she repeated to herself.

Anxiety and fear gripped her, threatened to tear her apart. Evie stared back at Lucca. She recalled the blood on her clothes. She remembered the stifled screams from the boys she'd heard raging through the darkness. There was so much more to Lucca that she had yet to understand. Still she was pulled. And to resist him was futile.

He is you and you are him.

She wanted to cry, but fought the compulsion. With a long toke of salty sea air and the cryptic encouragement from her inner voice repeating a choral refrain in her head, Evie stepped out of her car. She leaned up against the door, closed it while watching him with cautious eyes. Lucca leaned forward. His sly smirk beckoned her. He licked his lips lasciviously. Her body would never let her rest until she'd unraveled the mystery of him. The wind whipped her bright red locks about her face. The tug in her chest threatened to rip her in two.

***

As Evie approached the front stairs, ascending towards him, Lucca stood and stalked closer. By the time they reached each other, his breath wafting down on Evie's skin just inches away, still not a word had been spoken. She could feel the heat emanating off of his body, that scent of orange blossoms, mint, and rusty metal. Evie's fingertips pulled down on the seam of her tunic. She forced a large knot free from her throat down into the pit of her queasy core. Lucca's fingers twiddled through the air with anticipation.

She looked up into his eyes and was lost in their darkness. Fire danced across the rim of their irises like golden rings of candlelight. The desire to hold her breath and plunge to the nothingness of their depths held her still. Evie was crushed by the gravity in their shimmering nadir.

"Just, please, don't hurt me," she said, surprising herself with her own timidity. Her lips pursed and eyes shut to hold in tears from trickling down her face. Her body was tense as she felt his hand reach out to touch hers. The image of the Devil card spun out of view.

***

Lucca grinned in satisfaction and dragged her through the great entrance of the Carver Estate. As if gliding on air, he rushed her through the foyer, up the grand staircase, and down the hallway to his room.

She could feel other fiery orbs of light glaring at her as she swooped past them in the foyer. Khan cackled his amusement, revealing his position through the shadows. Evie was glad not to have noticed Mae anywhere; she'd be stabbed to death by the blonde's dagger eyes if she were near. Evie was also relieved not to see Evan lurking in the shadows. Somehow, she knew her actions would displease him. He might have even intervened with whatever it was she was trying to accomplish.

Lucca maintained his grip on her wrist until he had propelled her through his chamber door. He locked the door behind him. Evie's feet strived to keep up with his force, which thrust her in front of the fireplace. The fire blazed heat against her already flushed face. *I can do this*, she thought. What she was doing remained a mystery, but what she needed to know about him was more compelling than oxygen or her next heartbeat—even Rob.

Lucca approached her. He stopped inches away and peered down at her with intent and deviousness. He never released her from his gaze, like predator on prey.

"Are you that afraid of me?" he asked, basking in her current state. He lifted a long finger to pull her bottom lip down like a plaything.

"Terrified," Evie said. Her voice cracked under the pressure.

"Then why are you here?"

His devilish smile was unwavering and exposed elongated canines that Evie was sure hadn't been there before. His smile was beautiful, pearlescent, and foreboding.

"I don't know."

He chuckled. "Do you want me to let you go?" His composure remained constant, never faulting in his solid tone. He reclined into one of the high-backed lounges. As he lowered down from her line of vision and released her from his mesmerism, Evie blinked.

"What?"

"You've just said you're terrified of me, and you're locked up in my room. I seem to have the upper hand here. Would you like me to let you go?"

"I… don't know what I want."

"You came here for a reason. You're looking for something. I can show you, Evie. I can show you the pleasure in your pain. Is that what you want?"

Pain.

The word seized her. Her breathing halted. Her heartbeat arrested. Evie regretted ever listening to her damned inner voice, all due to the one little word. Drifting off Lucca's tongue, the word was almost tempting. But no, she should be home. She should be with Rob.

"I'm sorry. I shouldn't have come here. Will you please let me go?"

"First, I want something from you."

"What's that?"

"Dance for me."

Dance.

Her arrested heartbeat sputtered back to life. The lap dance he'd been asking for since they met, why was that so damn enticing? Then again, her body still thirsted for him. If that would bring her safely to Rob's arms, so be it. Her body pulsed as she forced her fear aside, tucked it far back in the corner of her mind where the dark shadow clung to it tightly, constricting it into submission.

"Fine," she breathed.

"Good," he said as he settled in his chair, like a king on his throne.

Just then, Evie noticed the soft melody of a somber tune playing from the stereo. She recognized it after just a few short chords, knew its lyrics like a prayer. It was one of the songs she played at home. The soft, suffering voice of the vocalist singing about love and death echoed throughout the room accompanied by building percussions, wailing horns, and the haunting strum of a guitar. Searching the room for orientation, her eyes settled on Lucca awaiting her performance with a crooked brow and pursed lips.

"By all means, Evie." He lifted an offering hand in the air. "Proceed."

The pounding drum of blood rushing between her ears threatened to do her in, but she needed him. For some unknown reason, she felt liberated, giving herself to the music. Evie closed her eyes and proceeded to sway side to side in tune with the rhythm.

Her hips rotated in a serpentine motion, seducing the air around her. Snake arms reached up and around for an unseen lover. Her own fingers tickled the surface of her pale skin. Like a charmed cobra, her spine curved, lifting her black silk tunic over her head, spreading her hood. Her body rode the waves of rhythm as she twisted her hips, peeling the skintight layer of denim off of her hips. A roll, a whirl, Evie's body undulated down to thin lines of violet satin and lace against creamy white flesh.

She blocked her surroundings out from her mind. The High Priestess emerged and set her gaze on Lucca, dancing so close she brushed up against him.

He sat forward in his chair, close enough to feel the air pushing off her body as she whirled about him. His tyrant smile stretched its boundaries across his face. He marveled at the warm glow of the fire playing off her skin. The firelight danced over her back and up around her neck, playing off each curve on her body.

A flick of her hips, and her High Priestess twirled her body around with a fluid movement. Twisting at her center, Evie turned her back to him. The intricate black wings across the expanse of her delicate shoulder blades fluttered, creating the illusion that at any moment she could take flight, escape out the window. She lifted her arms up and around the back of her head, scrunching her auburn lock in her hands. Lucca gripped his fingertips into the chaise, holding himself back from chaining her down, clipping her feathers, caging her.

The song ended and another began, as sad and lonesome as the last, and Evie danced. She continued working onto Lucca's lap, straddling him, careful not to graze against the denim-clad prominence reaching up to her. Whisper-thin gaps of air separated his body from hers. Her hips swayed up and down, in and out, riding her invisible lover. Her arms waved up over her head feigning ecstasy, but never giving in. Building up to the moment, Evie cupped Lucca's face, then ran her hands through his dirty blond hair. She lowered her face to his, allowed their breaths to commingle in the air between them, their lips denied the satisfaction of connecting.

Lucca held his hands by his side. His mouth opened enough to breathe her in, to taste her salty sweat. His eyes never released hers from his gaze. He stared with intent, peering deep into her soul. Her intensity strove to match his. The creature occupying the dark shadow in the corner of her mind had devoured her fear. She wanted to kiss him, to feel him inside. How long would this foreplay last? Pure longing took hold. There was little doubt in her mind they were connected in that moment. She felt her body come alive, wings lifting her and sucking her back down to him.

She released a tiny moan. Lucca attacked. He jumped up, clawing at her hips, around to her ass, grasping her with both hands, firm and determined. She clamped down on his mouth in return. Her tongue invaded his body. He reciprocated, biting at her lip. Her hands explored the contours of his back, mapping out the muscular tissue of his shoulder blades bisected by the ridge his spine. His fingers dug into her, hurting her, but arousing her more. Cradling her in his hands, Lucca carried her over to the giant bed, tossed her down, and hovered above her.

Once on the bed, Evie lay back, his body towering over the horizon of her hips. His conqueror's satisfaction spread across his face. His deep, dark eyes pulled her in. Her hand reached out to grab him, pulling at the air to bring him closer to her. His touch softened. His hands, still aggressive, glided over her body. She found him, ran her fingers through his hair, tugged and evoked the faintest groan from him.

"Come down with me, Evie. Fall from your graces into the depths." Lucca placed delicate kisses down the length of her neck. "I know it calls you. I can take you. Let me show you how sweet the darkness can be."

His voice, so soft and so pure, brought tears to her eyes. She wanted more than anything to fall into the dark abyss of his eyes, to occupy the bottomlessness of his inner being. She longed for its nothingness to overwhelm her. She continued to run her hands through his hair, clawing at his scalp, savoring his touch. Her body arched under him.

She felt his secure grip down the length of her back, pulling her up closer to him.

"Come with me, Evie. Come with me," he demanded in a low, vibratory tone.

She released a moan, joy and frustration fighting to speak first. She pulled his mouth to hers. Her tongue reached up into his body, searched and sucked at his very life-force. Her heart pumped and her mind raced. The physical need to feel Lucca under her skin stoked her carnality.

He held her head in his hands. With his eyes closed, he continued to place kisses across her face and along her jaw line. The tip of his nose caressed her skin.

"Come with me," he said in his luscious, soft, melodic whisper. "Tell me to take you."

She taloned his shoulders, hooked into his skin like barbed wire. Her body wriggled under his in anticipation. A primal hunger escaped her body with every breath in a whimpering moan.

"Tell me, Evie."

His demands became more urgent. She felt her senses on the verge of exploding.

His hand roamed across her body, pulling and tugging at her skin with more aggression. His weight on top of her increased, pushing her into the mattress. Neurons flared; her body's natural instinct, alerting her of a much darker intent, darker than her own lustful desires. Images flickered behind her closed eyelids. Red hot flashes of Lucca's eyes burned through her. The memory of his blood-smeared face rising up from between her thighs. Muffled screams from the back of her mind. Hope's frightened reaction with her hands flung up in the air. A deck of tarot cards scattered about. Anxiety flooded the very tips of her capillaries.

Evie's inner voice begged her not to run, too enthralled with the heavy sensation of Lucca's body smothering hers. She recalled the last time she was in his room, the fear, and the threats. Evie's lustful moans distorted into worried pants as she fought her own psyche for escape.

"Tell me, Evie." Lucca's voice grew stern, impatient. "I want to hear you say it."

She blinked. Her surroundings blurred in the fireplace's glow. The muscles in her chest contracted under the tension building within. She dizzied. Her panic intensified, searing from the inside out with each strained breath.

"I can't breathe," she wheezed.

Whatever it was that she felt for Lucca, she couldn't shake the fear bellowing from her core, encouraging her attack. The dark shadow growled from within. Her vision grew hazy. She needed fresh air and escape from the shadow's threat and sudden surge of overwhelming anxiety.

Lucca lifted himself from her body, allowing oxygen to find her lungs. The small consideration was enough for Evie to scramble out from under him, collapsing to all fours on the floor. He snapped back, confused, enraged.

Heart pounding, anxiety seizing her, convincing her that she'd find her death under his body, Evie scrambled to her feet. She dared not look back at him as she scooped up her belongings and bolted for the door. Putting her entire body's weight into her efforts, she managed to yank the latch free.

"Evie!" Lucca roared after her as she made chase down the hallway.

She didn't look back to see if he'd run after her. He hadn't the last time she fled the mansion, and her resolve this time was far firmer. She needed to get away from him. She needed to search within herself for answers before she could face him with confidence.

The Devil had gazed down upon her, and the High Priestess wailed, beat her fists against the walls of Evie's temples, begged the beast to take her down.

THIRTY

Evie's heart thrummed fast and uneven. Tears streamed down her face as she struggled back into her clothing during her retreat. The way she fumbled down the stairs and into her car would have given Lucca, Khan, or anyone else in the house ample opportunity to stop her, but no one came. Safe in her locked car, she looked up to Lucca's bedroom window. He was nowhere to be seen. Whatever had just transpired did nothing to dispel her desires or her fears. She remained in limbo. She cursed at herself for allowing herself to fall into such a confused state. She threw the car in gear and screamed off of the estate.

The tiny confines of her coupe could not contain her screams. She cried wildly as she scanned her mirrors, fearing someone would follow her, track her, hunt her. Her body convulsed in frenzy as her car hurtled down Black Cross Road.

She looked at the clock on her dashboard. Her daring and stupid excursion had cost her well over an hour of futility. She needed to get home. Rob would be there waiting for her. Or worse, she feared, perhaps he'd gone by her house already and left rejected. The thought of Rob leaving her doorstep betrayed and heartbroken made her nauseous.

She pushed her foot down on the gas, and was startled by the icy glare caught in the review. Cold blue eyes glowered. Anxiety pumped her irregular heartbeat.

"He needs to leave," she argued to her reflection.

No, we need him.

She whipped her head back and forth. "There's something dark about him. It's not right. He needs to leave."

Stupid, stupid girl. He is you and you are him.

"Stop it," she cried out. Nothing good could come from loving the Devil, Evie was convinced of that. She wanted Rob. She'd settle for Nate if need be. She wanted to fix the constants in her life. She didn't want to be aroused by her own fears any longer.

The icy blue glare held firm in the rearview.

"He has nothing to do with that fucking card reading. It's all bullshit."

Is it? Stupid girl, you know better.

"No. No, it's not possible."

Why don't you go drink or smoke yourself stupid? Run and hide. You can't deny what he is to us.

"Stop telling me what to do. Leave me alone."

As long as you exist, so shall I.

Evie sobbed her way into town. As she drove by the club, she saw Rob's truck still there. She wondered, was it still parked in the same place it was when she stopped by earlier?

"Fuck, he's still there."

Or he thinks we left him high and dry.

She screeched the tires against the cold asphalt. Her car skidded to a rest alongside his truck. She glared at her reflection, inhaled a deep breath, and wrestled her body's quivers into submission. She wiped away tears from her puffy cheeks, able to address most of her ailments. Not her hands. They trembled. Evie wrapped her arms around her chest, buried them under her armpits to conceal their tremors.

Pull it together, Evie. Pull it the fuck together.

***

When she walked through the front door, the first thing she noticed was the smell. There was an unusual funk in the air. The club's stink of must, sweat, smoke, beer and lust was overpowered by an acidic scent that stung her nostrils. She walked further into the club. The odor increased. It was rank and nauseating. Evie detected a hint of something sweet laced in the air. She looked around, but Rob was nowhere to be found. The stage lighting cast a rainbow glow across the open space.

What is that smell?

Her stomach turned, and anxiety built. She was unable to place the rotting sweetness in the air. She called out a few times for Rob. He didn't answer. The trembling of her hands coursed up her arms and rattled her rib cage.

She checked his office. It was empty. She walked back to the kitchen, expected the odor to increase. She presumed the source to be some bad meat in the freezer. The odor dissipated as she walked further away from the main floor.

Rather than searching for Rob, Evie stuck her nose in the air and fought back the urge to vomit as she traced the scent behind the bar. She walked closer, shaking. Shards of glass scattered about the floor, the bar top, and the shelves. Her eyes bulged from her face in awe and fear. Bottles along the mirrored shelves were missing or shattered.

When she came around the back of the bar, Evie spewed the contents of her stomach. Rob's body lay shredded to pieces in a thick, syrupy pool of his own blood. Splintered bones jutting up into the air and chunks of flesh rendered his geisha tattoo into a tapestry of gore and gristle. Evie found the nerve to call the police before collapsing unconscious to the floor.

***

Sitting on a gurney in the middle of the parking lot, Evie was surrounded by red and blue flashing lights. Sounds were muffled. The back of her head throbbed. She tried to lift a hand to the back of it to inspect the source of the pain, but her arms were so weak, she couldn't lift them above her head.

"She's awake," a voice said. Evie was flanked by two paramedics whom she recognized; Joel, an old flame of Blythe's, and Eddy, who held the distinction of being Evie's first drunken one-nighter.

Joel pulled at her eyelids and shined a bright light at her. Evie winced. Eddy was talking to her, but she didn't understand. The chaos in her mind was too loud. Her eyelids fluttered.

Too loud.

A familiar voice reined in her focus. "Evie? Holy shit, Evie. Are you okay?"

She looked up at Jerry's big, round face, panicked. Jerry *never* panicked. He must have been called in after Evie called the cops. "Evie Westvale. Can you hear me? Evie," he said, yelling. Her eyelids fluttered.

A rush of adrenaline pinged her awake. "It's Rob," she said, crying out in panic. "Oh my God, it's Rob. Is he okay? Jerry, tell me he's okay." She babbled and her heart raced. He helped the paramedics pin down her arms and her legs, now flailing as shock set in.

"Evie, he's gone. He's gone, Evie," Jerry said and held her face in his massive bear paws. Her body shut down. The image of Rob's body in a bloody mess gripped her. She began to hyperventilate. All went black.

***

By the time Evie came to again, the parking lot was lined with yellow tape and a crowd had formed. Her gurney was loaded up into the back of an ambulance to shield her from onlookers. Eddy sat at her side, monitoring her vitals.

"Hey Evie, how are you feeling? We gave you a little something to help calm you." She was grateful for the injection. She couldn't feel the drug coursing through her veins, but the numbing effect was needed. She had a composed and quiet voice now.

"What happened, Eddy?" He turned and grasped her hand.

"Everyone's kind of hoping you could tell us. You were the one who found him."

Her heart wanted to jump from her chest, but the sedative they'd given her kept it in place, thankfully.

"Where's Jerry?"

"He's with the police. Are you ready to talk to them?" he asked, checking her blood pressure and logging her stats on a laptop. She nodded in agreement. There was no use in prolonging the inevitable. "Okay, I'll go get someone."

Eddy left her alone, but her solitude lasted only a minute. Blythe would have scared her to death as she popped her little brunette head around the back of the ambulance had it not been for the drugs.

"Evie, oh my God, are you okay?"

That question was going to get old quick. Evie was surprised to see Evan's face surface from behind Blythe's. His features were shrouded in sorrow.

"What's he doing here?" she asked.

"He's the one that called me to say something happened at the club." Blythe rolled her eyes. "And he insisted on coming."

Even through her sedation, Evie could taste the resentment permeating from Blythe's pores. Evie looked past her to Evan. His determined glare fixated on her. He didn't seem fazed by the anger he caused Blythe.

Evan stumbled as a hand pulled him to the side. Eddy returned with two police officers, one a portly, older gentleman she didn't recognize and the other a taller fellow Evie had waited on more than once at the club. She never caught his name.

"Evie, the police want to ask you a few questions. Do you think you're up to it right now?"

Her heart sank at the thought of retelling what she saw when she walked behind the bar. The sickening sweet tang of rotting flesh—Rob's flesh—lingered in her nostrils. Her stomach churned and her head spun, but nothing came up. She nodded her head.

"Are you sure?" Eddy said. "You can take all the time you need. It's okay, Evie."

She smiled, but more than anything at that moment, Evie wanted to be done with the questions and go home. Before Eddy disappeared beyond her line of sight she called out to him.

"Where is he?" she asked.

He sighed and offered a sympathetic nod. "They took him away already. It's going to be okay, Evie." She nodded back, and the police officers directed Blythe and Evan away in order to conduct their questioning.

The older one stood closest to her. He rattled off questions and jotted down answers. The taller officer stood hunched over, staring at her out of the corner of his periphery. Something about his expression unnerved her.

"What's your name?"

"Evie Westvale."

"Is that your full name?"

"Err, no. Evelyn Westvale."

"Where do you live?"

"One Wayward Lane."

"Date of birth?"

"October nineteenth."

"And what do you do for work?"

Evie paused and teared up. She worked for Rob. She loved her boss, more than most. All that was lost to her now.

"I was a waitress at the club."

"The club?"

"Sirens."

The older chubby officer snickered as he noted that in his paperwork. Evie's expression hardened.

"And what brought you into the club tonight?"

Great. This isn't going to sound good at all. Evie hesitated, a pause not unnoticed by the officer.

"I came here to see Rob."

"Did you have a personal relationship with Mr. Miller?"

"He was my boss."

"Is it normal for you to come see him on your days off?"

"No, I—" Tears streamed down her face, but she maintained a solid tone. "No, Rob and I were close friends. He was supposed to be heading over to my house. When I saw his truck still parked outside the club, I stopped in and found him." She cringed.

"He was supposed to be at your house, why?"

The sedative given to her by the paramedics couldn't hold back the anxiety attack building inside. She remembered the kiss she and Rob shared the last time she saw him—alive. She pictured the image of the geisha on his back, twisted and clawed. Impaled by his broken bones and covered in his blood, her expression a destiny fulfilled. The police officer stared at her, awaiting her response.

Taking in a deep breath, Evie answered. "He was coming to see me. We were close friends."

"How close were you?"

"Rob and I were—we—" Evie fumbled over her words, there was no way to avoid it. "We cared a great deal for each other. He was coming over my house to *be* with me, if you know what I mean." She blurted this out hoping it would quell any further discussion on the topic. The chubby officer seemed to take extra time on this statement in his notebook.

"But you weren't home. You said you were driving by. If you were expecting him at your house, why weren't you there waiting for him?"

The realization hit her; Evie wasn't being treated as a witness, but a suspect. The thought that she could have anything to do with his death made her sick, red with a heavily sedated anger.

"I had to run an errand," she said with a huff and crossed her arms across her chest. There was no way the police officer would bully her into divulging more details about the nature of her errand. And then he asked a question Evie hadn't anticipated.

"Miss Westvale, you have a boyfriend, don't you? A fisherman?"

"Yes. Why?" The question was odd and out of place in her mind. What would Nate have to do with Rob's murder? It took Evie a moment to tie the pieces together.

Nosy little fuckers in this town, they know everyone's business.

"Nate's out on one of the boats right now. You can't think he did this?" The thought was ridiculous. Did Nate and Rob get along? No. Was it because of Evie? Yes. Was Nate capable of murder? Absolutely not.

"Did he know about you and Mr. Miller?"

"There was nothing to know. Everyone in this town knew we were close friends. We weren't having some drawn-out affair, if that's what you're insinuating."

"You know, Miss Westvale, we're not leaving anything to chance these days. You might recall the death of your co-worker from a couple of weeks ago, perhaps," the police officer said.

Evie jerked up on the gurney. "You can't compare Nate to Scotty. Nate didn't—He's not capable of—" Evie broke into tears, unable to describe what she'd seen. What happened to Rob was nothing short of monstrous. No normal person could have done something so heinous.

"Can you think of anyone else who may have had it out for Mr. Miller? Perhaps another friend you were *close* to? Other than your boyfriend that is."

It took all of Evie's nerve not to knock the fat bastard out. His suggestion that she had multiple lovers around town was... well, it was plausible, apparently. The sight of the broken glass, the way Rob's body was mangled, it was apparent he had put up a fight. There was enough evidence to suggest as much. And Rob was so strong. Evie's heart constricted. Whoever did that to him was no normal junkie.

I'm just a very jealous person. I would have ripped the fucker's throat. Lucca's words echoed in her head like a phantom lover whispering in her ear. The vision of the Devil card spun in her mind. Evie tried to maintain a calm demeanor, but inside her inner voice cried out.

Goddammit, it's not possible.

Evie stared wide-eyed at the chubby police officer. She shot a sideways glance to the taller one who turned his head away as their eyes met. There was a curious and apologetic recognition in his subtle movement. He looked off into the distance, shuffled his feet, fidgeted with his radio and excused himself.

***

After exchanging contact information with Evie, the portly cop excused himself and vanished into the flashes of blue and red. She sat a while longer in a state of silent panic. If it was possible that Lucca had something to do with Rob's murder, then how was she to reconcile that with her inner voice, her High Priestess whom she was told to let guide her? How could she trust a voice that would thrust her straight into the arms of a murderer? Not just any murderer, but Rob's murderer. Of course, she tried to convince herself that her paranoia was due to the delusions of a misguided psychic fraudster who had given Evie the heebie-jeebies over a stupid card reading. Hope's theatrics had driven Evie over the edge. As a result she had spent the past couple of weeks in a state of paranoid grandeur. Nothing more.

Nothing more. Keep telling yourself that, Evie.

The paramedics came back over to Evie. After taking her blood pressure one last time and recording a few more stats, they helped her stand on her own two feet behind the vehicle. The simple act of standing proved more difficult than she'd anticipated. Evie felt like she was standing on waves chasing each other across the bay. Her knees buckled and her head spun from the injury she must have sustained when she'd fainted in the club. Blythe hurried over, offering a delicate little shoulder to lean on.

"C'mon. Evan's talking to that cop over there. As soon as they let you go, we're driving you home," she said.

She looked over to Evan as he chatted with the taller officer. They both stared down at the ground between them, inconspicuously holding their conversation in plain sight. Evan glanced over to Evie and her heart dropped. His face was stern, his brow furrowed. She wondered what the cop must have been telling him to make him look over at her like that. It was an unsettling glare.

When Evan approached the girls he made no mention of his conversation with the cop.

"The cops are just checking on a few things and then, with any luck, releasing you," he said, observing the mass of bodies lining the parking lot. "Blythe, why don't you drive Evie's car. Evie you can ride with one of us." Evan's tone was solid and directing.

Evie followed his monitoring glare. Dozens of eyes rested on her, most were faces she knew, some she didn't. They all stared at her, like she had the answers to Rob's murder. The effects of the sedative were waning. Evie wanted to fade away. She wouldn't have to wait long to escape the public's scrutiny, as she saw the taller officer approaching.

"You're free to go, Miss Westvale. I'm sorry for your loss. We caught a lead." His voice was so mild and high pitched in comparison to his portly partner's. She stared back at him in disbelief.

They have a lead?

"Do you mind if I ask who?"

The cop cleared his throat and glanced towards Evan who stood tall with his jaw clenched. The cop paused before responding.

"I can't say much at the moment. But there was a nasty car crash off of Black Cross Road reported not too long ago. A couple of kids from the college just south of here. They had Mr. Miller's ID and wallet in their possession." Evie's pulse quickened as he continued. "The bouncer says the kids had been in recently and had a bit of an altercation with Mr. Miller. Seems pretty clear-cut. They came up to confront him again and things must have gotten out of control. Again, I'm very sorry for your loss."

Four Eyes?

"What happened to them?" Evie asked, dread filling her heart.

"Their car careened off one of the cliffs into the bay. There's very little left of them to identify."

A massive anxiety attack threatened Evie again as she listened to the officer's retelling of the car crash. She tumbled back and was held by Blythe's hand against the small of her back. Evie was incredulous. She knew Lucca had roughed those kids up. She had seen the amount of blood on her clothes. She knew it. Something was very wrong. But how did those kids have Rob's ID on them? She felt a gentle nudge against her elbow. Before following the hand which pulled her away towards the car, Evie shouted out to the police officer.

"The cameras," she said. "Did you check the cameras in the club?"

The cop looked back with sympathetic eyes.

"The cameras weren't functioning properly. Not sure why. I'm very sorry, Miss Westvale." He bowed his head and walked away.

Evie's breathing increased pace. She searched the faces in the crowd once more. This couldn't be happening. This wasn't real. She'd wake up from one of her horrible nightmares and Rob would be at her side. The hand on her arm pulled at her with a hint of urgency. She turned and thrust herself straight into Evan's arms. The tears flowed now, wetting his shirt. She pulled on him, used him to keep her grounded. Evie was afraid if he let go she'd sink into the nothingness. She was terrified.

THIRTY-ONE

Evie could feel Blythe's eyes burning as she chose to ride with Evan in his car over Blythe in her own. She didn't care. Her little outburst back at the club was justified in her eyes. Rob was her friend, her boss, her big brother, and her would-be lover. Evie felt she had every right to fall into Evan's arms as they offered themselves up to comfort her. The current condition of her friendship with Blythe was menial in comparison to her loss.

Therefore, it came as no shock to Evie when Blythe declined to follow her inside the house. "I'm sure you want to be alone," Blythe said and handed Evie her keys.

Evan, however, could not be swayed from walking her safely inside. "Blythe, I'm going to make sure Evie's set. Do you want to wait in my car?" he said. Evie watched Blythe's cheeks redden, her eyes bulge, but Blythe bit her tongue. Evan followed Evie into the house.

***

Once inside, he turned on the lights throughout the first floor and brought her over to the sofa. Evie passed through her home like a ghost.

"Do you think you'll be okay alone?"

Evan held her hands in his and watched her with cautious eyes. Evie stared into their hands clasped together on her knee. His were soft and warm. She didn't want to let go. A tear fell onto her lap.

"I'll be fine," she said with a whimper. Evan at her side wasn't going to help matters. Not with Blythe out in the car stewing in her jealousy. "You should bring Blythe home, anyway."

Her comment about Blythe rolled off Evan's shoulders. He dipped his head down to force Evie's eyes to meet with his.

"I'm not concerned about her at the moment. I won't leave if you don't want me to. She can take my car for all I care. All you need to do is ask, Evie, and I'll stay as long as you need me."

His sympathetic shoulder was welcome, but curious to Evie. He still didn't know her all that well. They'd only interacted a handful of times, just enough to break up his relationship with her best friend. She was grateful for his thoughtfulness, but found his sensitivity displaced. She wanted to ask, but thought better of it. Now was not the time to explore Evan's fascination with her. There were, however, a few things that had captured Evie's interest in him this evening.

"What were you talking to the cop about?" she asked.

"I was asking him when we could take you home."

"You were talking for a while. It looked kind of secretive."

Evan lifted the corner of his mouth in a tiny smirk. "Nothing gets past you, does it, Evie?" he said. "They thought you were involved with the attack. I was persuading him to let me take you home. I was trying to convince him you aren't a suspect. Are you?"

Evie whipped her head up, sitting straight and ripping her hands from his, ready to slap her open palm across his face.

"Are you fucking crazy? Why would you think that?" Pure rage echoed in her voice. She could feel it beam through her crystal blue eyes. Evan threw his hands up.

"I'm sorry, Evie. I didn't mean it like that."

"Did you know about those kids?"

"The college kids? Not until he told me."

"Were those the same guys from the party? The ones who slipped me something? Jerry told the cops about what happened with them at the club last week. They think they did it."

"Well, they found his ID on them. What else could have happened?"

"I don't know. Maybe someone you know who has his own... *penchants*, we'll call them. Someone who may be staying at your house, *charmed by my beauty*. Is that how you described him?" she hissed at him.

Evan's eyes grew wide.

"You think Lucca did this?"

"Well, there was a lot of blood on my clothes. You said so yourself, you couldn't clean it off my shirt. I know something happened that night that no one is telling me. I know you know, Evan. Did Lucca do this to Rob? Are you covering for him?"

Evan sat back, collecting himself. He stared, studying her. She watched as his features twisted into something more pensive, hardened.

"Evie, you're hurt. You're scared, and you've been through an immense ordeal tonight," he said in a calm voice. "I get that you think you saw things—" Evie opened her mouth to cut him off, but he shot a finger up over her mouth to silence her before continuing. "I get it, okay. It's no secret I don't like Lucca. And yes, he has a bizarre

292

fascination with you, but he is not a murderer. Understood?"

The finality in his words kept Evie quiet. She looked down into her lap again. Tears continued to dampen her clothes. Evan wrapped an arm around her shoulder and pulled her into his chest, resting his chin on the crown of her head.

"It's so easy to point a paranoid and judgmental finger at times like these, Evie. But let's be grateful that karma found her retribution. Those boys got what they deserved for what they tried to do to you. Take that as a tiny piece of closure and let yourself heal."

His words passed through her ears like the soft whispers of a lover. Her body shook fervently. Evie squeezed the fabric of his shirt tight around his waist, wringing it free of every last drop of truth. She wanted to believe him. Those boys died a horrible death. Did they repent in those precious few seconds as their car plummeted to the jagged rocks below the water's surface? She forced the image of Rob's shredded body out of her mind and conjured the contorted image of their broken bodies mangled in the surf. A tiny piece of closure, something to give her peace, she'd languish in that image as long as she could. With a mucus-lined whimper, Evie pushed herself off Evan's chest. She sat up with a strained smile across her face.

"Thanks, Evan."

"Can I check on you later, at least?"

Evie thought for a moment as to whether or not that was a good idea. Blythe was already fuming outside in his car, but the thought of being alone for any great length of time swayed her.

"Sure," she said with sore eyes.

Evan smiled. "I'd offer to leave you something, but that sedative is still doing its work on you. I don't think you should take anything. Okay?"

Evie laughed under her breath. She didn't feel any of the effects of the sedative anymore. Her whole body ached. Her heart felt as though it had imploded. She needed to be numb. The look on Evan's face was enough to tell her that he had no intentions of leaving her any pot. She'd have to find something else once he'd left.

She nodded her head and stood to escort Evan to the door. As he walked through the front porch and stood in the open doorway, Evie felt Blythe's incinerating glare from the passenger seat. She looked at her out of the corner of her eye. Blythe's evil eye didn't stop Evan from turning back to Evie to place a soft kiss on her forehead. Her skin seared where his soft lips made contact. He shook her hand, pulling at it as he walked away. His sad eyes fixed on Evan as he opened the car door and lowered himself into the driver's seat. The car roared to life and crept down the dimly lit street.

***

Evie turned back into the house and stood in the silence. Leaning up against the front door, she sobbed without restraint.

She'd wished she'd asked Evan to stay. She'd wished Nate were back from his fishing excursion. She'd wished Blythe would have come inside and scolded her for no good reason. She didn't want to be alone. Her hands trembled. More than anything, Evie wished she was holding Rob in her arms.

"What am I supposed to do?" she blubbered between the swelling of tears rounding over the crest of her cheek bone.

Damn, I need a drink.

Evie pushed off the door, stalked through the living room and into the kitchen, but there was no alcohol left in the fridge or on the counter. She slammed the fridge door shut and cursed at it. She flipped the cupboards open and slammed each door shut, finding no release. Her pulse quickened.

She thought of going out to the package store to buy a bottle of whiskey, but the thought of leaving her solitude petrified her more than being alone in her house sober. She remembered the glass pipe in her living room and the green nugget Evan had given her. She scurried to the living room, but the pot was nowhere to be seen. Did Evan take it? Could he have taken back the little cellophane-wrapped nugget without her noticing? Did she smoke it already?

Damn him. Damn Evan. Damn it all.

She stood in the middle of her living room confused, furious, and longing for a hit of anything that would subdue the pain. She spun around looking for the tiny emerald. She tossed seat cushions over, knocking a lamp off the end table in the process. Evie threw pillows in the air as a primal growl built up and released itself from her throat, scratching her from the inside out along the way.

She stopped. Panting, Evie looked up at the series of family photographs lined along her mantle. She looked at the picture of her mother holding her as a baby. Her mother was no more than sixteen in the picture and looked like a child. A child with a worn face, Evie thought. She scanned through the pictures, stopping at a picture of her with her grandmother at her high school graduation. That was right around the time her grandmother died. Evie could recognize the sickness in her grandmother's eyes, even through her proud smile. She shrank at the sight of it. She glanced over to the face of her namesake, the original inhabitant of the house, Evelyn, who was murdered there. The murder, more than ever, resonated through her mind. She looked at the woman's eyes in the photograph. They echoed her own as Evelyn glared back. It was like the ghostly image in the mirror. Evie hated her for it.

"Enough fucking death," Evie screamed at the top of her lungs and whipped the Evelyn's photograph across the room, shattering it against the hard wood floor at the bottom of the stairs. Her body folded into itself, left her cowering in a ball against the hearth.

She wanted to race down to the waterfront, to jump into the darkness of the water and wash away. She craved the sweet release of the murky depths suffocating her. She needed the feel of the water dissolving her, breaking her apart into her most basic elements. Evie allowed herself the moment to collapse inward. She stood wiping tears and mucus off her face with the bottom of her shirt. Bells chimed; the safest place for her was upstairs in the solace of her bath tub, with the hot steamy water enveloping her. With any luck, drowning her. As she walked over towards the bottom of the stairs, an object caught her eye.

The old picture frame that held the image of Evelyn had shattered. In doing so, it ejected the flimsy paper photograph across the hard wood floor. She paused, staring at the piece of parchment. The photograph was folded, not crumpled, like it was originally too big for the tiny frame. Leaning over to pick up the creased photograph, Evie found the photo of Evelyn was a snapshot of multiple individuals. Evelyn stood in the forefront, a soft and demure figure. The photo was folded at each end into a triptych. Evie had never paid attention to the background of the photo, but it appeared to be a family portrait, or rather a portrait of the family's fishing crew. The captain stood to Evelyn's side, recognizable as the woman's father. A few other crew members scattered around them in the background. Evie felt acidic bile lurch its way up her throat. She saw him off to the right. The same long and lean build, broad shoulders and long wispy hair, perfect. His sharp angular jaw line hid the hint of a smile, the same crooked grin that made her inner voice swoon. The crew member in the background, the one watching Evelyn from behind, was Lucca.

"Fuck!" Evie shrieked, tossing the photo across the floor like a contagion threatening to spread its fatal disease. Millions of invisible spiders skittered over her skin. Her stomach flipped upside down as she rubbed her fingers against her shirt to wipe away the picture's taint. The sedative given to her by the paramedics had been cried out of her bloodstream, no longer holding her anxiety at bay.

She watched the inanimate photograph laying on the floor, terrified to see Lucca jump from the image towards her. Clocks stopped as she waited for her pulse to even and her breathing to regulate, but still she watched the photo.

Following her recoil, she crept closer to the picture and picked it up a second time. Studied it hard. It was Lucca. Not just a likeness, like Evelyn was to Evie. It was him. It was his body. He could have posed for the photo yesterday and he would look the same. His dirty blond hair hung low to his shoulder. His hip was cocked to the side, just as he stood in front of her in his bedroom. His tongue traced the inside of his teeth through the beautiful grin he wore when he saw her. And he looked at Evelyn the same way he looked at Evie—hungrily.

Evie's heartbeat pounded against the cage of her chest. Complete fright engulfed her body. Her breathing burned and tears welled up in her eyes. How could it be? Who was Lucca, and who was the image in the photograph? Where the hell did the photograph come from? She turned and looked at the fireplace mantle, like it had betrayed her. She spun back around to look at the photograph in her hand. She carried it with her up the stairs, examining it, certain she'd find some feature that would differentiate the man in the photo from Lucca, himself.

THIRTY-TWO

The image of the man behind Evelyn burned into her retinas like a sunspot; she could see his outline as she stepped into the darkness of the second floor landing at the top of the stairs. Making her familiar path into the bathroom, she flooded her mind's eye with the bright light illuminating the pristine white tile room. She maintained her sights on the image. She drew a bath, twisting the faucet handle and filling the room with steam.

Evie paced out into her bedroom and fixed the photo on her nightstand. A soft light cast on it through the bathroom doorway. Stripping out of her clothes, she turned to face herself into the mirror. The ghostly image mocked her.

He comes. And to resist him is futile. He will bring the change you need.

Evie hated herself, hated what stared back at her in the mirror. Her inner voice proved to be a deceitful bitch. She wanted to gouge her crystal blue eyes out. She glowered into the mirror as Hope's words repeated over and over in her head. The sound of the old woman's voice grew louder and louder. She grabbed at her ears, clawed at her scalp, but the voice wouldn't stop.

He comes. And to resist him is futile. He will bring the change you need.

She stormed into her bedroom and cranked the stereo in order to drown out the voices. They wouldn't relent. They cried louder between her ears.

He comes. And to resist him is futile. He will bring the change you need.

She ran back in front of the mirror and shrieked. "Stop it!"

The voices stopped. Huffing and puffing, she stood naked before the mirror listening to the guitar and the singer's voice, but not her own. Her inner being stared back at her, noiseless from beyond the glassy surface of the mirror. Her tears subsided and she was left feeling numb, but not in the way she wanted, not how she needed. Out of the corner of the mirror's reflection, she saw the sweet amber reflection of a bottle. She turned and her eyes danced at the sight of the bottle of whiskey she'd found and placed near the tub's claw foot for safekeeping.

Thank fucking God.

***

She lowered herself into the scalding hot water, grateful for its burn and more grateful for the burn she'd feel down her throat as soon as her body allowed her to rest in the steam. Her stomach flipped as it passed down below the surface of the hot bath water. Her heart raced. She was settled and could reach out to the bottle. Evie licked her lips in anticipation. Sweat beaded on her brow.

She was about to take a large swig from the bottle when she paused. The anticipation on her face vanished, replaced by a sorrowful frown. Rob's sweet face flashed in her mind. Memories of him tending to her, night after night, shot after shot. He always knew what she needed. At the moment, she needed this whiskey, but Rob would never pour her a shot ever again.

Heartbroken by the thought, with a shrill cry, Evie chucked the bottle of whiskey across the room.

It burst against the wall, shattering in a sticky mess across the floor. She pulled her knees up to her chest and hugged them, rocking back and forth in the tub. Water crashed against the walls and splashed onto the floor. She tried to bury her face in her knees and cry, but the tears wouldn't come. She'd used up her reserve of emotions and sat suspended in her bath. Agony spider-webbed across her face as her body pulsed with hopelessness. In two weeks' time her life had capsized and she'd lost one of the true loves of her life. All because she met him. She was drowning.

He comes. And to resist him is futile. He will bring the change you need. He is you and you are him.

As if conjured up from her very thoughts, Evie became aware of a presence in the room. She didn't flinch. She didn't react. Her body continued to quiver as she shifted her gaze through the corner of her eyes' sights to see Lucca staring down at her. His dark eyes glowed with excitement.

***

With no words exchanged, Evie and Lucca stared. His exuberance gleamed against the white porcelain while Evie struggled to hold her gaze to his. The only sound was the wailing lovesick singer that serenaded her night after night.

"What are you?"

Lucca shook his head with a smirk. "It's not what I am, Evie. It's what I'm not. And what I'm not, is like you are now. What I'm not, is patient. And what I'm not, is playing games anymore."

"You're a jealous person."

"Yes," he said with a hiss.

"Did you kill Rob?" Her voice cracked under the pressure of being incapable of creating a single additional teardrop.

"Yes." His eyes gleamed.

"Why?"

She buried her face in her hands, unwilling to accept his affirmation. Her body shook as her chest threatened to snap in two. Through her hate, she was still enraptured by Lucca's beauty. Terrified by his monstrosities, she was overwhelmed by his being. Her fists clenched tight with white knuckles as the tempest raged inside her. Her head felt as though it were about to burst.

"Shh," Lucca knelt down beside the bathtub. He traced his fingertips along the water's surface.

Evie lashed out and tossed her hands up in the air to fend off his advance. With very little effort, Lucca restrained her in one hand's grip while water spilled onto the floor. She winced in pain from the force around her wrists.

"You said yourself, Evie. I'm a jealous person. And he would try to stop you from coming to me. It had to be done." Lucca spoke through gritted teeth.

You won't see the good in your sacrifice, but you must understand, it is all for you.

The levees burst. Evie cried violently. Her tears poured down over her knees, down her legs and mixed with the frothy suds in the bathwater. She continued to flinch in fear as he came closer and closer to her. She couldn't bring herself to look at his beautiful face. To lock her eyes with him meant abandoning all control. She feared her own inclinations almost more than she feared him. She was arrested in a catatonic state. Her hate for him burned so deep from within her core that it took all her control not to tear through her own flesh for escape.

"I haven't been to Fallhaven in over a century. Imagine my surprise and delight as I returned to find you right where I left you, like you were born again for my return. How can I leave you a second time?"

Her heart pounded, rushing the blood through her body and pounding between her ears like a tympani. She felt her face flush as a chill sent shivers down her spine. The old photo of her namesake flashed in her head. She saw him standing by Evelyn's side. It was him, not his likeness. And though inconceivable, Evie knew it to be true. Somehow the man in that photograph and Lucca were the same person. The presumption of Lucca as some immortal being was too much to bear. Her body was wracked with its own efforts to combat the urge to hyperventilate.

With his free hand, Lucca stopped playing with the water. He took a loofa off the bath tray, soaked it, and wrung it out on her shoulder. He dragged the loofa across the nape of her neck and down her back. Her quivering body, unwilling to relent, found the soothing water a formidable foe. She fought back.

"Fuck you," she said and tried to pull away from him. Lucca paid no attention to her request and held her in place.

"Evie, my patience has worn thin, along with the welcome from both Evan and his uncle." He spoke with authority now. "I've learned from my past mistakes. I have no intentions of killing you, but I will *not* leave this town a second time empty-handed."

Evie turned to look at him with a contemptuous glare. "What are you talking about?"

His menacing sneer widened. "Your eyes—your beautiful crystal blue eyes are so much brighter now. You're an improved, refined version of her, you must know that."

"Who?"

"Your namesake, of course. Evelyn. We are destined for each other. She feared it. You realize it, as I do. She was beautiful, but you, Evie, you are radiant by comparison." He continued pouring the steaming bathwater over her, soaked her head, caused it to tilt back revealing the full length of her alabaster neck.

The thought of him being something greater than she imagined, something more than human stirred a curiosity inside her. It quelled her anger for the moment. While it pained her, she forced the images of Rob to the back of her mind. The need to confront the creature in front of her overwhelmed. The unknown was far too enthralling not to take precedence above all other thoughts and emotions inside.

She searched in Lucca's eyes, with the loose hope of extracting any truth from inside their dark irises. Her head rested on her knees as she remained curled up in a ball, safe under the water.

"Did you kill her, too?" Her stomach dropped as she realized what she had asked. She flushed again.

"Yes," Lucca said with satisfaction.

Evie gave herself a moment to process his answer. She had so many questions. In silent acknowledgement, Lucca put the sponge down. He used his own hands to rub her back. Her skin crawled from his touch. She wanted to scream from the inside out, but found her inner voice controlled her actions. Her body was left motionless and dumbfounded.

"I have spent my entire existence searching for you. You've rejected me in the past, unwilling to accept our truth. I won't let that happen again." Lucca rubbed her back. His touch hardened and his face contorted as he continued. "I see now that Evelyn was not prepared for what we share. But you are, Evie. You've been searching for it. I can see it in your eyes and I can feel it in your reaction to my touch."

Lucca paused. His eyes burned red. He removed his hands from her back. She watched as his mad stare trailed off into a deep pool of fury. She wanted to reach out and touch his face. Too afraid of his reaction, she remained still. After a moment of silence, broken from his own trance, Lucca continued, his gaze unsoftening.

"There will be no anger, Evie. I will not kill you, but I will not leave without you."

He stopped and she knew the words he had spoken to be true. She needn't hear the rest. Her fate came full circle. Before Lucca, she was uncomfortable, unaware of her purpose. Here now, with him, this is where she belonged, with him. *He is you and you are him. It is inevitable.* The Devil card danced in her mind's eye and her inner voice cooed.

"Are you going to hurt me?" she asked in a strained voice, broken from her recent tirade against his touch, skating along the thin line of her nerves.

"Yes…" he said, sneering. "And no."

Without a word, Lucca stood, keeping his eyes locked with hers. She remained in her safe little ball under the bath's warm soap-clouded waters. Lucca lifted his shirt over his head. Effortlessly, he kicked off his boots and unzipped his grimy jeans. He lowered them to the floor, stepping out and revealing his perfect naked body.

Teased by the opportunity to regard his body in all its glory, Evie kept her gaze locked with his as he lowered himself into the bathtub behind her. She flailed, a prioress protecting her temple of solace from a savage nonbeliever. Again, Lucca deflected her attempts with ease as he straddled her from behind, restraining her with his entire body.

With the sanctity of her bathtub compromised for the first time, uncertain of what was about to transpire, and just as she did with his private dance, Evie grabbed hold of her nerve and gave in to her surroundings, to Lucca himself. He continued washing her, cupping water in his hands and pouring it down her back, his hands chasing the water down her skin. As his hands found her hips, he traced them down along the sides of her thighs. His fingertips sent shockwaves through her body. Her knees loosened and her legs sprawled out against the length of his.

With his left hand, he roamed down Evie's outer thigh. Using his right hand to navigate its way up the side of her torso, Lucca traced the outline of her breast, across her collar bone, and up her neck to her jaw. He coaxed her head to the side so that his own face was inches from hers. He leaned in, touching his lips to hers and split her lips apart with his tongue. Her tongue met the interloper and entwined it.

Lucca paused. He lifted his lip from over his elongated canine. Its sharp point dragged along her tongue. It tore through her taste buds through the outer layer of muscle. A line of crimson blossomed forth. And then he sucked, devouring her mouth. Evie didn't notice the pain or the metallic taste filling her mouth. While Lucca drank in her flavor, his left hand found its way between her legs. In and out—In and out. He was under her skin. Lucca massaged her insides, sent a rush of warm blood through her entire body, overpowering the pain inside her mouth.

He kissed her, pumping his fist between her legs, drinking in the sweet coppery fluid trickling off her tongue. His right hand groped her body, hungering for her, taking her in at every angle. Evie's back arched back in rapture as her body arrested. She moaned and broke free from Lucca's kiss to cry out loud.

Lucca pulled his fist out from between her legs to embrace her body in both arms. He lifted her from the tub. In one fluid motion he had her aloft in his arms, splashing the tub's contents across the bathroom floor. Lucca and Evie, having finally found each other, lapped at each other's face, competing to consume the other first.

They fumbled their way to the bedroom. Lucca tossed her across the bed. She landed on her back, and propping herself up at her elbows watched as his statuesque body descended upon her. She lay back and closed her eyes, willing to accept whatever fate Lucca saw fit to administer in that moment. He leaned over her, rubbing the length of himself along the tender structure between her hip bones, taunting her with the threat of his invasion. His devilish grin was the last image burned into her mind before hearing the front door slam shut.

THIRTY-THREE

"Evie." A low and gruff voice she recognized rumbled out from down stairs.

"Shit, it's Nate," she said in horror. Climbing out from under Lucca, Evie scurried to the closest article of clothing near her, Nate's green plaid shirt. The massive thud of Nate's footsteps reached the top of the stairs. Unenthused, Lucca turned into the bathroom to slip on his jeans. By the time Nate burst through the bedroom doorway, he found Evie standing frozen in shock near the bed and Lucca zipping up his jeans. His body seized with disbelief. Rage flooded his face, eyes ablaze with anger and teeth grinding to dust.

"Nate, wait, let me explain," she pleaded, and rushed towards him, barring him in the threshold. Lucca pushed his hair up away from his face and shrugged, not allowing Nate to shake his demeanor.

"Let you explain?" Nate barked. "I think it's pretty fucking clear what's going on."

His eyes ricocheted about the room. The bed looked untouched. Evie's hair was soaked, as was Lucca's. A small line of water trailed across the floor leading to the bathroom, where Lucca's boots and t-shirt lay in a pool of water and broken glass. In anger and jealousy, Nate looked towards Evie, a look which made her fear for her life.

"You better watch what you drink, little girl," Nate said in a low growl, pointing a massive digit in her face.

Fuming and defensive, she shouted back. "I'm not drunk, Nate. I wasn't drinking."

"Are you fucking high?"

"What? No."

"The goddamn Coast Guard brought me back in fucking handcuffs. They were one step away with charging me with Rob's murder. I was worried sick about you. In the meantime, you're here fucking this son of a bitch? If you're not drunk or high, what the fuck is wrong with you?"

"I didn't fuck him," she said. "Don't you dare throw Rob's death in my face. You weren't there. You didn't see." She paused to catch her breath before she passed out. "And I'll fuck who I want when I want, thank you very much."

Without hesitation, Nate wound up a backhand with every intention of cracking the side of Evie's face. She flinched, anticipating the blow. Lucca jumped forward, catching him by the wrist with one hand and slamming him against the bedroom wall with the other. Faded wallpaper and horsehair plaster crumbled around him from the impact. The animalistic rumble which bellowed from the pit of Lucca's core froze Nate in fear. He glared wide-eyed. The two men snarled inches from each other. Evie jumped back, and in an effort of self-preservation, cowered behind the bed.

"I wasn't feeling like a threesome tonight," Lucca said, taunting with a controlled tone.

"Fuck you." Nate spat in Lucca's face.

Both men braced each other at their shoulders as Lucca spun Nate around and tossed his massive body across the bed. The impact collapsed the frail antique frame, the box spring and mattress crashing to the floor. Evie shrieked and scurried behind the recliner.

Nate sprung up and lunged for Lucca, throwing his shoulders down to tackle him to the ground. He caught Lucca in the gut, knocking the wind out of him. Lucca stumbled backwards, but held his footing. He lashed back with a stone fist crashing into Nate's ear. Nate howled from the deafening impact.

Bodies flipped. The men growled, trading blow for blow. Nate connected with a right hook to Lucca's temple, stunning him a moment, just enough to pull Lucca into a chokehold.

Lucca wriggled free with a hammer blow to Nate's groin and a heel to his kneecap. Nate doubled over, roaring in pain. Lucca lunged, grabbed the back of Nate's head, and slammed it down to his rising knee. Nate's eyes rolled to the back of his head as his body slumped backwards, defeated.

Seething as he regained his composure, Lucca was on Nate. He hooked the crook of his elbow around the grizzly's neck, squeezing, cranking his head back. Lucca hissed and bared his sharp teeth ready to lock in on his reluctant prey.

"No!" Evie jumped out from behind the chair towards Nate, onto Lucca's back. He jostled her off with a turn of his shoulder, sending Evie tumbling to the floor near Nate. She scrambled to her hands and knees, swooping in between Lucca's face and Nate's exposed neck.

"Lucca, stop, please," she pleaded as tears poured down her face. He looked into her eyes, pure crystal blue. "Please," she said, begging once more, letting all her energy carry the word from her body. She'd seen more than enough blood for a lifetime. She couldn't bear to lose the one person left in her life that could possibly love her.

Releasing him, Lucca stood and looked down at his fallen foe. He said nothing, and then turned away with a disgusted sneer. Evie looked down to evaluate Nate's injuries. His face was a broken and bloodied mess, a haunting memory of the horror she saw at Sirens not so long ago. Her heartbeat raced arrhythmically. She couldn't lose Nate too, and sobbed as he struggled to maintain consciousness.

"Nate, please leave," Evie said. "Please."

Lucca remained still, glaring through dark and guileless pools at his opponent. Nate fumbled, but managed to lift his body off the floor, using Evie as a rickety crutch.

"I'm not leaving you with this piece of shit," he growled, spitting a wad of blood to the floor, and glowered at Lucca, ready for round two.

Anger burned inside Evie. *No more death*, she fumed.

"Get out," she snarled. "Both of you, get the fuck out."

It obviously pained him to do so, but Nate stood his full height, puffing out his chest and standing his ground. "I'm *not* leaving you with him."

"Nate, it's over. I want both of you out," she shouted and stepped a fair distance from both men. The three stood, tense, defensive, all unwilling to surrender. As Evie's eyes connected with Nate's she wordlessly begged him once more to leave. She lifted her arm straight out to direct him to the stairs.

His glared back, defiant, and shook his head, but Evie wasn't backing down. Nate wiped a ribbon of crimson running down the side of his face into his beard and scowled at Lucca. "I see how it is. Five fucking years, and this is how you want to end it?" Nate's nostrils flared.

"Yeah, it's over." He pointed into Lucca's face. "You're a dead motherfucker."

"Nate wait," Evie reached out for him, but he threw his arm up to deflect her advance and, with a low growl, headed down the stairs.

She turned to Lucca, incredulous. He snickered at Nate's threat. His snicker morphed into a cocky smile. Evie's heart burned.

"I don't know who the fuck you think you are, but you need to get the fuck out of here before I call the cops." She pointed towards the door.

"I've not thought to give you much choice in the matter," Lucca said and stepped closer to her.

"You're a fucking murderer," she said. Her voice cracked, and tears welled up in her eyes.

"Come with me, Evie. Come feel the nothingness. You'll understand once you feel it."

"You're a fucking psycho, get away from me."

She lashed her fingernails at him, swiping him away, frantic and afraid. A footstep back, and Evie was cornered by the toppled-over bed frame. Lucca wrapped himself around her. It didn't take long for her exhausted body to collapse in his embrace.

"Please," she whimpered. Her head lulled back in defeat.

"You realize I've made up my mind. There is no choice here to be made, Evie. I will have you. Make no mistake, you are mine. I've tasted you. I will *never* give you up."

"Please," She begged once more, looking around to the shattered glass and broken furniture. Out of the shadows and debris, a sinewy figure crept forward.

"Just like I said—" Mae scoffed. Lucca's smile soured at the sight of her and Evie found herself again frozen in fear.

"Yet another unwelcome guest," he growled.

Evie remembered the rage in Mae's eyes at the party. She felt their burn on her once more.

She stood watching the two predators size each other up, inhuman sounds rumbling from each like territorial animals. The moonlight glinted off the pair's matching pearlescent smiles.

"Poor Lucca," Mae teased with a sarcastic frown. "He can't hurt the wittle girl. Wouldn't want to scar that pretty wittle neck."

Mae slithered her way past Lucca towards Evie. She circled around her, looming over Evie by a full foot. Lucca declined to protest her stalking movements.

"Did he fuck you?" she cooed, placing extra emphasis on the crisp tail of the expletive. Mae dismissed the notion, however, as Evie's eyes shifted down to the floor. "No, of course not. Pity; he has a great cock, you know," she said, "I mean, I've had a lot of men in my day, but Lucca is—he's just so—perfect. Isn't he?" She giggled and shook her lower half like it was a key shimmying into a lock. Evie wanted to punch the smirk right off the bitch's face, but considered that if she were anything like Lucca, she could probably snap Evie in half.

"Do you know what he loves?" Mae whispered, breathing hot against the back of Evie's ear. She gripped hard against Evie's hipbones and thrust her bony frame up against Evie's backside. Evie stifled a yelp from Mae's force. "He loves to watch. I'm sure you were aware that he's been watching you these last couple of weeks."

313

Evie looked over towards Lucca. In the pale light of night, she made out the shadowy silhouette, the shadow she'd caught watching her. Dread pulsed from the pit of her core through her body. Frothy bile surfaced in the back of her blood-tinged mouth. She forced it back down.

"Would you like to watch us, Lucca?" Mae posed the question to him but her gaze remained fixed on Evie, running her fingernails up and down the length of her arms. Lucca's smile faded to a scowl, a low gruff growl building up inside him. "You could watch us, the same as you did with her little friend. What was her name? Natalia?"

Evie twitched and turned to gape wide-eyed back at Mae. Then she turned to Lucca with disbelief and pain.

"What did you do to Natalie?"

"We bled that bitch from top to bottom. And in the end—in the end it's always me and Lucca enraptured in the blood. It's beautiful."

Evie's stomach turned. The bile returned and refused to sink back down to her acid-churned stomach. She doubled over, hugging her body tight. Mae cackled. Lucca lashed out with a firm backhand. The force sent Mae spinning down to the ground.

"Too far, Mae," he warned. "I told you, Evie is mine."

This was her fate, Evie realized, disbelieving. This was her purpose for being born, just to die another meaningless victim, another of God-knows-how-many at the hands of this man, this creature. Lucca's ruthlessness dispelled the allure which for so long clouded her judgment. Rob's smiling face crept out from the back of her mind. She spit bilious phlegm on the floor and shuddered.

"I thought she should know her place," Mae said.

"I think it is you who should learn your place, whore," Lucca snarled. "How many times have I warned you not to overstep your boundaries? You are not *her*. You will never possess her essence. I tolerated you for Khan's amusement. Nothing more. And he's not here to protect you now, is he?"

Mae hissed back at him. Without hesitation and in one fell swoop, Lucca lunged. With both hands, he grabbed a firm hold on Mae's neck and snapped it to one side, disconnecting the wires in her spinal cord. Mae's expression froze in death. Her body slumped to the floor. Either unaware of the damage he'd inflicted, or simply unsatisfied with it, Lucca leaned down and gnashed at her throat. Evie heard the loud crunching of bone and the tearing of flesh as she saw his teeth lacquered red in the moonlight. Blood cascaded forward as he tossed the girl's body to the floor. He spat Mae's own gore back in her face.

Evie screamed in fear. She flinched and covered her mouth. Her anger had been replaced by terror. Too much had been witnessed, too much had been revealed; he would surely kill her now. Lucca leaned down to Evie. She trembled on the floor at his feet. He lifted her into his arms. In a desperate act of self-preservation, Evie tried to fight back. No matter the hate, no matter the adrenaline pumping through her body, she was too weak to raise a hand to him.

"No, God no, please," she said, crying. Lucca pinned her arms down against her midsection with a quick thrust. He nearly snapped her body in half.

"I told you, God has nothing to do with this."

He jolted her to face him. Evie shrieked at the gore smeared all over his face. It was stuck between his teeth and dripped off the tip of his chin.

"Please don't do this," she begged with what little breath she had to let out. "Please, I can't." Her body deflated.

Lucca looked down on her. His eyes shifted over to Mae's lifeless body soaked in her own viscera. With a huff of annoyance, he loosened his hold on Evie.

"Make no mistake. Our time will come, and I will have you" He paused, irritated. "But not like this, not with her taint everywhere. When the time comes you will taste me—*only* me."

Tremors ran through her body as he released her. Lucca ran his hands through his filth-smeared hair, lifting it away from his bloodied face. He turned. His naked back shone in the moonlight as he walked away.

"Lucca." Her inner voice urged her to call out to him. He turned in acknowledgment, didn't answer at first, but just smiled.

"You'll see. You'll come to me. We were meant for each other, Evie. I know you can feel it. We will have our time."

Lucca turned down the stairs and out the front door. Evie raced to her bedroom window and watched him walk down the street concealed by the night's darkness.

The Devil comes. To resist him is futile. He will bring the change you need. It is inevitable.

Alone, Evie's knees buckled and she found herself lying among the wreck of her room in the fetal position. Her tears would not abandon her now. The events of the last two weeks raced through her mind. She feared him. She desired him. She loathed him. She needed him. After the atrocities displayed before her, the image of Rob's body soaked in his own blood, the thought of Lucca in the throes of passion with Mae, the two of them feasting upon Natalie as she died, and the inexplicable concept that he was more than human, Evie's body collapsed. She fell, deep into her own nothingness. Feelings of love and hate, passion and desire, fear and horror dizzied her. She cried dry tears until the sun rose over the water out in the harbor, at which point exhaustion took hold and sleep claimed her body.

THIRTY-FOUR

Evie awoke to find Evan sweeping up broken glass. The blood had been washed away. Mae's broken body was gone, and Evan was there. He had propped Evie up in her cushy rocker-recliner, cradled in its arms and covered with an old afghan made by her grandmother. Even Lucca's boots and t-shirt had been neatly folded on the floor near the bathroom doorway.

She exchanged curious eye contact with him before he left her to herself. Clinging to the fringes of the afghan, Evie sat and stared, unable to muster sound from her dry throat. The events of the prior evening spooled up in her mind's eye like a grindhouse horror flick. The sweet and sour pain of Lucca's fang ripping into her lingered on her throbbing tongue.

***

Once she'd dressed and the pounding in her chest subsided, she followed the sounds of Evan's bustling downstairs to the kitchen. Evan had coffee and juice laid out for her. Drifting through her living room, her house felt foreign to her now. Evie noticed he also cleaned up the mess she made searching for her tiny package of weed. He sat at the kitchen table, stoic. Evie sat across from him. She had a million questions, all seeming too vague and inconsequential, but all so very important. She had no clue where to begin.

"Were you part of this?"

He stared back at her. A tortured gaze etched his face, one so pained that Evie knew he played some part, however small. And he was unwilling to admit it.

"I'm sorry, Evie," he said. "I owe you an explanation."

"You owe me a lot more than that," she said, lashing back. The simplicity of his words was insulting. "You owe me Rob."

Evan bowed his head with a heavy sigh. Evie forced herself back down to her seat. She clutched onto her scalding hot coffee mug to displace the pain.

"Will you let me explain before you start yelling at me?"

Evan's voice was remorseful. He stared into the space between them.

Explain? How will that bring Rob back?

Evie's lower lip quivered. His ridiculousness continued to insult her. How was she expected to sit quietly long enough to allow someone to explain how and why a man she loved had been killed? The anguish in Evan's expression pulled at the one tiny piece of her heart left to feel anything. Much to her inner voice's chiding, she allowed him the one little courtesy.

"Can I have a drink first?" she asked, staring into her cup but not wanting caffeine. The quivering at her bottom lip spread in waves down her body and settled into her hands.

"No." Evan frowned before opening his hands. He produced a rolled joint, lit it and passed it her way after taking the first long toke. "You don't need a drink. There's nothing left in the house anyway."

Evie scowled at his authority. She wanted to be numb, needed to be numb to tolerate Evan's explanation. She snatched the lit joint from him. It was sweet, tangy, and potent enough to send a rush of sedated relief down her body. She let the smoke roll across her wounded tongue.

"We're not like you, Evie," he said.

"Yeah, no shit," she scoffed. Evan shot her a warning glare, so she continued to suck at the tip of the joint.

"I said let me explain. I—Lucca and Khan and me, we're not like you or anyone you've ever known. We're not human. Not anymore."

As he paused, Evie passed the joint back to him. He seemed glad to relieve his own anxieties. For whatever reason, she detected a hint of embarrassment from him, as though it pained him to talk about this.

"What are you?" She sipped her coffee.

"Well, for one thing, we're not mortal. We can't die. Not like you, anyway. We may have been human at some point, but we're altered, genetically poisoned with self-preservation. Some of us have been alive for hundreds of years, even thousands. As long as we sustain ourselves, we can conceivably live forever. We are eternal."

A range of emotions, swirling from awe to anger to utter confusion washed over her. A pinch in her gut convinced her that Evan was sincere in his words, as preposterous as they were. She was grateful for the weed. It hid the continued waves of tremors afflicting her body.

"What are you, fucking vampires or something?"

"Something like that. We are known as the Sempiternal," Evan confirmed.

She shook her head back and forth. "You're fucking vampires," she affirmed, feeling rather childish entertaining his absurd explanation.

"Not exactly. Look, Evie, there are so many truths and untruths in fiction," he answered with a chuckle. "Like I said, we are eternal, but our immortality is not unconditional. I think you saw that with Mae. We can be killed through trauma."

Evie sat back, replaying the moment Lucca snapped the blonde's neck like a twig in his hands and tore her throat out with his teeth.

"We possess strength greater than humans, as nature grants any predator strength over its prey. There are millions of us around the world. We're governed by houses, bodies of state which exist outside of human visibilities. History has coined the phrase 'vampire' over the years through one culture or another, but in truth, we have existed for time immemorial. For as long as we know that man has existed, so have the Sempiternal."

"Sunlight?"

He smiled. "Haven't you seen Lucca and me during the day?"

"Garlic? Crosses? Any of it?" Evie found that with each word, Evan's proposed explanation seemed plausible. Her mind raced back to Lucca's words the night before. *I haven't been to Fallhaven in over a century.* She felt it was true last night, and Evan confirmed it today. They were not human. They were something… other.

"Evie, forget about the movies. Forget what you've read. We're not undead. We've been cursed by something that keeps us living beyond any natural means. We're not subject to superstition or magical control. We simply exist just like you. You would be the same if you were infected."

"But there has to be something supernatural about you. I mean, you're defying the laws of nature, aren't you?"

Evan forced his next smile before answering her. "I don't consider anything about us to be supernatural. As I've said, there are truths and untruths. There will always be things in this world that science can never explain. If you feel the need to associate our existence to some supernatural or magical belief, you'll need to go back to the beginning of recorded history, and then some."

"What do you believe?"

She watched the pain in his expression spread across his furrowed brow. Whereas Evie had become more and more comfortable with their conversation as the joint burned down, Evan was noticeably more disquieted.

"I believe humans are blessed with their mortality. I'm not sure anyone should able to walk this world forever."

***

Evie's buzz waned. She watched Evan cautiously. He was bitter, unappreciative of what Evie presumed was a precious gift, immortality. What could be so terrible about living forever, she wondered. And as she recalled recent events, a new thought crossed her mind.

"So you *have* to kill?"

"Unfortunately, it is kill or be killed. Though society's romanticization of the vampire has helped a bit," Evan explained. "There are some humans who choose to offer themselves up to be bled. They are considered friends of our kind," he paused and stared into the palms of his hands. "But there are always victims too. We've tried to create a structured society to protect our life source and conceal our existence, but there are some who are power-hungry, violent, and don't care for what we've built over the centuries."

"Like Lucca?"

Evan nodded. "Lucca and Khan operate under their own rules. They're nomads, unwilling to conform to the rules set forth by the houses. If they are caught in a spectacle that might expose our kind, like a murder spree in a small fishing town... well, let's just say we tend to frown on such behavior, and it's grounds for prosecution."

Evie paused to digest their conversation and produced the folded piece of sepia paper from her back pocket. She stared at the image of Lucca standing behind her forebear.

"Lucca said he'd seen me before. In a past life. Was this it?" She tossed the photo into the center of the table. Evan flinched at the sight of the image.

"What I've learned in my time as one of the Sempiternal is that history repeats itself, Evie. And try as we may, we can never run from our fate."

A hard knot formed in her chest. She found it difficult to breathe under Evan's gaze. If she closed her eyes, she saw the Devil tarot card dancing with its deformed body and twisted grin. Opening her eyes to meet his again, tears trickled down.

"How old is Lucca?"

"I first met the man that was Lucca when we began construction on the estate here in Fallhaven. He worked down on the docks. As far as I am aware he was human at the time."

"What about Khan?" The contempt lining Evan's face was enough to answer.

"Khan is much older. He's said to have been one of the *khans*, a faction of the Sempiternal bred by the young

Ottoman kings to wage war and expand their empire. He changed Lucca when he was visiting with my uncle."

"And how old are you?"

Evan didn't answer her at first, lips pursed with reluctance. "What should it matter?" He paused. "What do you think about everything I've just told you?"

"It all sounds a little hokey to me," she said in earnest. Evan released a tiny hint of laughter from under his breath.

"I suppose you're right. It is a bit hokey, but it is what it is."

With his sad eyes and hesitant laughter, Evie felt that Evan posed no real threat to her. She didn't feel the same fear with him as she had in Lucca's company. In fact, quite the opposite. Evie realized every time she was around Evan she didn't want him to leave; realizing her feelings, a guilty thought passed through her mind.

"What about Blythe?" she asked, wondering how much of his true life Blythe was privy to.

"She knows nothing. I'd like it to stay that way. I didn't want her getting hurt. I don't want her to be part of this life."

"You know she was hoping for a future with you. What were you going to tell her?"

"There was no way for me to explain that I was only seeing her to keep an eye on you. I would have had to end things with her eventually."

"Me? Why were you trying to keep an eye on me?"

Her mind was fucked up enough after dealing with Lucca, Nate, and of course poor Rob. She didn't need or want the increased conflict Evan posed.

"I'm sorry, Evie. I really can't say, but remember, we are a structured group," Evan said. "I didn't want him to hurt you, or worse. I wish I could, but I can't elaborate further... It's not my place."

A cold shiver rushed through Evie as she watched Evan choke on his words.

"But why were you trying to protect me? How did you know Lucca would find me?"

The corner of Evan's mouth pulled into a grin, and he shifted his gaze away from her. "History, Evie. He knew you'd be back eventually. We all did."

The hair on the back of her neck stood on end as she listened to him. He spoke with such authority. She forced the uneasiness deep down into her core. She had so many questions to sort through, so many uncertainties. And the Devil's tarot card continued to dance in her mind.

A soft buzzing came from Evan's pants pocket. He reached down to retrieve his cell phone, silencing the ringtone and placing the phone atop the table near the ashtray between them.

"So how often do you need to..." Evie was unsure how to finish her question, "... feed?" She winced at the thought of Evan, sweet, handsome Evan, sucking the life out of anyone. The same bittersweet sorrow caused a crease in his brow.

"I don't know if '*feeding*' is the right word, per se," he said, searching for an answer in the swirling smoke lifting from the tiny roach between his fingers. "We need to ingest a human's... essence, in order to sustain our own. It just so happens, someone's life force transfers easily through the blood." He shifted his narrowed eyes up towards the ceiling.

She stared back at him for a moment, questioning whether or not he would continue to elaborate on the process by which he kept himself alive. He didn't.

"So you—"

"I feed off of blood." The shame in his face was unwavering. Evie could see this was difficult, but appreciated his honesty. "I've heard of some of the Elders who can literally suck the life out of you through the air. I've never seen it done. Maybe I think we all consume blood and someone generated the myth to stir a false sense of reverence for the Elders."

Sucking the life out of you through the air? Elders? It was all too much. How was she supposed to keep up?

"So how often do you need to feed?"

The word made Evie's stomach turn. The thought of consuming someone's soul shrouded Evan in a dark cloak. Somehow she could see the menace in Lucca's eyes, but not Evan's. It was an unnatural thought to envision Evan killing anyone.

"We're all a little different, I suppose," he answered. "I need to sustain myself every couple of weeks."

Weeks?

Evie presumed that a short expanse of time in the realm of immortality. Was that the equivalent of having the munchies and eating every five minutes to a normal human being? She continued to watch him. His face was beyond pale. His eyes, more than sorrowful. He looked waned and worn.

"When was the last time you..." She let the question trail, unable to say the words. She knew he understood. Evan fidgeted, poking out the roach in the ash tray.

"It's been more than a month," he said, unable to lift his eyes to meet her wide-eyed gaze. Evie took a deep breath.

"And how does that make you feel?"

"Empty. Hungry. Wanting—It's a difficult emotion to explain."

"Should I be worried right now?"

"A little." His eyes lifted to meet hers, a deep set russet gaze tearing through her center.

Her heart jumped. She was afraid the beating of her heart would not just burst from her chest, but also call out to his hunger like a beacon. She sat back further in her chair but she was held back by the flimsy wood frame. She had seen firsthand what Lucca was capable of. Could Evan be so capable? What does a rabid dog do when it's hungry? What does a junkie do when he's jonesing for a hit? They react erratically. They're unpredictable and dangerous. Evie choked on her cottony mouth. She dared not move.

"How are you going to, you know..." Evie still had trouble forming the words. "Feed?"

Poor beautiful Evan, a monster.

"Just like you'd presume. There are plenty of friends willing to offer themselves up to us. We never have to outright attack anyone. Not unless..."

"Unless what?" A desperation in her voice made itself evident. Her volume increased.

"Unless you get off on that kind of thing," he said.

"What's that supposed to mean?"

She watched as Evan again paused to choose his words wisely. Whatever he was, whatever Lucca was, she needed to know the truth. She stared in anticipation.

"For most of us, this is our way of existence. We do what we must to survive, sparing lives when and where we can. But for others..." Evan paused. "Like Lucca, they take pleasure in the killing, the thrill of the hunt."

The thrill of the hunt?

"But I asked you once if you thought Lucca meant to hurt me, and you said no. Now you're saying he's a killer. How does that not put me in danger?"

Evan looked up at her with his soft, pained eyes.

"He's promised never to *hurt* you. He doesn't want to kill you. He wants to change you," he said. "Into one of the Sempiternal."

A new kind of dread washed over Evie. "Why?"

"He believes you are his destiny."

THIRTY-FIVE

As much as Evie wanted to continue probing Evan for details about the Sempiternal, Lucca, and her past with his kind, she didn't. Evan may have turned the ringer off on his phone, but throughout their conversation, he continued to receive messages and calls. Evie left him downstairs to tend to his phone. Standing in front of her bathroom mirror, she stared at the ghostly image. His words ricocheted between her ears. His destiny. Her destiny.

To resist him is to resist yourself, Evie. To resist him is futile. Do not try to resist. He is you and you are him. Hope's words crept back to haunt her. She could feel the bile churning in her stomach burning its way up her esophagus. With a great heave she doubled over the toilet to void it of its contents.

Up against the cool porcelain, she pictured Rob. He'd died as the result of Lucca's domineering jealousy. Her body was washed over with heated anger. She vomited again. Evan tried to watch over her, to protect her, but he failed. *That's not fair to Evan*, she told herself. He hadn't failed her, he had failed Rob. In truth, Evan hadn't failed anyone at all. It was Evie who had failed. In her heart, she promised Rob that she'd find a way to make up for her pathetic attempts at loving him. She stood back in front of the mirror and scowled at her image.

To resist him is futile.

"Fuck you," she said to her reflection and turned back down stairs to Evan.

***

She found him in the kitchen, right where she'd left him, playing with a plastic bag of pot. Snatching up her glass bowl from the living room, she placed it down on the table in front of him to be packed. The two sat there in silence, passing the glass bowl back and forth, numbing their senses.

"I don't know that I trust or believe you yet, Evan," she said. "I don't know that I can believe. Maybe I don't want to."

Evan nodded and accepted her admission without questioning along with the glass piece. Evie watched him work, not a word spoken, his brow furrowed, his eyes warm.

"I'm leaving town, Evie."

She flinched when he spoke and stared at him with questioning. "Khan and Lucca are gone. I have matters to tend to back home. Whatever you want to believe, I know for a fact I can't do anything to protect you from here anymore."

He passed her the bowl and she stared into the colorful swirls of the blown glass piece.

"Take me with you," she said in a whisper, still staring into the glass. When she raised her eyes to meet his, he stared back, stunned.

"I can't," he said. "Evie, you wouldn't be any safer in my house than out here in the middle of nowhere."

"But I'd be near you. You could still keep an eye on me. Evan, I'm not ready to admit I have no control over my own life. Now that I know what you are, it'll be easier for you to help me, right?"

He reached out for the bowl and took another long toke. Through the smoke, he stared, contemplating her proposal. She could see it in his eyes. His gaze, predatory, reminded her of someone else's, and she forced the trepidation creeping up her throat back down.

"Fine," he said. "But you'll need to break all ties here. If you want me to hide you, you'll need to leave Blythe and Nate behind for good. No one can know where you are."

We are not running from him.

She shook her head at her inner voice's protests. Evan gave no indication he noticed her internal strife.

"How do I know you won't kill me yourself?" she asked.

"Evie, I can't convince you of anything. All I can say is that the last thing I want is to see you die."

His answer was genuine, that much she knew for certain from his tone.

"Fine. What do I need to do?"

Evan didn't answer her right away. The longer he paused the more opportunity her inner voice had to spew obscenities in her mind. But she wasn't ready to die or turn into something she didn't understand. She needed time. If Evan could afford her the time to sort through things, if he could educate her on what potential fate lay ahead, she needed him.

"I can take care of setting up residence for you, but in the wake of Rob's murder you shouldn't just disappear. You need to tell Blythe and Nate that you need to get away for a while. Sort things out following Rob's death and take some time to yourself."

"What if they ask me for details?"

"Refuse to give them. If they love you, they'll have to accept your privacy," Evan said, curt. "Whatever you say, do not tell them that I am involved in any way, okay?"

She was finding it increasingly difficult to keep her trepidation bottled. She was about to trust her very life with a man she just met. Not a man, a thing, a monster.

"Okay," she said with a hesitant breath.

***

Though Evie was terrified at the thought of leaving Fallhaven, the only place she had ever lived or known her entire life, part of her was relieved by the notion of anonymity in a far-off place. She would be alone and yet not. She would have time to come to terms with her emotions, wants, and needs. She thought of Nate. Hurt and confusion over how they ended things were sure to haunt her. Would he even care that she left? She wondered how long she could keep her distance from him suffering such uncertainty. Like Fallhaven, Nate was a constant in her life. The thought of moving on without him terrified her.

Evie thought about Blythe, who could never know of Evan and the role he was about to play in her life. Blythe had asked Evie to stay away from him. What she was about to embark on would require her to rely on him, heart and soul.

She gazed up at him across the kitchen table. The two monitored each other. Evie thought for sure he looked just as worried about what they were planning as she was.

"Why are you so willing to help me?" she asked.

The pain in his eyes increased. He grabbed the pipe into his hands. Pounding ash and resin from the empty bowl, he placed it back down on the kitchen table and dropped a plastic bag full of bright green bud beside it.

"I'll help make the arrangements. You'll want to speak with Blythe, Nate, and anyone else you feel is necessary," he said and stood to leave.

"You didn't answer my question, Evan."

Evie chased him out into the front entry way. His answer was relayed in his pale skin and tortured gaze that she'd come to associate with Evan's uniqueness, just as she would the sticky sweet taste of the cannabis he carried. She wanted to press him for explanation. Before she was able to push him further, Evan turned and both fell slack-jawed by the unexpected face at the door. Blythe stood with her surprised glare burning them.

"Evan," she said, fed up. "What are you doing here?"

"I wanted to make sure Evie was okay," he answered.

"I bet you did," she said, hissing back, glowering in Evie's direction.

"I'm so sorry, Blythe. Truly, I am."

Evan exchanged a sorrowful expression with Evie before walking past Blythe, out of the house. Evie shrugged. Blythe's impromptu entrance wasn't going to make leaving any easier. She wasn't prepared to face her friend. She hadn't thought about what she was going to say. To be confronted in Evan's company made it all the more awkward. Without a word, she turned into the house and sat on the couch. Blythe followed, slamming the door behind her.

THIRTY-SIX

"I came to see how you were coping. I see you're just fine," Blythe said following Evie into the living room.

"Blythe, Rob's dead. Okay? Murdered. And I found his body. Evan was just being a concerned friend. Get over it."

"A concerned friend? Get over it? Evie, when did you get so chummy with Evan? Please, you just can't help yourself. To think I apologized for insinuating anything happened between you two."

"Nothing has happened," Evie argued back. Tears were welling up again. She looked down and her hands were shaking. She wanted a drink. "He brought me pot, okay? Look," she said and snatched the bag of weed and glass bowl from the kitchen as evidence.

"Great, so you two sit here, get high, and have sex? Sounds like Nate all over again, Evie."

"Who said anything about having sex?" Evie said. "You know what, fuck this. You think what you want. I'm getting out of here."

"That's it, Evie. Go run and hide yourself at the bottom of a bottle like you always do. There'll be a guy in your bed later anyway, I'm sure."

Evie balled up her fist and forced the tears to relent. Fighting the urge to release her pent-up anger onto her supposed best friend was not how she planned to say goodbye.

"You have no idea what I've been through. Don't you dare judge me from on top of your pedestal. I'm not going to buy booze. I'm leaving town."

Blythe reciprocated her glare. "What do you mean you're leaving town? With who? Evan? Is that why he was here, so you two could make plans to run off together?"

Evie scoffed. Blythe was blinded by jealousy. Her reliance on Evan had nothing to do with emotions, not for him. But her perfect little brunette friend, with her perfect little family, and her perfect little life would never comprehend what she was going through. Arguing about it was pointless.

"With nobody. I can't be around anyone right now. I can't live my life like this anymore," she found a certain amount of freedom in her words. "I'm sorry, Blythe. For whatever I may have done to make you think I've betrayed our friendship again, I'm sorry. This isn't about you, or Evan, or Nate. This is about me. I need to walk away from this life for a while."

She sat back and watched her friend attempt to reconcile her feelings. It wasn't an easy task, Evie could tell. Blythe's eyes squinted with hate. No matter what truth may lie within Evie's words, she'd never buy into it. She'd lost Blythe over a man, a thing she didn't quite comprehend just yet. She wanted to tell Blythe about Evan, to try and preserve what could be salvaged from their friendship.

"Blythe, Evan's—" Evie cut herself short. She'd promised him that Blythe would remain oblivious to the Sempiternal. The promise she made to him was of far greater importance to the one she made to Blythe.

"He's what, Evie? Evan's what?" Blythe said, standing defiant to Evie's mirrored stance.

"Evan's—He's nothing," Evie answered, quiet, repentant with her head hung to the floor.

Blythe answered her by spitting at her feet. "I thought we were sisters," she hissed and clipped Evie's shoulder as she pushed past her to the front door. Evie wanted to run after her. Instead, she stood her ground, and let Blythe walk away.

Sometimes it's just better to let them walk away, she told herself.

***

Evie sat by herself in her living room. The silence in her house was deafening. Retreating upstairs to the sanctuary of her bathroom, she stared at the tub. It was tainted now, no longer a sacred vessel. It had been dirtied by Lucca. A warm thrill made her flush. A throbbing made her cringe. Her body wasn't ready to relent. Her inner voice still wanted him. Frustrated, she turned into her bedroom and blared her stereo. She drowned out the silence of the house and the chiding of her inner voice. Damn the music, its lyrics only stoked the fire inside of her.

Stupid, stupid girl.

"I need a fucking drink," she said aloud to herself and marched down the stairs.

She left her stereo blaring inside the house and neglected to lock the front door before tearing down the street to Nate's apartment across town. Following his altercation with Lucca the night before, she owed him a greater explanation than what she afforded Blythe. She couldn't think beyond the thirst or the guilt.

***

She approached his tenement house and rang the buzzer over and over. When he didn't answer, she grabbed her cell phone and began calling him, hanging up at his voicemail greeting and redialing until, on the fifth attempt, Nate finally answered her call.

"What do you want, Evie?" he growled through the phone.

"I want to sit down with a drink and talk."

"I'm not feeling well. Not now."

"Nate, please," she said, begging. "Listen, I'm sorry about last night."

"Not now, Evie," he repeated.

"No listen, I didn't want to do this over the phone but I'm leaving town for a little while. I need to sort some things out for myself. I don't want to leave like this, Nate. Please, let me in."

After a long pause she heard him groan, whimper even. He was crying, not something a burly man like Nate did. She began tearing up herself on his dilapidated front porch.

"Evie, I don't feel well. Please don't go until I can talk to you face-to-face."

"I'm sorry, Nate. I really am. I never wanted to hurt you. Please let me in."

She continued to plead, but he didn't respond. The call ended. She stood with her head hung low for some time.

"Fuck," she said, cursing into the warped screen door and kicking it with her unlaced boot. She looked to her right. Nate's neighbor, a little old lady with greyed skin and toothless gums watched her through squinted eyes. Evie sunk back and retreated to her car. Both attempts to cut ties had failed. She was running off to hide, rejected and alone. More than anything, Evie wanted a drink.

***

She stopped by the package store, all swollen eyes and puffy cheeks. The clerk shook her head in disgust while ringing up a bottle of Jim Beam.

"It's a sad thing, what happened to Rob Miller, isn't it?" the clerk said.

Evie glared back. *This whole damn town knows what happened.*

Denying the clerk the satisfaction of a response, she completed her transaction and marched out to her car.

Evie sat in her car, twisted the cap off the bottle, and licked her lips at the clean lip. She peered up, pausing before her swig, to see a police cruiser sitting across the parking lot. The cop was watching her, waiting for her to commit the misdemeanor. She rested the bottle back down in her passenger seat. As she drove home, she spent more time looking through the rearview than the windshield.

***

She sat in the solitude of her living room, surrounded by the melancholy soundtrack of her life as she found the bottom of the bottle. When Evan returned to her that evening, he found her drunk off the bourbon whiskey and stoned from the bag of weed he'd left behind.

"Why, Evie?" Evan sat down by her side.

"I said goodbye to Blythe and Nate," she said, slurring through her drunken stupor.

"Okay."

They remained on the couch for some time before speaking. Evie hiccupped and pushed the whiskey back down her throat each time it threatened to come back up. She stared in front of her, unwilling to look over at Evan's beautifully pained expression. The eternal monster was all she had left in the world. The fear of his judgmental glare froze her in place.

"Evan?"

"Yeah, Evie?"

"Why can't I just go tell the cops about Lucca?"

"The past cannot be changed. What's done is done," he said and took her limp hand in his. "Who would believe a girl with known depression and alcohol dependency issues that vampires had ravaged their tiny little fishing town?"

She wanted to cry. She should have been insulted by his comment, but she wasn't. She was numb.

Evie's life changed. Lucca had changed it. Whether it was the change she needed, she couldn't be sure. What she did know for certain was the Devil had come for her. He did change her, and her want for him was undeniable. She hoped that when he returned, she would know herself well enough to remain strong and resist falling into his dark nothingness.

Epilogue

Evie curled up in a tiny ball, cradled by the downy white cocoon of her comforter. Her nostrils were bombarded by the familiar scent of fabric softener, fresh linen, and body sweat. Her body pulsed from the waves of convulsions raging through her. Tiny whimpers escaped her pursed lips. She squeezed her eyes shut, forced the light out.

"I fucking hate you."

"I know. You've told me repeatedly the past few days," Evan replied. "And I've told to each time that I'm not taking you until you're clean."

"Fuck you."

Evan sighed.

Evie felt his cold and dry hand wrap around her clammy forehead. His contact was a cool burn. She flinched when he touched her.

"I'm going to fucking die. Just give me a fucking drink."

"You don't need it."

Evie's body jolted. She slumped over the side of the bed, voiding the contents of her belly. She felt Evan's hands support her as she retched down the side of the crisp white linens. Her mind went blank, unable to see beyond the physical pain. She gasped for air and choked on her own frothy sickness.

You wanted this. You wanted to run from him.

Regret slapped her. Evie howled in pain as Evan lifted her off the bed. She wrapped herself into his arms, then yelped in shock from cold porcelain and frigid water overwhelming her body. The shock cut straight through her soiled clothing, suctioning the cotton to her skin. Evie trembled in the tub. The air burned her lungs as she heaved violently from the shock.

"I want to die," she said.

Evie pried her eyes open, expecting to wince from the sun's blinding light. But it was past midnight; there was no light to strike her. The moon glowed from across the room. Disoriented, she gazed up. She focused on Evan's face. His brow furrowed with concern as he rinsed her forehead clean.

"I'm so sorry, Evie. But you need this. It will pass."

She cried louder still. The spasms increased. Her eyes burned from sweat-salted water droplets falling down from her brow. Rolls of cramping churned in her core like a wild hurricane. She squeezed her eyes shut once more. All went black. That's when she heard his voice. Panicked, she searched the dark for him.

I can make it all go away. I can bring the release you need. Lucca's voice echoed in her darkened mind. For days, she had heard him. She searched, each time unable to find him amidst the dark swirls of pain.

Evie licked the sweat lining her lips. "Yes. Yes please, make it stop," she said, barely coherent. The cool burn of Evan's palm on her forehead pierced through the darkness.

"I'm right here, Evie. It's okay," he said.

Let him find us. This is fucking pointless.

Fall with me. Lucca's voice echoed.

"Yes, please."

341

Glowing orbs flickered through the black. Her chest twisted with apprehension and fear, but still she craved the release. Her inner voice reached out to the golden light twinkling in the darkness. Weight, hot and heavy, fell on her chest. She gasped for air. She swiped through the dark. The orbs disappeared. Panic cracked through her apprehension and fear.

"Please," she said, whimpering. "Make it stop."

"It's okay, Evie," Evan replied.

"I want to die."

"No, whatever it takes, I'm not going to let you die."

"Just let him take me." Evie felt her body burning, swirling in the tempest, raising the temperature of the water around her.

"No, Lucca's not here."

Evie cried some more. "I want to die." Each time she managed to utter the request, she hoped Evan would give in. He never did. He just kept rinsing her soaked head, hushing her cries, consoling her, and tending to her tortured aches.

"No, I know it hurts. It will pass—but not this time. I'm not letting you fall this time."

ABOUT THE AUTHOR

J.C. Stockli is inspired by music, the past, and possibilities. Also an established full-time professional with her MBA, over the years she's moonlighted as a magician's assistant, a roadie for a metal band, a dance fitness instructor, and even dressed up as a promotional character at public events. Why not explore writing?

She lives along the Massachusetts coast with her husband and two children. You'll likely find them dancing around the house, or out on the water soaking in the sun and breathing in the sea salt air.

Sign up for her mailing list or follow her at:

www.jcstockli.com

https://twitter.com/JCStockli

https://www.facebook.com/JCStockli

Acknowledgments

Thank you to my love, for his support and understanding through countless days and nights of endless writing, and for being my best inspiration.

Special thanks to my close friends for believing, most notably my nearest and dearest, Diana, for being my positive energy and guide through this journey. Your support is nothing short of beautiful.

To the early adopters of my madness: Becky, Lindsay, Lindsey, and Linda (to name a few), thank you for embracing Evie and her vices.

Thanks to my editor, Andy Holmes, for the tough love. Support comes in many forms.

Lastly, thank you to my past, present, and future for supplying me with the tools to make it this far.

COMING IN SUMMER 2015
The

SAVING

Addictions Of The Eternal: Book Two
(excerpt)

After work, Evie walked home alone. Before ascending the three flights of stairs, she crossed the street over to Carson Beach, unwilling to sit in her once-craved solitude. She removed her shoes and let her toes sink into the gritty sand. The sun hadn't quite settled for the evening. It glittered gold and silver streaks across the water. Its orange glow was warm and soothing. The salty air tugged at her memories. She felt like she was home, even if only in spirit.

Life in Boston proved so much more complex than it had been in Fallhaven. As much as she hated herself and her inner voice for antagonizing her, she couldn't stop dreaming about Lucca. She hated him for what he did to Rob. She wanted nothing to do with him, but when night came and she curled up under the sheets, she couldn't keep herself from dreaming about his silky skin against hers, his warm breath lingering on her body, pulling her down deeper and deeper into his darkness. Pulses of agonizing pleasure rushed through her bones. Evie knew that no matter where Evan hid her, she'd never escape her own desires for Lucca.

She sighed, as visions of Evan flashed through her mind, the Evan from her dreams, the Evan she'd been wrongfully objectifying—*her* Evan. Better than her mind's image of him, his body standing in front of her at work constricted her chest. Tall, slender, tousled hair, and pin-straight tie tucked behind his tailored suit, those big brown eyes locking with hers, aghast. She remembered what Dawn said about the bet the girls had running around the office.

Evie hugged her body tight while caramel ribbons of hair flailed around her face in the warm summer breeze. She scowled at the sand between her toes washed over by the surf as the tide rolled in. She lifted her foot, twirling her pointed toes around in circles through the foam.

"Those skanks don't deserve you," she whispered aloud to herself.

Do you?

***

"I'm leaving now. Do you need anything before I go?"

Evie's eyes opened. Senses alerted, heart thumping, she looked over at Evan now standing by her side, his trousers rolled up and bare feet firmly planted in the sand next to her. His suit jacket and tie were gone. He had his shirt sleeves up past his elbows, hands tucked into his pockets. He met her gaze with a cautious stare through his periphery.

"I thought you already left," she said.

"I told you, I had some business to wrap up. I didn't think I'd run into you at the office. I hope that didn't embarrass you."

She huffed and turned to stare back out into the harbor, transfixed by its golden beauty, its gorgeous warm light. "It shocked me a little. I didn't realize you went by there so often."

"I told you I did business with the company," he said joining her gaze out to the water. "And what do you mean, *so often*?"

"Nothing. Some of the girls there enjoy when you grace the office with your presence, that's all," she said with a snicker and a smile and continued twirling her toes through the wet sand.

Evan cracked his sweet crooked grin, maintaining his sideways glance. "Is that so?"

"Mm-hmm. I'm pretty sure they're all trying to get in your pants. It's safe to say I'm the only girl there who doesn't want to fuck you."

Who said we don't want to?

Evan's amusement waned, eyes shifting down to the movement of Evie's toes in the sand. "So you're all set then? I'm going to leave tonight." His tone saddened her, such poignancy made all too prevalent in her eyes. She kept them hidden from his view. No, she wasn't ready to be alone. She wasn't ready to be without him.

"I'm sorry, I told the girls I wouldn't say anything. I didn't want you to feel embarrassed next time you went into the office," she said. "If it makes you feel any better, I was tempted to bitch-slap one of them. I can't stand her anyway, and I know how you feel about sex and all. It's not right that they—"

"It's fine, Evie," he said, curt. "I have to hit the road. Do you need anything or not?"

She straightened her posture from his terse response. "Geez, Evan. I was only joking about the whole sex comment. Do you even know how to goof around?" She batted him playfully across the chest, searching for a bit of levity in their otherwise awkward accord, beaten to death on multiple accounts. She looked back up to the harbor.

There was a long pause between the two, and Evie watched Evan through the corner of her eye. His jaw flexed as though mulling over a thought in his head. She'd seen that contemplative stare before—on her—on Lucca.

Before Evie could decode his thoughts, Evan nodded, decisive. He cleared his throat and pulled his hands from his pockets.

"Goof around, huh?" he said with a crooked brow. He bent down, tossed Evie over his shoulder, and then marched in a determined line into the surf.

"Whoa! Evan, what the fu—" she yelped out in protest before being submerged under the waves. Evan dropped both their bodies below the surface and clung to her, preventing her escape as she floundered.

Evie closed her eyes and sucked in a deep breath. Her hands searched through the waters to find his body while he adeptly handled her, raising her back up above the surface. Her legs whirled through the surf and found themselves anchored to his waist. She coughed thick salty water from her lungs as she clawed at his shoulders for stability.

"What the fuck was that?"

Evan smiled. "You said I didn't know how to goof around."

"Yeah, but that's not what I meant," she argued, wiping her face and licking at her salt-lined lips.

They remained submerged for a few more moments before Evie looked down at her drenched white blouse, now transparent, revealing the black brassiere underneath. Self-consciousness had always been an emotion reserved for the unwarranted glares of strangers, but floating so close to Evan, those insecurities seeped into her pores. Her short skirt floated under the water's surface like seaweed, doing little to prevent his hands from reaching up to cup her rear, preventing her from washing away with the tide.

He was equally soaked. His white shirt, equally translucent, clung to his body. She ran her fingertips across the wet linen, inspecting a black mark showing through along his shoulder.

"What's that?"

Evan's smile faded as he looked down to her fingertips. "It's nothing," he answered. "Now let's get you home before you float away."

He carried her over his shoulder back up onto the beach. Evie mocked protest, but enjoyed every second of playful Evan, carrying her from the sea like a prize. Her savior—*her* Evan. She slid down him, safe and secure to the sand, unwilling to tear her arms away from his neck. Her body trembled, a faint quake deep within her core. She recognized it—the nearness, too close to be decent. Her inner voice purred, craving the flesh.

Feels good, doesn't it?

***

They walked hand-in-hand and smile-to-smile back up to her apartment. Once inside, Evie disappeared into the bathroom for some towels. Tossing a few in Evan's direction, he placed one or two along the floor to prevent the pooling water from damaging the floors. She disappeared back behind the door to shower and change.

When Evie stepped out from the tiny bathroom fully clothed, she was taken aback by Evan standing in the middle of her living room wearing nothing but a soft pink towel around his waist. She gasped out loud, her hand held up to conceal her startled outburst. He turned to face her with apology before her inner voice crept up from the confines of her core.

"Sorry, I don't have any extra clothes to change into. I'm just using your washer and dryer, and then I *really* need to hit the road," he said.

It took Evie a minute or two to roll her tongue up from the floor and snap her jaw shut. Her inner voice chided her to remember to breathe, but the sight of Evan's body reminded her how long it had been since she'd seen a man naked, and the last was not just any man—it was Lucca. Their bodies were so similar. Long, lean, and expertly carved. They were almost identical—almost. Evie noticed the black mark she saw under his shirt on the beach was a tattoo, a broken wing across his left shoulder, a very crude rendering, but artful and detailed nonetheless.

"When did you get that?" she asked, waving a hand towards the ink. Evan looked down to his shoulder and scowled.

"A long time ago."

He turned his back to her. She studied his ink-capped shoulder, cut over to the muscular formation of his shoulder blades, and lowered her eyes, drifting down to the base of his spine.

"Must be rough regretting a tattoo when you'll see it forever… literally," she laughed, nervousness set off small tremors in her vocals, and her smile soured when Evan didn't respond to her humor. She shook her head and dismissed her jest. Gnawing at her lower lip instead, she used the self-inflicted pain to divert her attention from his flesh, a task that proved difficult. She forced her sights away before she assaulted her friend with her eyes or her mind any further. Her legs proved weak as she attempted to walk towards the futon.

"Are you hungry?" Evan asked.

Evie shot him a look of complete astonishment. "Am I what?" she said, feeling herself flush from the innuendo.

"Are you hungry? I'm guessing you didn't have dinner yet. I can make something for you in the kitchen while I wait for my clothes," Evan replied in the most innocent of voices.

Evie hated her hormones.

"Oh... No, thanks."

She grabbed for her glass bowl without hesitation. Evan sat next to her in his towel. Evie's hands fumbled over each other as they fought their compulsions to rip at Evan rather than break up the marijuana bud therein. Head held down to the drug in hand, her eyes wandered to their corners, aching for a glimpse at the pink towel and what lay hidden beneath it.

Stop that, unless you plan on doing something about it.

Evie jumped up off the futon, disturbed by the proximity of his near-naked body. She marched over to the computer desk and plopped down in front of the laptop, allowing her licentious fingers to take out their angst against the touch pad instead of Evan. Damn the first track that played on their playlist—one of Evan's, tender musings, piano and acoustic guitar. Sweet, painfully beautiful music, just like Evan.

He made no comment. Instead, his eyes revealed all the sorrow her recoil may have caused. He resumed her efforts at packing the bowl and took a hit before extending the piece in her direction.

"Want some?"

Evie looked at him with wide and wanting eyes, incredulous.

Yes!

"What? No. I mean, yes but… no," she growled with frustration. "Give me that," she exclaimed and ripped the glass piece from his hand to take a long hard toke. She hoped the effects of the weed would numb her senses, calm her hormones, and silence her inner voice. She put all of her wants and needs into that hit, closing her eyes and holding the smoke in. Her head dizzied in an instant.

"I'll go wait out on the balcony, so this isn't so awkward," Evan said and motioned by her.

Evie shot up from her chair in protest. "No, you can't!" He turned to her, shocked, perplexed no doubt by her outburst. "You can't go stand outside in a towel where everyone can see you. That's got to be considered indecent exposure or something," she explained. "No, I'll go wait outside. You stay here where I can see y—where no one can see you," she corrected and stormed past him onto the balcony.

Evan stood frozen and confused. She didn't bother to explain her behavior further. *Let him think what he wants,* she thought. Hell, maybe he could shed some light on the whole conflict of emotions raging through her body, because Evie was lost in her own darkness.

***

Neither one acknowledged each other through what felt like the longest hour of her life. Through it all, she stood with her back to her apartment, eyes closed and summoning visions of Lucca in her mind. At the moment, her murderous conquest seemed the lesser of two evils. Her efforts proved dismal as she evaluated their perfect bodies together. Her mind's eye arranged the apples-to-apples comparison, and melted her. They were so much alike.

Where are you, Lucca?

She dared to peek through a cracked eyelid at the darkening streets. He was out there somewhere. And for the first time since she went running from Fallhaven, Evie knew she'd run into his open arms willingly to escape the torture of hurting another friend.

***

Evan dressed and left without as much as a word to her. She was grateful for that. She stood on the balcony, listening to his sad music waft through the open French doors. Lovesick lyrics nipped at the nape of her neck. A single tear escaped and rolled over the crest of her cheekbone. Too afraid to turn around and miss his sticky sweet aroma, she stared out at the moon now hanging high above the harbor.

Why won't you let me have him?

"No. He's a good friend. Too good for me."

You can't hide forever.

"What is wrong with me?"

They're so very similar—and yet not.

"What are you talking about?"

Lucca and Evan—the Sempiternal.

"Hope said you were supposed to guide me. What are you saying? Who's the monster and who's my destiny?"

Do we really need to choose?

"There has to be a choice. It wouldn't be fair to Evan."

What about what's fair to Lucca?

"What if he decides he doesn't want me once he finds me?"

So you're choosing Evan then?

"No, I'm not. Even if I wanted to, I'll never shake Lucca."

He is perfect.

"They both are. What do I do? What do you want?"

I want out of this human existence. I want to rule the Sempiternal. He can help us.

A burst of crazed laughter came thundering past her lips. "Rule the Sempiternal?" She snorted. "I'm fucking crazy." Evie planted her forehead into the palms of her hands. "What am I going to do?"

You'll know. You'll feel me.

Evie released a heavy breath, unsure of even her own obscure reasoning. "I'll feel you," she whispered to herself. "I'll feel you."

***

At about half past midnight, Evie told herself to go to bed. Evan was gone. Before long, Evie was alone in her bed and dreaming of Lucca. She dreamt of his perfect body stalking across the room sopping wet and naked. His ever-present sideways smirk teased as he loomed overhead, just as he did in her dreams each night. He purred. He clawed. Her body tingled as he ravaged her throughout the night. His adept fingertips traced nonsensical shapes along the contours of her body. She accepted whatever demeaning punishment he saw fit to administer.

"Fall from your graces," his melodic voice called out. "I know it calls you," he said. "I can show you the pleasure in your pain."

Her body quivered in his dark nothingness, wanting nothing more than to embrace his disease. His elongated canines scraped along her flesh, scratching, but never breaking the surface. Even in her dreams, she pined for his bite.

Thankfully, Rob's geisha remained in the shadows, unable to work her way into Evie's frustrated psyche. Just before Evie awoke the next morning, she peered up at his beautiful face. She gazed at large warm chocolate orbs floating overhead, framed with soft pale skin and pink pouty lips.

Evie whispered, "Evan."

CREDITS

Cover Art © 2015 J. Coulombe

Cover Girl © 2015 J. Coulombe

Cover Boat © 2015 J. Coulombe

Editing by Andrew Holmes